THE LITTLE PARIS TOYSHOP

LAUREN WESTWOOD

BOOKS BY LAUREN WESTWOOD

The House of Second Chances

The House of Hidden Secrets

The House of Love and Dreams

Moonlight on the Thames

My Mother's Silence

The Daughter She Lost

My Secret Sister

Published by The Empowered Author Limited

Cover artwork by Emma Graves

THE LITTLE PARIS TOYSHOP

PART I

In the tangled streets of Paris, there is a toyshop. A place of the imagination, a landscape of dreams, a repository of memories. Some of the objects are shiny and new, others old, worn, tattered. Some are lost, others forgotten or discarded, by children who long ago became adults.

And who have those adults become now? What stories are they telling? What stories are they living? What happened to the dreams, the magic? Have they lost them? Or did they never exist at all?

An old man sets the animals in the cars of the miniature train: a tiger with a jewelled collar, a monkey in a pillbox hat, a poodle, a dancing bear, an elephant, an ostrich with plumed tail feathers.

They too have a story, though the old man does not know it. Once, a long time ago, they were lovingly carved, carefully painted. Unwrapped on Christmas morning by a small pair of hands, played with, delighted in: a seal with a ball on its nose, the ringmaster in a top hat, a leopard, a lion, a piebald pony.

Once, they stood in a circle in a soft-lit room, on a shelf above a small bed, watching over a tiny, sleeping child. Once, they were complete – but now one is missing: the little giraffe on tiny wheels, its horns chewed, its painted spots worn and loved off. It is gone.

The old man connects the circuit. The music plays; the animals trundle around the track. Now, they are here, in a toyshop window. Their gentle faces have seen everything and reveal nothing. The joy, the sorrow, all the spaces in between. On the outside they are smiling. Inside, they mourn the one that was lost.

1

SARAH

FRIDAY, JULY 14TH

Fireworks exploded in the skies of Paris, dazzling like jewels overhead. Crowds of people flocked onto the bridge, slowing the traffic to a halt. Fountains of sparks fizzed in the colours of the *tricolour*, reflecting in the dark water of the river. In the distance, the national anthem blared over a loud speaker – *La Marseillaise* – with onlookers joining in the refrain. The Bastille Day celebrations were every bit as enchanting as she'd been led to believe. Beautiful, magical…

The last thing she needed.

Sarah checked her watch – she was cutting it close. The wine shop in the Latin Quarter closed at eight, and it was already a quarter to. Her assistant, Jeanette, had phoned around to all the local shops, but only one had a bottle of the new investor's favourite vintage. The proprietor was leaving tomorrow for an extended summer holiday in Antibes and wasn't going to wait around. The shop was on her way home; Sarah had hopped in a taxi to collect the bottle herself.

Now, the car ground to a halt as the crowd overflowed

into the street. 'Can you pull over, please?' she said to the driver in schoolgirl French. 'I'll walk from here.'

The driver glared at her in the mirror and began speaking rapidly. She only caught every other word, but the gist was clear: he was on the bridge thanks to her; she might as well pay to be dropped on the other side.

'Here.' Sarah handed him a ten euro note – double the meter. 'Keep the change.' She opened the door and joined the throng of people on the pavement, jostled on all sides as people made space with their elbows. Her black patent court shoes had a slender heal – totally wrong for walking. Her chest felt tight and constricted as she tried to push her way to the end of the bridge. A man hoisted a squirming toddler onto his shoulders, and she was nearly kicked in the face. So many people, children – the heat, the noise – by the time she reached the other side of the Pont St. Michel, she could barely breathe. She twisted the St. Jacques lanyard around her fingers, willing the feeling to pass. Over the river, the fireworks continued, the rockets booming and whistling. Keeping her head down, she hurried away down the boulevard.

According to Google Maps, the wine shop was located down a small street that branched off from the main boulevard. She passed several cafés, their entrances flanked by striped awnings, potted plants, and frowning waiters looking to usher in customers after the fireworks. Pulling out her phone, she checked the map again. The street should be located just past the next shop – a bookstore – but it didn't seem to exist. All she could find was a dark, narrow gap between two buildings that stank of rotting vegetables and worse.

The explosions reached a deafening finale. The noise pounded inside her head; she longed to abandon her errand and retreat to the relative quiet of her flat. She'd been working nearly seven days week for the last few months – surely no one would blame her for calling it a night. Besides, there was time before the grand opening to phone more wine shops, or else Javier, the new bartender, could find a substitute.

While she debated, two *voitures de police* raced past her, their sirens on, blue lights flashing. Dark spots formed in front of her eyes. The flashing lights… the sounds… too much.

Sarah plunged forward into the passage. The explosions died away and in the distance, a cheer went up. She held her breath as she passed a row of overflowing bins, the way twisting and turning until it eventually forked into two smaller roads. Sarah stopped long enough to check the map again. But the signal was poor in the labyrinthine streets, and the little circle went round and round. She chose a direction blindly as a church bell began to toll the hour.

The buildings loomed around her, tall and claustrophobic, stealing the last of the light. Some of the shops at street level were dark and empty, with boarded-up windows and 'to let' notices on the doors. The street seemed lost in time; it made her feel dizzy and disoriented, and well and truly lost.

As she rounded the corner, the heel of her shoe caught in the cracked pavement. She cried out in pain as her ankle turned; the heel twisted and snapped, hanging on by a thread. As she regained her balance, she saw a light up ahead. Sarah limped onwards – this must be the place.

The light came from an old-style shop with an art nouveau display window. A faded sign hung above, the name written in cursive letters: *La Boutique Fantasque. Joeuts.*

A toyshop. Sarah shuddered. Of all the places she didn't want to be… the wine shop must be further down the road; there was still time to find it. As she hobbled past the window, the display came to life.

Coloured lights twinkled; bright carnival music began to play. Spotlights shone on the elaborate tableau: an old-fashioned circus with a red and gold big top hanging from the ceiling. Sarah stopped to watch – she couldn't help herself – the display was like nothing she had seen before.

A troupe of mechanised figures performed complex movements: a tightrope walker in a spangled costume teetered along a thin cable, trapeze artists performed aerials, a fortune teller rotated a crystal ball filled with swirling smoke. The ringmaster cracked a whip at a fantastical lion made of folded paper, horses in jewelled harnesses moved on wheels around a track, mechanised clowns formed a teetering pyramid, an audience of dolls held paper roses and glass toffee apples. It was a scene from a bygone era, dreamlike and fascinating. At the top of the window, a harlequin banner unfurled from a miniature aeroplane with a name in old-style writing: *Le Cirque du Lune.*

As she continued to watch, a model steam train trundled out of a tunnel at the side of the display and made its way around a track. The shiny enamelled cars crossed the window in front of her, each one carrying a carved wooden animal from an antique set, their paint patinaed with age.

Sarah blinked rapidly, her fascination turning to shock. This couldn't be happening, couldn't be real. The train entered a tunnel, then reappeared on a higher track, snaking its way around the tent. Pain blindsided her as she stared at the animals in the cars, looking for answers in their expressions. Lost forever – so she had thought. And one was missing: the little giraffe – where was it?

She had to do something – get to the bottom of this. If this was a nightmare, she needed to wake up. Sarah went to the door at the far side of the window and tried the knob, finding it locked. 'Hello!' she shouted, banging her fist against the wood. 'Is anyone there?'

No one answered, but she found a bell inset into the wall. She leaned her weight upon it and heard ringing inside. Would anyone reply? Was anyone here *to* reply?

Once again, no response. She slumped back, defeated. What should she do? More than anything, she wanted to turn back the clock so that she'd never come here – five minutes would do, or better yet, five years. Failing that, she wished she could convince herself that it was all her imagination. She tried the bell one more time.

This time, a buzzer sounded; the latch clicked. Sarah flung open the door, her heart racing as she stepped inside.

2

TOMAS

Tomas's hand ached as he wrote out the inscription – *To Laura, Bonne Anniversaire* – and signed his name with a flourish. Who knew so many people would choose to come to a bookshop rather than attend the Bastille Day festivities? He put down his pen and pushed the book across the table. 'Happy birthday,' he said. 'You can pay up at the till.'

The woman hovered, giving him a shy smile. 'I was so glad that Agent Clarke got together with Dr Clint,' she said in heavily accented English. 'Can I ask if they stay together?'

Tomas didn't have the heart to tell her that he'd already killed off Dr Clint, the handsome but slightly dim museum curator. Shot him point blank in the head with a Glock 9 and then dismembered his body, hiding his head in a reproduction Assyrian temple, arranging his hands on a plinth in Neoclassical European Sculpture, and stuffing the rest of him into an already-occupied Egyptian sarcophagus circa 945 BC. Agent Lucinda Clarke, MI6, was left frantically trying to pick up the pieces of her short-lived love affair. Literally.

'I think, Laura,' Tomas said, 'that you will just have to wait and see.'

'*Ah, mais oui.*' As the woman leaned over the table to collect her book, the neckline of her blouse gaped down to reveal a hint of cream-coloured lace. He could smell her perfume: *Trêsor*. She met his eyes, her smile moving by degrees from shy to confident, seductive. Her finger caressed the spine of the book. The words were on his lips: *would you like to have a drink? Come back to mine?*

No. He took a breath. 'It was nice to meet you. I hope you enjoy the book.'

The woman frowned. With a flick of her hair, she moved off, clearly put out by his cool response. He watched as she teetered off in high heels, hips swaying. What was wrong with him tonight?

'Ahem.' Tomas was startled by a throat clearing. An elderly man stood at the table holding the last book open for Tomas to sign. He tapped his finger on the page.

'To Delphine,' he said in awkward English.

'Of course,' Tomas replied in French. 'It will be my pleasure.'

The language barrier broken, the man launched into a diatribe of how much he hated Tomas's books.

'They are just so violent and none of the characters show any feeling. It is just bang, bang, bang!' The man pointed an imaginary gun at Tomas. 'Who cares if they save the world in the end?'

Tomas laughed. The man broke off, embarrassed. 'I am sorry, Monsieur Mercier,' he said. 'My wife loves them all.'

'No need to apologise.' Tomas respected the man for

expressing his opinion – one he secretly agreed with. 'What do you like to read?'

'My eyes are not what they once were,' the man said. 'So now, I struggle. I like the old books, though. The ones that speak of real people. Not killers and ticking clocks and heroes out to save the world. Just those that are trying to make sense of life.'

'Have you read Proust?' The words came from nowhere – Tomas wished he could take them back.

'But of course! *À la recherche du temps perdu*! That is true literature. A book that lives and breathes! It creates life and takes it away.'

Tomas stared down at the blank leaf, pain flashing as Tom Willowfield fought his way into his head. Tom Willowfield, the golden boy from Beaconsfield; the youngest ever winner of the Curtis P. Whitney prize for literature whom critics had likened to a youthful Ian McEwan, José Saramago, and even William Faulkner. An author able to create 'paintings with words', 'the tragedy and exaltation of the human spirit leaping off the page'. Tom Willowfield, who had, for all intents and purposes, disappeared off the face of the earth and not written a word for fifteen years.

'In English, we call it *Remembrance of Things Past*,' Tomas said. 'That used to be one of my favourites, too.' He signed the copy of his own book – *To Delphine with best wishes, xx* – and handed it back to the man. 'You can pay up at the till.'

With a curt nod, the man ambled off. The clerk brought over another stack of *The Art of Death*.

'No more today.' Tomas stood up. Hopefully he'd missed the fireworks, but he wanted to leave before the crowds dispersed and more customers came in to browse.

'But of course, Monsieur Mercier,' the clerk said. 'We can schedule another signing very soon.'

'Fine. I'll let you know.' It wouldn't be soon – that was for sure. Being in a shop surrounded by books was making Tomas ultra-aware of the empty hole inside him. The one he usually kept filled up with work and distractions.

'Very good, monsieur,' the clerk said. 'Before you go, could I get a photo for the window display?'

'No photos,' Tomas said quickly. 'Sorry.'

'Of course.' The man seemed a little perplexed by his attitude. Tomas knew from his own long-ago days as a bookstore clerk that most authors would jump at the chance to get their photo in a bookshop window. But not him. Other than this shop, which he liked to support because it was local and independent, he sold his books strictly online – which suited him perfectly.

As the clerk stacked the books back in the box, Tomas browsed the crime books on the nearby tables. He picked up a copy of his first book, *A Mind for Murder*, and set it down again in disgust. 'Where can I find a copy of *À la recherche du temps perdu*?' he said.

The clerk looked surprised – like he'd expected Tomas to ask for the latest Jack Reacher instead. 'We have several editions. Come, I'll show you.'

Tomas followed the clerk through a maze of shelves to the classics section. Had he taken leave of his senses? As the clerk busied himself arranging a nearby shelf, Tomas chose a plain brown leather volume with the title etched in gold. It was expensive, but he'd sold enough books today to cover it.

The clerk was still hovering. Tomas wished he would leave; he gave the man a pointed stare. When he turned away, Tomas went to the end of the shelf, from 'P' to 'W'. And there it was, like a poisonous snake, coiled up and ready to strike. A single copy in English and two copies translated into French.

The Rites of Spring by Tom Willowfield.

He picked up the book and opened it. The words melted off the page, taking him to another place, another part of his mind.

'Frost flowers bloomed on the window. Sam made a circle with his fist in the cloud of his breath. The sea in the distance was a heavy quicksilver. The dune grass, poking its head out between the weathered boards of the path, was dusted in soft white.

A lone figure stood facing the water. Albie. He would be seeing the sky and the water and hearing the strange sounds of whales and mermaids calling to him in his head. When Albie smiled, there was an impossible joy in those eyes, a whole world in his mind that no one else could see.

Albie took a step forward towards the foam edge of the waves. Sam tried the window, but it was frozen shut. He tried to call out, but he knew his brother wouldn't hear. Albie walked forward. The waves welcomed him. Sam's fingers clawed at the glass. The waves embraced him; swallowed him.'

Tomas's hand quavered as he shut the book and shoved it back on the shelf, spine first. When he turned around, the clerk was holding his mobile phone; he lowered it quickly. Had he taken a photo? Surely not. Nonetheless, Tomas felt a stab of the old fear – this was a mistake, he should be more careful. He went over to the clerk and handed him the heavy volume of Proust. 'I'll take this one,' he said.

'Of course, Monsieur Mercier. And naturally, you can have a special discount of ten per cent.'

Tomas left the classics section, relieved to be back amongst the tables of crime and commercial fiction. As he went up to the till, the woman, Laura, gave him another lingering glance as she went out the door. Not too late…

he let out a long sigh. Time to go home and spend another night of his life alone.

Tomas paid for the book, put it in his bag, and left the shop. The last of the firework explosions died away, and the onlookers were starting to disperse. Getting home from here would be like a salmon swimming upstream. For a second, he sympathized with Andre – the outside world was pretty overwhelming when it came right down to it. Had the boy watched the fireworks from the window, or stayed in his room with his head under the duvet? Maybe he should go round and check on him and Mathilde – bring them something sweet; or better yet, bring Andre something to occupy him besides playing games on his iPad. But what? A book? No. He checked his watch. If he hurried, he could just get to the toyshop before it closed.

3

SARAH

A toyshop. This was all wrong – she shouldn't be here. As Sarah pulled the door shut behind her, the shop surprised her senses. The room smelled of varnished wood and oiled metal; clockwork gears clicked and whirred behind the big top; *Carnival of the Animals* played from a CD player. Her eyes were drawn to the many childhood treasures displayed on shelves, tables, and even hanging from the ceiling.

But as she looked closely, the cavern of wonders fragmented into something lost and unloved. Every surface overflowed with old wooden toys and antique puzzles and games. Broken, faded, repaired, dilapidated, the objects covered with a thin patina of dust. On one side of the room, a row of wooden carousel horses stood sentinel, their manes and tails matted, their dappled paint pocked. On the shelves behind, armies of toy soldiers faced each other, the battlefield crisscrossed by cobwebs. She avoided the glassy eyes of a cabinet of dolls: old-fashioned and probably never played with. Above her head, kites and papier mâché hot-air balloons drooped with dust, frozen and still.

Interspersed among the old things were signs of modernity. On a table at the front, an Eiffel Tower had been constructed from colourful pieces of magnetic Perspex – Sarah moved past it carefully for fear of knocking it down. One rack displayed building toys that were boxed and new. Another cabinet held musical boxes: beautiful confections of inlaid wood, brass, and painted enamel.

The mismatch filled her with unease. Even more unsettling was the emptiness – the complete lack of any customers, or children, or even an assistant.

But someone had buzzed her in; someone must be here. She needed to find the proprietor, and then what? This was madness! What business could she possibly have at a toyshop? The wooden circus animals... yes, they looked familiar – very similar to the ones that had stood in a circle on Rowan's bureau – but they couldn't be the same. It just wasn't possible.

At the back of the room, an archway led to another room. Beyond, an art deco foyer contained a labyrinth of low shelves crammed with second-hand books and old-time Paris postcards and memorabilia. On the top of the shelves was a city of doll's houses – perfect replicas of famous Parisian buildings: Notre-Dame, the Arc de Triomphe, Les Invalides. In the Place de la Concorde, a miniature guillotine had been erected with a head, coiffed like Marie Antoinette's, in a basket. Sarah shuddered and stopped looking so closely. She had the strong urge to leave the shop, but now that she was here, she was determined to speak to someone. She made her way to another door, this one flanked by heavy velvet curtains.

Sarah gasped at what was beyond. The vast, high space was dimly lit by a bank of orange lights – an old theatre, by the looks of it. But instead of a stage and seats, a gigantic clockwork castle filled the entire room. Multiple levels tapered upwards like a sumptuous layer cake: part carousel, part adventure playground. On the bottom layer, shiny painted horses pranced and tossed frozen manes. Above, protected by a golden net, was a castle play area with criss-crossing walkways and staircases, ball pits, and slides. Higher still, life-sized mechanical figures peeked out of windows and hid in nooks and crannies of the clockwork tower: princesses, knights, court jesters, minstrels. At the top of the fly space, a glittery dragon was affixed with cables, ready to swoop downwards on vast papier mâché wings.

The layers of the clockwork castle were still. Sarah half expected them to come to life at any moment. But like the rest of the shop, something was not right. At the bottom of the castle, exposed rebar sprouted like a forest, huge banks of gears were attached to nothing, and loose wires and cords littered the floor. It was like stepping inside a broken musical box. Sarah felt an unexpected flare of anger. Someone had clearly gone through a lot of trouble to create something unique, but had failed to get it over the line. All that potential, all that creative spirit – all for nothing. What could have been a child's paradise – but for the lack of children – looked instead like an accident waiting to happen.

A sound – hammering.

'Hello?' she called out.

The hammering paused, then started again. In the gloom, she'd failed to notice the crack of light at the far side of the room. Another door. She went towards it tentatively, fearful that all she would find was some sort of mechanised Santa's workshop.

She pushed the door open. An old man with a riot of white hair stood hunched over a workbench, holding a hammer in his gnarled fist. He glanced up, his brow knit with tension, as though he was expecting an unwelcome visitor. When he saw her, however, he smiled, his face growing as round as a cherub's.

'Ah, madame,' he said. 'Welcome to the Fantastic Toyshop.' He greeted her in English, with a strong accent. Behind him, the workshop was a study in organised chaos. There were more deconstructed clockwork cogs and gears in all shapes and sizes, life-sized papier mâché animals and figures, and a half-finished puppet theatre. On the workbench itself was another miniature building under construction: a perfect replica of the Paris Opera House.

'Thank you,' Sarah said. 'Your shop certainly is…' what, exactly? She decided to go with '…interesting.'

The old man's smile broadened, a gold tooth glinting in the incandescent light. 'I am glad you think so. I believe that an interesting shop draws interesting people.'

'Maybe.'

'Though not all interesting people are brave enough to venture inside.' His smile drooped.

Sarah came closer to the workbench, curiosity getting the better of her. The miniature building was truly spectacular in its detail and construction. 'You made all this yourself?'

The old man set down the hammer. 'Yes,' he said. 'I make the doll's houses, the mechanical figures, and anything that has wood or clockwork. I repair old toys, and I work on my castle, which is – shall we say – a work in progress. You must come back another day when it is finished.'

Sarah had the distinct impression that the castle had been a 'work in progress' for a long time. Given the state of the shop, the old man probably didn't get many visitors, and she felt a little sorry for him. But she would not be coming back another day.

'I came in to ask about the window display,' she said.

'Ah, yes, *Le Cirque du Lune*.' He frowned. 'It needs oiling.'

'The animals in the circus train – where did they come from?'

'The animals?' The old man raised a single bushy eyebrow. 'They, like many other treasures in my shop, came from an estate sale. There are people who bring me things, you see.' He took out a battered ledger from beneath the counter and opened the book, running his finger down a page of entries. 'Yes, here it is: *set of wooden circus animals circa eighteen ninety. Attributed to Gustav Bayol*.' He glanced up as if expecting a reaction. 'He was a famous maker of carousel horses. Possibly, the animals were a study for larger pieces. They are quite rare, I believe.'

'Really?' Sarah said. 'That's interesting.'

'It says here that I bought them last winter – yes, I remember. From a dealer who lives in Chantilly.'

Chantilly. Victor's mother had lived near Chantilly. That was a coincidence – it had to be. The animals might be rare, but they were not unique. And even if, by some strange twist of fate, they had ended up here, then what was it to her? It was best if they found a new home – a child to love them – and became part of someone's new memories. Sarah steadied herself against the workbench, trying to stave off the feeling that something inside her was crumbling, falling… dying, all over again.

'Are they for sale?' She gripped the cord of the lanyard around her neck. 'I know they're part of your display. But I'd like to buy them.'

The old man gave her a curious look. 'Are you all right,

madame? You look a bit pale. Can I get you a glass of water, or some tea? Then we can discuss your purchase.'

'What?' The offer startled her. What was there to discuss? She wasn't here to adopt a kitten or a puppy. Just to buy some toys. The old man's face fell. Only then did she realise she'd spoken aloud.

'I'm sorry,' she said. 'I didn't mean to be rude. It's just, I was supposed to be somewhere.' She sighed, her original errand all but forgotten. 'Too late now.'

A chime sounded from a small speaker wired to the wall. The old man startled at the sound, looking worried as he pressed a buzzer next to the speaker. He gathered together some papers and envelopes from the top of the work bench and shoved them underneath. Sarah caught a glimpse of red writing at the top. She was pretty sure they were bills and that the writing translated as *Final Notice.* Who was he expecting – a debt collector? Whatever his troubles were, Sarah felt bad for making things worse.

The old man bowed his head. 'I am sorry I upset you, and I wish I knew more about the animals. I am interested, you see, in the history and the memories. Every object has a story. Most of them, we will never know.' He stared at his hands wistfully. 'Those animals are well over a hundred years old. Who knows what they have seen?'

Sarah sensed the old man's loneliness in every shadow, every cobweb that smudged the corners of the room. Sensed his love for the objects around him, his vocation, which had somehow gone astray. In her glittering world of hotel consortiums, rich investors, and economies of scale, she rarely encountered emotion of any sort unless it related to share prices or cost overruns. Of her own warring emotions, compassion won out, rippling inside her like a deep, quiet pool.

'How long have you been here?' she asked gently.

'Years,' he said. 'I have forgotten how many. When I arrived in this country, I had nothing – no French, no job, and no place to live. I saw an advertisement for work at the shop. I washed my clothing in a fountain and came to seek an interview. The previous owner, Monsieur Courbet, was a good man. He took me in, and we worked together until he retired. But even that was long ago.'

'And where did you come from—'

Before she got an answer, footsteps drew up to the workshop door. The old man looked past her; his face bloomed into a grin. 'Ah, Tomas,' he said. 'Come in, come in. It is good to see you.'

Sarah turned as a man entered the workshop. Late thirties or early forties, tall with wavy brown hair, a delicate nose, and a strong jaw. He wore a smart linen blazer over jeans and carried a well-used leather satchel.

'Hi Franz. Hope you didn't miss the fireworks.' The newcomer spoke English like a native.

The old man snorted. 'I have no use for fireworks,' he said. 'Far too noisy and busy.'

The man laughed. 'I hear you. I'm steering clear of the main streets myself.'

'Good. And I hope your Lucinda and Andre are well?'

'Sure they are.' The newcomer gave Sarah a bemused look like they were sharing a secret joke. His eyes drew her in: the colour of an aquamarine marble, sparked by a light of intelligence. His assured manner made Sarah feel self-conscious, not knowing what to do or say. She noticed him glace at the St. Jacques lanyard around her neck; she tucked it into her blouse.

'The lady was good enough to come inside and keep me company,' the old man said. 'She is interested in the circus display.'

'It's amazing, isn't it?' the man addressed Sarah. 'Herr

Himmelberg – Franz – is quite the genius. Did he tell you about his glockenspiels back in Germany?'

'No,' she said. The man was clearly just being friendly, nonetheless she felt tense and annoyed. He'd barged in and interrupted her conversation as if he had every right. In her mind, she categorised him: an Englishman living in Paris – handsome and successful – maybe a lawyer or a doctor. A regular at the quirky little toy shop with plenty of money to buy handmade toys and antiques on his way home to his beautiful Parisian wife, Lucinda, and their son, Andre. The ghostly fingers of panic tickled at her throat. His life – everything hers could never be.

'Well, the castle will give you some idea of the scale,' he continued. 'You worked on some that were two or three times as big, didn't you, Franz?'

'Some of them, yes,' Franz said. 'But in those times, after the Berlin Wall was built, such things were – shall we say – not fashionable in the East. But my father was once allowed to travel to München to repair the Rathaus-Glockenspiel, which was for him a great honour.'

The man was blocking her path to the door; Sarah dug her nails into her palms. Glockenspiels, circus trains, antique animals. How had this happened? She'd been out to buy a bottle of wine – failing miserably – and a wrong turn had brought her here. To this strange, childless toyshop full of misplaced memories and dusty, broken things.

'That's fascinating,' she smiled mechanically, 'and I wish I could hear more. But I need to go. I'd like to buy… what we talked about. How much do I owe you?'

The old man hesitated. 'You see, madame, it is not a matter of money—'

'If you want a recommendation,' the newcomer said,

'then I'd go for the magnetic building kits.' He glanced at Franz. 'Andre loves them.'

'A bright, clever boy,' Franz muttered.

The man turned again to Sarah. 'You probably saw the Eiffel Tower in the first room. You can build almost anything.' He winked. 'They're great for boys or girls – whatever you need.'

The man's comment, though surely well-meant, was the last straw. 'I don't need anything,' she said through her teeth. 'I just have to go.'

'But madame? The animals?' The old man sounded distressed.

She shook her head. 'Thank you, but never mind.'

Turning, she hobbled on her wonky shoe past the other man and out of the workshop. Despair welled up inside her as she made her way out through the dim labyrinth of rooms. Dusty, broken, shattered… *empty*. So terribly, terribly empty.

She was breathing hard as she went outside into the slow-hot Paris night. In the toyshop window, the odd, amazing, horrific *Le Cirque du Lune* continued its relentless motion. The little train trundled on its track, but she couldn't see the animals.

Her eyes were too full of tears.

4

FRANZ

'What was that all about?' Tomas said.

'I do not know.' The woman's tension had made his bones ache, making Franz aware of every long, painful second he'd been alive. Far away in another room, the door slammed. She was gone. He wished he had asked her name.

'I should have given her what she came for,' he said. 'Whatever her pain is, I do not wish to add to it.'

'I'm sure you haven't,' Tomas said. 'Maybe she was just in a hurry.'

'Yes, maybe. Most people do not want to stay and talk – and why would they?' He shrugged. 'Sometimes, Tomas, I think I have lived too long. I am an antique – something to be put on a shelf and dusted once a fortnight. Sealed away in a box and shoved in an attic.'

'Come on, Franz. That's not true.'

'Is it not? I don't know anymore. Toys are so much easier than people.'

Tomas laughed. Franz forced himself to smile. The toyshop looked unfamiliar, as if he was seeing it through a stranger's eyes. A curiosity at best, but more likely old-fashioned and sad. But to him, the shop was his life. He'd hoped to keep going until his hands became too shaky to hold a hammer or a paintbrush, his vision too blurry to glue or solder, his mind too scattered to puzzle together clockwork and mechanisms. But lately, many of the nearby shops had closed and doubts had crept into his mind. If he could not keep the shop going, then what would be left of Franz Himmelberg?

'In the beginning, Tomas,' he said, 'I had great plans for this place. It would be full of children, and I would create a world straight out of the imagination. A place of laughter and joy. A place of magic.' He smiled sadly. 'But now the years have passed, and I have barely noticed. Now, most children and their parents would rather go to a shopping mall in the suburbs or to a department store—to the Disney Store. If things had been different, Tomas, I would have been like Walt Disney.'

'Yes, I can imagine that.'

'So many things happen that are an accident of birth. Walt Disney came from America. Franz Himmelberg came from East Germany.' He spread his hands. 'As they say, never the two shall meet.' He looked down at the miniature opera house he was gluing together. The pieces like a puzzle, and yet to him they came together so easily. Not like real life.

'Do you know,' he mused, 'that many of today's children do not even know there once *was* a place called East Germany?'

'They'll probably learn someday,' Tomas said. 'When they're old enough to understand.'

'They may learn, but they will never understand. They will have their own problems and heartbreak. Perhaps suffer even worse than we did. But they will never understand the *why* of it. Why we did what we did – and why we failed. The memories – and even our guilt – will be lost in time.'

Tomas looked thoughtful. Franz worried he'd said too much: danced, in his awkward old man's gait, too close to the truth. He took a long breath. 'Most of all, I wanted to create a place of memories that would last long after the children are grown up – and long after I am gone. But whatever my vision was, I fear I have left it too late.'

'It doesn't have to be,' Tomas said. 'I know times are hard, but so far you've survived when other shops have failed. If you opened more – did some advertising – then you'd have more customers. If you'd put your sign board out tonight, you could have got lots of foot traffic. And I'm no expert, but I would think you could do more with the place. If I'm being honest, mate, it's looking a little tired.'

'Yes, yes.' Franz was grateful for his friend's candour, but the words chafed. Tired? Exhausted was closer to the mark.

'It might help if you hired an assistant. Or found an apprentice you could train up. Like your father taught you, right?'

'Yes,' he said, 'I was once my father's apprentice. Though I did not appreciate or value the teaching. Back then I was…' he shook his head. He didn't want to think about what he was back then, let alone say it aloud.

'And you never wanted children?' Tomas indicated the theatre behind him. 'You seem like a natural.'

'Being a good toymaker and a good father is not the same thing,' he said.

'Fair enough.'

'And I suppose if we are being so honest,' Franz said, 'I could ask you the same question. You are young. Do you not want children?'

Tomas laughed, but his eyes were guarded. 'I'm forty. That's hardly young. And being a rubbish human being and a good father is not the same thing either.'

'Ah,' Franz said. He knew better than to argue. Tomas was a man whose life, on the outside at least, seemed full of possibilities. But who was he to say for sure? Once, when Franz had looked into the mirror, he'd seen the same thing. Too bad mirrors lie.

'Besides,' Tomas added, 'I've got Andre. He keeps me on my toes. That's why I'm here. I'd like another one of those magnetic building kits.'

Franz studied the face of the younger man. In his day, he'd seen people capable both of great altruism and dog-eat-dog selfishness. If he'd seen Tomas on the street, he wouldn't have thought him the former. And yet, taking such an interest in his young neighbour… it was this human side of his friend that interested him most.

'Yes, take a building kit,' Franz said. 'Take two. In making sculptures, bigger is better.'

'Great.' Tomas took out his wallet. 'How much do I owe you?'

'Nothing.'

'That's kind,' Tomas said, 'but unnecessary. I've got cash.'

Franz felt a pang of distress. He counted Tomas as a friend – one of very few – and surely a friend would not insist on giving him money. Even if he desperately needed it.

'Please,' he said, 'take the kits as my gift to young Andre. He sounds like such a clever, artistic boy. My father used to say that if you can touch the heart and mind of even one child, then you will have done something worthwhile. I hope that someday, Andre will come to my shop. I have many things I could show him. To have a child who appreciates my work will be payment enough.'

'But those kits are worth fifty euros each,' Tomas said. 'I looked online.'

Franz snorted. The true value of the toys in his shop could not be found *online*. Or anywhere else.

'I have named my price.' He crossed his arms.

'You're an odd one, Franz.'

'I take that as a compliment.'

'Yes, well…' Tomas spread his hands. 'I'd bring him here if I could. Sometimes, I think he's on the edge of a breakthrough. But so far it hasn't happened.'

'Healing cannot be rushed,' Franz said. 'Take the building kits on your way out. After that, we shall see.'

'Thanks.'

As Tomas turned to leave, Franz stopped him. 'Can you do me a favour? Bring me the animals from the circus train? You will have to stop the mechanism. The switch is by the door. I could go myself, but at my age, walking across my own shop is tiring work.'

'The circus animals? That's what she was after?'

'It does not seem right to keep them in the window. I will keep them safe in case she returns.' He hoped the woman would find her way back. The shop might once have drawn interesting people, but these days, he was glad when anyone stopped by.

'Sure.' Tomas left the workshop. Franz looked around for a box and packing material for the animals. As he searched, he found a box of cogs he'd ordered for his castle that had gone missing. Tomas was right – things did need sorting out. If only he had an apprentice to follow in his footsteps. Then it would be easier to tackle all the tasks – big and small – that the shop required. He'd be able to focus all his time and energy on finishing the castle.

But there was no such person. Sadness leached into his bones. Each day he felt more tired, his joints stiff and sore. The area was changing – soon the other shops would be redeveloped, transformed into something new. His shop would remain the same, drawing fewer and fewer people, his great work unfinished.

'I've got them.' Tomas returned a few minutes later and set the animals on the workbench one by one. 'They look pretty old.'

'They are in good condition,' Franz said. 'And quite valuable. Though, the woman did not seem like the ordinary sort of collector. I was hoping to discover the story behind her interest. I am always curious to find out the stories behind the objects – and the people that come into my shop. Stories are very powerful, are they not?'

'I guess so.' Tomas gave an offhanded shrug.

Franz gazed quizzically at his friend. He knew all about Tomas's novels and had even read a few of them, because it seemed the right thing to do. He was fond of imagining the exciting life Tomas must lead in the great city of Paris, inspiring his mysterious and romantic characters. But each time he mentioned the books, Tomas acted oddly evasive, his eyes wreathed with shadows. Franz suspected there was another story – a darker one – that Tomas was hiding. He was curious, of course, but it did not seem right to ask.

He gave Tomas two large bags for the building kits. 'Please give my regards to Andre,' he said. 'And let him know he is welcome anytime. As are you.'

'I will. But Franz…' Tomas frowned, 'are you sure you're OK?'

Franz gave him a smile he didn't feel, dodging the question he couldn't answer. A part of him longed to tell his friend the truth – the whole truth – not just the ones that mattered in the short term: the stack of bills, the feared visit from the landlord, the health and safety report. Tell his young friend the real story of why Franz Himmelberg was troubled, and why he could never achieve his dream. But the other part of him – the part that had learned to keep silent – won out.

'I am fine,' he said, 'really. Thank you for stopping by. And for being a friend.'

5

SARAH

The street that led to the wine shop was a block further down the main boulevard. Sarah threw her shoes in a bin and limped her way back to her flat in her bare feet, angry and frustrated with herself. If she hadn't been in a hurry, if she hadn't been stressed by the crowds, then she wouldn't have misread the map. She never would have got lost in this shabby area of empty shops; she never would have found the toyshop. A cruel and unwanted twist of fate that could not be unravelled.

She checked her messages as she walked. Jeanette had called asking if she'd bought the wine. Monsieur Forman, the manager of the St. Jacques, had called as well. Sarah was overseeing the modernisation of the historic art deco hotel, and even on a public holiday, she could only imagine what crises had occurred in her absence. The building inspectors were due in the next few days to check the new lift, and the construction manager was on holiday. The new investor, a rich property developer from Eastern Europe, was coming for a private tour of the refurbished hotel before next month's gala, and might arrive unannounced at any moment. The consortium had grand plans to increase their property holdings in Paris and, if she played her cards right, she could be in line for a big promotion. All in all, when she returned to work tomorrow, everyone would expect her to be on her game. Her most of all. *Work* – that was her safety net. Emails, meetings, and spreadsheets were the best way to eclipse the unwanted thoughts and memories that lurked at the edges of her mind.

Her small serviced apartment was in a building owned by the consortium. Although she could have stayed in luxury at the St. Jacques, Sarah preferred to have her own space. The flat was located on a narrow street near the Luxembourg Gardens, just around the corner from a little hotel where she'd stayed with her mum on their trips to Paris before her marriage. As she passed the hotel, she recalled long weekends spent combing the stalls of the famous Paris flea market, Le Puces de Saint-Ouen, for treasures, fabrics, and trims that her mum sold in her shop in Surrey. Glorious autumn days, crunching through golden leaves, enjoying the pale watery sun on her face, sitting in a café watching the people go by. Innocent days, a lifetime ago.

Now, Paris held nothing but ghosts. Although she'd spent most of the last six months in the city and had a guidebook with places circled – museums, galleries, theatres, monuments – she hadn't managed to visit any of them. It was easy to make excuses: work was all consuming, she was too tired, she didn't know many people in Paris. But the truth was, it seemed pointless making new memories. In the last five years, she'd tried to get her life back on track – and in many ways she'd succeeded. She'd landed a top job and excelled at it, successfully managing people and projects. She'd picked up the broken pieces one by one, gluing them together like the fragments of a broken vase. On the outside, the repairs looked complete. But tonight had proved that the cracks would always be there.

The apartment building was modern and ugly, but it was also clean and quiet, and the café next door did morning coffee and croissants. '*Bonsoir*, *madame*,' the guard greeted her as she came inside.

Sarah didn't correct him. Most people she'd met in Paris called her madame. At thirty-six, the term might be a nod to her age rather than an assumption that she was married. Still, it was a tiny barb, a reminder of everything that had gone wrong.

'*Bonsoir.*' Sarah padded her way to the lift. Inside the flat, she rinsed off her feet and put the kettle on. The flat seemed unfamiliar, as if she'd entered the life of a different person. This morning, everything had been in its place, her thoughts and feelings compartmentalised. She'd enjoyed the walk to the St. Jacques, prominently positioned on the Right Bank near the river. She'd been calm, polished, and professional in every way.

Now, her mind was in disarray.

She had to pull herself together: her job was too important not to. When the kettle boiled, she made herself a cup of tea and made a few calls – to Javier, asking him to sort the wine disaster; to Monsieur Forman, saying she was available if needed. Normally, it felt good to take action and be in control, but tonight, everything seemed off-kilter.

Sarah finished her calls and went to run a bath. As the tub filled, her phone rang. 'Mum' came onscreen. She debated letting it go to voicemail, but her mum had been her rock when the world was crumbling around her. When she'd been unable to leave her room for the better part of two years, overwhelmed by the world outside.

She grabbed the phone and answered it.

'Hello, Mum. You OK?'

'Yes, love, fine. You?'

Hearing her mum's voice almost made her break down. They'd seen each other recently – she'd gone home to England in May to celebrate her dad's birthday – but they hadn't really caught up. The garden party had been a success, with family and neighbours dropping in on a sunny Saturday afternoon. Sarah's brother had brought his wife and their young twins. The children had been so happy and ebullient running around the garden, and her sister-in-law was friendly and interested in her work in Paris. Sarah had tried to show an equal interest in school trips, summer camps, and family-friendly holidays. Tried not to dwell on the fact that the twins were too young to remember their cousin. It had been five years. For everyone else, life was 'back to normal'. The harder she'd tried, the more the sadness had eroded her smile until her face felt ready to crack.

In the end, she'd changed her ticket and come back after only two days. The flat in Paris – empty, soulless, and lacking in memories – was infinitely preferable to the pain of home.

Her mum gave Sarah all the updates: the library book sale, the state of the garden, the heatwave, the neighbour's dog. She asked whether Sarah was eating enough and had any plans to leave the city in August the way Parisian locals did. Sarah gave the obligatory answers, but her mind kept wandering back through the tangled streets that led to the strange toyshop. It had seemed like fate, destiny – not that she believed in such things.

'Mum,' she said, 'can I ask you something?'

'Sure.'

'What happened to Rowan's things?'

A long pause ensued. When her mum spoke again, Sarah was aware of the distance between them. 'You said at the time you didn't want anything,' her mum said. 'I have a few suitcases of things I picked up from your flat – mostly your clothes. Victor cleared out the rest.'

'OK.' Sarah schooled her voice into normality. 'That's what I thought. Thanks.'

'Why are you asking?'

'No reason. Actually, Mum, my battery's low. I'll ring you in a few days.'

'OK. But try and enjoy yourself while you're there. Maybe you'll meet a tall, dark, mysterious Frenchman.'

The statement was a punch in the stomach. Her mum meant well, but sometimes her attempts at cheer bordered on thoughtless. Though Victor had been only *half* French.

'I mean…' her mum backpedalled, '… just try to have some fun. You work too hard.'

'Sure, Mum. Thanks.'

Sarah said goodnight and ended the call. She was grateful that her mum had never sounded the battle cries of 'get back out there' and 'meet someone new' – until now, at least. Sarah had decided long ago that she didn't want that. Her memories, kept safe inside her heart, were enough.

She undressed and slipped into the bath. Closing her eyes, she tried to clear her head. Focus on tomorrow, go through her mental checklist, steel herself for the tasks ahead.

She couldn't do it. Her mind spun and looped, relentless. Animals, acrobats, a circus train on a track, and another face that her mum's comment had unwittingly brought into her head. Of a tall, dark-haired Englishman that she'd met only for a minute and would never see again.

6

TOMAS

It was five flights up to the flat. The building had a lift, but Tomas rarely took it. He liked the fact that each step he climbed took him further away from the real world.

Tonight, the stairs winded him; the magnetic building kits were surprisingly heavy. In truth, he was worried about Franz. So many local shops had closed due to rising costs and low foot traffic, and, if the Facebook forums were to be believed, nefarious plots by landlords to buy out the struggling shops for 'redevelopment'. Could Franz survive that? It was hard to see how.

The top floor had only two flats. The flat opposite his belonged to his neighbour, Mathilde Villere, who had lived alone for many years until two years ago, when her grandson, Andre, had come to live with her.

It was tempting just to go home. It was already past nine, and after jostling through the crowds in the street, Tomas was dying for a cup of tea – or something stronger. But it had been a few days since he'd last visited Andre – the only thing he did of any real value – and he wanted to see the look on his face when he gave him the present.

Mathilde answered, her grey hair pulled back in a tight bun, her brow knit in its usual frown. 'Tomas,' she said, 'we were not expecting you tonight. Are you not joining in the celebrations?'

'Fireworks and parades aren't really my thing,' he said. 'Is Andre OK?'

'The noise bothered him. He has not left his room—'

'Tomas?' The bedroom door banged open. A few seconds later, Andre ran out, his face lit up like a sparkler. He flung his arms around Tomas.

'Easy mate!' Tomas grinned, hugging him back. Although Andre, who had recently turned eleven, never left the flat and had trouble communicating with strangers, he was always excited to see Tomas. His energy was infectious. *One child* – what was it Franz had said? To touch the heart and mind of even one child makes everything worthwhile? For Tomas, Andre was that one child. The boy was the son he might have had, had things been… different.

He untangled the boy's arms, indicating the bags. 'I brought you those,' he said.

Andre let out a breathless cry of delight; Mathilde pursed her lips in disapproval.

'You shouldn't have,' she said. 'You will spoil him.'

'I'll take that as a thanks.' Tomas smiled fondly.

'Yes,' she said with a sigh. 'And while you are here, would you like a coffee?'

'I'll make it,' he said. 'You sit down – have a break.'

'May I have two sugars, please?' Her mouth eased into a line. 'Last time, you only add one.' Her English was halting, but they'd agreed to speak it around Andre so that he could learn. For 'someday' when he was 'cured'.

'My mistake,' Tomas said wryly. He watched Andre tear the lid off the first box, then went to the kitchen to put the kettle on.

He spooned coffee into the cafetière as he had many times over the last two years. Before that, despite living across from Mathilde for years, he'd never set foot inside her flat, or had any conversations beyond 'may I borrow an egg?' or 'can you sign for a package?' They were from different generations, and both content to keep themselves to themselves. The polite anonymity might have gone on indefinitely, but one day when he passed her on the stairs, he noticed she was crying. He'd made a very un-Tomas-like decision: bought some croissants and knocked on her door. For a brief time, he'd felt like Tom Willowfield again.

In fact, 'Tom' was how he'd introduced himself to the thin, gangly boy with the haunted blue eyes that held all the darkness in the world. Mathilde had talked like Andre wasn't in the room, telling Tomas all about the cancer that had taken her daughter, Renée, the boy's mother. The boy was in shock – which was only understandable – he would barely speak. Tomas had made another uncharacteristic decision. He'd sat down on the sofa and began telling a story. One that didn't involve murder or international intrigue, or a heroine racing to save the world. The words flowed from his mouth, the images spinning from thin air. A dark wood, a princess in a tower, a sorcerer who had stolen the moon. When it was done, Andre had uncurled himself from the sofa and taken a sketchbook from the bookshelf. In only a few minutes, with swift, bold strokes of the pen, he'd created a tangled wood, a tower with vines snaking upwards, and a very life-like princess, capturing all the details of the story with skill and imagination.

Tomas finished making the coffee and brought it to the table where Mathilde was seated, knitting shapeless winter garments for the local refugee centre. '*Merci*,' she said, as he set down the cup. Her tone was brusque but held a genuine note of thanks. Over time, he'd got to know her –

she had no family in the picture: no one else to perform even a small act of kindness like making her a hot drink. Her small annuity from her late husband's pension provided enough to live on, but no frills. She still sometimes spoke like Andre wasn't there, lamenting the fact that nothing had 'worked': not the psychologists or the home-schooling teacher sent by the local authority. More than once, Tomas had taken her out into the corridor for a private word. Andre's anxiety and panic attacks prevented him from going outside to experience the world, and words like 'autism' and 'agoraphobia' had been bandied about. But the fact remained that Andre was affectionate and worthy, not to mention one of the brightest people Tomas had ever met.

Andre had one of the kits scattered on the floor: a huge pile of flat, geometric-shaped pieces in rainbow-coloured Perspex. There were wheels and pistons, cords and pulleys, doors and windows, and pieces shaped like clockwork gears. Tomas knelt down and fit some pieces together. With the help of the magnetic edges, it was possible to make three-dimensional shapes: towers, walls, turrets.

As they worked, Andre asked for a story. Tomas sat back and thought for a moment. Sometimes it took him a while to come up with a good story, but thanks to the earlier conversation with Franz, something sparked in his mind. An idea… a vision. Stories *were* powerful – another thing Franz had said. Once, in another lifetime, Tomas had believed in that power. He chose his words carefully, nurturing them like the tiny seeds of a garden.

'Once upon a time, there was a man,' he said. 'He'd lived through many difficult times and spent much of his life trapped behind a high wall. But the man barely noticed because he lived in his own magic world. He was an artist who made things out of metal and electricity. Clockwork toys, carousels, doll's houses. He lived in a fantastic toyshop.'

Andre looked up and smiled.

'The man had a dream. He was building a great work: a huge castle with rotating layers, life-sized moving figures, jousting knights, and imaginary animals. But the man was sad because he was getting old, and his great work wasn't finished. He had no child or apprentice to take over his shop when he was gone. To continue his work and maintain the shop as an oasis of history and memory in a world where everything else was changing beyond recognition.

'And, make no mistake,' he continued, 'not just anyone would do. He needed to find the right person to share his vision. A person with the right kind of love in his heart.'

Tomas stopped speaking. Andre continued to build.

'So, what happened?' Mathilde pressed. 'Did he find someone to help him complete his great work?'

'No. Not yet. He's still searching.' Tomas looked at the structure Andre was making. It had many layers, rooms, and doors. A staircase crisscrossed the space. It reminded him of Franz's creations. But already, Andre was running out of pieces.

Andre tried to place a turret made from four elongated triangular pieces on top of the structure. As he did, his knee hit the perimeter wall. The entire structure juddered and hung in mid-air for a moment before crashing to the floor.

Tomas and Mathilde both started forward. This kind of thing could set Andre off into one of this 'states'. When the boy's pent-up frustration and rage became too much, he'd start smashing things. Sometimes, when Tomas heard a commotion in the night and went over to help Mathilde, he'd seen real fear in her eyes. He felt for Andre, but Mathilde was all alone, doing her best in a tough situation.

This time, Andre just shrugged. He picked up the pieces and started again.

Mathilde sat back, visibly relieved. 'Too bad your magic toyshop is not real. Perhaps, if there is one place Andre could be persuaded to go, it would be there.'

'Maybe it is real. Or… it could be.' He winked at Andre.

'Sometimes, Tomas, I think you get too caught up in your stories for your own good,' Mathilde said.

'Is it wrong to be caught up in a story when it's better than real life?'

Mathilde shook her head and tsked. 'A man like you. How can you even ask?'

A man like him…

Tomas gave her a kindly smile and stood up to leave. 'I'm sure you're right, Mathilde.' He brought the second bag over to Andre. 'There's another kit in there, mate. Make something awesome, OK?'

'I will,' Andre said. '*Merci.*'

'Hey, you're welcome.'

Mathilde walked with Tomas to the door.

'You are too kind,' she said. 'And I wonder why that is. Why do you care so much about a damaged boy?'

Tomas stared down the corridor for a long moment. He knew the answer, though not how to voice it. Franz, Andre, Mathilde – all living their lives at the margins – inhabiting the edges of his own liminal space.

'Maybe because that's how you see him. And he knows that.'

'Maybe.' Mathilde sighed. 'But sometimes it is too hard. I want so much for him. But there is so little I can do.'

'You can love him the way he is.' As soon as the words were out, Tomas wondered what possible right he had to speak to Mathildc about love, or self-sacrifice or any kind of real human feeling. Except maybe loss…

In an instant, the woman in the toyshop came, unbidden, into his mind. Huge, complex eyes, a face that couldn't hide her anguish – the cause of which he couldn't fathom. Seeing her in that state had triggered something inside him. He'd been acutely aware of his own pain, which he normally kept under lock and key. Was it the same for her? He'd never know – and that was a good thing. Just as well that he'd never see her again.

'Yes, you are right,' Mathilde said. 'I can love him and continue to hope. That someday a miracle will happen.'

Tomas fished his keys out of his pocket and went to the door of his own flat, unlocking it. 'I guess that's all any of us can do.'

7

MATHILDE

As she closes the door to her flat, Mathilde's chest aches with a familiar tightness. The boy, however, is still occupied. She understands the meaning behind Tomas's story; she wishes with all her heart that Andre could understand too. The boy needs a purpose: a reason to escape the prison of grief, the prison of this flat. If only there was a destination, a key. A magic toyshop; if only such a place was real. If only... so many things. Tomas truly is a saint to try to help. Who knows what his reasons are – but does it matter in the end? She needs help – never more so than now. The letter... a single sheet of paper. So light in the pocket of her cardigan that it weighs nothing. Yet, it contains the weight of all her fears, all her regrets.

She tiptoes her way carefully through the pieces of coloured plastic scattered on the floor. Andre does not look up or speak to her. She does not look at him or speak. It is almost as if she has forgotten how to speak. One of so many things...

Mathilde goes to the kitchen to make soup for dinner. The chicken is not in the fridge or on the worktop. Cursing under her breath, she opens the freezer. She's forgotten to defrost it. Again. She can almost hear Jean-Louis's voice, as if they were back in their old flat in the 12th arrondissement. 'Always defrost the meat thoroughly, and never forget to preheat the oven.' And Renée, looking up at her papa with love in her eyes. 'I will not forget, papa.'

No, Renée would not have forgotten. She and Jean-Louis had loved to cook together, making decadent meals and desserts from a little cookbook he'd inherited from his mother. Mathilde once again feels the pride – and the phantom stab of jealousy. Seeing them together in the kitchen always made her feel like an outsider, a third wheel.

And what did she do? Complain. About the mess, about the waste, about the money. Endlessly. It is just as well her husband and daughter are both free of her. Just as well that she cannot speak to Andre. And the letter: just as well it has confirmed the worst. Even the memory of her own voice sickens her.

'*Grand-mère*?'

Cheese on toast – it will have to do. Mathilde puts two slices of bread in the toaster; the walls of the kitchen close around her. This flat is much larger than the old one, with its thin walls, noisy plumbing, and tiny wardrobes. Her life is different, and yet she still feels the same clawing discontent. Never appreciating how blessed she was until everything was gone. Will she make the same mistake again?

Undoubtedly.

'Come look what I've made.'

Letting out a pent-up sigh, she goes to the door of the kitchen. Andre has set the remaining coloured tiles in front of his tall structure, making a wide, colourful plaza. A dance floor. The memory… it hurts. Dancing with Jean-Louis in her special pair of silver shoes. She can feel his arms around her, breathe in the scent of his skin. The rush of pain is overwhelming. The shoes… she has not seen them for years. What happened to them? Where can they be?

'*Grand-mère*?'

Andre speaks louder now, impatient. The shoes are not important. Clinging to the memories is not important. Andre is important. If only it was not so painful to look at him. He has Renée's eyes. Eyes that once danced with wonder and delight. Eyes glassy and cold… dead.

'It is…' she swallows '… very colourful.' She must continue to make an effort, the way she has done every day of her life. The letter is not an excuse for giving up.

'Can you ask Tomas to bring me another set? I need more pieces.'

'Don't be so ungrateful,' she says more sharply than she intends. 'Tomas has done enough for you. You should appreciate more of what you have, not what you don't.'

A barb of loss pricks her heart. Renée was never ungrateful or discontented in any way. She was a girl who laughed a lot – smiled a lot. Wanted to experience life to the full. Andre is not like his mother. No – Mathilde knows the source of the friction between herself and the boy. Andre is too much like *her*.

'Sorry, *Grand-mère*,' Andre says, his eyes huge and hurt. *So like hers*… Mathilde feels a fluttering sensation deep inside her chest. The urge to fly away. From this room, from this life. Once, she had been like a butterfly. Spinning, dancing, light on her feet. That was how Jean-Louis had seen her. Jean-Louis tried to help her break free of the cocoon that imprisoned her. But she had resisted, complaining even more. Her feet hurt, the pay was bad, she was fat with the baby – no point to any of it. She'd seen the disappointment in his eyes each time she chose to remain stuck in that sticky mass of want and discontent. A failed chrysalis. That was all she had ever been.

Renée has flown away. Not by her own choosing, but flown away nonetheless. And Jean-Louis… he too is gone. She believes they are together in the beyond, inseparable as always. The thought gives her no comfort. They have left her behind, trapped in this life, this cage. Leaving her with this boy.

'It is fine,' she says. 'But please clean up this mess.'

She returns to the kitchen and takes the letter from her pocket, shoving it in the drawer. The words do not lie. She knows them to be true. Time is slippery; she is struggling to grab hold of it. Already she has forgotten so much – the shoes, the chicken. But what does any of that matter? She has forgotten the most important thing of all. She has forgotten how to love.

8

FRANZ

FRIDAY, JULY 21ST

Franz frowned as the music played and the clockwork ballerina spun *en pointe* along her figure of eight. The male dancer skated forward and lifted his arms. The two figures collided, the ballerina pushed from her track. The mechanism began to tick and whirr over and over again. He untwisted the electric wire and the whole thing ground to a halt.

'*Scheiße*!' he muttered, annoyed and perplexed. He picked up his tiny tweezers and screwdriver and once again checked the mechanism under the magnifying glass. He'd been working on this for hours, and he'd made similar things hundreds of times. But for some reason, no matter what he tried, the two dancers continued to collide.

He had decided to replace the circus in the window with a Nutcracker display. The figures were complete, but the gears and mechanics of the theatre refused to cooperate. It was good in a way. The difficult clockwork puzzle kept his mind off other matters. Like the stack of bills with red writing on top; like the other shops on the street that had darkened one by one, their owners taking with them the memories of more prosperous times and leaving behind only empty shells. Like his castle: the embodiment of his dreams, which wasn't going to build itself.

'I am open to suggestions.' Franz glanced disapprovingly at an antique bear he'd re-stuffed for a woman from Montmartre who'd bought it for her niece. Next to the bear was a porcelain doll whose head was cracked from a fall from a shelf. Franz had painstakingly glued every piece back in place. Sometimes, he felt like his shop was nothing more than a hospital for old toys.

At the other end of the worktable, the wooden circus animals looked on as he worked. He had little sense of time passing, but surely it had been at least a week since the woman had come into the shop. He had been so certain she would return – but so far, he'd been wrong. Perhaps she could not find her way back through the tangled streets, or perhaps she had not cared as much as he'd thought. Or perhaps something else was keeping her away. Whatever the reason, Franz wished she would return. He wanted her to have the animals – to take them away to a new life and a new home. At the end of the day, the shop was more than a hospital for old toys – it was an adoption agency. His role was to find the right toy for the right person. Spread a tiny bit of magic, a glittery speck of love.

He fiddled with the screws, struggling to focus. Already, he'd taken down the window display, but maybe that was a mistake. The circus was in good working order, and he needed to make progress on his castle. A part of him feared that he was focusing on a smaller problem to avoid a bigger one – something he'd done all his life.

His father had been the same, Franz recalled as he loosened the screws to realign the track. He'd chosen to devote his life to musical boxes and glockenspiels: the tiny part of the universe he could control. He never spoke of the war or showed any interest in the political tensions between East and West. Franz remembered that long-ago trip to München they'd taken together. When his father had asked him to come along, Franz had been uncomfortable about going to the West even for a few days. But when he'd told Anna about the proposed trip, she'd been impressed. He hadn't wanted her to think he was a coward.

When they'd got off the train, Franz had been both amazed and bewildered by the colours, the sounds, the advertisements, the cars – a bombardment of the senses. They'd visited the Bavarian Christmas Market, which had been full of delights: iced gingerbread, pungent glühwein, shiny decorations, and the beautiful Rathaus lit up in the centre of the square. Some of the shops sold nothing but Christmas decorations. He could still recall their window displays: miniature winter wonderlands with sparkly crystal snow and glittering lights. A magical world – one Franz loved and despised in equal measure. He'd learned in school that decadence and capitalist consumption were bad things created by greedy people. Americans. His world might be less bright, but its simplicity was clear: shades of brown and grey, a three-metre-high wall that had gone up almost overnight when Franz was ten years old. Franz had been glad to return home; content to choose his own prison. Now, as he looked around him – at the old toys, the mess, his great work unfinished – he realised that although the walls were different, it was still a prison.

He adjusted the track and rewound the mechanism. Once again, the dancers collided. It irked him, like an itch he couldn't scratch. Perhaps thinking about Anna had darkened his mood. He should go back to his flat – call it a night, as they say. Or perhaps he should make a list of materials needed to finish the castle. Or tackle the pile of bills… even the thought made him feel sick.

As he was about to put away his tools, a noise startled him. Metal on metal, the sound coming from the back of the theatre where a secret door led to the main street. A burglar? Franz tightened his grip on the screwdriver. How could it be a burglar when there was nothing to steal?

'*Bonsoir.* Monsieur Himmelberg?'

Franz's shoulders drooped as a man came into the workshop: tall and thin, grey hair combed over a nearly-bald pate, wearing an expensive suit. His landlord. He'd used his own key.

'Monsieur Rouveau,' he said. 'What a nice surprise.'

Rouveau wrinkled his long nose into his signature frown. Franz felt like a small child who had made a bad smell.

'I see you are hard at work,' Rouveau said.

'Yes, yes. My work – it is everything to me.' Franz tried to make his mind recall the right French words and stem the awkwardness. 'My castle, you see. I am getting back to work on it. After I change the window display and finish my commissions….' he rambled on, hoping if he talked long enough, Rouveau, who was bound to have some important appointment elsewhere, would decide to leave.

The man cleared his throat. No such luck.

'I will keep this brief,' Rouveau said. 'You know why I am here?'

'The rent…' Franz spluttered. 'I will have it. Soon.'

'You are three weeks overdue. And this is not the first time.'

'Yes, yes, I know. I am sorry.'

'And then, there is the matter we discussed last time. Especially for a shop that purports to cater to children.'

Health and safety. Three little words: bullets to the heart.

Rouveau had given Franz the report almost gleefully. The trip and fall hazards, the fire safety measures, accessibility. The costs associated with putting everything right. Franz had ignored it, hoping it would go away. Obviously, it had not.

Rouveau was talking. Franz tried to listen, but the fear clouded everything. He'd been given time and had failed to take the necessary actions. What would happen now?

'… been very patient with you. You know I've always admired you and Monsieur Courbet before you.'

'I remember those days.' Franz smiled faintly. 'And your son, when you brought him round. He liked the doll's houses best, did he not? The ones of the Paris buildings? Is he well?'

Rouveau flicked a manicured nail. 'My son is divorced now. I am training him up to take over when I retire. He has no need of doll's houses – not when he owns real Paris buildings.'

'I see.'

'I admit that your shop has a certain "sentimental" value to the area,' Rouveau said. 'But times move on and things change. I can't let you stay here out of charity. This is an up-and-coming area.'

Franz swallowed hard. It had not been up and coming for the pet shop, the hairdresser, or the green grocer. Though Franz kept largely to himself, even he had heard the rumours. Shops forced to close because of rising costs, leases that were terminated due to minor infractions, elderly patrons offered money to retire, landlords with council inspectors in their pockets. Franz had grown up in a world of power and authority – others had power and he did not. The more things changed, the more they stayed the same.

'Please…' the word sounded small and insignificant.

'Please, monsieur. I appreciate everything you have done for me. I will have the rent and make the changes. I promise.'

'I will give you three months,' Rouveau said. 'Which is more than generous, I think you will agree. If things do not change, then you will need to vacate the premises so I can pursue other options. You will need to be out by Christmas.'

Out by Christmas. Franz felt his bad knee begin to quiver. How had it come to this? Times were hard – yes, of course – and the problems were not going away. But to actually lose the shop? Somehow, he had not considered that outcome, clinging instead to the idea that eventually he would finish the castle and things would turn themselves around. But if he lost the shop, the castle would be dismantled. His great work would remain forever unfinished.

'It is more than reasonable.' Rouveau's frown deepened as he swept his gaze around the workshop. 'I am trying to be helpful.'

Helpful. Yes, he probably thought he was. But nothing in the world could help now. How would he ever find the energy, the money – the will – to turn things around? What would happen if he was forced to close the doors of *La Boutique Fantasque* forever? Would he become just another old man sitting on a park bench feeding the pigeons? Hating himself and the choices he'd made; wondering what had happened to his life?

'Yes, you are being very helpful.' Franz hung his head in anguish and defeat. 'Thank you and goodbye.'

PART II

The old man is sad, and that makes the animals sad. They may be only wood and paint, but they have seen so much, felt so much, lived so many stories. They understand grief; they understand loss. Most of all, they understand regret. Why do we not appreciate our gifts until they are lost? Why do we wait to speak up until it is too late? These questions trouble the old man and trouble the animals too. For a heart filled with regret can spare no room for love.

9

SARAH

FRIDAY, AUGUST 4TH

'Madame, the champagne is not cold!'

'Madame, we are missing three flower arrangements.'

'Madame, the sous chef has called in sick!'

'Madame, the glasses are not clean.'

At times, Sarah felt like the only sane person in the world. Or, the only insane one. As the days passed, preparations continued for the grand reopening, and she dealt with disaster after disaster, she couldn't stop the soundtrack running through her head: *What is the point?*

The bizarre little toyshop haunted her dreams. Had she really come upon it by chance – or had destiny led her to that particular spot at that particular time? It was such an odd catalyst for a war she hadn't even known was raging inside her. It wasn't like she was avoiding the pain: she thought of Rowan every day. Though the memories cut as sharp as knives, Sarah welcomed and cherished them.

But the toyshop had rippled the surface of the hidden pool of rage and shame. She'd tried so hard to rebuild her life, but all her efforts had been pointless – she saw that now. Some wounds were too deep to heal, some holes too dark to climb out of. Why had she even tried?

The day of the gala arrived, and by late afternoon all the little fires were put out. Sarah finished checking the table settings in the dining room and went to the reception desk where Jeanette was on duty. 'I think we're all set,' Sarah said.

'Thank you, Sarah,' Jeanette said. 'You have done such a great job. Even Komitov has made no complaints so far. He must be happy with the Presidential Suite.' She winked. 'And the wine.'

'Good,' Sarah said. After her wine shop failure, she'd had Javier prepare a selection of wines even older and more expensive than the requested bottle. It had obviously done the trick. She was glad the problem was sorted, but any sense of achievement eluded her.

Her thoughts veered to the toyshop and the old man – Franz. The money spent on the bottle of wine could probably pay his bills for a month. She was used to dealing with members of the development consortium, most of them rich and spoiled. To them, one hotel was very much like another. Whereas the old man had real passion – however misguided – for his little shop and cherished treasures. *Cherished treasures…*

A sudden wave of panic swept over her. What if the animals were gone? She'd resisted going back, mentally beating herself up for being foolish and nostalgic. Was it too late?

She checked her watch – the guests were due to arrive in just over three hours. 'Can you hold the fort for a little while, Jeanette? I have an errand to run.'

Jeanette cast her a worried look. 'Is everything all right?'

'Yes,' Sarah assured her. 'I'll be back soon.'

'*Parfait*,' Jeannette said. 'Then I will see you later.'

'*Parfait*.' Feeling a little sick, Sarah asked the doorman to hail her a taxi.

Although many Parisians were away on summer holiday, the streets were teeming with tourists and souvenir sellers. The weather was hot and sticky, the afternoon still and airless. The taxi dropped her in front of the bookshop. She found the passageway, thinking it would be easy to retrace her steps. If anything, the tangle of streets was even more impenetrable. Anxiety knotted in her chest – this was another bad decision and a distraction she didn't need. At the same time, it seemed imperative.

At last she saw the sinuous art nouveau window and faded signboard. *La Boutique Fantasque*. She prepared herself for the sight of the circus animals. But the window was dark and still. A new sense of loss blindsided her. It was one more thing she'd taken for granted, slipping through her fingers like sand in an hourglass. She was tempted to leave; to allow her pain to scatter into the wind. But she found herself at the door, ringing the buzzer, half hoping no one would respond. After an eternity, the door clicked and she pulled it open. Her heart pounded as she went inside. The circus had been dismantled; she almost tripped over a pile of broken train track. In the dim glow of a forlorn security light, the rocking horses cast monstrous shadows, the dolls in the cabinet dark except for the glint of their glass eyes. Sarah hurried forward through the labyrinth, unable to cast off the feeling of resigned sadness that pervaded the shop.

The light from the workshop shimmered like a mirage. The old man was working on what looked like a puppet theatre – a new window display? He greeted her with a hearty hello, but his eyes looked troubled. She felt sorry for him: toiling away in his shop, maybe not realising how it looked to outsiders. She'd encountered people like him before – people who didn't see the need for change. In any case, it wasn't her concern. She needed to finish her errand, return to the St. Jacques, and get on with her life.

'I came back for the animals,' she said. 'Please say you still have them.'

10

FRANZ

When the doorbell rang, Franz almost decided not to answer it. He had no joy to share; failure crushed him like a weight. After Monsieur Rouveau's visit, he'd put down his tools and stared at his hands. His fingers were crooked, the skin calloused. He was unused to seeing them so still. But if things stayed the same, he would have to get used to it. The thought made him want to cry.

But when the woman walked into his workshop, his spirits lifted. She was so beautiful, so fragile. Her face was a mask finely carved from marble that might crack at any moment. Yet he sensed her strength underneath. She'd had the courage to find her way back to the shop and face whatever demons were inside her. Something Franz had never managed.

'I have been keeping them safe for you,' he said, indicating the little menagerie at the end of the bench. 'I am glad you came back.'

The woman picked up the tiny poodle and turned it over in her fingers. Her face gave nothing away, but her hands trembled as she set it down again. Franz was curious, but it was important to give her time and space. Let her talk if she wanted to. If she was ready.

'Thank you,' she said, 'I appreciate it.' She opened her handbag and took out a small purse. 'How much do I owe you? I really have no idea what they're worth.'

Sadness pooled in his chest. He hated talk of money and owing – such poor substitutes for the value of a treasure or memory.

'I think only you know their worth,' he said.

The woman did not meet his eyes. 'OK, then I guess they're not worth anything. I had a similar set… once. But it can't be the same. My set, you see, had a giraffe. That was the most special.'

'I am quite sure there was no giraffe when they came from the sale,' Franz said. 'I am very sorry.'

'So am I,' she said softly.

She picked up the seal with a ball at the end of its nose. 'I know it's a lot to ask, but can you give me the details of the person you bought them from? Maybe he would know. It's a long shot, but I'd like to try.'

'I do not have his details,' he said. 'Sometimes he comes to the shop with things for me to buy. We talk, have a coffee. That is all.'

Her face clouded over. 'But surely you keep details of your suppliers. Otherwise, how do you run your business?'

The force of her emotions scared him a little. 'A good question.' Franz hung his head. 'I only know that I do not run it very well. Tomas tells me that I should open more and advertise. You are telling me that I should keep track of what I buy and sell. And the landlord tells me I must fix up the shop or else he will find another tenant. And how will I complete my castle then?'

He looked up, hoping she might have an answer. She was staring at him, her face unreadable.

'You came from Berlin, is that right?'

'Yes.' Her unexpected interest gave him courage to continue. 'When the wall came down, I left to seek freedom – or at least to escape the past. At the time I thought they were the same thing. I had nothing but the clothes on my back and the skills my father taught me. Skills I did not value at the time. Over the years, I have tried to do him proud.' He looked around at the shop, sickened by what he saw. 'I have not succeeded.'

She smiled sympathetically. 'Whether you have or not, it's a fascinating story.'

A fascinating story! Franz had heard many stories over the years from his customers. But never before had he thought of his own life as anything other than a series of mistakes and a catalogue of regrets. He sighed. He had other stories he could tell her – darker ones. He did not like to remember those. But lately, the shadows of the past had been lengthening in his mind.

'Thank you,' he said. 'And if you wish to tell me your story – about your set of wooden animals – then I will gladly listen.'

The woman hesitated, clearly uncomfortable. 'The animals I lost belonged to my daughter, Rowan,' she said. 'They were antiques that were passed down in my husband's family in France. Victor and I got divorced, and they got lost when I moved out.' Her eyes shifted evasively. 'But that was in London. And there was a giraffe. So obviously they aren't the same.'

'And your daughter, Rowan?'

'She… liked the giraffe best. I'd like to get it back.'

There were a thousand things he could say. Ask your ex-husband. Ask the removal men. It was easy to give advice to other people. But in this case, compassion seemed more valuable than advice.

'I understand,' he said. 'And if my supplier comes back, I will certainly ask him. I can send you word at your hotel. The St. Jacques, right?'

She stared at him. 'How did you know?'

'The badge you were wearing last time.'

'I'm not actually staying at the St. Jacques. I'm working on the refurbishment.' She took out a card with a corporate logo and set it on the counter. *Sarah Williams, Design Management.* 'Please do call if you hear from your supplier.'

'Yes. I will.'

'I appreciate you taking the trouble,' she said. 'And I'm sorry for the way I acted before. It's just, I'm very… busy.'

'I understand.' He didn't really. She had chosen not to tell her story, and he had to respect that. He put the animals in a box, nestling each one in tissue paper. He found a carrier bag and handed her the parcel.

'Thank you. And really, I'd like to pay you something.'

Franz waved a hand. 'When you find the giraffe, then we can talk of payment.'

'But are you sure?'

'Yes,' Franz said. 'I like things to find their proper home. But if you wish to do something for me, then perhaps you can come back again. For a cup of tea. I would like that.'

He crossed his arms to stop any further protest.

'OK.' She rewarded him with a smile and made to leave. 'Your castle truly is amazing. And the window display – it's a shame you took it down. The shop is so quirky and unique. But I think your friend Tomas is right. You could do more with it. A lot more.'

Franz looked down at the card. She was right. Everyone was right. Right – and wrong. For they did not know the truth about Franz Himmelberg and why he could never achieve his dream.

'Yes, perhaps.' He let out a long sigh. For a moment, their eyes met. It was like looking into a mirror and seeing a reflection of his own loneliness, his own despair. He tucked the card in the cashbox. The woman waved; then she was gone.

11

SARAH

Sarah returned to the St. Jacques, her head aching. Although she felt sorry for the old man and his dilapidated shop, she was angry too – at herself. Five years ago, she'd walked out of her life, never wanting to look back. She'd convinced herself it was best to block that time out of her mind and memories; immerse herself in work and get ahead in her career. Now, the memories had emerged from the shadows. Despite taking responsibility for her professional success, inside, she'd wallowed in her own grief and shame. She'd allowed others to make decisions and take action for her. Something as insignificant as a set of antiques in a shop had brought it all to the surface. It was ridiculous. She had to pull herself together – right now.

At the reception desk, she retrieved the bag with her dress and shoes and got a key to a hotel room so she could shower and change. The room was one that hadn't yet been renovated. Until the new investor signed on the dotted line, the hotel was on a tight budget and needed to fill the refurbished rooms – at the new, higher price – to pay for the rest to be upgraded.

She rode the new lift to the top floor. Though Monsieur Forman had baulked at the cost, Sarah had insisted on modernising the lift. Out with the old and in with the new. There was no point in having brand-new five-star appointed rooms if the guests had to wait ages for a cramped and creaky lift.

The corridor smelled of fresh paint and stargazer lilies. She'd found the vase at the flea market – one of the few places she'd ventured since beginning work on the project just after the new year. Then, the weather had been cold, rainy, and miserable, the pavements all but deserted. When spring arrived, the city became rejuvenated, with crowds of people flocking to parks and shops. Sarah had retreated. Paris might be a city for lovers, but it wasn't seeing couples that triggered her loneliness – it was families. A glimpse of a new-born baby, a toddler launching a miniature sailboat in a fountain, a dad swinging a child onto his shoulders. She never knew when or where the feeling would hit. Just that she feared it worse than anything.

The room faced the busy Boulevard de Sébastopol. The décor was tired, but the shower was hot. Afterwards she dried her hair and put on the hotel dressing gown. Exhaustion hit her full force. She sat down in the armchair by the window, staring at a thin crack in the plaster. All she had to do was get through the evening. She closed her eyes…

The room has the soft, clean scent of baby powder. The nightlight casts a gentle glow of stars onto the ceiling. The animals form a circle on the bureau, all except the giraffe. The baby is lying in the cot, her hands wrapped around the small wooden toy that she likes to suck on. Sarah reaches out and puts a hand on her daughter's cheek.

Cold. The coldness stuns her. Sends her mind spinning out of control. Rowan is wearing a sleep suit and tucked up in her sleeping bag. Should be warm…

Sarah lifts her, listening for the soft 'whu whu' of her breath. But there is no sound, no breath at all. She staggers under the weight of the little body. A silent scream rises in her throat. She clasps her daughter to her chest, willing her own breath, her own heartbeat to connect them once again.

But there is nothing.

Rowan is gone.

Sarah awoke with a start. The agony hit her like the wake of a passing train. The gaping sense of loss that nothing could ever fill. The memories exploded: the flashing lights of the ambulance; the tiny, baby-sized stretcher. The policewoman asking questions. And then… Victor had come home.

Breathe, she commanded herself. In and out. Gradually her surroundings took shape – a Paris hotel room, twilight descending over the city. She'd closed her eyes for a second and must have fallen asleep. The rhythm of her heart began to slow. But the pain of the dream remained, sharp and agonising. The only thing that had dulled over time was her memories of Rowan. The warmth of her body, the scent of her velvet-soft skin, the gentle motion of her lips as she suckled in her sleep, her eyelids tiny half-moons. The memories she wanted to keep were slipping away, leaving the rest.

The carrier bag from the shop was near the door. She had the urge to open the box, unwrap each animal. Check to see if she was mistaken. Where was the giraffe? Why hadn't she kept it safe? At the time, Sarah had been swaddled in grief, trembling and panicking at the world outside. She'd let her mum and Victor take care of everything. Now it was too late. If only she had something – something Rowan had loved; held in her tiny hands; her eyes shiny and delighted. Alive…

Her phone beeped with a reminder. Sarah forced herself to rise and put on her dress and shoes. Brush her hair, do her make-up. More heartbeats, more moments of her life… gone.

The guests would be arriving soon. The crème de la crème of the city and beyond. They were expecting a glittering party – and she would give it to them. Sarah pushed everything from her mind but the here and now. Time was relentless – it would pass. That was all she knew.

12

TOMAS

Tomas balled up the paper and threw it in the bin. He was distracted, unable to focus on his work. It had been that way for a few days, though he wasn't sure why. Maybe he should go see Franz – see if the woman had come back for the animals. He wasn't sure why he kept thinking about her. Yes, he'd been intrigued and wondered why she'd been so upset. But it was none of his business. She'd probably returned home to wherever she was from. Most likely she had a nice life with a husband and child – or children – maybe one of each. Why else would she come into a toyshop? In any case, he'd never see her again which should be enough to put her out of his mind. What was real and staring him in the face was the email from his editor. His deadline was looming; he had to crack on with the revisions to his manuscript.

He made himself a cup of tea and a sandwich and brought them over to the table where his laptop was open, the screen accusingly dark. The old ghosts whispered in his head: *imposter*. No point in even trying to silence them. He ate slowly, staring out the window at the lights of Paris, shining below like cold stars. He was just one tiny, insignificant speck in the world. His problems, such as they were, didn't matter. All the years of lost work, lost so-called genius, didn't matter. Nothing mattered when it came right down to it.

The printout of his current draft was like a heavy white brick on the table. He forced himself to read:

'The stockings would have to be sacrificed.

As the phone buzzed on the bedside table, Lucinda rose to her feet, completely naked. She picked up the crumpled stocking from the floor, balled it up and shoved it in the mouth of the man who had introduced himself at the bar as 'Simon from Leeds', but she knew was really Simeon Meyer, Mossad specialist in counter terrorism. He squirmed, but Lucinda had made sure the knots in the second stocking, tying him to the bedframe, would hold, at least until the maid found him the next morning. She picked up the phone and muted the call. The number of Meyer's contact would come in handy, as would the other files that she'd send over to be decrypted. She put on her bra and pants and slipped the tight red dress over her head. It was a shame to cut the evening short, but needs must. She put on one black patent Louboutin and held up the other, pressing the sharp point of the heel to the soft flesh of Meyer's throat. 'Traitors will be punished. Remember that.'

It was satisfying to hear him whimper as she put the shoe on her foot, picked up the phone, and left the room.'

Tomas sighed. There was nothing *wrong* with what he'd written. It was good enough for the next draft, even if it didn't quite get to the heart of his editor's comments – ten solid pages of changes and clarifications. He'd been ticking off the points one by one, trying to ignore the black despair rising inside the hidden part of him. Truth be told, he didn't give a monkey's about Lucinda Clarke's feelings as she entered her office after hearing about her lover's death. He didn't give a monkey's about the fact that she came across as too cold and unsympathetic, like she'd already moved on. Maybe she had. In Tomas Mercier's books, feelings didn't matter. What mattered was the ticking bomb and whether or not Lucinda Clarke was wearing the right shoes to save the world. His old editor understood this. But the publishers had recently been acquired by a behemoth entity, and his new editor was some fresh-out-of-college girl with big ideas and no clue.

Now, he'd been tasked with giving Lucinda Clarke more 'human' emotions. What did she feel when she looked down the barrel of a gun? What did she feel when she returned each night to her cold, empty flat? Did she have friends that she talked to? He almost laughed at one of the comments for Chapter 3: 'Maybe Lucinda considers getting a dog'.

Pushing the manuscript aside, he stood up and paced in front of the window. If he craned his neck, he could see the traffic crawling over the Pont Neuf. The sight made him restless. He checked his watch. Seven-thirty. Plenty of time to go out and get a proper meal at a brasserie. He could ring Anne-Marie, a local acquaintance who ran the neighbourhood Facebook page – they'd had an on-again, off-again thing going for a few years – and had been 'off' for over six months. If she wasn't keen for him to come round 'for old times' sake', then at least he could get some news about the status of the local shop closures – something that had begun to worry him the last time he'd visited Franz. Or, he could start fresh and go to a bar in the Latin Quarter. Get chatting to a woman, buy her a drink, let one thing lead to another, come home and do a few hours of work. It was a drill he knew well.

Too well.

God, was this really his life?

He continued to pace.

At the very least he should go to the supermarket – he was out of almost everything except wine, coffee, and half a packet of smoked salmon. He looked towards the door trying to summon the will. His eyes snagged on the brown leather book on the coffee table. He picked it up, running his fingers over the binding. *À la recherche du temps perdu.* In English, it translated to 'Remembrance of things past', or, more accurately, 'In search of lost time'. He'd spent the last fifteen years trying to forget the past, trying to lose the details of his memories in the labyrinth of his mind. He really ought to return the book to the shop.

Instead, he sat down on the sofa and began to read. The words were beautiful and familiar, and yet brand new. The mark of a true classic. As he read on, page after page, he was no longer Tomas, or even Tom. He became the words on the page, climbed inside them. He saw the world through different eyes, experiencing emotion in a different way. Time ran in a parallel clock. He was here and yet not here.

The pictures swam in his head, blending, changing, like the movement of clouds, the shimmering of light on water. Images from the book, images from his own life. The farmhouse on the edge of the village, his mum baking gingerbread and cakes for her WI friends, his dad reading the newspaper by the fire. Friends from school, skimming stones on a lake, building sandcastles on a beach, looking through a telescope at the stars. The little shed down the bottom of the garden where he'd spent long summer hours dreaming of faraway places, reading books, writing in his journal, and planning an epic novel about a young man's journey to find himself. Friends, family, real and imagined, flitting across his memory.

And then, like a reflection in a deep pool, he saw *her* face—Jessie. His stomach twisted involuntarily with revulsion and desire. The half-remembered scent of her perfume, her midnight hair, eyes that drew him like a moth to a flame. Memories of those early days: a sunny afternoon at the bathing pool on Hampstead Heath… a secluded picnic… he'd woven daisies into her hair and they'd made love on the blanket, laughing when a jogger ran by and caught them in the act. And then, the other memories, drunk and indistinct. Spiralling downwards; an ugly place riddled with doubt and insecurity. Those eyes no longer filled with love, but dark with malice. Staring at him from the hospital bed. Her words whispering in his head like restless spirits. *You hurt people, Tom.*

He stared at the page until her image dissolved and Proust's words took shape again. Lost time. Lost words. He'd written millions of words since it happened. Words that held no other meaning. Words to describe cardboard cut-out people who lived their lives by a ticking clock. There were good guys and bad guys, and occasionally, even people in between. But all of it was manufactured. There was no part of *him* in any of it. No part of Tom Willowfield, the man who had been lost.

Tomas closed the book. Reading it, he'd felt things he hadn't wanted to feel, remembered things he hadn't wanted to remember. His own scorched-earth policy had not dulled the memories at all – it had only served to sharpen the landscape of regret that he navigated every day.

The room suddenly felt oppressive – he needed to get out; into the warm, sticky buzz of the Paris night. He left the flat, taking the stairs down to the street. He suspected he'd end up in one of the usual places, that this night would end the same as any other. Still, his mood felt momentous. As if his thoughts and routine had been elbowed aside by a greater power inside his head. A voice that was trying very hard to speak but could not yet find the words.

13

FRANZ

It was time to close up for the night. The visit from the woman – Sarah – had revitalised Franz enough to do his work for a few more hours. But he'd been so engrossed that he'd forgotten to eat supper and needed groceries. It was nearly half past nine, and the *supermarché* closed at ten. Franz went out through the secret door that led onto the main street. Once he'd planned on making the secret door the main entrance to the shop to draw more customers. It was another thing he regretted not doing. In all honesty, he hated leaving the shop these days. To go out in the world, into the busy, bustling night – it was exhausting.

Tomas had told him about the *supermarché* where he could get everything in one place. Another magical world, almost like his own shop. Some Parisians turned up their noses at the idea of buying things anywhere besides the little shops they'd visited all their lives. But Franz was not a Parisian. In his country, people often had to queue for hours for food. Once, when his local shop had got a shipment of bananas, a small riot had broken out. Somehow, he'd managed to get two bananas. He'd given one to his father and one to Anna. He could still remember watching her eat it, savouring each bite. When he'd kissed her, her mouth tasted of bananas...

He had not eaten a banana since.

His legs ached; he leaned heavily on his cane. This pain in his knee was only arthritis, the doctor said. *Only* arthritis, but likely *only* to get worse. Franz sighed. How could his body be ageing so rapidly when the memories only grew sharper and more painful?

Music and laughter filtered into the street from cafés and restaurants; lights in the trees along the boulevard twinkled like stars. So many people: lovers, families, tourists; strolling on the pavement, sitting outside under striped awnings, a delicate crescent moon shining overhead. No one alone, no one marginal. No one like him.

Franz hobbled on. Perhaps it was best if he did retire and become a pigeon man. The shop could be redeveloped for people like these. People who inhabited their lives and stood up to be counted. If Anna had lived, would he have been one of them?

The *supermarché* was at the end of the block. Not far. There was a cashpoint on the other side: a hole in the wall that spat out money when you inserted a card. Magic!

A woman stood at the cashpoint; she took her cash from the machine. From around the corner, two shadows emerged. In the blink of an eye, they pushed her down and grabbed her handbag. The woman screamed. Someone ran out of the *supermarché* and went to her. The two shadows ran.

They were coming towards him. Franz didn't think – he reacted; his body possessed with a jolt of youth and a flash of superhuman strength. The shadows ran, closing the distance between them. Franz lifted his cane.

The force of the collision knocked him off balance.

One of the shadows swore and got up again. The other was on his knees, the wind knocked from him. Franz regained his balance and brought the stick crashing down on the shadow's head. The figure reeled back. More people came out of the *supermarché* drawn by the commotion. Most of them stood by and watched, their mouths gaping in shock.

Franz brought the stick down again. Adrenalin coursed through his body. He was blinded by rage and fury; transported to another time and place. Another moonlit street, another gang of bullies – ones he kept watch for, laughed with, unwittingly condoned their actions with his presence and camaraderie.

This time, however, he did more than just watch. This thief, this hoodlum, had attacked a woman and deserved to be punished. Franz grabbed at the shadow's hood and pulled it back. For a second, he glimpsed his own face—

'That's enough, stop!' A voice he recognised. Hands pulled him back. A siren droned, blue lights flashed as a gendarme pulled up.

Two officers jumped out of the car. One rushed over to the figure on the ground. The man wasn't moving. Franz snapped back to his senses. *Oh God.* Had he killed him?

'Looks like you're the hero of the hour,' the voice said again. As the adrenalin ebbed away, Franz's knees turned to jelly. He wavered… strong hands gripped him.

'Is he…?'

The figure on the ground shifted and groaned. The policeman quickly had him on his knees with the handcuffs out. On the ground was a lady's handbag.

'He'll be fine, Franz.'

Franz turned at the sound of his name. Who…? His eyes were hazy, and everything was spinning.

'And you're recovered the purse. Great stuff. I'll have to put it in my next book.'

Tomas. It was Tomas.

'The woman…' Franz's voice was hoarse and dry. 'Is she injured?'

A small crowd gathered near the cashpoint. The woman shouted and swore at the mugger, shaking her fists.

'Everyone's fine,' Tomas said. 'You're the hero – you saved the day. If you hadn't done something, the thief would have got away.'

The words reached Franz's ears like a foreign language he couldn't quite work out. He'd *done something.* A hero.

'Come on, mate. Let's get you a cup of tea. I live just around the corner. There's a lift up to my flat.'

Franz didn't protest as Tomas took his arm. All of a sudden, he wanted to get away. Before the police could take his name, question him. Before he could find out if he'd hurt the mugger – the man was standing now, his hands cuffed behind him – so it appeared not. Before anyone else could call him a hero, or thank him, or act in any way grateful.

'How did you come to be here?' Franz leaned heavily against Tomas.

'I was in the supermarket. I was just coming out when I heard the commotion.'

'The supermarket?' Franz noticed Tomas was carrying a shopping bag. In his mind, he'd built Tomas up as a man who lived an exciting and mysterious life. Bars, women, penning his mystery stories, occasionally taking an interest in his young neighbour. Now, he began to wonder. Going to the supermarket at night did not seem very glamorous. Could Tomas be as lonely as he was? No – he would not believe it!

Tomas steered him around the corner to a handsome

Beaux Arts building just off the main boulevard. It would be noisy, but it fit his vision of Tomas to be in the centre of things. The foyer was decorated in black and white marble tiles. The lift had an intricate iron gate over the door. 'I'm on the fifth floor,' Tomas said, 'so I hope this thing is working.'

The whirring of the lift made Franz feel instantly calmer. The elevator was slow, trundling up to the top floor. 'It's a lovely building,' Franz managed to say. Right now, he felt so tired.

'Yes,' Tomas said. 'Built in the eighteen sixties. I was very lucky to get my flat.'

The lift came to a halt. Franz leaned heavily on his stick as he came out. The lift shaft was in the centre of an atrium, the stairs spiralling around it like a nautilus shell. Vertigo overcame him as he looked down to the bottom.

'Thank you, my friend,' Franz said.

Tomas led him inside the flat and went to make tea. Franz sank down on the sofa. The bright city lights twinkled and blurred before his eyes.

'I forgot the milk. What an idiot!' Tomas swore from the kitchen. 'The shop will be closed now.'

'Yes.'

'Just a second, I'll be right back.'

Franz was vaguely aware of Tomas going back out into the corridor. He heard a knock and voices speaking in French. Tomas and a woman.

'… think he's in shock,' Tomas was saying.

'… asleep so it is fine,' the woman replied.

'Yes. Thanks, Mathilde.'

Franz closed his eyes. The images flooded back: the dark street, the shadowy figures, the droning of a police siren. The floodgates in his mind wrenched open, the memories rushing in.

The freezing block of apartments, the radiators that were always cold. The constant noise: neighbours talking, fighting, making love. No such thing as privacy or your own thoughts – such things were bad for the state, and the state was all that mattered. He had learned to be vigilant: to keep his eyes and ears open. Heinrich, his best friend, had a father in the SSD – the Stasi – doing great and important work. All the boys wanted to be like him; Franz wanted a father like him. Not a lowly clockmaker who repaired glockenspiels and musical boxes.

Heinrich's sister, Anna, however, loved the musical boxes and glockenspiels. Franz had loved Anna since he was a small boy, and as they grew older, he dreamed of making her proud. He knew the best way was to go out with her brother and his friends who were doing their bit.

Doing their bit. *Setting fire to the shop of a man who was suspected of distributing leaflets. Informing on a student who'd tried to get a message to his relatives in the West by flying a model aeroplane over the Wall. Bullying, threatening, ransacking. Listening at keyholes. Heinrich and his friends received commendations from the citizen's police. Though he most often kept watch rather than joining in directly, Franz basked in his friend's glory.*

So why had Anna stopped speaking to him? Why did she refuse to acknowledge him? Franz didn't understand her reaction. When he thought of the things he and his friends were doing, he felt sick. How much more would it take before Anna deemed him worthy—?

'… will he wake up?'

Franz shuddered away from the edge of sleep. Cold – he was so cold. The voices were not the sharp voices of Heinrich and his friends; not the voice of the youth group commander as he revealed Anna's fate—

'I have made the tea,' a woman said.

Franz opened his eyes. Except – he was still dreaming. He must be! A woman stood before him: thin and delicate with grey-streaked hair pulled tightly back from her face in a bun. It wasn't *her*… the eyes were different: blue instead of brown. And yet something in her expression reminded him of the girl he had once loved.

'Anna?' The word slipped from his mouth.

The woman frowned. 'I am Mathilde Villere. Tomas says you have had a shock. Drink the tea now, all of it.'

'Thank you.' Franz sat up on the sofa, his hand shaking as he took the cup and saucer. The hot tea burned his throat.

'You can sleep here tonight, Franz,' Tomas was saying.

'You seem... familiar.' Franz focused on the woman, her image swimming before his eyes. He thought of his dancer on her track. Her face – it was the same.

'I am quite sure we have never met,' she said. 'But I know who you are. You're the toymaker.'

'Ah. Then you must be the grandmother of Andre.'

'Yes, that's right. He is the light of my life, and yet, a heavy weight to bear.'

'I understand.'

Her face blossomed into a smile. She wouldn't be smiling if she knew about all the things he'd done – or failed to do. But for now, he was content just to look at her. The phantom taste of bananas flooded his mouth, bringing a feeling he'd not experienced for a very long time.

He felt happy to be alive.

14

SARAH

It was painful. These evenings always were. The luminaries of the Paris property development industry had turned out in force – investors, architects, CEOs, property owners, hoteliers. So many attractive people, rich people, confident, put-together people. Looks could be deceiving though – and Sarah hated the deception. How many of them were hiding heartbreak underneath? All of them, most likely. Domestic rows, affairs, ailing parents, irritating children. But how many had suffered the loss of a child? To Sarah, this was the dividing line for the world. There were people like her – and there was everybody else.

'I must say, Mademoiselle Sarah, you have truly worked wonders.' The man who handed her a glass of champagne already acted like he owned the place. Ivo Komitov, a big-time player in hotels, was in the process of finalising a deal with the consortium to buy a controlling stake in the St. Jacques. The financing had put extra pressure on Sarah to do a top-notch job.

'Thank you,' Sarah said. 'I appreciate your saying that. But it wasn't just me, but the entire team…'

'Yes, yes.' Komitov drained his glass. 'But we all know you are the brains behind the transformation. The vision.'

He laid a hand on her arm, friendly but assured. She appreciated the compliments about her work – though, once or twice she'd worried that he'd looked a little *too* admiringly at her. Above all, it was important that he viewed her as put-together and professional.

'As you know, I have other hotels,' Komitov said. 'In Kraków and Sofia, and many other beautiful cities in the east. I can provide you with many opportunities – a promotion. You could have your pick of projects anywhere in the world.' He smiled at her, his teeth unnaturally white. 'It would be good to have a discussion.'

'Thank you,' Sarah said, taking a small step back. This was the opportunity she'd been waiting for. A new city, a new project, another new start. Instead of excitement, she felt a strange ache inside. 'I'll schedule something with your assistant.'

'Yes,' Komitov said. 'Do that. And let us not spend all evening talking shop. We must sample the delights of this party. We will speak more later, Sarah. But for now, go and enjoy yourself. After all your hard work, it is much deserved.'

'Thank you.'

She excused herself as a commotion at the door – a local journalist arriving with a camera crew in tow – demanded her attention. She helped them get settled and took the opportunity to slip out of the ballroom. The noise and the crowd were making her light-headed, and she needed to gather herself before her inevitable speech.

The bar across the corridor had been refurbished with shiny black glass, chrome, and mirrors. She'd managed to poach the perfect bartender, Javier, from an upscale bar in Saint-Germain-des-Prés. She sat down on a stool and thanked him again for sorting out Komitov's wine. 'It is no problem,' he said in Spanish-accented English. 'I believe your investor may need a little education when it comes to wine.'

'I'm sure he'd love to know that.'

'Speaking of which, I have found an exquisite Côte de Nuits just for you.' Javier took a bottle from behind the bar. 'A beautiful garnet red, with a hint of chocolate, leather, and mint.'

'OK,' she said. 'Educate me.'

Javier poured an inch of wine into a crystal glass. Sarah lifted it to her mouth, tasting only delicious, fruity red wine. Victor would have been able to distinguish the flavours. In the wake of his worldly sophistication and upper-crust French upbringing, she had felt unworthy and insecure.

Sarah drank the wine down swiftly. 'Nice,' she said. 'Can I have some more?'

'Not if you drink it like that,' Javier said. 'This is a wine to be savoured. Made love to. Like the body of a beautiful woman.'

Sarah laughed. 'I don't think your boyfriend would appreciate that.'

'Maybe not. But seeing you in that dress, it is my loss.'

Sarah almost began to enjoy herself. It was fun flirting with Javier because it could go nowhere. It was safe. Just the way she liked it.

Two men came up to the bar. Javier fell into his patter, chatting and mixing them his 'Mystery Mojito'. Sarah stared at her reflection in the mirror. She did look good. The blue fabric came down into a low V and hugged her waist before falling in a sparking cascade skimming her hips. She'd been slim before her pregnancy, and afterwards her body had filled out, making her curves more voluptuous. Not that she'd ever use that word to describe herself. That word implied a woman with a sense of her own sensuality. Whereas her body might as well be carved from marble like the Venus de Milo. Cold and functional, that was all.

Sarah went over to the French doors and the balcony that faced the main street. They'd had to get special permission to raise the height of the wrought-iron railing and line it with safety glass. Although the night was warm and muggy, she pulled her pashmina around her shoulders like a cocoon. She should be enjoying herself – a glittering event, a possible promotion. Why did she feel so cold and paralysed inside?

Across the street, an orange neon sign flashed on and off. It was nearly eleven o'clock. Soon, she could gracefully bow out and go back to her flat. She breathed in deeply, letting the night air fill her lungs.

People walked by under the golden circles of the street-lamps. Two couples, a teen in a hoodie. A man in jeans and a button-down shirt—

The man stopped walking. He looked at her, and just for a moment, she felt something. A flash of recognition, a flicker of something awakening inside her. He smiled up at her and gave a little wave. She stayed rooted to the spot. It couldn't be the same man… and yet…

Her emotions churned: terror, annoyance, curiosity. He crossed the street, his eyes locking with hers as he headed for the front door of the hotel.

15

TOMAS

Tomas hadn't planned on crossing the river. He hadn't planned anything at all. And yet, from the moment he'd encountered Franz giving a mugger a good thrashing, the night had become extraordinary.

Tomas didn't believe in love at first sight, or karma, or astral twins. He understood loneliness and wanting to fill the hole inside, but that was a far cry from love. But when Mathilde had come to his flat and he'd seen the look on Franz's face – the melting away of years – he'd known his presence was no longer required. His two friends were transformed before his eyes. It might have been his imagination, but Tom Willowfield's voice kept piping up in his mind, whispering that it was possible.

If he were honest, he was a little jealous of Franz and Mathilde's instant connection. The last time he'd met a woman at a bar, they'd ended up at a shabby hotel near the Cluny. She hadn't bothered to take off her wedding ring; he hadn't bothered to take off his socks. It had been as mechanical as one of Franz's window displays. The only interesting thing was the despair he'd felt afterwards. That this thing between two human beings that was supposed to be beautiful and life-affirming, was just… sex. Once, Tom Willowfield had written about human emotions: joy, love, and most of all, wonder. He'd had the rare gift of being able to pass that wonder on to others. *Painting pictures with words.* Tomas had slipped out while she was in the shower. If the feelings were gone and even sex held no pleasure, then what the hell was left?

He walked across the bridge. The river below was sleek and dark like a sinuous creature, lying in wait, biding its time. He continued through the streets of Île de la Cité, past the scaffolded shell of Notre-Dame. Lovers in dark corners, hidden cafés, secret haunts. He doubted Franz and Mathilde had noticed his absence. It was sweet, this idea of two people making a connection – even finding love – at their age. Sweet and remote. He'd been lost in his own self-loathing for so long that such feelings were hazy and vague, like the smudged orange pools of light from the streetlamps. Love was possible – for some people.

Not for him.

You hurt people, Tom.

Somewhere in a different city and country, Jessie was living her life – such as it was.

Once, at a particularly low point, he'd looked her up on Facebook. Her profile was private, but a Google search had revealed that she headed up a charity helping disabled women integrate into the workplace. A path she never would have taken if—

As he was about to cross the road, the light changed; cars sped past him. He closed his eyes against the dizzying sense of vertigo. Jessie – his head hurt to think about her – especially twice in one day. It was the Proust, it was Franz and Mathilde, it was… what? Why had he come this way? He should cross over at the next bridge and head for home.

It was pointless to keep going. No matter how hard he tried, he could never outrun his own thoughts. But something subliminal told him to keep going.

A little way along the river, one of the older hotels was lit up like a Christmas tree. Torches blazed and limousines were lined up outside. Tomas recalled reading one of Anne-Marie's posts on the local Facebook page about a hotel refurbishment project that was nearing completion. A banner hung above the door: *Welcome to the grand reopening of the Hotel St. Jacques*. The St. Jacques. The toyshop… the lanyard.

He looked upwards, taking in the intricate details of the Beaux Arts facade. He saw the woman on the balcony. And suddenly, he *knew* why he was there.

16

SARAH

It was him – the man from the toyshop. Though they'd only met for a minute, the recognition was mutual. His smile glowed with magnetism and charisma. Her pulse darted as he headed up the steps to the hotel. Which was silly, really. She wasn't vain enough to imagine he was coming inside to see her. *Lucinda*, *Andre* – this man was obviously married, obviously had a child. Whatever his moral compass was, she didn't want to be attracted to someone unavailable – or anyone at all.

'There you are, *chérie*, I have been looking everywhere.' A hand slid down her back. Sarah tried to move away, but Komitov was blocking her path. While she was chatting with Javier, he'd clearly had a few drinks; his breath smelled sour and he was standing too close.

She'd had high hopes that the new investor would be an upstanding visionary who would respect her work and involve her in interesting projects. So far, however, she was not impressed.

'Mr Komitov. Sorry. I… needed some air.'

'Some air, yes, I understand. Perhaps when you are

finished here, you could come and meet me in the presidential suite – the air is very pleasant, and we have so much to discuss—'

'The room is lovely, isn't it?' Sarah went from being unimpressed to annoyed. She was a professional woman – was it too much to ask to be treated like one? She grappled for an excuse. 'But I'm afraid I'm meeting someone afterwards. My… friend… Ah! There he is now.'

She gestured to the man who'd come in from the street. The light was gone from his eyes as he sized up the situation.

'Hello!' Sarah took the opportunity to move past Komitov. She stood on tiptoes and, married or not, gave the stranger a kiss – on the lips. 'I'm so glad you could make it.'

'Wouldn't miss it.' The warmth in his voice made something cold and hard inside her begin to liquefy.

'Who is this?' Komitov said icily.

'He's my—'

'I'm her fiancé,' the man cut in, his tone unmistakeable.

'Fiancé?' Komitov turned to Sarah. 'But you did not say. Where is your ring?'

'At home in the safe,' she said, seized by a strange recklessness. 'It's very old and valuable – I don't wear it out very often.'

'I see.' Komitov looked bemused. 'And what is his name, if I may ask?'

'Tomas Mercier,' the stranger said.

The name meant nothing to Sarah. But Komitov stepped back, instantly all charm. 'The *author* Tomas Mercier? As in *The Art of Death*? *A Mind for Murder?* As in, Agent Lucinda Clarke?'

'Yes. That's the one.'

Sarah looked from one to the other. An author? Lucinda? Had she got the wrong end of the stick? Was Lucinda not his wife? Was she not… real?

'I bought the series for my niece last time I was here,' Komitov said. 'I ended up reading two of the books myself. I do love a page-turner. Tell me, does Lucinda stay together with Dr Clint? I was so pleased when she found love.'

The glint returned to the stranger's eye. 'I'm afraid the good professor meets with an unfortunate mishap early in the next book.'

'A shame.' Komitov nodded grimly. 'I hope she can find another love to console her in her grief.'

'I can't say,' Tomas said, 'because I haven't finished it yet.'

'Perhaps that is how you keep the reader guessing? If you yourself do not know the ending—'

Sarah couldn't process the conversation or the revelation. Lucinda was a fictional character – she almost wanted to laugh—

'Ah, Sarah, there you are.' Jeanette came up and took her arm. 'Monsieur Forman wants you to say a few words.'

'Of course.' Sarah was glad to extricate herself from the whole messy situation. Jeanette looked questioningly at Tomas. '*Bonsoir*, *monsieur*. Have we met?'

Komitov's eyes instantly narrowed. 'Allow me to introduce Sarah's fiancé,' he said. 'The author, Tomas Mercier.'

Jeanette's mouth became an 'O' of surprise. Tomas gave her a little wink and kissed Sarah on the cheek. 'Knock 'em dead, darling,' he said. 'I'll wait for you at the bar.'

'You don't have to…' Sarah started to say. Now was the time to walk away and end the charade. It had been…

fun… while it lasted. But she stopped herself mid-sentence. 'OK.' She turned and walked towards the ballroom, her cheeks burning, his eyes following her.

17

TOMAS

Her name was Sarah. Tomas went to the bar and ordered a glass of Burgundy grand cru – expensive, but worth it. He took a long drink. Now was the time to make a graceful exit. The incident had been diverting, even a little exciting. But it was over.

He left the empty glass on the bar, planning to leave; but as he walked past the ballroom, Sarah was standing at the edge of the stage as the hotel manager made a speech. Tomas hovered by the door, then took an empty seat at the back. The evening had been unexpected on so many levels, just like the ending to one of his novels. He felt duty-bound to discover where it might lead.

'And now I'd like to introduce the woman who is the brains and vision behind this transformation: Sarah Williams.'

Applause rang out as she came onstage. Tomas took in all of her. She was a beautiful woman, but not in a conventional way. She had an otherworldly quality about her, like the subject of a pre-Raphaelite painter. Her hair was long and honey-blonde, and her face had a slight asymmetry that was arresting to the eye. In her stiletto heels, she was as tall as he was. She took the microphone with an air of practised confidence, but he sensed a vulnerability underneath. The contrast was enchanting – he couldn't take his eyes off her.

'I can only add my thanks to all of you for coming tonight,' she said. 'This project was particularly important because it involved such a beautiful and historic building. I believe it is our duty to preserve a building's glorious past while allowing it to evolve in a way that is relevant to the future. I've tried to achieve that here. Please raise a glass to the success of the Hotel St. Jacques.'

Glasses clinked as the manager took the mic again, heaping praise on their new investor, 'Mr Komitov'. He invited everyone to stay for dancing. Sarah came off stage as a few couples filtered on to the dance floor. The band played *In the Mood*. Tomas stood up and moved towards her, but she was absorbed into a crowd of well-wishers. He hung back, annoyed with himself. Really, he ought to leave—

'... have a proposition for you. The area is ripe for redevelopment. A word in the ears of the planners, and it could be very lucrative.'

Tomas turned, his crime novelist's brain on high alert. An elegant man in an expensive suit was talking to the smarmy little man, Komitov, who'd been hitting on Sarah. Tomas squinted – something about him was familiar. A local businessman? Tomas couldn't place him.

'I have heard about your efforts, Mr Rouveau.' Komitov patted the elegant man on the arm. 'Get in touch with my assistant and I'll hear your proposal. It sounds very interesting – if you can deliver.'

'Oh, I can, I assure you—'

Komitov suddenly looked in Tomas's direction. He'd

made a rookie mistake standing too close – one that Lucinda never would have made. Good thing he was just the writer, not a secret agent himself. Komitov's eyes bored into him – hawklike – before recognition dawned.

'Evening.' Tomas raised his hand in a goofy wave, and made a point of moving away, knocking into a waiter and almost toppling at tray of vol-au-vents.

He regained his balance and made a beeline for the door. Being amongst all these glamorous A-listers and corporate types made him queasy, and Sarah was clearly one of them – a rising star by the sound of things. Once, he too had aspired to be part of a world of glitz and glamour. It had ended in disaster.

As he neared the door, he caught sight of Sarah surrounded by a group of men in black tie. Though she was smiling, he sensed a restlessness in her, as though she were going through the motions for the sake of appearances. She extricated herself from the group, glanced towards the door – and caught him looking at her. Against his own better judgement, he went to her. Without thinking, he brushed his hand over her arm, feeling a liquid heat as he touched her skin. Her eyes flashed with surprise; he withdrew his hand.

'Sarah, I should go.'

'Thank you for playing along before,' she said. 'And I hope I haven't kept you from anything.'

'You haven't,' he said with a grin. 'I happened to be passing and saw the festivities. As a starving author, I rarely say no to free food and drink.'

She smiled, but only for an instant. 'And did you find what you were looking for at the toyshop? For whatever you have – boy or girl.' If she meant it as a joke, it came out laced with disapproval. He didn't laugh.

'Boy,' he said. 'My neighbour, Andre. He can't leave

the flat, so I like to bring him things from time to time that will stimulate his mind. He's very bright. And he loves those magnetic bricks.'

He was rambling – this woman wouldn't be interested in a psychologically damaged eleven-year-old. But it seemed important to explain that he wasn't just some prowling tomcat ready to play fiancé with the first beautiful woman that needed rescuing.

'He can't leave the flat?' Sarah said. 'Why not?'

'He's got an anxiety disorder. He's been that way since he lost his mum – long story. Anyway, it was nice to meet you – and be your fiancé for a few minutes. But I'll go now. You've done a lovely job with the hotel.'

Two other guests swooped in on Sarah; Tomas walked out of the ballroom. He needed to get home. Forget he'd met her again; forget that she still intrigued him, drew him with a strange, inexplicable gravity—

'Wait.'

Tomas turned. Ignoring the other people, she came up to his side.

'I'm sorry if I was rude,' she said. 'Tonight – and before. Would you like another drink?'

'Only if you'll join me.' He risked the smile he relied on to work its magic with women.

'Yes, OK.' She seemed unaffected by his charm. 'But give me a few minutes to wrap up here.'

'I'll wait,' Tomas said. The sudden surge of joy felt unfamiliar. It felt wonderful.

18

SARAH

Every voice in her mind shouted that she was an idiot, yet her body told a different story. The empty place inside her was filled with warmth and excitement. She was aware of Tomas's presence as she said her goodbyes, as if he was imprinted on her mind.

A few people were still dancing, though the party was winding down. Komitov eyed her from across the room. Sarah made her way over to Jeanette. 'I'm going now,' she said.

'Who's the handsome stranger?'

'No idea. But Komitov knew who he was – he saved me from an embarrassing situation, and I got a few brownie points. I figure I owe him a drink.'

'Sounds good,' Jeanette said. 'And you deserve to have some fun. Just… be careful.'

'I will.' Sarah glanced over at her stranger. Too handsome for his own good, just like Victor. But unlike Victor, he had a sense of humour – he'd readily played along with her escapade. She'd have one drink and never see him again. It was perfectly safe.

Sarah made her way back through the crowd. The air felt electrified as she came up to Tomas. 'I'm finished. Thanks for waiting.'

'My pleasure. Shall we stay here or go somewhere else?'

'Somewhere else,' she said. 'Maybe across the river? My flat is on the Left Bank—' She broke off, not wanting to give the wrong impression. 'But just for the record... I'm not inviting you...'

'Sure, I get it.' He grinned. 'We're going for a drink, not a one-night stand.'

'Right.' She blushed.

He reached into his pocket and pulled out a business card. 'And if I act like anything other than a gentleman, you can one-star me on Amazon, OK?'

The card showed a row of novels with dark covers and weapons dripping with blood. She recalled seeing them displayed in the local bookshop. 'Your covers don't exactly inspire confidence,' she said.

'Maybe not. But don't worry. In my books, the good guy – or, actually, the good woman, Agent Lucinda Clarke – always comes out on top.'

'To be honest, when I first heard the name, I thought she was your wife.'

'My...' He laughed. 'Oh... I see. No – she's not really the wife type. She is beautiful though. *And* she saves the world in four-inch stilettos.'

'She sounds like a triumph for feminism.' Sarah arched an eyebrow.

'What – so those aren't comfortable?' He looked down at her high heels.

'Only for saving the world,' she said. 'But it's a little late for that tonight.'

'We'd better get going, then. I live on the Left Bank

too. Not that it matters.' He gave her a cocky smile. 'Since we're not going to... well, you know.'

Sarah laughed – the sensation felt unfamiliar. She retrieved her bag and changed into flats, leaving everything but her handbag at reception. Her stranger was funny and charming. A gentleman. Though this evening could go nowhere, she liked the illusion forming between them. That she was open to adventure and romance. That she was something other than dead inside.

In front of the hotel, a sea of expensive cars and limousines blocked half the main street. The doorman enquired if they wanted a taxi.

'It might be nice to walk,' Tomas suggested.

'Yes, let's,' she said. 'It's good to be outside.'

They headed down the wide street to the brightly lit bridge. As they walked, she asked him about himself. She discovered that he was originally from Buckinghamshire – not far away from her hometown in Surrey – and that he'd been living in Paris for over fifteen years.

'That's a long time.' She stopped at the edge of the bridge to admire the view, the Eiffel Tower just visible in the distance along the curve of the river.

'I guess it is,' he said. 'My parents still live in the same house where I grew up. But I like it here. Time passes, and yet, the city is timeless. So full of history and beauty. It's a place where you can lose yourself. Sometimes that can be... refreshing.'

'Maybe.'

Sarah stared out at the dark water, scribbled with peaks of golden light. She'd been trying to find herself for so long – and hadn't succeeded. Maybe getting lost was exactly what she needed.

'But what about you?' he asked. 'How long have you been in Paris?'

'A few mouths. But work has been so busy – I haven't really seen much of the city. Every time I plan to go someplace…' she shook her head, 'it just never seems to happen.'

'I understand. It's a tough city to be alone in.'

'That's not it,' she said, even though it was. Her loneliness, however, was the kind that could never be filled by another person.

They walked on, reaching the end of the bridge and crossing over to the Left Bank. Many of the cafés were closing for the night, but Tomas stopped at the corner of a dark street with a single light shining halfway down the block.

'Well, if you want to experience the real Paris,' he said, 'there's a nice wine bar just there.' He pointed towards the light. 'It's mostly locals, and they have a piano. Shall we have that drink?'

'OK,' she said. 'But just the one.'

The basement bar was dark with candle-lit tables and walls covered with photos of jazz legends. The piano player's fingers danced over the keys; the singer belted out an Édith Piaf song. They found a table in a secluded corner. Sarah ordered sparkling water; Tomas ordered a beer.

'What do you think of the bar?' he said, as their drinks arrived.

'It's wonderful,' Sarah said. 'It's just the kind of place that I'd associate with Paris. Though, we tourists rarely find the best spots.'

'Maybe that adds to the mystique. Knowing something exists but not finding it.'

'True. But sometimes, it's nice to find it.'

'I agree.'

She turned to watch the piano player. Surely, it was best to stick to small talk: questions about his novels, where to go in Paris, meaningless chat. But for some reason, it seemed unnecessary. In their brief meeting at the toyshop, he'd caught her at a vulnerable moment; her mask had slipped and he'd looked beneath. What had he seen? Did she dare find out?

'You must have thought I was very strange getting upset at the toyshop,' she said.

'I did wonder.'

'It was silly. The circus animals… they brought back memories.'

Tomas smiled. 'Franz prides himself on his shop being a repository of memories. Lost things found again and given a new life. Every time I go in there, I see something that triggers a memory – though I'm not sure it's my own, if that makes sense.'

'It does. It seems an odd place, but special too.'

'Yes, though, in this day and age, special has a way of becoming obsolete. The past giving way to shiny new things.'

'I'm not sure that's true.'

'I liked what you said in your speech,' he said. 'About the importance of making the past relevant to the future. But not everyone shares your views. In fact, I overheard a few of your "guests" tonight discussing more of a "scorched-earth" approach.'

'What do you mean?'

He waved a hand. 'I'm sure you saw the empty shops around *La Boutique Fantasque*. Small shops owners being bought out. Making way for redevelopment and gentrification. For progress. A lot of the older shopkeepers have chosen to retire. I wonder what happens to them. Do they enjoy a new start, or just fade away?

'I don't know, but if a property is being underutilised, that's what happens.' Sarah felt a little defensive. 'Sometimes it's best just to move on. Out with the old, in with the new.'

'Maybe.' He sounded unconvinced. 'And speaking of Franz, there was an odd incident tonight.' He launched into an animated account of Franz defending a woman against a mugger.

'What a story!' Sarah said. 'That poor man.'

'I think he liked being a hero, though it did take it out of him. He's at my flat right now, recovering. My neighbour, Mathilde, is with him.'

'I'm glad someone's looking after him.'

'So is he, believe me.'

The piano player and singer went for a break; the music gave way to a background of whispered conversations. She sensed him take a breath and ask the unspoken question that lingered between them.'

'What did the animals make you remember?'

He cared enough to ask. But what could she say? The urge to lie was overpowering. But the question itself demanded the truth.

'They reminded me of a set that belonged to my daughter, Rowan. It's probably not the same one.' Pain made her ramble on. 'Her set had a giraffe. That was the most special of all. So very special.'

'And Rowan?' he said gently.

Sarah turned away. 'She died.'

He didn't speak; didn't say he was 'sorry for her loss' or that it was 'just awful' or 'such a tragedy' – things she'd heard a thousand times from others. Instead, he reached out and took her hand. The gesture was caring, intimate.

Sharing her daughter's name made her live again, if only for an instant.

Then, he spoke:

'Autumn flame of fiery red,
Your berries are beacons in the gathering darkness.
Giver of life, nurturer of the soil.
Your boughs sheltering beneath an impossible sky.
But all too short is your glorious blaze.
And then the winter comes.'

Sarah watched him as he finished speaking, his profile softened by the golden glow of candlelight.

'I… I haven't heard that before.' The words of the poem reverberated inside her head. It was as if he'd looked into her soul and uncovered something hidden – something frightening, but beautiful too. 'You didn't just make that up? Did you?'

'Was it terrible?' His eyes glinted as he gazed at her.

'No. It was… beautiful.' She reined in her emotions. 'But not what I'd have expected from a crime writer. Unless Agent Lucinda Clarke happens to be a poet?'

'No. Definitely not.'

He seemed pensive as he let go of her hand and took a sip of his drink.

'I'm sorry,' she said, feeling shame, feeling desire – how had Tomas managed to make her feel so much in such a short time? 'I shouldn't have mentioned it. It's not something I usually broadcast at dinner parties and soirees – or to complete strangers.'

'You don't need to apologise.' His hand brushed hers again, sending off another firework. He felt it too – she knew he did.

'Thanks. It's just that seeing the animals was like a dam

breaking inside me. I felt the loss all over again. And the giraffe – it's lost too. I let others take care of clearing out the flat,' she said. 'My mum, and my ex… Victor.' Her face clouded over. 'I wish I'd done things differently.' She stopped herself as reality overcame her.

'You needed time,' he said gently. 'You needed to become someone else. I don't know…'

She looked at him; his eyes had darkened.

'It sounds like you do,' she said.

19

TOMAS

Tomas looked away so she wouldn't see the truth of it in his eyes. Over the years, he'd trained himself not to feel. His characters could experience life and he was their medium. But

the connection between him and Sarah was so unexpected that the strength of his own feelings fascinated – and scared him. If she'd been beautiful only on the outside; if she'd been a corporate puppet through and through; if she'd been like most of the women he met, then he wouldn't feel so off balance. As it was, however, her revelation and vulnerability made him feel protective of her. Though a part of him longed to tell her the truth – test the strength of the connection between them – he knew it was best to keep silent.

The piano player began a new set, playing a rendition of *Let's Call the Whole Thing Off*. Sarah began humming softly to the song. In the glow of the candle she looked ethereal, otherworldly, her profile softened by the waves of her hair and the curves of her body.

The singer crooned the familiar words of 'tom-ay-to'

and 'tom-ah-to'. A warning not to let down his guard or even think about getting too close.

A warning…

He chose to ignore it.

He stood up and reached for her hand. 'Would you dance with me?' There wasn't a proper dance floor near the piano, but there was space next to the table. 'Right here.'

She hesitated. 'I don't really dance.'

'That makes two of us.'

Someone inside his head did, though. Just this once, he decided to listen to the whisperings of that long-silenced voice.

Despite her reluctance, he drew her to her feet and she slipped effortlessly into his embrace. She twined her arms around his neck. When the length of her body pressed against his, she tensed, but didn't move away. She began to relax as they swayed together to the music, the pianist throwing in a crystalline gliss that sparkled in the darkness of the bar.

He ran his fingers along her bare shoulder. She shivered and melted into him, pressing against his chest. So close that he almost forgot that they were strangers with secrets and separate lives. Was this real? Could she feel it too?

No. The song came to an end, the last notes dying away. She pulled abruptly away as background noise filled the space and the moment was lost to the relentless heartbeat of time.

They returned to the table. Sarah perched on the edge of her chair, clearly uncomfortable. 'I'd like to go home now,' she said. 'It's been a really long day.'

'Sarah. Stay. I'm sorry if I came on too strong.'

'No. Don't apologise. I shouldn't have agreed to come

out – it was a mistake. I'm sorry if I gave you the wrong impression. I just… can't do this.' She stood up, scattering some coins on the table and taking her bag from the corner.

Tomas could sense the undercurrent of pain and desperation flowing through her. The loss that had decimated her soul, leaving behind an empty shell. There was no answer, no solution to losing a child. He tried to speak, but the words jumbled on his tongue. What right did he have to say anything? He didn't understand the landscape of his own pain, let alone another person's. He was the ultimate imposter: a coward who had run away from his own demons. He was more closed off than anyone.

Sarah walked swiftly to the door; he could barely keep up. The host gave Tomas a knowing look. 'Have a *lovely* evening,' he said.

Tomas ignored him, following her out into the night. 'Thanks again for everything,' she said when they reached street level. 'But I can make my way back from here. I'm staying at Aparthotel Sevres. It's only a few blocks.'

A clear dismissal. She was done with him. Normally, that would be fine – Tomas Mercier could handle rejection. It happened sometimes. But this had felt so different – so right. How could he stand it if she just walked away?

'It's not safe this time of night,' he said. 'I'll walk you to your building.'

'I'll be—'

'And then I'll leave. I promise.'

'Fine.' His would-be chivalry had clearly annoyed her. She turned and began walking in the wrong direction.

'It's this way.' He pointed.

She didn't look at him as they walked on in silence. A hollow sadness spread over him. Would it really end this way? He wanted to apologise again – shout out that he was sorry for everything. But 'sorry' was completely useless. Instead he spoke words that formed deep inside him, that hadn't even risen to the level of conscious thought. Whispering to him in a language he'd thought he'd forgotten.

'What if it had been you who died, not her?'

Sarah stopped walking. 'What? What did you say?'

'What would you have told Rowan? Would you have told her to grieve forever, to close herself off from life? Or would you have told her to go out and experience as much as possible? The pain that's always waiting. But the joy, too.'

'How dare you.' Her voice was low and icy. She began walking again, more quickly than before. He stayed rooted to the spot.

After a few paces, she stopped and turned back.

'You don't know what it's been like,' she said. 'Remembering her, forgetting her. Each day, I feel the pain all over again. Every moment, I miss her.'

Tomas said nothing. His own despair glittered like a dark pool inside him. Once again, he wanted to tell her exactly why he did understand. But it seemed best to stay silent and absorb her anger.

'When Rowan died, I walked out of my marriage – and my entire life.' She shuddered with emotion. 'My daughter was all I needed in this life; and she's gone. So please don't try and tell me what I should or shouldn't be doing. Just because we laughed and flirted; just because we danced, and maybe… felt something… it means nothing. Do you understand? Nothing at all. I'm not looking for a lover, or a relationship, or a one-night stand.'

'I understand,' he said softly. 'But how about a friend?'

'A… friend?'

He took a silent step forward, bridging the distance between them.

She collapsed into his arms.

He held her close, stroking her hair. It was the strangest feeling – wanting to take away her pain. Had he ever felt that way before? It didn't matter. All he wanted to do was be here with her, two human beings together on a Paris street. The moment would pass; it would come to an end. But right now, it was enough.

20

MATHILDE

She is spinning, dizzy. Silver shoes on a black and white floor. Music playing, figures moving, clocks ticking. As Franz speaks, weaving a web of magic, Mathilde feels the half-remembered sensations in her body, even though she has never seen a glockenspiel or a mechanical castle in real life.

She has been to the toyshop, however; this she knows for certain. Long ago when she was a girl – long before Franz ever worked there. His words open the curtain of memory inside her mind to reveal a brightly lit stage. A rocking horse with a real mane and tail; a beautiful ballerina doll – her papa bought it for her, spending an entire week's wages. The doll was long gone, of course. But suddenly, Mathilde longs to stroke her soft hair, feel the silken fabric of her petticoats. Suddenly, just for a moment, she is young again. That is the toymaker's gift. One that is very precious.

And somehow, he coaxes her to tell her story too. She speaks haltingly at first, but his interest gives her the confidence to continue. Before she knows it, the threads of time have begun to unravel themselves. The cocoon has spun around her again, the chrysalis reformed. No longer sticky with disappointment and lack. But loose and silky, cradling the butterfly inside.

In her flat across the hall, the boy sleeps, oblivious of her brief transformation to dancing princess, young girl. If he wakes and finds her gone there will be consequences and broken things. At this moment, Mathilde doesn't care.

Franz's voice lowers as he continues to tell his own story. A memory of bananas; Mathilde can taste them in her mouth – their soft sweetness hidden beneath the skin. But then the tale begins to twist and tremble, leading down darker paths. Ones she does not want to travel.

'I was young and stupid,' he is saying. 'And people got hurt.'

'But all of us were once that way,' she says. It seems important to convey this point. 'I, too, have made mistakes. Too many to count. And I still make them. Every day.'

Her companion's eyes are glassy with unshed tears. Nonetheless, he smiles at her with such warmth and compassion that she feels something hard and sharp inside her start to melt like a lump of molten metal. Mathilde has the sense that he sees the girl she once was. The girl she *should* have been. There is magic in his smile.

The magic of possibilities she cannot allow.

Mathilde stands up unsteadily. The movement cripples the memories of dancing and flight. 'Would you like another cup of tea?' she says.

'Tea?'

The sparkle disappears from his eyes. Mathilde stifles a sigh. She has broken the enchanted web. All that remains are the severed strands of failure and regret, and a letter shoved at the bottom of the drawer. Franz will be seeing her now as she truly is. An old woman. All she can ever be.

'Yes, if it is not too much trouble, that would be nice.'

Mathilde walks a few steps, but the kitchen is not where it should be. The lights of Paris, they are the same but different. A mirror image… of course. She is in Tomas's flat, not her own. How stupid to forget that. The boy is sleeping across the hall.

The boy.

Somewhere inside her head, a clock begins to chime. Time has stood still but now it races forward. If Andre wakes and finds her gone there will be consequences and broken things. At this moment, it is *all* she cares about.

'I must go,' she says. 'My grandson needs me.'

The old man nods sadly. 'I understand.'

She blinks rapidly. The kitchen… she has promised the old man something. But what…? The boy… he needs her.

'Thank you for the story,' she says.

Her feet feel heavy, her limbs stiff as she moves towards the door. She has the aching gnaw that she has forgotten something. Again.

'Mathilde…' he calls out after her.

'Good night.'

She slips out like a wraith, a memory, closing the door softly behind her.

21

FRANZ

The door opened and closed. The beautiful dream faded away. Franz thought of Clara in *The Nutcracker* ballet, awakening from her vision of giant mice, snowflakes, and sugar plum fairies. How painful it was to have such loveliness snatched away, to question what was real and what was fantasy. Had she been real? *Mathilde*… her name was Mathilde.

She'd found a blanket and tucked him in like a child. He'd watched her moving about: fetching a plate of biscuits, straightening Tomas's papers, folding a pile of laundry. Her movements were graceful, her figure slight and ethereal. She'd spoken half in French, half in halting English; half to him, half to herself. What *was* he doing attacking thugs on the street and almost getting himself killed? Yes, it was very noble, but really, at his age, he ought to know better.

Eventually she'd sat down and sipped her tea. He'd managed to tease out some of her story. Once she had been a dancer at the Paris Opera House, pursuing her dreams like a ballerina doll come to life. Reality was long, painful hours rehearsing for low wages, but as soon as she'd stepped on stage, she'd felt beautiful and special. He could imagine her, pure and delicate as a beam of moonlight sparkling on water. She'd told him about a pair of silver shoes in a shop window that she'd wished for, more than anything. By the time she had saved up the money, the shoes were sold. The clerk, however, found her a pair from the window display that fit perfectly. She had kissed him full on the lips. And voila! He was the man she would marry. She'd walked up the aisle in those shoes… still had them somewhere…

Franz was enchanted. He could picture her as a young woman, which surprised him. He knew this sometimes happened to couples who'd been together for many years, but he and Mathilde had just met. How could this be?

He told her stories too – nice ones about glockenspiels and musical boxes. Things he'd once despised but which were now part of an enchanted world he wanted to share. He told her about the shop and his castle; he explained his vision. To create a place that drew children and adults alike: a place with a particular magic that could not be found elsewhere. As he talked, she smiled. The crushing weight of regret he carried became as light and delicate as the wings of a dragonfly.

But he had faltered… failed. He'd felt duty-bound to tell her the other stories: the darker ones. She'd become unsettled and left to look after her grandson. Once he had stayed silent and it had led to disaster. Now, he had spoken, and the result was the same.

'Franz?'

A voice. Her voice? No. *Tomas.* Franz came back to the present; he was lying on Tomas's sofa. A lamp illuminated the dark room. *She* was gone. A dream that he could not get back again.

'Tomas,' he said in a rusty voice, 'I should be going.'

'It's the middle of the night,' Tomas said. 'Lie down. You need to sleep.'

'Yes – I will. But won't you stay a minute?' Franz felt wide awake. This feeling… he needed to share it.

'OK.' Tomas went over to the window. Far below them, the lights of Paris pierced the darkness like glittery stars.

'Your neighbour is a wonderful woman,' Franz said. 'So beautiful and special.'

Tomas laughed. 'You're an old softy.'

'How does it happen – this business of attraction between people? I am somewhat of an expert in clockwork and mechanics. But this shocking electrical feeling – it defies the laws of physics!'

'Maybe,' Tomas said. 'But just like a scientific experiment, you need the right ingredients and conditions. And then a catalyst. Say, for example, interfering with a mugging. Ending up on a friend's sofa.'

Franz chuckled. 'You are right, I'm sure. But what about you?'

'What about me?'

'Do you not wish for that feeling? To be… in love?'

'Who says I don't feel it?' Tomas said. 'Maybe I feel it every night for a different woman.'

He frowned. 'And do you?'

'No.'

Tomas turned back to the window. Franz felt bad for saying the wrong thing. But how could he say the right thing when he did not know Tomas's story? His elation drained away.

'I suppose it is foolish to dream,' Franz said. 'I am an old man. I have made many mistakes. It is only right that love has eluded me over all the years.'

'Come on,' Tomas said. 'I'm sure that's not true.'

'Are you?' Regret rumbled inside him like a roll of distant thunder. 'Do not be so sure. You see me as Franz the toymaker, no? An old man who is eccentric – maybe even a little mad? An old man who deserves your pity?'

'I think you're eccentric, but I don't pity you.'

'And well you should not. You don't know what I've done. The pain I have caused in the past by my actions – and inactions.'

Tomas turned. 'Now, I'm definitely curious.'

Franz had a strange sense of vertigo like he was standing at the edge of a tall building looking down. Stories had power – the power to gnaw away at you over many years. But also the power to free you. Which would he choose on this momentous night?

He closed his eyes and began to speak, recounting the things he had done. The beatings, the arson, the intimidation. He even told Tomas about Anna – the musical boxes, the bananas – the only woman he'd ever loved. The words spun themselves into the terrible shapes of his memories. Tomas listened without speaking, his face half in shadow. Franz knew what he must be thinking. His friend would judge him, hate him even.

'So you see, my friend, I am not worthy of love. I do not deserve a wife to comfort me in my old age or a child to follow in my footsteps. I do not deserve my shop, and most likely, I will lose it. I do not deserve a good friend like you to show me kindness.'

Tomas came over and sat next to him on the sofa. Franz felt a clawing panic as he waited for the verdict to be delivered. But he glimpsed something unexpected on his friend's face. Compassion. Almost as if, on some level, he understood.

'That's an extraordinary story,' Tomas said.

'Tonight was the first time I have told it. I am sorry to burden you. It's just, when I met Mathilde—' He broke off in despair. 'It was foolish even to dream of a different life.' He threw off the blanket. 'If you will be so kind as to call me a taxi, I will leave. You don't need a thug sleeping on your sofa.'

'Come on, Franz. I'm not going to judge you for what you did back then, and I don't think Mathilde will either. Do you really think she's going to call the police and tell them that she knows an old bloke who was a rabble rouser fifty years ago in East Germany? Do you think they'll come with sirens blazing?'

'Maybe not.' Franz frowned. 'But the passing of time does not change the right or wrong of a thing.'

'True. But it does change us as people. The grief changes us. It doles out its own retribution. Think about it – are you still the same person you were back then?'

'No. Not at all.'

'How long are you going to punish yourself for what you did?'

'That, my friend, I do not know.'

'We only have one life,' Tomas said. 'One precious, unique life. You're not too old to dream of something different – and to make it happen.' Franz was surprised to see the pain on the younger man's face, deep and defining, a landscape of hidden scars.

'Perhaps that is true,' Franz said. 'But are you trying to convince me, or yourself?'

Tomas shrugged. 'Maybe I haven't been punished enough.'

'I have told you my secrets,' Franz pressed. 'Will you not tell me yours?'

'Who says I have secrets?'

Franz sighed. Tomas's flippancy had returned – the mask slid firmly back in place.

'No one. I am sorry.'

Tomas waved away the apology. 'No worries. But what's this about you losing the shop?'

'Oh.' Franz wished he had not mentioned it; he wished that by staying silent, it would all go away. 'It is nothing new. I am an old man, and I have made a bed and I must lie in it. I am late in my rent and there are health and safety matters to address. If I do not, then I must be out by Christmas.'

'Out by Christmas?' Tomas looked stunned. 'Is that what you want?'

'No.'

'Well, surely you have a lease. If you put things right, they can't throw you out on your ear.'

'That is not so easy to do.'

'Then maybe this is a sign from the universe that it's time to retire. If you get the landlord to buy out your lease, you could get some good money out of it.'

'Money.' Franz blanched. 'What is money in the face of a life's work? I do not wish to retire; to become a pigeon man in the park. I wish to stay in my shop and complete my castle. That is my vision. It is all that matters to me.'

'Look, I get where you're coming from,' Tomas said. 'I'm no expert, but there's someone I could ask who might have a few tips.'

'Really?'

He smiled cryptically. 'It's someone you know, in fact.'

'Me?' Franz drew his eyebrows together. 'This is a conundrum. Who could it—'

A face popped into Franz's mind. An angry, troubled, beautiful face. 'Ah-ha!' he said. 'It is Sarah. The woman who came to the toyshop. Am I right?'

'Got it in one,' Tomas said. 'She's working on a hotel renovation across the river. The grand opening was tonight. I just *happened* to be passing and ran into her again.'

Franz smiled wistfully. 'It sounds very romantic.'

'It wasn't like that.' Tomas's voice lowered. 'I found out she had a daughter – a baby girl – who died.'

'So that is her secret.' Franz's heart squeezed like a fist.

'She was glad to get the animals back. Though I gather there's still one missing?'

'The giraffe. It was not in the set I purchased. I will speak to the man who sold them to me, but I don't hold out much hope.'

'It's better than nothing. Now, time for bed.'

'Yes, my friend, you are right. This business of living a life – or thinking about living a life – is tiring work.'

'You can say that again.'

Tomas gave Franz a pat on the shoulder and left the room. Franz listened as the water ran and an electric toothbrush buzzed. He thought about Sarah and Tomas – and about Mathilde. He closed his eyes, picturing the dancers colliding on their track; a flock of pigeons scattering to the sky. Grief, guilt, punishment, joy. The clockwork of the human heart worked in mysterious ways.

22

SARAH

SATURDAY, AUGUST 5TH

The alarm beeped. Sarah groaned and rolled over, knocking her phone off the bedside table. Her head was pounding. Last night… the gala… Tomas. Were they dreams or were they memories? She feared the latter. He had played along with her charade – her *fiancé*? God, he must have thought she was either completely deranged or an easy lay – or both. She'd let him walk her halfway across Paris, take her to a bar, and *dance* with her. That dance…

A rush of *wanting* swept over her. Somehow, like Pandora's box, Tomas had picked the lock and prised open the lid. Encouraged her to get her pain out in the open and look at it. That in itself had been momentous. And what had she done? Gone into the street and shouted like a mad woman. Ended up back in the danger zone with his arms wrapped protectively around her.

The last thing she remembered was him walking her to her door, giving her a double kiss on the cheek, and asking her to meet him again at the café on the corner – this morning. She'd agreed – how could she have done that?

Surely it would be best to cancel. Chalk up their connection to a trick of the night and wrestle her mind back to reality. Her life – empty, childless, loveless. Exactly what she deserved.

And yet, something was different. The cracks in her heart were still there – that wasn't going to change. But a thin ray of light was shining in.

She pulled up Amazon and did a search for Tomas Mercier. Disappointingly, no author photo was displayed. His latest book, *The Art of Death*, involved an international art smuggling scam that was a front for human and weapons trafficking. She downloaded a sample and began to read. In the first few pages, two people were brutally murdered. Sarah shuddered. She'd never met an author before: someone whose job it was to invent a whole story; visualise it, live it. What did it say about Tomas?

She continued to read. Agent Lucinda Clarke was a beautiful woman with long legs and voluptuous breasts. A male fantasy. Sarah felt oddly jealous. If this was the kind of woman he wrote about, why was he bothering with her?

Abandoning the book, she got out of bed. The room spun – she'd had too much to drink, and she didn't have Tomas's number to cancel. She showered and dressed, trying not to think or feel anything. But as she got ready to go out, her eyes snagged on the carrier bag near the door. The toyshop… the animals…

One by one, she took the wooden figures out of the box and set them on the table. They stared back at her with gentle, benevolent expressions.

Tomas's poem had perfectly captured the love she'd felt for her daughter. *Rowan would want you to live your life.*

It was an audacious thing to say; her anger had been justified. She picked up the tiny monkey in the pillbox hat and turned it over in her hand.

'You would want me to be happy, wouldn't you?' she whispered into the air.

A pang of intense longing was the only answer – but it was enough.

A waxy lemon sunlight warmed her face as she left the flat and went to the café. She'd been inside a few times to grab a coffee and croissant on the way to work but had never sat down. The shop smelled of fresh bread; the glass case was filled with delicate patisserie – it was like she was noticing it all for the first time.

She ordered coffee and a *pain au abricot* and sat down at a table by the window. A bell tolled the hour. Tomas was late. Or more likely, he wasn't coming.

Of course he wasn't. The connection between them was nothing more than a chimera. He'd been a friend when she needed it, but now that moment was lost in time. Maybe she should have invited him to her flat. Slept with him. At least then, she'd have had the memory of something real—

'Sarah?'

His voice sent a sparkle of electricity down her spine. She'd been so busy wallowing in self-pity that when Tomas appeared – against all odds – she wasn't ready. A flush crept up her neck. Why was she so nervous?

'Hi,' she said. 'I didn't think you'd come.'

His smiled wavered as he sat down opposite her. 'Is that what you were hoping for?'

'I don't know.'

The memories of the night floated between them like a soap bubble. The nice moments and the not so nice.

The waitress brought Sarah's order on a tray, and

Tomas ordered an espresso. The pastry was light as air, the apricot sharp on her tongue. 'I read a sample of your latest book,' she said. 'A bit gory for me – though definitely a page turner.'

Something flickered across Tomas's face. Concern, annoyance? He sat back in his chair. 'Let me guess. As you were reading, you started to wonder if someone who could write that stuff is someone you want to see Paris with?'

'The thought did occur.' She gave a little laugh. 'Though I also wondered about the main character: Lucinda. She seems, well, I don't know…' *Like a hot, male fantasy*, she didn't add. 'Is she based on someone real?'

'Not really. Like most characters, she's an amalgam. Of people I know, people I see, people I imagine.'

'And are you in love with her?' Sarah said it teasingly, but Tomas took a long moment to answer.

'Maybe I wanted to be,' he said. 'Years ago, when I wrote her for the first time. I liked escaping into her life. But in the end, she turned into something created by readers and editors. Their version of a fantasy heroine. That's it really.' The waitress brought his espresso, and he drank it down. 'The truth is, I just put random words down on a page. My stuff is nothing special.' He frowned at the empty cup. 'And contrary to popular belief, the life of a crime writer is far from exciting. At least – until I ended up rescuing a beautiful stranger at a bar from the attentions of a smarmy little man.'

'Actually, he's likely to be my new boss.'

He arched an eyebrow. 'My mistake. I hope you wouldn't rather be seeing Paris with him.'

'It's probably better to see it with a *friend*. But I guess that depends on you.'

'Fine. I like a challenge. Let's do it.' He gazed across at

her as if sizing her up. 'I've got a place in mind that I'd like to show you. Somewhere I find… inspiring.'

'OK. As long as it doesn't involve rappelling off the Eiffel Tower – I really don't like heights.'

'I'll keep that in mind.' He rose from the chair and held out his hand to her. When she touched his skin, she felt that glitter again.

'Great,' she said. 'Surprise me.'

23

TOMAS

Tomas had been hoping the magic would vanish in the light of day. He'd lain awake much of the night alternatively reliving the evening with Sarah and thinking about Franz's story. Had he been wrong to comfort the old man with sentiments he didn't believe himself? Some wrongs simply could not be put right.

Sarah had suffered a terrible tragedy. He was a fraud, living a lie. What was done could not be undone. Surely, the song they'd danced to, *Let's Call the Whole Thing Off*, was prophetic. The best option all around.

Despite his misgivings, he'd come to meet her at the appointed time. When he spotted her sitting in the café, possibility sparked like a firework inside his chest. He wanted to spend time with her. Show her *his* Paris; see if it resonated with her. Surely, that couldn't be a bad thing. She made it clear that she wasn't looking for a lover or a one night stand – it was enough to be friends.

She'd looked him up, of course. If she dug deep enough, she might connect the dots and that would be the end of their story. His anxieties whispered from the wings.

Usually, he silenced them by summoning up Lucinda Clarke, his mirror image and alter ego. Cold, dedicated, and distant, with no subtlety or artifice, Lucinda was exactly what it said on the tin. Tomas wasn't in love with Lucinda – it was more that he wanted to *be* her.

Just not today.

As they left the café, his senses were on high alert to the poetry of the city: the rhythm of their footsteps on the pavement; the smell of urban decay punctuated by the scent of fresh-baked croissants and coffee; the gradients of light and dark as the sun chased away the last of the morning shadows. Most of all, he was aware of Sarah. She seemed glad to be outside taking in the sights: the architecture, the people, the little shops and cafés. They chatted amiably, and she seemed happy enough to talk about herself – her job, at least – when he asked her.

'I studied business and design at uni,' she said. 'I love art, so I thought I might open a gallery or something. But then I got offered a job at a London hotel that was undergoing refurbishment. I helped manage the project, which was great – I got to be creative and practical.' Her voice dropped. 'Then I met Victor.'

'Your husband?'

'Yes. He's half French. We met when he was interviewing for jobs in London. He was… very charming.' He sensed she was skipping over vast areas of her life. 'It was the usual story. We fell in love, got married, had a child…'

Her mouth set in a line as they walked onto the bridge. Sunlight sparkled on the ripples of water. The city was lit up like a jewel. But a shadow had fallen across her face.

'After Rowan died, I didn't leave my mum's house for almost two years. That's why I noted what you said about the boy – your neighbour?'

'Andre.'

'I don't know if I was suffering from the same thing. But I couldn't face the outside world. It seemed so full of terrible things. So full of… death. Every time I even thought about going out, I had a panic attack. My heart would race so fast I thought it might burst open. I couldn't breathe. I couldn't fathom why I was still alive when Rowan wasn't.'

'Survivor's guilt. I think Andre has that too.'

'Probably.'

'So how did you get over it?' He tried to sound casual – to hide his true interest in the answer.

'My mum wanted to turn my bedroom into a sewing room. She started bringing me magazines from the supermarket. About gardening, of all things. I'd never done any gardening in my life! But it helped bring the outside in. Those magazines saved me. Finally, I decided I was ready to start looking for jobs and landed an interview with the hotel consortium. I had to leave the house for that. The first time I tried, I thought the panic might suffocate me. But I survived, and that was the turning point. It still took a long time before I went anywhere willingly, but gradually, the panic attacks became less frequent. I learned to close my eyes and trust that they'd pass.'

Tomas smiled gently. 'I'm glad they did.'

'Yes, well… I've found it's best just to focus on work. When phase one of the St. Jacques is over the line, I'm hoping to be promoted. Mr Komitov is a big player in the industry.'

'He's certainly a big something.'

She laughed. 'Well, hopefully he got the message. I may not have a real "fiancé", but I'm not looking, either.'

'Good to know.' The hint was clear. He took it. *Friends*… It made things easier for both of them. No games, no meaningless flirtation, no need to find a room or think up an exit strategy. It made the day *possible*.

'And you like your work?' He steered back onto safe ground.

'I love it,' she said. 'The projects are interesting – a lot of it is dragging failing hotels kicking and screaming into the modern world. Refurbishing, changing things that aren't working. Striking a balance between the old and the new. That's the part of the job I like.'

'Sounds interesting. And if you've got any advice I can give Franz, let me know. His shop is struggling.'

'I guessed as much. It's sad, really. The shop is unique, but it would take a huge effort to turn things around. Not to mention, heaps of cash.'

'That's what I thought,' Tomas said, resigned. It just wasn't going to happen.

They crossed the bridge to the Île de la Cité. 'Speaking of old,' Tomas said, 'that's where we're headed.' He pointed to a thin green spire peeking out above the other buildings. 'Sainte-Chapelle – one of my favourite spots in all of Paris.'

'I wondered what that was,' Sarah said. 'I thought it was a government building.'

'Yes. The Palace of Justice. The chapel is inside the grounds.' He felt secretly pleased that she hadn't been there. 'It was built by Louis IX around 1248. It's… well… you'll see.'

They stood in a queue to go through the metal detector. Crossing the courtyard, they entered the chapel at its upper level.

When they were inside, Sarah gasped. 'I've never seen anything like it.'

He knew exactly how she felt. Each time he came here it took his breath away. The ornate gothic ribs of the chapel gave the impression of height and weightlessness, drawing the eye heavenward. The windows contained some of the most spectacular stained glass in the world. An explosion of colour and light. Blue, red, green, and gold, sparkling like the rarest of jewels. The vaulted ceiling was speckled with hundreds of golden stars.

'Apparently, it was designed to house the king's most valuable relic,' he said. 'The crown of thorns.'

'It's like being inside a jewel box.' Sarah craned her neck upwards, her face lit with fascination. 'I can't believe I've never been here.'

'I'm glad there are still a few surprises in store.'

It surprised him how much he wanted to share it with her.

24

SARAH

Sarah squinted as the beautiful jewel-like colours and spectacular light blurred into an abstract mass. The beauty was exhilarating – and frightening. 'It's… amazing,' she said. 'But overwhelming too. I find it hard to let myself to be moved by beautiful things.'

'Because of her?'

Sarah stared straight ahead. Had it been a mistake to tell him her story – her secret? Rowan was present in everything she did – every breath she took. Now, her daughter was part of her and Tomas. The connection between them was full of energy and life, but there was also a sliver of death.

'She'll never see this. Never see any of the beauty in the world. Never fall in love, or experience anything.'

He took her hand. Caring, intimate. *Rowan would want you to live your life.* Last night the words had made her angry. But today…

She squeezed his hand and then let go. 'I'm sorry,' she said.

'You don't need to apologise for your grief.' His voice was gentle. 'I would never ask that of you.'

Sarah shook off the yoke of melancholy and gave him a fragile smile. 'Where did you come from? I haven't met anyone like you before.'

'Thanks… I think.' Tomas laughed.

As they left the upper chapel, she felt suffused with a warm glow. In the lower chapel, the arched golden ceiling was held up by columns decorated with golden castles and stencilled fleurs-de-lys. The space felt intimate and cosy, heightening her awareness of Tomas and the spark between them that was unexpected, and yet undeniable.

I think he's right, Sarah spoke the words inwardly to her daughter. *You'd want me to experience this.*

But could she risk wanting it for herself?

25

FRANZ

Franz's back was aching when he awoke. It took him a second to recall where he was – in Tomas's flat – and the momentous events of the night before. He levered himself up with a youthful surge of energy. He had to get back to his workshop. The clock was ticking and he had so much to do!

He gathered his things and hobbled out of the flat. As he closed the door, he heard a loud crash: glass shattering, a woman crying out. It was none of his business; he should ignore the commotion and leave. In his youth he'd spent too much time sticking his nose into other people's business and ended up hurting them. And yet, when the crisis point had come – when Anna had needed him – he'd stayed silent and lost her. Which was worse?

He began walking towards the lift—

'Stop it, Andre! Pull yourself together!'

Mathilde's voice. Franz turned around and went back, rapping on her door with the end of his cane.

'We're fine, there is no problem,' Mathilde called out. 'Sorry for the noise.'

'Mathilde? It's me, Franz.'

He waited for what seemed like a long time. Was she ignoring him? And what of Andre?

Eventually the doorknob turned – slowly, reluctantly.

Mathilde seemed shorter, slighter, and more diminished than his memory of her. Her face was drawn and pale, with dark hollows below her eyes.

'Monsieur Himmelberg.' Her words were clipped and formal. 'I'm sorry, but this is not a good time.'

Her coolness dismayed him – so different from last night. He should apologise for bothering her and walk away. That was the right thing to do.

'Please, Mathilde,' he said instead. 'You helped me before. Let me help you.'

Emotions flitted across her face: irritation, shame, regret. Franz longed to run his finger down her cheek and memorise each line on her face the way a blind man would. He'd been blind and deaf, divorced from his senses for all these years. Now, in what seemed a miracle, everything was reawakening. He didn't want to let the feeling go.

'It is not necessary,' she said. 'Andre, my grandson, had a bad night.'

Franz pushed gently on the door. Inside, colourful magnetic building tiles were scattered across the floor like a smashed stained-glass window. Beyond, near the kitchen table, he noticed broken crockery. On the sofa near the wreckage, a boy was curled up like a snail, vulnerable and robbed of his shell.

He felt Mathilde's anger gathering force. Ready to shout at him; ready to tell him to mind his own business and leave—

Wordlessly, she stepped aside.

Franz came inside the flat, careful not to tread on

anything. He made his way to the sofa and sat down next to the boy.

'Andre?' he said in a calm voice. 'I am Franz. A friend of Tomas. He has told me all about you.'

The boy buried his face in the cushion.

'I own the toyshop. *La Boutique Fantasque*. A wonderful place – full of possibilities and magic. Would you like to hear about it?'

The boy didn't answer. Mathilde shook her head and tsked. She swept up the broken crockery and disappeared around the corner into what Franz assumed must be the kitchen.

'I make many of the toys myself,' he said. 'It is painstaking work. My favourite toys are the mechanical ones. I have made a mechanical circus and a ballet theatre. And I am working on my greatest project yet – a castle. It has many layers that move and rotate; a carousel at the bottom and figures and animals above. For the sky, I am making a huge dragon that swoops down. I do the drawings first, and then I assemble the pieces. Do you like building things, Andre?'

The ball shifted a little.

'He spends his time playing games on the iPad.' Mathilde re-emerged from the kitchen with a tray of coffee and croissants. She set them down on the table and picked up her knitting. 'Too much time.'

'Ah, the iPad.' Franz felt a momentary stab of doubt. 'A wonderful thing – I am sure of it. Though I prefer to work with my hands.' He took a breath, desperate to make a connection. 'When I was your age, I had a building set too, but mine was made of wooden blocks. I spent hours making things, tearing them down, starting again. But when I was older, I stopped building.'

The boy moved. Unwashed hair fell in a curtain over his face.

'Have you heard of the Berlin Wall, Andre?'

The boy nodded. It gave him the courage to keep going. Andre too was trapped in a prison of a sort. If his story could help in some way, then he needed to tell it. Franz allowed the memories to escape and flow outwards, recreating and reliving the guilt of his youth.

'We were like rats in a cage,' he said. 'We did what we were told – we did bad things to innocent people. We *believed* what we were told. But it was not the truth.'

His unburdening was met by deafening silence. The past took on a life of its own, huge and monstrous like a shadow puppet. Shame and fear clawed inside him. But having begun, he was determined to finish. Even the most terrible story deserved an ending.

'When the wall came down, it was very frightening. Yes, people were happy; they were dancing and cheering. Finally, we could see the world on the other side. The world we'd been taught to fear and hate. Freedom is a scary thing.' He sighed. 'In the end, I decided to leave Germany. I hitched a ride with some friends who wanted to see the world. I learned to think for myself, even if I could not come to terms with what I'd believed – and done – before. Eventually, I found a place where I belonged. A little toyshop in Paris. And now…'

Was he doing the right thing? Was there ever a *right* thing? 'Now, I am ready to find someone who will work with me – someone who understands the joy of making things and sharing them. Finally, I am ready to create the place of wonder and magic I have dreamed about. To be open for business.' He smiled wistfully. Mathilde had put down her knitting and was staring at him, her face unreadable.

'I would like you to come to my shop, Andre,' he said. 'Someday, when you are ready. I have so many things to show you. So many things that a clever boy would enjoy and understand. Would you like that?'

The boy made no response. Franz finished the coffee, leaving the croissant. He would do the noble thing and leave.

'Thank you for having me, Mathilde.' He stood up stiffly. 'I should go now.'

'Andre?' Mathilde looked over at the boy. 'Monsieur Franz has asked you a question. You must let him know you've heard.'

'Perhaps I should not have—'

'He's leaving now, Andre. Do not waste this opportunity!'

Andre lifted his head; Franz sensed the war going on inside him: continue the sulk or sit up and respond. He kept silent, waiting.

The boy moved, raising his torso, his legs still wrapped underneath him. Slowly, he uncurled his body and stood up. He went to the bookcase and removed a messy, loose-leaf sheaf of papers. When he returned to the sofa, he looked at Franz for the first time. The boy's blue eyes were deep-set, his skin pasty from lack of sunlight. His sandy-coloured hair was scraggly and too long. He was wearing a pair of old denim shorts and a faded blue T-shirt. He shifted on the sofa – a clear invitation for Franz to sit back down.

Franz glanced at Mathilde who gave a small nod. He sat down again as the boy opened his folio, overflowing with pencil drawings, sketches, and cartoons. There were vast, imaginary buildings, drawings of people and animals, storyboards of superheroes, pirates, and jungle treasure hunters. Franz felt a painful sense of recognition. Andre lived entirely within his own head. He didn't need anyone's pity – he needed an outlet for his creativity. A real-world place to break out of his shell and spread his wings.

Franz pointed to the drawing of a towering skyscraper formed from a mosaic of shapes. 'Tell me about this,' he said.

An hour later, Franz sat back, tired but exhilarated. The boy spoke little beyond a simple 'oui' or 'non,' but it was amazing what could be accomplished without words to interrupt the flow of ideas. Andre sketched: Franz showed him how to make his creations more structurally viable. The boy got down on the floor and began to build. In the end, the whole structure came crashing down, but instead of getting angry, Andre began to laugh – a high-pitched sound that took some getting used to. Tomas was right – the boy was special – intelligent, creative, focused. Everything Franz would have wanted if he'd had… a son.

No. Franz glanced at Mathilde who seemed lost sewing beads onto a knit garment. He refocused on the boy. Life happened, and regrets meant nothing. In the last twelve hours he'd been shaken to the core: first by the mugging, then by meeting Mathilde and Andre and telling his story. It was more excitement than he'd had in years!

'You need another support on the right side.' Franz held his breath as Andre's newest creation began to wobble. The boy put a long Perspex beam across the top of his structure. Franz exhaled. 'And now the last piece.'

With a rock-solid hand, Andre put the cupola on top. The structure juddered again. This time, it held.

'Brilliant!' Franz really could keep this up all day. But he needed to return to the shop. There was so much to do. He wanted to savour this new, bizarre revelation that had come to him, like Saul on the road to Damascus.

That maybe he had punished himself long enough.

26

MATHILDE

The toymaker, Franz, has a strange gift, a particular type of magic. Or maybe it's just more forgetting. Mathilde doesn't know, and somehow, it doesn't matter. He arrived at the least opportune moment – a moment she would like to forget, but has to live through first. The boy awoke from a nightmare – or perhaps it was simply a dream of his mother that he wished to savour. He cried out, and when Mathilde summoned the courage to go into his room, his face was etched with disappointment. She told him to get up and get dressed. He got angry and smashed the dishes. Was his reaction her fault? She doesn't pretend to know anymore.

Now, however, Andre is spellbound, the laughing and dancing back in his eyes. As Franz teaches the boy to build things, Mathilde sweeps up the shards of the cup and saucer that got broken, brings the coffee, and sits at the table with her knitting. The scarf is knit from soft cashmere wool in robin egg blue. At the edges, she is sewing tiny pearls and glass beads. The lady from the refugee centre will tut and tell her to make something simple and functional. But as Franz speaks, bringing the past to life in the present moment, Mathilde remembers what it's like to want special, elegant things. Why do the refugee women not deserve such things? Even in grief and hard times, a woman should not be deprived of beauty.

She threads the needle and begins to sew. Her fingers fumble with the first tiny bead, smooth and slippery. She secures it with the thread, and sews on another. The old man talks; the boy listens; Mathilde sews. With each bead she affixes, a memory rises to the surface of her mind, like bubbles in a crystal glass of champagne.

Walking along the streets of Paris; gazing at beautiful things in the window of the Galleries Lafayette. Trying to imagine a life beyond the cramped and tired bedsit shared with three other dancers. A future of happiness, love – and most of all – luxury. A future she expects to obtain. Expects to deserve.

She sews on another bead. The shop floats into her mind – infinitely smart and infinitely expensive.

The silver shoes in the window are sharp heeled and beautiful. The perfect shoes for a dancer. The perfect shoes for taking flight. Each day she walks past the window; terrified they will be gone, delighted to see them still there. Living on water, cigarettes, and day-old bread from the bakery on the corner. Scrimping and saving all of her wages. The other girls laugh – it would be so easy to get a man to pay for the shoes – and so much more. Why does Mathilde always insist on doing things her own way?

Another bead…

A purse full of money. Walking past the door of the shop several times before mustering the courage to go inside. The clerks are so well dressed, so worldly and sophisticated. Frowning at her with disapproval, as if she is a common thief – or worse. Inside she is shrinking. But she keeps her back straight, her head held high.

She finishes the row of beads on the scarf. The boy is laughing now. She picks up a seed pearl to start the next row. It was hard to enter the shop, but the next memories hurt even more.

'Oh, but mademoiselle, we do not have your size.' The clerk's words, distant and indistinct.

'Non. Non.'

The shock of it, the disappointment – too much to bear. She puts her head in her hands.

'Mademoiselle?'

She looks up, roused by a kind voice. A man with neat brown hair, a thin moustache, and a well-pressed suit. His badge reads Jean-Louis, Manager. He kneels down; takes her foot in his hand. Directs a clerk to bring the shoes from the window display. Just her size… and he will sell them for half price. She twines her fingers through his hair, kisses him on the lips…

The bead slips from her hand onto the floor. Her back hurts too much to retrieve it; even the good memories hurt. Jean-Louis. A good man. Together they had Renée – a beautiful, special girl. And Andre… she looks up at the boy, still happily building things with Franz. There is a genuine kindness in the toymaker's eyes, a genuine joy. Another good man, though she suspects he does not see himself that way.

She runs her fingers over the row of beads. Each one has evoked a memory – but now, she has already forgotten. Something painful – something beautiful. One and the same.

Mathilde looks out at the city stretching below her, the morning sun glinting off rooftops and chimney pots. Had she ever noticed it before? The moments pass, even the beads cannot secure the memories. But right now, she has this…

'Careful… easy does it.' Franz's voice is coaxing. 'Yes. Yes!'

He claps his hands. Andre jumps up with a cry of delight.

She sets down her knitting and stands up to go to them, surprised to find herself smiling.

A strange gift, a particular type of magic. It is too late for her, of course, but Andre… can she dare to hope? The ache in her chest gives way to a stirring sensation. Silky, loose… a fluttering of wings.

27

SARAH

MONDAY, AUGUST 7TH

The weekend seemed like a dream. At first, Sarah wanted to preserve the memories so she could relive them. After leaving St Chapelle, she'd felt dizzy as Tomas had walked her back to her flat and given her a double kiss on the cheek the Parisian way. She'd agreed to meet him again, though they hadn't made a firm plan.

But since then, her misgivings had crept back. Finding the animals had made her vulnerable to unwanted feelings, and she needed to keep her head. She'd made it clear that she wasn't looking for a lover or a relationship, so why was Tomas spending time with her? She didn't want to believe the cliché that 'all the good ones are taken', but if Tomas was single, there must be a reason. Maybe he'd been burned in the past, or maybe he was a consummate bachelor who enjoyed taking his pick of women. Or maybe, the charm and good looks hid a darker truth underneath. Was Tomas too good to be true? One of them had the wrong end of the stick, and she didn't want it to be her.

As she walked to work, she passed a group of school children entering the Métro. Little girls in neat dresses, boys in shorts and blazers. The pain blindsided her, as it always did when she saw children. The poem Tomas had composed – its simple imagery had magnified her every emotion. Emotions she could not afford to feel. Looking away, she hurried past the group. Now, more than ever, she needed to focus. She needed to look beyond Paris to the next escape.

The office building was near the river on the Right Bank. An incongruous structure of glass and steel at one end of a small square. Her feelings were wrong – she knew that. Only a few days ago, she would have been excited to be meeting with Komitov: a man of wealth and power who could put her in charge of the best projects all over the world. He could give her a lifestyle that she could only dream of. The ultimate forgetting.

So why did she feel on edge? Komitov was nothing like Victor, and yet, as she walked into the lobby, ghostly sensations from the past rose to the fore. Of playing a role; out of place in a strange pantomime where she didn't know the plot or the lines. She rode up the elevator and emerged into a plush modern waiting area. The PA ushered her into the corner office where her new boss was dwarfed behind an enormous desk.

'Ah *chérie*, how lovely to see you.' Komitov got to his feet and made a show of kissing her hand. Sarah made a conscious effort not to cringe. Although his unctuous display was annoying, she schooled herself to remain detached and professional as she took a seat across the desk.

'Thank you for agreeing to meet me, sir,' she said.

'Please, call me Ivo,' he said. 'For if you are to be part of my special development team, then we should be on first name terms, yes?'

Special development team. Sarah listened as he outlined his plans for the consortium. It was everything she'd dreamed of and more. He was developing glamorous hotels in exotic locations: Dubai, Abu Dhabi, Singapore, Malaysia. Mixed retail and residential projects in New York, Los Angeles. Her head swam with the possibilities.

So why did the image of a tired old toy shop continue to leak into her mind like an overexposed old photograph? Tomas, Franz – people she'd just met. They'd reminded her that she was a human being – with heartbreak, pain, and memories.

'What about Paris?' she heard herself saying. 'Are there opportunities here too?'

'Ah Paris. A city for lovers. You and your delightful fiancé.' He winked. 'I can see that he took his inspiration for Lucinda Clarke from you. So beautiful… and sexy.'

'Well, no.' She blushed. This really was too much.

'And when is the happy day, may I ask?'

'Oh.' She waved a nonchalant hand. 'We haven't set one yet. But he knows my job involves lots of travel; and he can write anywhere. It's not a problem.'

'No, it is not a problem. For I have recently met a man who owns retail space on the Left Bank and wants to present an opportunity to us. I shall put you in touch to discuss the plans. That is… if I can count on you to be my right-hand man – so to speak.'

'I'm honoured to be working with you.' Speaking the words aloud was the first step to making them true.

'Likewise, *chérie*. Likewise.'

28

TOMAS

SATURDAY, AUGUST 12TH

Tomas had tried – and failed – to put Sarah out of his mind. He had edits to be getting on with, a deadline, a life – such as it was. But she continued to linger at the edge of his thoughts, present in everything he did. He debated and argued with himself, hovered his finger over the button to delete her number. Ended up calling her instead. *Stupid, reckless... inevitable.*

At first, she'd sounded a little cool; she was busy – working hard for a promotion and a new project. But he persuaded her to meet him at the Cluny museum, another of his favourite haunts. She met him at the appointed time, beautiful and flustered in a summer dress, cardigan, and sandals. Her skin was soft as he kissed her cheek. *Friends* – it was what she needed, and as long as they could spend time together, it worked for him too.

They spent the morning exploring the museum's exceptional collection of medieval art and decorative objects, including its *pièce de résistance* – the tapestries of *La Dame à la licorne*: the Lady and the Unicorn. Tomas felt like he was seeing everything through new eyes, as Sarah walked slowly around the room, studying each tapestry in silent awe. Five of the tapestries represented the senses: touch, smell, hearing, taste, sight. They were intricately woven in the *millefleur* style, with spectacular hues of red, blue, green, and gold that seemed as bright and vibrant as the day they'd been made, many hundreds of years earlier.

'She reminds me of you,' he said, referring to the honey-haired lady, wearing an intricate jewelled gown, and flanked in each scene by mythical beasts.

'I wish,' Sarah said, both embarrassed and flattered. 'It's all so spectacular. I have no words.'

'There's a mystery associated with the last tapestry,' he said, pointing to the sixth hanging. 'The words along the top: *À mon seul désir*.'

'My only desire,' Sarah translated. 'What does it mean?'

'That's the question. Does it mean she's seeking something more than the sensual pleasures, like knowledge or enlightenment? Or maybe, she's seeking the culmination of the senses. Love.'

'Maybe she just wants to be happy,' Sarah said. 'At the end of the day, isn't that what we all want?'

'I suppose so,' he said.

À mon seul désir.

In this moment, he'd achieved it.

After the museum, Sarah agreed to lunch. The wide streets of Saint-Germain-des-Prés teemed with life: tour groups, street performers, artists and souvenir sellers. They chatted amiably as they walked past the famous Café de Flore and Café Deux Magots. Tables spilled out onto the pavement beneath colourful awnings, occupied by throngs of tourists served by hassled-looking waiters. Tomas directed Sarah down a small alleyway, enjoying the cornucopia of delicious smells. The small local market was full of traditional bakeries, butcher shops, and fruit sellers, frequented by Parisians who bought their food fresh every day.

The café was a hole in the wall – another place most tourists would never find. Dark and atmospheric with drippy candles in wine bottles and red and white chequered tablecloths. Tomas ordered coq au vin, and Sarah the beef bourguignon. The conversation stayed on safe, neutral ground. Wine, food, places to visit in Paris. Neither of them acknowledged the sweet undercurrent of desire humming between them. It was a little dangerous. It was delicious.

But as they waited for their mains to arrive, Sarah steered the conversation in a different direction. 'You know so much about me,' she said. 'But I know very little about you.'

He gave her an off-handed smile, trying to ignore the clawing urge to evade the question. 'There's not much to know, really. What you see is what you get.'

'Good to know.' She leaned forward. 'But I'd love to hear everything. From the beginning.'

'OK…' He took a long, hesitant breath. 'I grew up in the home counties. Had a pretty normal upbringing. You'll be bored silly.'

He provided a few details of schools and friends, ice creams and seaside holidays. He was an only child, his parents were teachers, his upbringing was unabashedly middle class. 'In my twenties, I worked at a bookshop in London,' he told her. 'I lived in a tiny bedsit in Clapham. I wrote at night – just rubbish really. Then I met someone, and we moved in together. But she and I…' *You hurt people…* he winced. 'Let's just say, things didn't work out. I was ready for a new start, so I moved here.'

'Oh.' Sarah looked a little puzzled. Immediately he

knew his answer had been a mistake – saying too much and too little, leaving too many questions unanswered.

Before she could ask him anything else, he took a long sip of his wine and asked her about Victor. Her answers were equally short and free of painful details. 'He was a good husband,' she said. 'But when Rowan… well… we couldn't come back from it. There was no point to our marriage. No point to us.' She looked away.

'Hey, it's OK.' He reached over and refilled her glass. 'You don't have to talk about it.'

'Thanks,' she said. 'I appreciate that.'

29

SARAH

Their food arrived, putting an end to the conversation. Afterwards they shared a dessert: a *mille feuille* with layers of air-light pastry with chocolate, crème, and raspberry sandwiched between. Sarah pushed the past from her mind. *Focus on the present. Enjoy this moment.*

Being with Tomas, it was easy enough—

'Tomas!' A female voice jarred her from her thoughts. 'Long time no see, *chéri*.'

A gorgeous dark-haired woman came to their table in tall stilettos, an expensive suit, and a waft of perfume.

'Tomas,' the woman said, 'you are a *hard* man to pin down.' The innuendo was clear. Tomas looked suitably embarrassed. 'But now I see why – you have a new lovely companion.'

'Um, Anne-Marie, this is Sarah. Sarah – Anne-Marie. She runs the local Facebook group.'

'*Enchanté*,' the other woman said. 'But I know who you are, of course. You work with the redevelopment consortium.'

'Yes.' Sarah frowned. The woman's manner put her on her guard. 'That's right.'

She turned to Tomas. 'So you are now in bed with "Big Business".'

'Whoa,' he said, frowning. 'That's hardly fair.'

'Which part?' she said.

'Look, Anne-Marie, it's great to see you. But maybe we can catch up another time.'

'Another time, yes…' She narrowed her eyes seductively. 'I will look forward to a much longer catch up very soon.' Still smiling at Tomas, the woman blanked Sarah. The waiter came up and ushered her to a table – fortunately on the other side of the room. But Sarah could still feel the woman's eyes upon her: judging, mocking, hostile.

Sarah deliberately turned to stare out the window, uncomfortable.

'Sorry about that,' Tomas said. 'Anne-Marie's an old friend.'

'Seems like she was more than that.' Sarah couldn't keep the edge from her voice.

'Oh well, you know how it is…' He laughed awkwardly.

'I can guess.' She could. Tomas must have his pick of beautiful woman. Which still begged the question – why was he here with *her*?

Their coffee arrived, but the conversation had fizzled out. 'I'm sorry,' he said as he flagged down the waiter and paid the bill.

'It's fine,' she said. 'Really. I've had a lovely morning.' She made to leave.

'Look,' he said, 'all that stuff about "Big Business" – I know it's not true, and so does she. I saw a piece she did on the St. Jacques – she was very complimentary of your work. It's just, her godfather ran a barber shop and lost his lease – she's touchy about that sort of thing. She sees herself as a champion of small shops and loves to ruffle people's feathers.'

'Well it's nothing to do with me,' Sarah said. 'Most likely I'll be off to Dubai or Singapore very soon.'

'Really?'

She stood up. 'I work for a big developer, and I'm very focused on my career. I do what I'm told. When the St. Jacques is finished, my next project is likely to be somewhere other than Paris. And speaking of which, I need to go. "Big Business" calls.' Her pulse was racing, her cheeks flaring – the damn woman was still looking in their direction.

She walked to the door, half expecting him to stay and talk to his 'friend'. Instead, as she left the restaurant, he was there beside her.

'Do you really have to go?' His voice was gentle. 'I mean, of course you do – sorry. I know you're busy.' He gave her a lopsided smile. 'It's just, I was looking for an excuse to avoid my edits a little longer. And anyway – I should probably go see Andre. I haven't checked on him this week, which is my bad.'

'Well, it's good he has someone.'

'Franz told me something along the lines of: "If you can touch the heart and mind of even one child, then you will have done something worthwhile." That's what I'm trying to do.'

Sarah looked at him thoughtfully. 'That's very admirable.'

He shrugged. 'I don't know about that, but actually, I was thinking – maybe you could come with me?'

'What?'

'It's just that you have a special insight – an understanding of his condition. Maybe meeting you is just the thing he needs to "bring the outside in".' His face shone with hope.

Sarah let out a breath, softening. As strange as it seemed, maybe Tomas needed a friend as much as she did. At the very least, it was kind of him to want to help the boy.

'I'm not sure what I can do,' she said. 'I'm no expert.'

'You mentioned magazines,' he said. 'We could try that.'

We. A short word; so full of meaning. She hesitated, but only for a moment. 'Fine,' she said. 'I have to go to the St. Jacques later, but I guess it's on the way.'

Against her better judgment, Sarah allowed herself to get caught up in Tomas's charismatic gravity, walking swiftly beside him as they left the restaurant. Obviously he was a man with a past, and it wasn't surprising that women – beautiful ones – were drawn to his suave charm and easy sense of humour. The fact that the woman in the restaurant reminded her of Lucinda – leggy, voluptuous, and stunning – shouldn't make her jealous. The fact that the woman had clearly judged her – as some kind of cold corporate tool – shouldn't bother her either. *Friends*. That was the boundary she had set, and she was grateful that he was respecting it. She was determined not to let anything else spoil the day. Tomas too seemed keen to put the incident behind them. He directed her to a news kiosk, and they had a lively debate on which magazines to buy for Andre.

'Electronics?' Sarah suggested.

'No – he spends too much time on his iPad. How about art?'

Sarah laughed as Tomas held up a posh magazine. 'Would you have been interested in that at age eleven?'

'No,' Tomas's eyes sparkled, 'but isn't that kind of the point?'

'Fair enough. How about *National Geographic*? That will bring the outside in.'

'Do they still have naked people in it?'

She laughed again. 'Um… I'm not sure.'

'OK. How about that *and* the art magazine.'

'Fine,' she said. 'That one can be from you.'

They paid for the magazines and stopped at a patisserie to get some *pain aux abricots* for Mathilde. By the time they reached the elegant apartment building, the sky was darkening and the wine had worn off. Sarah felt a prickle of misgiving.

'I'm on the top floor,' Tomas said as he called the lift in the striking black and white-tiled foyer. 'Andre and Mathilde are in the flat opposite mine.'

'I hope we won't be imposing.'

'We won't. Mathilde will enjoy the company. Sometimes I stay with Andre so she can have a break. I don't mind though. He's a great kid.'

The lift was one of the slow, trundling types that Sarah made it her personal mission to get rid of. But in this old building, it seemed appropriate. The doors opened onto a long corridor with two doors at the end. Being so close to Tomas's flat felt strangely intimate. Sarah's pulse began to race with anxiety. She replayed their earlier conversation – she was here to help Andre, that was all. She was safe – perfectly safe.

Tomas knocked on the right-hand door. 'Mathilde? It's me, Tomas.'

No answer.

'I've brought a friend,' he called out.

A shuffling came from inside. The door was opened by a small, trim woman with grey hair pulled back in a tight bun. 'Come in,' she said in French. She looked at Sarah carefully but not unkindly. 'We've had quite the morning.'

Inside, the room looked like someone had smashed up the stained-glass windows of Sainte Chapelle. Colourful geometric shapes were scattered all over the floor, the sofa, and the coffee table. A tower of cubes in the centre of the room leaned precariously. The vibration of a single step might send it toppling over. There was no sign of Andre.

'What happened?' Tomas asked.

'Your friend Franz. He met Andre last week and came back again today. They spent the morning building and sketching; talking about geometry and engineering. If the man was not seventy-two I would have thought him a boy of seventeen.' The lines on her face softened, and for an instant, the years melted away.

'That's brilliant,' Tomas said.

Mathilde offered Sarah coffee which she declined.

'Sarah has to go to work,' Tomas said. 'But I've told her about Andre – she wanted to meet him.'

'Only if he wants to,' Sarah added quickly. 'I don't want to overwhelm him.' Her own insecurities rose to the fore. She could relate to Andre's predicament, but that didn't mean she'd be of any use. She was no expert in the psychology behind agoraphobia or anxiety disorders.

'I will see,' Mathilde said. 'He has enjoyed meeting Franz – maybe it is good for him to have visitors.'

When the old woman left the room, Tomas grinned conspiratorially. 'I think Mathilde is enjoying Franz's visits just as much. They both came down with a fatal dose of love at first sight. If you believe in that sort of thing.'

Sarah blushed. She didn't believe in it – she reminded herself. She was here to meet Andre and see if she could help. If that resulted in her becoming more of a part of Tomas's life, well, that was what friends did, wasn't it?

30

TOMAS

Tomas's neck was tight with anxiety. Running into Anne-Marie was bad luck – and clearly, she'd enjoyed taunting Sarah. In fact, it put into sharp focus how jaded he'd become. Seeing Paris through Sarah's eyes had reawakened his own sense of wonder at the beauty of the city. Already, her friendship was becoming more to him than all his encounters with Anne-Marie or her ilk. Never before had he considered bringing a woman friend to see Andre – the boy was fragile and none of Tomas's romantic encounters were important enough to risk unsettling him. In contrast, Sarah understood exactly what Andre was going through, and he trusted her sensitivity and compassion. Now that they were here, however, he wondered if it was one act of intimacy too far.

It was several minutes before Mathilde returned, followed by Andre. The boy shuffled into the room, his shoulders slumped. His face had its usual pallor, and his too-long hair was falling into his face. But when he pushed it back, his eyes were bright.

'Hey mate,' Tomas said. 'I've brought a friend to meet you. This is Sarah.'

Andre stared at Sarah. He leaned in, cupping his mouth with his hand. 'Is she your girlfriend?'

'No, Andre, just a friend.'

'She's pretty. Are you going to sleep with her?'

Tomas looked at him, stunned. Andre spent a lot of time on his iPad. The boy might be getting the wrong sort of education off the internet. He leaned down and spoke close to his ear. 'That's not the kind of question a man asks in front of a lady. Do you understand?'

Andre grinned. 'Are you?'

Tomas cuffed his arm gently. 'Be polite.'

Andre drew himself up solemnly and walked over to Sarah. He pressed his hands together and made a small bow, like a courtier before a queen.

'Hi Andre.' Sarah smiled at the boy. If she'd heard what Andre said, she made a good show of hiding it. 'Tomas has told me a lot about you. He says you like to draw wonderful buildings. He's taken me to see Sainte Chapelle and the unicorn tapestries at the Cluny. Places too beautiful to be real.'

Andre dashed over to the bookshelf on the opposite wall. He returned with an A3 sketchbook and opened it, turning the pages quickly. Tomas felt an almost fatherly sense of pride as the imaginary worlds leapt off the page in vivid technicolour.

'These drawings are amazing,' Sarah said. 'Do you have an art teacher?'

Andre flipped to a drawing that had lines of correction drawn in blue pencil.

'Monsieur Franz is helping me,' Andre said in halting English. Tomas was surprised the boy spoke so easily around Sarah. 'He says that a great building must stand up properly.'

'That sounds like very good advice.'

'He said he will show me his workshop. I can make buildings – small ones – like doll's houses. I can use his tools—' Andre broke off suddenly, a flash of terror on his face.

Tomas's tension returned. Sarah, however, seemed unfazed. 'So you want to visit Monsieur Franz at his toyshop?'

Andre nodded.

'That's a wonderful goal,' she said. 'And you'll make it happen when you're ready. I know you will, because once I was like you. I needed to stay where I felt safe. The outside world seemed too big. Too loud and too… frightening. Even the thought of it made me panic. Like I couldn't breathe.'

Andre's eyes widened. 'You?'

'Yes, me. I thought I had to wait until the fear and panic went away. But one day I woke up and realised I had it wrong. I had to face up to the feelings to make them go away. I made a decision and followed through with it.'

Andre looked thoughtful. Tomas wasn't sure if the boy understood or not, but *he* admired her strength and vulnerability all the more.

She and Andre flipped through the book until eventually he began to squirm. Sarah put her hand over Andre's and stood up.

'I must be going, now,' she said. 'Would you walk me to the door?'

The boy stood up, shaking his head frantically.

'What's the matter, Andre?' Tomas said.

'She can't leave,' he said to Tomas. 'I need her to help

me go to the toyshop. And when I'm gone, then she needs to be here. To look after you—'

Tomas was startled. He avoided looking at Sarah as he reached out and ruffled the boy's hair. 'That's nice of you, old chap, but really, everything's fine. I want the best for you. You know that.'

'I'll come back and visit you again, Andre.' Sarah's voice was gentle but firm. 'And I almost forgot, we brought you these.' She handed him the magazines. It did the trick, arresting Andre's attention.

'Have a look through them. When I come back, we can look at them together.' She led Andre towards the door. 'In the meantime, start to imagine what it would be like to see those places for real…'

As she spoke, Tomas went over to Mathilde. She was standing by the window, staring out at the view. In the distant haze, the Eiffel Tower stood like a needle pricking the fabric of the sky.

'This is a good thing you have done,' she said. 'And now, you must make sure that you do not… what do you say?... screw this up?'

'OK?' Tomas said, bemused.

'Your Sarah is a wonderful woman. She is intelligent and caring. And beautiful too. You must treat her right.'

'Look, Mathilde…' he shoved his hands in his pockets, 'we just met, OK? And you know me. I'm not one for—'

'Yes, I do know you. And that is my worry.'

'Luckily, I've got you to keep me on the straight and narrow.'

His flippancy seemed to distress her. 'Do you know how difficult it has been to believe in anything over these last few years?' she said. 'Only now am I beginning to see the truth. Humans are not meant to live one day at a time.

We are meant to make plans, to fall in love. To allow ourselves to be hurt, over and over again.'

'Sounds like you think humans are pretty stupid.'

'Not all humans. But I think *you* are very stupid if you do not change your ways.'

'I'll keep that in mind.'

'You should.' She reached out and squeezed his hand. 'You have given us so much, Tomas. Your time and your care. You have brought Franz here. You have got Andre thinking about what is possible. And me too. Why do you hate yourself?'

'You wouldn't understand.' He turned away, staring out the window. 'I'll drop by in the next few days. If you need anything before then, let me know.'

'I will.' Mathilde let out a long sigh. 'Thank you for bringing Sarah.'

'You're welcome,' Tomas said flatly. At the door, Sarah and Andre still had their heads together. It was probably mostly a one-way conversation, but whatever she was saying, Andre seemed to be listening intently.

'It was lovely to meet you,' Sarah said. 'I'll come back and see you soon.'

Andre hung his head. Tomas came up and gave him a clap on the back. 'Come on, mate, don't look so glum. I'm around too.'

Andre ignored him. He held out his hand to Sarah.

'Goodbye, Andre.' She shook his hand as if there were an unspoken bargain between them. 'Take care of yourself.'

Tomas followed her out into the corridor. But the door didn't close immediately. For the first time since Tomas had known him, Andre poked his head out into the hallway. Tomas ushered Sarah into the lift, then turned and waved.

Andre was still looking down the corridor, waving back.

31

FRANZ

FRIDAY, AUGUST 25TH

Franz felt young again. No – not young, for his youth was tainted by all the mistakes he had made. He'd been given a second childhood, a second chance. The years had slipped away and could never be recovered, but he would make the most of the time that remained.

Andre wanted to come to the toyshop – and someday, when he was ready, he would do so. The boy needed him, which meant Mathilde needed him too. Each time he thought about her delicate beauty or spoke her name in his mind, he felt such a rush of joy that he wanted to break out singing in the street. To stop complete strangers and tell them that he, Franz Himmelberg, had a new purpose in life. He was in love. That in itself gave meaning to the unknowable. It gave him the desire to change.

If only change wasn't so hard.

He put down the paintbrush he'd been using to retouch the face of an old porcelain doll and blinked hard, hoping that somehow, the vision before him would match the one in his mind. Instead, he saw the shop through new eyes that troubled him. Reality was a far cry from the magical wonderland he'd promised Andre. He had no idea where even to begin.

Each passing moment felt like a new failure as he hobbled across the vast theatre, leaning heavily on his stick. The electrical plugs and switches on the wall were half-wired, some of them sticking out of their sockets. He flipped a switch and the room flooded with coloured lights. Another switch and music played: *Capriccio Italien*. Then, the final switch. A low grinding noise as the castle came to life.

The lower level rotated, the carousel horses and figures moving up and down. Franz watched, transfixed, the way he had as a boy when his father's creations came to life. People might doubt him – dismiss him – and the upper levels of the castle were not yet fully automated. But the effect was astounding. His great work. Andre would love it. Mathilde would be amazed. He could imagine their faces, he could imagine…

A memory floated to the surface of his mind. *Anna*… her face round and rapt like a shiny moon. But she would never see this.

She would never see it because of his silence.

Abruptly, he flipped off the switches. All the motion, all the music stopped. The room was plunged back into darkness. He'd told his friends something of his bad acts and the person he'd been. But he had not told them the whole truth. How could he possibly deserve the respect of Andre and Mathilde? How could he finish his great work when his great guilt was still eating away at him?

He went back to his workshop. It was just as he'd left it – a doll's house half finished, the broken doll, the dancers that would not stay on their tracks.

Anna was dead. Nothing would bring her back. But Mathilde and Andre were alive and needed him. He had to make the effort to transform the shop. He *would* do it…

Putting on his leather apron, he got to work. He coated clear glaze over the face of the doll, touched up the paint on the doll's house, and moved them both off the work table to dry. He next tackled hanging up his tools and organizing the loose fittings for the puppet theatre. It freed up space on his workbench, the top nicked with tool marks and drips of paint. It was the first time he'd seen the surface in years.

It was unexpectedly satisfying; he decided to continue. He cleared a shelf of half-empty paint pots and threw away some old brushes he'd been keeping 'just in case'.

Franz was barely aware of time passing. When Andre finally came here, what fun they would have. He imagined the boy eagerly experimenting with paints and glazes and learning to use his tools. Andre would have good, young eyes and wouldn't need the magnifying lens. Mathilde would sit at the end of the bench wearing her silver shoes. When the boy was occupied, he'd give her a kiss and make her blush. It was a beautiful vision – and so real. He was making a start – actually making a start—

A noise came from outside. A key turning in the secret door. His elation evaporated. As his landlord entered the workshop, Franz felt like he was swimming underwater and couldn't catch his breath.

'Monsieur Himmelberg,' Rouveau said gravely.

'Yes?' Franz sputtered. 'I am making progress.' He indicated the clean workbench. 'Great progress.'

'Yes, I see that.' Rouveau's long nose twitched. 'And getting rid of things is all for the best. I am afraid things have changed since we last spoke.'

'Changed?' That dreadful word.

'I have had a discussion with a powerful man. I will be

pitching him a plan to redevelop all of my premises. The planners are in favour of a mixed-use retail and residential development. As many of my properties are already empty, it seems a good time to get them on board. I am no longer a young man – nor are you.'

'What are you saying? What has it to do with me?'

'There may be an opportunity for you to, as they say, "cash out". Let me – or the new developers – buy out your lease.'

'Why would I want to do that?'

He was being deliberately obtuse, but he wanted every dreadful second to delay the inevitable. How could this be happening? Just when he'd been on the cusp of turning things around?

'Let me be plain,' Rouveau said. 'You are in breach of your lease, and I have grounds to evict you. I am offering you another way.'

'Your "offer" means I lose my shop.'

'With respect, you are going to do that anyway. There is no way you can save it.'

'Ah, but that is where you're wrong. Things have changed for you, but they have also changed for me. I have hired in some help – a business consultant. She starts… next week.'

'A business consultant?'

'Yes. You gave me time to make improvements. That is what we agreed. And that is what I will do.'

'And who is this "help", may I ask?'

Beneath his workbench, Franz gripped the business card – his last tattered ace.

'A powerful woman,' he said. 'That is all I will say right now. And even I know that the planners are also in favour of preserving local shops.'

Rouveau pursed his lips. Franz knew he was bound to

lose the battle, but he had thrown his opponent off guard, and that was worth something. He took a breath. The moment had come to put his dreams into words – to give them a chance at life. 'Just before Christmas,' he said, 'we will have a grand reopening. In that time, I will create a place like no other. A magical place: one that draws adults and children alike.' He met Rouveau's hard gaze. 'There are many other flats and hotels in Paris. But only one Fantastic Toyshop.'

Franz stopped speaking. He waited for his opponent to respond.

To his surprise, Rouveau laughed – Franz had not thought the man capable of it.

'You are full of surprises, Mr Himmelberg. I have listened to your offer, and now I will counter with two options. First, you can retire immediately and vacate by Christmas. I will forgive your arrears and you can walk away with your savings and dignity intact, and I will pay you a small sum on top.' The 'small sum' he named made Franz's eyes pop.

'Alternatively,' Rouveau continued, 'you use the time I have given you to transform your shop, pay your arrears, and have your opening. If you succeed, then I will let you stay for the duration of your lease.'

'And if I fail?'

'There will be no extension of time. You will vacate the premises without compensation and be liable for all past rent and repairs.'

Franz wanted to leap and shout and put his arms around his nemesis. Instead, he kept his tone measured and professional. 'Thank you,' he said. 'I choose the second option.'

'You are making a mistake.' Rouveau sniffed.

'It will not be the first time.'

With another short laugh, Rouveau turned and left the workshop. As soon as he was gone, Franz collapsed onto his stool, his legs shaking. This was a disaster of epic proportions – he knew that. And yet…

Sarah Williams.

He clutched the business card to his chest, over his heart. Tomas said she might be able to help. But would she agree, even if it could be done?

No. Why would she?

He was going to fail.

And yet… if that was his destiny, then he might as well fail in a spectacular fashion. He owed that much to Andre and Mathilde. To Tomas. To Anna. To… himself.

He picked up the receiver of the old telephone at the end of his workbench, surprised to hear a dial tone. His fingers were remarkably steady as he dialled the number on the card.

32

SARAH

Sarah picked up each of the animals, turning them in her hands and studying their gentle, painted faces. The colours seemed brighter, the paint less faded and worn. She'd been noticing things all around her: sounds, colours, textures, smells in a whole new way. Her senses had come alive, like kindling catching alight. Until recently, she'd been itching to start a new project in a new city. But now, she had met Tomas – and Andre and Mathilde. She'd allowed, ever so briefly, for the possibility of change. The toyshop had brought them together; it was a place that held not only memories, but also a simplicity and joy she had forgotten. Forgotten… because she had forced herself to forget.

It was a strange feeling to be useful to real people. Not just nameless hotel guests, not just rich businessmen. Of course, it didn't help to view her life that way – she had ambition, a job she excelled at, a career that gave her a purpose of a sort. But the look on the boy's face stayed with her. What had Tomas said? 'If you can touch the heart and mind of one child, then everything is worthwhile'?

It was ironic really. She avoided children like the plague. Andre was older than Rowan would have been, nonetheless, his innocence – his need – made her ache inside. If only she could do more. But what?

She set the animals back in a circle. Tomas was right – Rowan would want her to live her life. Andre's parents would have wanted that for him too, and Tomas was trying to help him achieve it. It was an admirable goal and one she wanted to be part of. Andre was a fragile life force, but she sensed he was on the cusp of breaking free. When he'd poked his head out into the corridor, she'd felt an unexpected sense of joy and purpose. Once, she had been just like him. Could she help him come out the other side?

Andre… Rowan… Her gaze snagged on the photo she'd put on the coffee table. Tiny half-moon eyes and rosebud lips; the baby swaddled in a crocheted blanket.

Inside, the dreadful pit of despair opened its jaws. Sarah's pulse pounded in her skull. Her breath grew shallow, laboured. No… her hands clawed at her throat. She was over this… no…

The memories marched in like an invading army. Sitting at the table with the policewoman. Victor coming home – his key in the door. The way he looked at her – seeing her for what she truly was – his eyes as cold as dying stars.

What have you done?

In the taxi to her mum's, she'd experienced the first of the panic attacks. Self-doubt and loathing had risen to the surface, flooding over her in waves. *She* was Rowan's mum. *She'd* had a duty to protect her child and had failed to do so. She'd failed to face up to her problems and get help. All of it was her fault.

When she'd arrived at her mum's house in the middle of the night, the driver had woken the household. 'What's the matter?' her mum had cried out. 'Where's Rowan?'

But Sarah couldn't tell her. Not then and not for days. Her mum handled most of the arrangements and made endless cups of tea for the stream of social workers sent by the council. Victor came to the house, his grief palatial and overwhelming. Sarah's mum handled him too, comforting him as a beloved son-in-law, reassuring him that Sarah would see him when she was ready. At the funeral, Sarah sat in the car alone as the little coffin was lowered into the ground. Victor and her mum both cried, but Sarah couldn't shed a single tear. The other mourners probably thought her cold and heartless, less affected by the tragedy than her husband. She was in no state to care. After the funeral, she returned to the room at her mum's house and stayed there for the better part of two years. Crawling inside her own Pandora's box; pulling the lid shut over her head.

Breathe, she commanded herself. *In, out. This will pass.*

Every nerve in her body was firing wildly. She put a sofa cushion to her face, blocking out the world, taking comfort in the darkness and nothingness. Maybe she should go back to London sooner rather than later. Ask her mum if she could stay a few nights in her old room…

Eventually her breathing slowed, though her heart continued to race. One by one she put the animals back in the box.

The attack had shaken her. She tried to deconstruct the cause and kept coming back to the same conclusion. Too much emotion was no good for her. She needed to keep her feelings under wraps and do what she did best. Focus on work and forget the rest. She shoved the box underneath the sofa.

Her phone rang. Perfect timing. Komitov's assistant was due to call to set up another meeting. She would ask to go somewhere other than Paris. A new start – that was what she needed. She picked up the phone.

The line crackled; no one spoke. A crank call? She was about to hang up when a breathy, accented voice spoke her name.

'Ms Williams? Is that Sarah Williams?'

'Yes.'

'This is Franz Himmelberg. I hope this is not a bad time.'

'No, it's fine.' Her hopes soared. He must have found the giraffe! The set would be complete. And then… what? She swallowed hard. Nothing would bring Rowan back.

But as the old man spoke, slow and halting, she discovered that he was not calling about the giraffe.

Half an hour later, Sarah was lost in the tangle of alleyways, her feet sore from walking in circles. Par for the course for a visit to *La Boutique Fantasque*. This time, however, when she finally reached the shop and the door clicked open, she entered with a new resolve.

This time, things were going to be different.

33

FRANZ

'I am very sorry,' Franz said. He was out of breath from explaining; from justifying what could not be explained or justified. The end of a dream, the admission of defeat. He'd tried very hard to make himself believe a different ending was possible. He'd failed at that, too.

Sarah Williams was having none of it. She was a strong and admirable woman. A woman like Anna was… or should have been.

'Don't be sorry,' she said. 'Sorry is not good for business. That's what this has to be about. Not your dreams or regrets – those things have got you where you are now. You need to accept that and decide where you want to be. Then, you need a plan to get from one to the other.'

'Yes. Yes!' For a second he recalled the rousing speeches of the youth leader – but this message was one he wanted to believe. This was about Andre and Mathilde. This was about the future. A new hope bubbled up inside him.

Sarah's reaction, however, was measured. 'I've seen the empty shops; and from what you've said, it looks like your landlord is keen to cash in and redevelop. If you hold out, you'll be an island in a turbulent – and expensive – sea. Is that what you want? It's not too late to take the money he's offered you. Retire in style.'

Retire. The word had only one meaning – failure. 'You think that because I am old that that is naturally what I want,' he asserted. 'But it is not. I do not wish to retire and become a pigeon man. You are friends with Tomas, no? You have met Andre and Mathilde?'

'Yes, I have.'

'Then you know that young Andre wants to come here – only, he remains locked in a prison of his mind. But the key is so near; I can feel the weight of it in the lock ready to turn.'

Sarah ran her hand over the tool grooves in the workbench. 'I admire your passion,' she said. 'More than you know. But passion alone won't turn things around. It would be a huge job, especially in a short time. It would require careful planning, and you'd need people in to help which would cost money.'

As his hopes evaporated, he let out a deflated sigh.

'I would like help, though it is hard for me to ask. And what is more, I cannot pay.' He hung his head.

'You've clearly got a cashflow problem,' she said. 'But on the other hand, this shop is unique. It's magical – or could be. Your castle is a true work of genius. And some of your stock might be valuable. I'm not promising anything, and I can't help out in any official capacity, but if you want to save your shop, then I can help you get on the right track.'

'Yes! I want to save the shop!'

'Wanting it is a start. But you'll have to invest in making it happen. Your time and your heart – and every ounce of strength and belief you have. You'll have to commit to opening more often. There's no point in creating value if no one gets to experience it. The place will need a total clear out and refurbishment. You'll have to write a business plan and convince a bank to give you a loan. You'll have to change.'

'Change.' The word felt foreign on his lips. A beautiful word full of hope and promise, but also, the biggest challenge of all. It would be easier to stay the same; easier to continue to let life pass him by. But he'd already made the decision to try.

'Yes,' he said. 'I would like to change. I would like to make the shop into the magical place I have dreamt about. I want to do it for Andre… and other children. For Mathilde, whom I have only just met, but feel like I have known all my life.' His vision blurred with sudden tears. 'I want to do it to make amends to *her*.'

'Mathilde?' Sarah looked confused.

'Anna,' he whispered. Inside his head, a monumental wave was forming. Rising, cresting. Talking to Tomas had been the first step. But he had not told the whole truth. The wave broke inside him. He had to let it out or else he would drown.

'She was the girl I once loved. The sister of my best friend, Heinrich. Their father was a captain in the Stasi – the secret police. The organisation was hated and feared by many, but revered by stupid boys like me.'

He paused as the memories pulled him under. 'She used to love coming to my father's shop to see the musical boxes. She loved music, and we used to listen to vinyl records together. We talked about music and books and things we dreamed and imagined. Despite her upbringing, Anna did not like to talk about the glorious state. She had her own mind and ideas. She was like a bird in a cage, longing to be free.'

'What happened?'

He let out a pent-up sigh. 'What happened is that she was smart and brave, and I was stupid and weak. As we got older, she stopped coming to the shop. She had other friends – friends her father and brother did not approve of. We stopped listening to records – we stopped talking. I thought that by spending more time with her brother, I could reclaim her affection. But I was wrong. She began to look upon me with contempt. I did not know why, and it made me angry. In that place, there were many outlets for an angry boy.'

He picked up a clockwork gear and turned it around with his fingertips.

'Eventually I tried another way. I made her a beautiful musical box with a golden ballerina inside. I brought it to her one night when her family was out.

'But when I got there, she was listening to a record with one of her new friends. A record of banned American music. I got very angry and broke the record across my knee. We shouted, and the musical box got smashed and broken. She screamed that she never wanted to see me again. She called me a conformist. A bully. A coward.' He closed his eyes to stave off the pain. 'Heinrich came home during the commotion. He burst into the room.'

His vision clouded with the darkness of that time. Sarah gently touched his hand. He was so ashamed, so grateful that she was still there listening.

'Anna's friend was part of a group who were planning publicity stunts under the direction of western agents. Heinrich searched Anna's room and found some leaflets.'

He clenched his fist; the teeth of the gear bit into his hand. 'He informed on his own sister! Anna was taken in for questioning. Heinrich got a commendation. I remember the speech the youth group leader gave: "It is sometimes difficult to do our duty to the state when a family member is involved. But you, Heinrich, have been vigilant. It is brave acts like yours that remove the bad apples from the barrel."

'That was the moment I should have stood up. Said something to try and save her. I should have defended her character. But instead, I saluted like everyone else. I was too afraid to speak up, so I stayed silent.' He wiped his eyes angrily. 'Anna was arrested and sent to a prison camp. She died there – I never saw her again.'

He waited for the judgement; for Sarah to leave in disgust. It was what he deserved. Maybe even what he wanted.

'Oh Franz. I'm so sorry.' She held out her arms.

Shaking, he went into them. The warmth of another human being was unexpected. He leaned into her, letting her strength flow into him, battling the tides of shame. Pulling away, he steadied himself against the workbench. 'I should not have stayed silent. I did everything backwards and wrong.'

'I know how that feels.'

He risked looking at her; her face mirrored his own pain. 'I am sorry for burdening you with this,' he said. 'For I think that you too have suffered. And now, you have come to help me, which is more than I deserve. You are right. It is my regret – the regret I feel every day for my silence – that has brought me here. To the brink of losing my life's work.'

She took a tissue from her pocket and handed it to him. The small act of kindness almost undid him.

'You said before that stories have the power to heal,' Sarah said. 'Now that yours is told, are you ready write a new ending?'

Franz looked around. Years of clutter, years of loneliness, years of tinkering with small problems to avoid the big ones. Sarah was right. It was going to be a huge job.

'Yes,' he said. 'I want to save the shop. I am ready.'

'Then let's get started.' She opened her handbag and took out a notebook. 'The clock is ticking, so let's get some ideas down on paper.'

PART III

The animals have a new home. A woman who treats them with care; touches them with a gentle reverence. A mother without a child; her eyes betray the sadness inside. The animals too know loss; they know what it is to be locked away without love.

Why are they here? Reminding her of her pain, of each agonising heartbeat. Holding her memories in their paint and wood and varnish;

memories that she would rather forget. They take more of what is left of her each time she looks at them.

But as she gazes on them through a fog of grief, they can give her something too. Will she allow it? Is she ready? As she places them in a circle on an empty shelf in an empty room she leaves a gap for their lost one. The giraffe that cannot be found. A break in the circle, a crack in the whole. A weakness, an imperfection. An opening… a space…

Will it break her, or let in a new precious light?

34

TOMAS

SATURDAY, SEPTEMBER 2ND

Time had passed. Days and hours. How had he spent them? Suddenly, Tomas couldn't remember. Because as soon as Sarah walked into the café, her hair wavy and soft, her cheeks rosy in the golden sunlight, the past evaporated as if it had never been.

'Hi.' She seemed a little nervous, her smile fragile.

'Sarah.' Tomas stood up. His lips lingered on her skin as he kissed her cheek. 'It's great to see you.'

In truth, he knew how he'd spent the time. By imagining her a thousand times in his mind's eye. He'd relived the wonder on her face as she'd experienced the beauty of Paris, the kindness and care she'd shown to Andre, the sound of her laugh, the look of anguish that sometimes took her unawares. The memories had been sweet and sustaining. Up to a point.

He'd also imagined the places they could go together; the things he wanted to show her and experience with her. His favourite museums, little hole-in-the-wall restaurants, tangles of alleyways leading to hidden squares and neighbourhoods. Holding her hand, feeling the warmth of her skin, the quickening of her pulse. Enjoying the anticipation of all the things they could discover together.

They sat down at a little table and ordered coffees. Now that she was here, two friends meeting up, he was having trouble getting the *other* visions out of his mind. The ones he'd tried to push away – late at night, in the middle of writing a scene, first thing in the morning – but hadn't succeeded. Imagining there was no more pretence of playing tour guide or seeing the city. No need to bother with words or small talk. Giving in to the wanting, the elemental force that drew them together…

'So… how's she doing?'

'She?' He blinked back to reality. *Friends*… That was what they were. That was best for both of them.

'Lucinda. Has she saved the world yet?'

His lingering fantasies dissipated. Lucinda was like a built-in cold shower. Before coming to meet Sarah, he'd been focusing on a scene where his star character was about to drink a poison cocktail bought for her by a double agent. Does she drink it and go into cardiac arrest or take him upstairs and sleep with him first? Maybe she needs a friend to rescue her. Or a dog… who the hell cared?

'I'm afraid not,' he said. 'She's got to survive the next attempt on her life. And the one after that.'

'Sounds tricky.'

'The action scenes usually write themselves.' He quickly changed the subject. 'What about you?' he said. 'How's the hotel coming?'

'Phase two is progressing,' she said. 'And I've been promoted to a Special Development Committee. At the moment, I'm waiting to hear what – and where – my next project will be.'

'Sounds exciting.' In truth, the news worried him.

She'd mentioned before that she might be leaving Paris. The thought made him feel hollow inside.

'It could be.' She shrugged. 'But you might be interested to hear about a new project I've taken on – strictly in an unofficial capacity.'

'A secret project? Now that is intriguing.'

As she went on to explain, his mouth gaped open in surprise.

'So let me get this straight,' he said. 'You're helping Franz save his shop?'

'I'm giving him some tips, that's all. Actually, I was surprised to get the call. In my experience, people don't change. Not really. Not when they're as set in their ways as Franz. It's going to be a huge job. When I tried to explain it to him, it was like I was speaking a foreign language.'

Tomas laughed. 'You probably were.'

'His books and accounts are total chaos. People owe him money, but he doesn't collect. You can't run a business in central Paris on the barter system.'

'You can't?' Tomas cocked a wry eyebrow. He found this side of her incredibly attractive. She was like a beautiful jewelled egg: gorgeous and sophisticated on the outside; full of humanity and vulnerability inside. In truth, he was delighted by this turn of events. She was helping out *his* friends. First Andre, now Franz. For now, at least, she would be *here*.

'Not when you have a bank loan to pay off.'

'A bank loan?' Tomas practically choked on his coffee. 'Franz is getting a bank loan?'

'Unless he can wave a magic wand and marshal his toys into action like Santa's elves, he's going to need it to pay for the refurbishment.' She set her coffee cup down with a sigh. 'And there's one thing he'll need to get to grips with sooner rather than later. The castle. Either he finishes it, or else it has to go.'

'No – surely not!'

'In its current state, it's the biggest health and safety hazard of all.'

'But it's his life's work. His link to his past.'

'Maybe he's best cutting that link. You know his story, right?'

He nodded. Franz had let his past cast a shadow over his whole life. Tomas understood all too well how that felt. Having one's life's work taken away – or losing it carelessly through shame and self-doubt – was the worst feeling in the world. Franz was eccentric, but he also had a dream. Tomas respected him for that.

'I do,' he said. 'But you mentioned elves – do you know the story of the Elves and the Shoemaker?'

'The fairy tale?'

'Yes. Brothers Grimm.'

'I think I knew it once. What is it?'

'Once upon a time at Christmas,' Tomas began, 'a poor shoemaker was about to lose his shop. The man cut out the leather for one last pair of shoes. In the morning, he found a pair of shoes masterfully made. He sold the shoes, bought more leather. The same thing happened – night after night. The old man discovered that a pair of elves had come to help him, doing the work while he slept. The old man became rich and prosperous, and eventually, he and his wife made the elves their own little clothes and shoes. The elves skipped away, delighted, and were never seen again. But thanks to the elves, the old shoemaker and his wife lived happily ever after.'

'That's a nice story,' Sarah said. 'Though I'm not sure it would fly with modern labour laws.'

'You're right,' he said. 'But do me a favour – let Franz

keep the castle for now. Maybe he just needs a little help.' He flexed his biceps. 'And maybe, I can use a little exercise.'

Sarah laughed, her eyes sparkling. 'So now we're elves to a shoemaker? I didn't know you were such a softy.'

'Neither did I,' Tomas said. 'Sometimes I even surprise myself.'

35

SARAH

It was so easy – that was the surprising thing. Being around Tomas, feeling light and carefree and fully alive in the moment – something she had never felt around Victor. Sarah liked the spark between them, although it scared her too. Meeting Andre and Mathilde was one thing, and now she'd agreed to help Franz as well. Elves to a shoemaker. Her life and Tomas's were becoming entwined. Was that why she was doing it?

It was a dangerous proposition. On the one hand, she was committed to her job, her promotion, and giving her all to Komitov's projects. Out with the old, in with the new. A new city, a new language, a glamorous new hotel. But the more time she spent trying to work out how to save the toyshop, something tugged inside her to do more, help more; to stay in Paris where she had new friends and a new purpose. It was the animals, it was the toyshop, it was Andre and Mathilde. Real people with lives on the margin.

It was Tomas. It kept coming back to that.

In the time apart, she'd wondered about him. She sensed there was a part of him that he was keeping hidden from her. Did it involve the tall Parisian, Anne-Marie? Or was it the other woman he'd mentioned – the relationship that 'didn't work out'? Was he willing to be friends only because he knew her grief made her unavailable? Or because he knew she was likely to be leaving Paris? Was that why *she* had agreed to the arrangement?

Now that she was with him, she found she didn't care. 'So where are we going today?' She loved asking the question. So far, Tomas's Paris had been a revelation to her. The sights, smells, and sounds of the city enchanted her. The Parisians were returning after their holidays. The summer weather had lingered, with people enjoying the warm balmy weather of *l'été sauvage* in outdoor cafés and bistros, relying on awnings and umbrellas for protection against the occasional rain shower. Tomas's easy charm and humour was infectious. He made her laugh, and that felt good.

'I thought we'd go to L'Orangerie. Have you been?'

'No. What is it?'

He gave her a cryptic smile. 'You'll see.'

They crossed the river and walked along the quayside where artists and booksellers were displaying their wares. Past the Louvre, the leaves of the trees lining the avenues of the Jardin de Tuileries were edged with the first hints of orange and gold. Tomas pointed out their destination: a low building of mellow stone with a green patinaed roof at the far end of the garden. He explained that the building had originally housed the orange trees of Napoleon III, but was now one of his favourite museums in Paris.

They joined the queue outside. The banner above the door read: *Les Nymphéas*.

'Waterlilies?' Sarah said.

'Yes, but not like you've ever seen before, I promise.'

Tomas bought their tickets, and they went down the ramp to the subterranean level.

Each of the two rooms was shaped like an elongated oval. Surrounding them, like a cocoon, were huge, room-sized paintings of waterlilies. No mug, tea towel, or tote bag could do justice to the size and majesty of Monet's artwork. The effect was total immersion in beauty: a magical aquarium of light, water, and colour.

Sarah felt a rush of feeling; her body lit up with pure joy. She turned slowly in a circle, immersing herself in the experience. Euphoria rippled inside her as they walked slowly along the perimeter of the room, taking in every glorious metre of artwork. The variations of colour were so subtle, so masterfully blended, the mood changing from light to dark and back again. People moved around them, like the long roots of lilies floating on a pond, each lost in their own experience of perfection.

In the second room, the contrast between light and shadow was more pronounced. Sarah let herself be pulled under the surface of the water: drowning, losing herself. She was hyperaware of Tomas next to her, sharing the spark of wonder. Whatever they were to each other, he had given her this – this experience, this enchanted moment.

'Thank you,' she said.

His fingers brushed hers. 'You're welcome,' he said. The moment shimmered in the air between them.

He took his hand away and moved on.

When eventually they came back upstairs, the bright sunlight was a shock to the system. Though they hadn't made further plans, Sarah suggested that they visit Andre. Tomas readily agreed, and she bought the boy a book of

Monet's works. 'If this doesn't bring the outside in, then I don't know what will,' she said.

'Right,' he said. 'Let's do it.

When they reached Mathilde's flat, Andre was delighted to see them, babbling in a mixture of French and English. Tomas made lunch in Mathilde's kitchen while Sarah described every detail of her experience at the museum. 'I've never felt so peaceful before,' she said. 'And yet, giddy at the same time, like breathing underwater. It was amazing. And someday, Andre,' she said, 'you'll be able to go there too.'

'*Oui*,' the boy said, focusing on the book she'd brought him.

Even Mathilde seemed brighter than before, if a little distracted. Sarah felt for the older woman – she too had lost a child – her adult daughter, Renée. Sarah could only imagine her pain, especially since she kept it so well hidden behind a mask of disgruntled making do. Once or twice, she'd seen a distant look in Mathilde's eyes that she recognised as memory. Memories of a better time – one that was lost forever.

When eventually Andre set the book aside, he showed her some of his favourite spreads in the magazines they'd brought previously. An article on German castles prompted Andre to ask about Franz and his life in Berlin. Sarah showed him a few pictures of the city on her phone. But then Andre asked her about Franz's sweetheart, Anna.

Mathilde cleared her throat from the door of the kitchen. 'Andre, I do not think we should talk about that,' she said.

'But why? What happened to her?'

Sarah drew a breath. 'She went to prison,' she said. 'It happened a lot back then.'

'I do not understand.' Andre crossed his arms.

'Neither do I,' Sarah said. 'But I believe that Anna wanted to fight for change. Most of us choose the easy path, but Anna wanted something different. She chose the hard path – one that required her to sacrifice herself. If she had lived, she would have been extraordinary.'

Sarah glanced towards Mathilde. She too was admirable; she too had chosen the hard path, raising her grandson in difficult times. It made Sarah wonder about her own choices. Was taking up her promotion and leaving Paris the hard choice or the easy one?

Was holding on to her grief easier than letting it go?

Mathilde went to help Tomas with the food; she heard their voices in the kitchen. Sarah handed Andre another magazine but the boy still seemed distracted.

'Franz says he likes to help lost things,' Andre said. 'Toys that are lost and need a new home. Is that because of Anna? Why didn't he find her?'

'It was harder back then,' Sarah said. 'They didn't have the internet.'

'No?' Andre frowned like she was describing the Stone Age.

'No. And speaking of which, I wonder if you might be interested in setting up a website for the toyshop.' She leaned in. 'I think Franz could use your help.'

'A website?'

'Franz wants to make a few changes. For when you're ready to come round. But a website is something you could do now.' She explained what she had in mind. Andre seemed excited to help, and Sarah felt hopeful that the day was coming when he'd be ready to venture out to the toyshop and the world. But after they ate lunch, he grew tired and fractious. They'd been there for over two hours.

'Time to go, I think,' Tomas said, looking at Sarah. 'Shall I walk you home?'

'Sure. I've got lots to get on with – for work, and for the shop.'

Why had she said that? Why was her pulse racing? His flat was just across the hall…

'Me too,' he said. 'My edits aren't going to do themselves.'

She sighed inwardly, disappointed and relieved in equal measure.

Friends. Both of them were sticking to the bargain. The easy path – the exit strategy. Neither of them were brave like Anna – or even Franz. Brave enough to risk themselves. Brave enough to change.

36

MATHILDE

The world is shifting, tilting on its axis. Mathilde can't grab hold of it or stop it. Nor is she sure she wants to. Tomas and Sarah. Franz. Has Renée sent these new people into her life? Or Jean-Louis? Does she believe in such things?

Mathilde stands at the door as they leave her flat. Sarah is beautiful and special; Tomas is charming and handsome. Electricity arcs between them – an undeniable attraction. Have they acted on it? Why do they keep coming here to spend time with two damaged people? So many questions she cannot answer.

When her visitors are gone, the door closed behind them, Mathilde waits for the expected sensations. Trapped, confined, frustrated – abandoned in the flat with a boy she cannot reach. Waits... but they do not come.

'*Grand-mère?*'

Andre speaks; Mathilde glances over. She waits for the expected twist of pain as his eyes become those of her daughter's. Instead, the memories scatter like pearls. In this moment, she sees a too-thin boy with hair that needs a trim. With his feet curled beneath him he is so small, so vulnerable.

The rush of love is staggering; she grips the edge of the door. Andre waves her over to see something in one of the magazines that Sarah brought. Mathilde goes to him; sits down on the sofa. Warm… the boy is warm and alive. He is more than just her daughter's son, more than just the embodiment of her pain, more than just a disappointment and a responsibility too big to handle. He is her grandson.

Her hand trembles as she puts it over his. For a second, she thinks he might pull away. Instead, he glances at her through his curtain of hair. 'Look,' he says.

The magazine has a picture of a ballet dancer in a white room, the floor strewn with red roses. The photo is soft, the dancer caught in the moment of *reverence*. The memories… Mathilde holds them back.

'She is lovely, no?' Mathilde says. 'Though I am sure her feet are hurting.'

Andre watches her as she studies the picture. She never speaks to him of the past – a conversation that can only lead to death and loss. He turns the page: more pictures of dancers, some stationary, some in motion. Her head whirls like it would after a poorly executed pirouette. *Jean-Louis*. *Renée*. All gone. A box of her old things… clothes and shoes… Renée's special recipe book… stored somewhere? But no… time is unstuck in her mind, that is all. Is there an attic in the building…? She must ask Tomas. What about the wardrobe? No – she has looked many times; the shoes are not there. But she did find something else…

'A minute,' she says to Andre. Her legs are unsteady as she gets up from the sofa and goes to the bedroom, opening the wardrobe door. Inside, an old lady's clothing, most of it from the charity shop. Sensible shoes, the soles worn down. She doesn't want to look anymore. But on the shelf at the back sits a bundle wrapped in cloth. She opens it and removes the small, leather-bound album. Is this the right thing to do? So painful… so dreadfully painful. But the boy – he deserves more than she has given him.

Returning to the other room, she sits down next to Andre. The boy's eyes are as round as moons. Instead of the usual pain, they hold curiosity.

'I will show you this.' She sets the book on her lap and opens it. 'Your mother may not have told you, but once I was in the *corps de ballet* for the opera.'

Andre takes the book from her. Tattered playbills, over-saturated photos. Memories she should have given him long ago, and soon it will be too late. But she can do it now, before they spin out of time. She can give them a new life before they are lost forever. She *will* do it now.

'Look here.' She points to a photo – the trio of cygnets in *Swan Lake*. 'Once that was me – can you believe it?'

37

TOMAS

THURSDAY, SEPTEMBER 7TH

'Easy does it… a little more. Ouch!'

Tomas winced at the sound of metal hitting masonry. The passageway was barely wide enough to swing a proverbial cat let alone fit a skip. The driver and his assistant cursed.

'So this is a skip,' Franz said, looking glum. 'I had expected something… different. A child's game: skipping rope, perhaps.'

Tomas laughed; the skip thudded to ground.

'Sorry mate, I know it's a lot to take in,' Tomas said. 'But a clear out is the first step on Sarah's list. Out with the old and in with the new.'

Threat of the new was all around them. The empty, boarded up shops now had signs in the window. '*New retail and residential developments coming soon.*' A phone number and a website to obtain further information.

'Remember, you're doing this to save the shop,' Tomas said. 'You've got yourself a stay of execution. Make the most of it.'

'Yes, yes.' Franz frowned. 'I understand. But I do not have to like it.'

They moved aside as the lorry inched forward, taking a few bricks off the corner of the building. Tomas waved to the driver as the vehicle pulled into the main street and drove away.

It would be easier, he knew, if Sarah was here. On the surface, she was calm and professional, but it was the warmth of her beating heart underneath that put frightened creatures, like Franz and Andre, at ease. But Sarah had made it clear that her involvement had to be strictly after hours. She was committed to her day job, especially now that she was on the cusp of being shipped off to some exotic location. Tomas understood her ambition, even if he selfishly wished she would stay here in Paris. With her new friends. With him.

They had begun as friends, but now they had evolved into partners helping Franz save the shop – elves to the shoemaker. After that, she would leave. Her giraffe would remain lost. His words, his true self, would remain lost. As long as they both remained lost, they would never be able to find each other. More than once he'd almost told her the truth. But each time, he'd backed away, unable to find the words. Each time, he'd looked inside himself and found only the cowardice.

You hurt people, Tom. The voice he'd worked so hard to put out of his head continued to whisper in the wings.

He didn't want to hurt Sarah. He didn't ever want to feel that kind of guilt again.

'Well, my friend…' Franz's voice brought him back to the moment, 'I suppose this is it. The transformation of *La Boutique Fantasque* must begin.'

'You're a brave man,' Tomas said. 'I'm proud of you.'

'Be proud of me when it is finished,' he said. 'When

Andre can come to a place that is magical and special. When my old shop is ready to be part of new memories.'

Tomas laid a hand on the old man's arm. 'You've taken the first step to change,' he said. 'That's more than most of us ever do.'

Franz sighed. 'Thank you, Tomas, for everything. Now, let us make a start so that Sarah will be proud too.'

'That might be easier said than done.'

Friends. Partners. Elves to a shoemaker. No one gets hurt. It would have to be enough.

38

FRANZ

FRIDAY, SEPTEMBER 15TH

Change was hard.

He'd hoped that in deciding to move forward, he'd broken the back of it. But he'd been wrong. Each moment required a new decision, a new commitment, a new challenge.

'That's one for the skip,' Sarah said.

Franz stared at the doll. Its face was cracked, its right eye rolling up into its head, its hair matted. 'But I could varnish over the crack,' he said. 'It could be fixed.'

Sarah took the doll from him and shoved it in the bin bag.

'Remember…' her voice held a note of strain, 'if you can't sell it, it has to go.'

'Yes, yes. What about this?' He held up a moth-eaten bear.

'Bin.'

Franz sighed. Sarah was right. His precious time was slipping by like a wriggling fish. He had to stay focused. Since the skip had arrived, Tomas had come for a few hours most days to help out, and Sarah dropped by in the evenings. So far, they'd managed to clear most of the workshop, like a team of explorers unearthing an ancient tomb. But Franz was finding it hard to resist the clawing urge to go back through the bin bags and take things out again. Finding it hard to let go of all the *things*, give up on the little projects he'd never made a start on.

I'm doing this for Andre… for Mathilde… for Anna. He repeated his mantra in his head. *I'm doing this for myself.*

'Franz – you OK?'

'Yes,' he lied.

'Sorry – I know this is tough. But you're doing great.'

Her smile boosted his spirits. Sarah was a hard taskmistress, and Franz felt like a naughty school boy, hoarding bits of string, sticky chocolate wrappers, and interesting stones in his pockets. He was grateful to her – more than he could ever express. She was putting a lot of time and energy into the project on top of her day job. She'd brought him a notebook full of lists and bewildering figures – a business plan. He'd tried hard to pay attention when she'd talked him through it, but mostly he'd marvelled at her. So smart, so dedicated. And so kind – that impressed him the most. She'd arranged for workmen to install broadband and wi-fi, and told him that Andre was keen to set up a website for the shop. They'd agreed to keep the extent of the project secret from the boy, however, until things were further along. Franz liked the idea of a 'secret project' – though many people seemed to know about it. Sarah hired other tradespeople to come in to poke around his electrics and check his fire extinguishers. It had taken courage to ask how the men would be paid – and more courage when she told him the answer. A bank loan! Exciting, he supposed, but overwhelming too.

He clutched the bear tightly. Sarah was still looking at him. 'You'll feel better for it, I promise.'

Muttering a heartfelt apology, Franz put the bear in the bin bag. Maybe he would feel better, but he was still waiting for that magic moment to arrive. Admittedly, it was exciting to unearth bits and bobs, tools and treasures that had gone missing over the years. Sarah took photos of his finds for the website, promising that it would open up new avenues for uniting old toys with new owners, and generate some much-needed cash.

When he was on his own, Franz worked on finishing his commissions and repairs with a new sense of purpose and energy. When the owners came to pick up their treasures, he found new homes for other unclaimed objects. A set of toy soldiers for a grandson, a rocking horse for a niece, a musical box for a maiden aunt, a doll's house for a daughter's birthday. He and Tomas had taken four whole boxes of toys to the refugee centre where Mathilde donated her knitting – practically just around the corner – and watched the faces of the children spark and shine with joy. At last, he was beginning to remember how satisfying it was to speak to people; how fulfilling it was to find the right toy for the right person.

He attributed his enthusiasm in part to Andre and Mathilde, but also to the fact that he was lighter for having told his story. All of a sudden, his head was clearer, and he could enjoy the good memories. His father's workshop, the Rathaus Glockenspiel, the look of wonder on Anna's face when she examined the musical boxes. He'd even bought a banana – not to eat, just to look at. The memories were out in the open: he didn't have to fear them anymore. Taking action made the pain more remote but also gave it more value. He decided not to question the how or why of it. Live in the moment, look to the future. Working side by side with Sarah, he was happy.

If only it was the same for her. More than once he'd

seen her pick up a toy, her face darkened by shadows. It pained him to tell her that he had spoken to the man who had brought him the wooden animals, and the man knew nothing of the lost giraffe. It was an unsatisfying end to a sad story. Franz hated the thought that the giraffe might have ended up in a skip somewhere, forever parted from its wooden companions, never again to be found; the circle broken, never again to be complete.

More than once he'd nearly asked her about Rowan and the ex-husband who seemed to hold some powerful sway over her emotions. But so far, he'd stayed silent.

Instead, he stuck to asking her mainly about her job, which she was happy enough to talk about. She was a high flyer with her eye on her next project. It sounded exciting, he supposed, but also like escape. Was that ever the right choice? What did he know about it anyway?

And then there was the matter of Tomas. He'd pressed his young friend, who kept insisting that he and Sarah were just friends, nothing more. He seemed content to see her only occasionally, like a blind man who preferred to stay in darkness rather than risk getting burned by the sun. There was a simple explanation, of course – Tomas preferred working on his edits and writing at night, which was the time when Sarah came to the shop after work. Franz did not understand the how or why of it – like the two dancers on the track who seemed determined to stay apart.

He glanced over at her as she rifled through the box of toys. So beautiful. Such a waste to be alone. He had a plan to act on that as well – one he'd come up with all on his own.

The clock began to chime the hour. Would his plan work out? 'Maybe I should make us a cup of tea,' he said. It was the most useful thing he could do.

'OK.' Sarah put something else in the bin bag. He

decided not to ask what it was.

As he hobbled off, voices came from the theatre. Two workmen were finishing up and getting ready to leave. All afternoon they'd been working on replacing the secret door with a more prominent one, with a marquee above – like an old-time cinema. It was to become the main entrance. According to Sarah, making the shop accessible from the main street would give a big boost to foot traffic. It was true, he suspected, though he felt a little like he was giving up a secret.

As the clock finished chiming, he heard another voice. 'Yeah, mate, he rang and asked me to come by tonight. That OK with you?'

Franz smiled. The call had been worth it – the plan a success so far. It was Tomas. Right on time.

He went to the kitchenette and made tea for Sarah and Tomas. Having brought them together, he was planning to leave early. In the fairy tale that Tomas was so fond of recounting, the elves worked alone while the shoemaker was asleep. It was time to let that story work its magic. It was another way in which he hoped he could create something special – not for the shop, but in the lives of his two friends. In his tenure at *La Boutique Fantasque*, Franz had had many jobs: toymaker, inventor, fixer, confidante. Now, he hoped to add another one to his resumé.

Matchmaker.

'… Didn't know you were coming.' Sarah's voice rose in pitch; he could imagine a pretty flush on her cheeks.

'Franz said you needed my help.'

'Did he now?'

His young friends began to laugh. It warmed his heart. He wanted for them what he was learning to want for himself…

Being in love. The source of all the magic in the world.

39

SARAH

She hadn't expected Tomas tonight. Hearing his voice made Sarah feel like she was at the top of a roller coaster on the edge of freefall. His blue-green eyes had the same spark she recalled from their first meeting in the toyshop. He was dressed casually, lean and muscular in faded jeans and a black Rolling Stones T-shirt. His hair was uncombed, and he hadn't shaved. He looked edgy and bohemian. He looked incredible.

In truth, he was never far from her mind. Over the last few weeks, her feelings had spun around like a carousel, out of control. Right? Wrong? She didn't pretend to know.

On the one hand, her days were glass and steel, glitz and glamour. Sitting at a desk poring over budgets, plans, and proposals. It was a far cry from the hands-on work she'd done at the St. Jacques, restoring a historic building to its former glory. Sometimes she felt like an imposter, as if the other members of Komitov's Special Development Team, mostly located in other cities, knew more – and cared more – than she did.

'Let's have a girl's night out to celebrate!' Jeanette had

suggested. She, too, was to be promoted within the organisation, though she was waiting to hear the specifics. 'Somewhere fancy – let's put a dent in our new salaries.'

'Sure,' Sarah had agreed, but secretly, her head and heart was elsewhere, her free evenings few and far between.

In the past, the nights after work had been long and lonely: walking home past cafés full of laughing people, lovers, and families. She'd felt like a child looking in a shop window at expensive toys that could never be bought or played with. She'd envied the lives of others – often without even realising it. The toyshop had given her a new purpose. Helping real people – Franz, Andre, Mathilde.

And Tomas – it always came back to him.

'So, boss,' he said. 'Where do I start?'

'Moving those bags out to the skip.' She leaned in closer. 'And you'd better put them deep down. Franz has a bad habit of unbinning the rubbish.'

'Got it.' His smile warmed her. 'It's good to see you,' he said.

'Oh well, I've been busy with work,' she said. 'How about you?'

'Same.' He hefted a bag. 'Got to keep things ticking over. I spend so much time with Lucinda that I almost forget what it's like to see real friends.'

'Great,' she said dryly. 'And has Lucinda managed to save the world yet?'

'Not yet. I'll let you know when she does.'

It was idle banter, certainly, but she also felt a little jealous. Lucinda might be a fictional character, but Anne-Marie was a real flesh and blood woman: tall, beautiful, and *French*. And then there was previous relationship he'd mentioned – and who knew how many others? Did she want to be one of them? There was no denying that she was attracted to him, and vice versa, she thought. And yet, he was continuing to be the consummate gentleman, the ultimate friend. He'd provided a listening ear, a shoulder to cry on, and companionship in a city that she was suddenly delighted to experience. Their friendship had done wonders for her spirts. But a part of her couldn't help but want more. Did he feel the same? Why hadn't he tried harder to make it happen?

'With your permission, I will leave you to it.' Franz appeared with an empty grocery sack and a twinkle in his eye. Clearly, he saw himself less as shoemaker and more as matchmaker. Either way, having him gone made things easier.

'Fine,' she said. 'Take as much time as you need.'

When Franz was gone, she turned back to Tomas. Whatever was or wasn't between them, there was work to be done.

'When you're back, we can get started on the painting,' she said.

'OK, I can handle that.'

'Good.'

He left with the bags. Sarah spread canvas drop cloths over the floor and opened a can of pristine white paint. For the showrooms and theatre, she planned on stretching the budget to get a professional team in. But for the workshop itself, a blank canvas, a fresh coat of paint – it would be just the thing to reenergize Franz for the clear-out.

When Tomas returned, she assigned him a wall and a roller. He took to the work eagerly, talking about how he'd helped paint a friend's flat in Paris. Sarah had the distinct impression the friend was a woman. Was it Anne-Marie? Really, it shouldn't matter.

'Hey,' he said, 'penny for your thoughts.'

'Sorry,' she said. 'Just thinking about the shop, and

Franz, and everything really.'

'Is there any word on your next project? Where you're off to?'

Her next project. Another damper.

'No,' she said. 'It's just. Well. Never mind.'

On the wall in front of her, the old paint was cracked in places. She painted a wide white circle with the brush. If only she could paint over the cracks in her life as easily.

'Do tell,' he said.

She hesitated for a moment. 'Before I started this project, I thought I knew what I wanted,' she said. 'Security, prestige, a job where I can make a valuable contribution. And what's more, I thought I had it.'

She stopped painting. 'But then, I don't know… it's fun to play elves. It's satisfying, and maybe even more valuable. Helping people like Franz who are the true beating hearts of Paris. Anyway, it's got me thinking.'

Tomas stopped painting and turned to face her.

'I had this idea that I could start my own business – someday. I could help out struggling shops. There are so many around here. If I could lend my expertise, then maybe more of them could turn things around and stay independent. There's so much character here: so much history. I'd like to help preserve it.' She sighed. 'But it's a pipedream, I realise that.'

'A pipedream? Why would you say that? It's bloody brilliant, that's what it is.'

'Well, I couldn't really—'

'Yes you could.' He pointed his brush for emphasis. 'I can't imagine anyone better to help out the people around here.' He grinned. 'Even if you are English.'

Without thinking, she flung a gloop of paint at him. It landed squarely in the centre of his forehead and dripped down the side of his nose.

'Hey, none of that.' He glooped paint right back at her. She laughed – it was too much.

'Seriously…' She signaled détente by putting the brush back in the can. 'It would never work.'

'Why not? It's working here, isn't it?'

'Well, for one thing, Franz isn't paying me. And I doubt any of the other struggling shopkeepers could either.'

'Couldn't you get creative? Take an equity investment or something?'

'You mean like on *Dragon's Den*?'

'Ah,' he lowered his eyes and smiled, 'you'd make one hell of a fierce dragon.'

They flung more paint at each other, laughing and making a right mess of the room. Finally Tomas came over to her. He dipped his finger in the white paint and made a heart on her cheek.

'Sarah…' he said.

She was too breathless to respond. This was it, then; he was going to kiss her. Was she ready? *In bed with big business* – the words of Tomas's 'friend' came back to her. She stepped back, practically sliding back on a slick of paint.

'I'm sorry… I—'

A loud thunk startled them both. A door, footsteps. Time raced forward. It was later than she'd thought.

Franz appeared in the doorway, overflowing grocery bags in hand.

'My friends… Oh— but I did not mean to interrupt.'

Sarah put her hand to her cheek smudging away the heart.

'You haven't,' she said. 'And in fact, we were just finishing up.'

Franz had arrived just in time to save her from herself. Sarah was beyond relieved… beyond disappointed.

40

TOMAS

What would have happened if Franz had not come in when he did? The idea terrified him, thrilled him. For a brief moment, he'd been Icarus: flying too close to the sun, the heat searing his skin, his wings starting to melt. A glorious sensation. But it was time to pay the price, spiralling back to earth. Sarah was embarrassed, the heart a white smudge on her cheek. She spoke too loudly, moved too quickly, busied herself with cleaning up the paint splatters. He'd overstepped the mark, but had he done irreparable damage?

You hurt people…

He hoped not.

He waited until Sarah finished with Franz, going over the work plan for the week, scolding him for minor infractions, praising him for his grit and fortitude. When it was time to go, she seemed a little surprised to see him still there, awkward when he offered to walk her home.

'Sure,' she said. 'I'm tired. It's been a long day.'

'Yes, it has.'

The message was clear enough.

It was already getting dark, though the lights were bright, the pavements busy, and shops were still open. He thought of asking her to dinner; a drink – anything to recapture the earlier levity – and the moment that was interrupted. Surely, he hadn't misread the signs. First they were friends, then they were elves; and now, in whatever time they had, they were evolving into something else. Something he wanted more than anything. But did she? Was he brave enough to find out?

They walked past the bookshop. The large window had been decorated with back-to- school books for children, but the smaller window displayed books for adults, including a pyramid of his own novels. And something else…

Sarah stopped walking, grabbing his arm.

'Look! It's you.'

Tomas froze, terror and shame creeping down his spine. 'What the—?' he muttered. Behind the pyramid of his books there was a new addition: a photograph of him blown up to poster size. He was standing near a shelf, a blurry book in his hand.

'You're famous.' Sarah gave him an admiring smile. 'I can't wait to tell my mum that I'm friends with a famous author.'

'I'm not famous,' he said sharply. 'The clerk must have taken it at the book signing – ages ago. I told them no publicity photos – and I certainly don't want to be in the window. I'm sorry, but can you give me a minute?'

Sarah looked a little stunned, but she followed him into the shop. He marched up to the till and had a sharp word with the clerk. The poster had to be taken down. Right now.

'And nothing on the website – OK? Delete it all.'

A manager was called. The window display was

altered. Profuse apologies and assurances were granted. Sarah browsed at a nearby table – he could tell from her body language that the incident was making her uncomfortable. He regretted the scene – regretted – everything. Their evening, their possibilities… ruined.

But that had happened a long time ago.

Sarah walked out of the shop; he followed her, stopping her with a hand on her arm. 'I'm so sorry.' He made a monumental effort to turn on the devil-may-care charm and charisma. 'Just a little misunderstanding.'

'It seemed like more than that.'

He laughed lightly. 'Maybe I overreacted a little.'

Sarah shrugged. 'I don't know anything about it. But if I was an author, I'd love to have my photo in the window of a Paris bookshop.' She resumed walking in the direction of her flat.

'Maybe.' Tomas kept pace beside her. 'But I write spy novels. It's better if my readers think I'm an "international man of mystery" rather than just an ordinary bloke with a dull sort of life.'

'Yeah.' She gave a tentative laugh. 'That must be it.'

Outside her building, he gave her a double kiss on the cheek; promised to text. The incident was a wake-up call. He needed to heed it. As he walked away, he could feel Sarah's eyes upon him as she stood at the door, watching… wondering…

41

SARAH

MONDAY, SEPTEMBER 25TH

Glass and steel, glitz and glamour. Sarah felt like she was trapped between two worlds as she waited in the foyer for her monthly catchup with Komitov. Perhaps it was the late nights, but she felt heavy and slow – and annoyed with herself. Her job was all important; she loved the possibilities it offered. Her work on the toyshop was nothing more than a diversion; a favour for a friend. Franz… not Tomas.

The incident at the bookshop had unsettled her. The time she spent with Tomas was like the swift brushstrokes of an impressionist painting – exquisite present moments that slipped away into a brief shared past. There was no time *before*, and no promise of an *after*. But although he'd told her the bare bones of his history, she sensed that there were layers that were hidden from her. His story about his author mystique as an 'international man of mystery' made sense, she supposed, and it was understandable that he might be careful with publicity. But his reaction had seemed over the top, and not at all like the Tomas she knew. Or thought she did…

'Ah *chérie*… so nice to see you.' Komitov's greeting included an unctuous hug and a kiss that landed at the edge of her lips. She forced herself to smile – and be grateful that Paris rarely seemed to be on her boss's itinerary.

'I have heard you are settling in well to the new job,' he said. 'And I am eager to discuss the future.'

'Yes.' Sarah managed. 'Me too.'

'And your fiancé? He is well?'

His eyes flicked to her bare finger. Sarah winced. 'Yes. Very.'

'Good, good. And since you are, as they say, "on the ground" in Paris, I have someone for you to meet. He ushered her into his office with a flourish. A well-groomed older man in an impeccable suit was standing by the window looking out at the view. As he turned to face them, she felt strangely cold.

'Have you met Monsieur Rouveau?' Komitov said, directing her to a chair across the desk.

Rouveau. The name sounded familiar, though she couldn't place it.

'We have not yet had the pleasure,' the older man said. 'Though I am familiar with your work on the St. Jacques. Which is why I am here. I have an opportunity that may be of interest to your organisation.'

'Good, good,' Komitov said.

Sarah stayed silent. Rouveau launched his presentation onto a projection screen. Instantly, Sarah's pulse quickened. She recognised the location: the tangled streets, the empty shops.

The situation was straightforward. Rouveau owned a number of vacant properties. The former tenants had mostly retired, though, Rouveau admitted, one or two of them had required 'incentives' to hand over their keys. His slides showed architect's drawings for a street of sleek, cookie-cutter shops and a modern hotel.

Sarah did all she could to keep calm and collected. When the presentation ended, Rouveau handed out a hard copy of the proposal, and Sarah posed a few questions. Did the council support the project? What about the local residents? What about the local directive designed to preserve independent shops?

Rouveau had an answer for everything. He had not yet approached the planners, but he had a vision – of glamour and cash. Komitov flicked his nails looking bored. He raised objections of his own. The project was too small. If there was likely to be planning red tape, then surely, they could find lower hanging fruit elsewhere.

Secretly, Sarah was glad of her boss's cool reaction. But as Komitov and Rouveau's discussion deepened, her fears floated back to the surface.

'There may be a way I can increase the footprint,' Rouveau was saying. 'I'm thinking of one particular premises that could be the *pièce de résistance.*' He flipped to a new slide – the doorway to *La Boutique Fantasque*.

Sarah's breath caught.

'It is currently occupied by an eccentric old fool with a long lease negotiated by his predecessor,' Rouveau said. 'Out of sentiment, I told him he can stay – for now. But these decisions can be reversed, no?'

'No,' Sarah heard herself saying. The two men looked at her; she was horrified that she'd spoken aloud. 'I don't think that's the right way to go about it.' Her hand shook as she flipped through the proposal; drew a few lines on the map; pencilled in a few provisional figures on the spread-sheet. 'Empty shops are one thing, but occupied ones are quite different. There's a local online group that's very interested in preserving independent shops. It benefits everyone to keep them happy.'

Komitov frowned. 'It is fine to keep them happy. But not if it increases costs and reduces profits.'

'Leave it with me to make some changes,' Sarah said. 'I'm sure I can make the numbers work.'

'She is magic,' Komitov said. 'If anyone can do it, she can.'

Rouveau raised an eyebrow, looking as unconvinced as Sarah felt.

'I hope so,' he said. 'For all our sakes, I hope so.'

What a mess.

Sarah walked out of the meeting, her head and heart pounding. How had she got herself in this position? A favour for a friend, a diversion – but now, it seemed she was walking a tightrope. She'd risked giving hope to an idealistic old man and a vulnerable boy. Risked her own heart in the process. And now she might be risking her job too – the one constant in her life. Why hadn't she tried harder to leave Paris – asked Komitov to assign her to a soulless project somewhere else? Was it too late?

Now that she was aware of Rouveau's plans, it seemed too late for Franz. She saw with new eyes the empty shops with for rent signs in the windows. With an investor on board they could be turned *en masse* into upscale high street shops. How could *La Boutique Fantasque* survive when the dominos started to fall?

When she got to the shop, she was terse with Franz for failing to have his signboard out and undercharging a collector who'd bought an antique musical box. Worse, Tomas arrived – she hadn't seen him since the bookshop incident – and she hadn't been expecting him. She was too stressed even to banter about Lucinda, or ask if he'd been to see Andre. Instead, she set him a task of sorting through a box of toy cars while she went to see the workman who'd come to check the electrics on the castle. The news was not good. More time and money would be needed to gain the necessary certificates. When the men were gone, Sarah gathered Franz and Tomas together in the theatre. She decided not to tell them about Rouveau's plans, focusing instead on her frustration with the lack of progress.

'OK.' She took a breath. 'Since we're all here – elves and shoemaker – it's decision time.'

'Decision time?' Franz's shoulders drooped.

'The castle,' she said. 'We've barely tackled the work that needs doing, and it's taking up space, time, and money. If we're going to save the shop, then we need to prioritise. Let go of things. If we can't get it safe, then it has to go.'

'Safe! It is perfectly safe!' Franz was adamant. My father was the best at mechanics and I learned from him.'

'I don't doubt it, but—'

'Show her,' Tomas said to Franz. 'You've got one shot – convince her.'

'Yes.' Franz's eyes flashed with a rare steel. 'Yes, I will.'

Sarah stood next to Tomas as Franz went to the side of the room and flipped a switch. Music played through the speakers, spirited and lively. The castle began to move and spin, the carousel horses bobbing, figures moving, lights flashing. Sarah stood mesmerised – suddenly, she understood Franz's vision. She could imagine children on the carousel, adults standing transfixed; laughter, joy, delight. Her head began to swim. The lights… the music… memories. *Victor*. The giraffe… the police car… the ambulance…

The music blared, the animals rotated. A toyshop, the circus animals. She shouldn't be here… dark spots appeared in front of her eyes, her skin felt cold and clammy as her pulse raced and her throat constricted and suddenly she couldn't breathe. *No*… this could not be happening. She was over this…

'I think I'm going to be—'

She staggered over towards the wall to steady herself. Her foot caught on a stray electrical cable. For a moment, she teetered in mid-air. Then, she was falling…

'Rowan,' she gasped. The darkness closed around her.

42

SARAH

When Sarah opened her eyes, the lights and music had stopped, though the bright tune lingered dizzily in her head. As her throat loosened, she gulped in breath after breath. Franz was holding a bag of ice to her forehead; Tomas had hold of her wrist, monitoring her pulse.

'What… happened?'

'You fell,' Tomas said.

'I am so sorry.' Franz sounded distraught. 'It is my fault. The castle – it is not safe.'

'We'll sort it out,' Tomas said. 'Another time.'

'Of course.'

Sarah took the icebag from Franz. She wanted to tell them to stop fussing over her; pretend they hadn't seen her in the throes of a panic attack. She was in charge; everything was back to normal.

But her pulse continued to beat too quickly; her body flooded not just with shame, but with grief and despair. She'd convinced herself that by taking on the toyshop project, she was facing up to her darkest fears. Fighting and vanquishing them. But her demons weren't going anywhere. Not until she let them out.

'Rowan,' Franz said in a gentle voice. 'Were you thinking of her?'

'Yes.' Sarah's breath caught again. 'Your creation… it's wonderful. But she'll never see it.'

Franz nodded, his eyes mirroring her pain. He understood – she knew he did. And Tomas… Both of them had seen something inside her worth saving. But they deserved more. They deserved the truth.

Tell me your story…

Franz was speaking.

… Ready to listen.

Ten minutes later, she was sitting on a wonky folding chair, her hands trembling as she sipped a cup of tea. Franz sat on his stool, Tomas leaned against the door. Even in the chaos of a half-renovated Paris toyshop, years on and hundreds of miles away, the grief was crushing.

'It was all my fault,' she said. 'I was there. Victor was not. He was right to blame me.'

She stared down at the brown liquid in the cup, searching for answers. There were none to be had. As she slipped back in time, the images formed and flew away. Her wedding on a sunny day at the Arts and Crafts chapel in Compton. A dreamy, perfect moment. She'd felt so beautiful in her Edwardian-style beaded dress and her grandmother's veil. The smiles on her parents' faces, the breeze that blew her hair as she walked up the hill to the chapel. She could remember every detail as if she was staring at a photograph. Of someone else's make-believe life.

'I was so lucky to have Victor,' she said. 'After all, I was just an ordinary girl from the Home Counties. He was so handsome and sophisticated. So French. I wanted to be perfect – to make everything perfect for him. I tried so hard, but he could be very distant. He travelled a lot for work and some weeks we rarely saw each other. When we were together, I tried my best to make him happy.'

The feelings came back in a rush. The *trying*, the *insecurity*, the *blame* – she'd taken it all upon herself when Victor hadn't responded.

'I always felt like I was doing something wrong. He was so serious – I could never make him laugh. That made me unhappy, and I felt guilty for that too.'

She took a sip of the cooling tea. The sweetness only just masked the bitter taste underneath.

'When I got pregnant, I was determined to be a great mum. I had everything all planned out, from the design of the nursery to the exact style of pram. Victor wanted to be a father, but with the baby on the way he worked even harder to get promoted. I was alone so much of the time. That's when I started to realise that something was wrong with me.

'Secretly, I felt awful. It wasn't just morning sickness. I hated my body and my lack of energy. The magazines said I was supposed to feel great. I was a mum-to-be; I was undergoing a life-changing and life-affirming experience. But my feelings were all *wrong*.'

'Wrong how?' Franz looked perplexed. 'They were yours.'

'I wanted to feel like all those perfect mothers,' Sarah said. 'The ones in the magazines and on Instagram. I pretended that I did – to Victor, to my mum, to my friends. I was one thing on the outside and another on the inside.' She shook her head. 'I was living a lie.'

'No,' Tomas said sharply. 'It sounds like you were depressed, that's all.'

'That's what they said later. I was suffering from post-natal depression, and in my case it started before Rowan was even born.'

She closed her eyes. The moment they'd placed the baby in her arms, she'd begun to drown. In love and fear. In inadequacy and insecurity. Feelings that she hadn't wanted to feel, so she'd kept them locked inside.

'For months and months after the birth, I barely ate and couldn't sleep. I didn't want to feed the baby; she was so tiny, and I was afraid I'd hurt her. My mum and Victor were great with her, but she always cried when I held her. I tried to smile through it, but I couldn't keep up appearances. Victor found me crying – he told me that I needed help. That's when I lost it. I'd failed even at pretending things were OK.'

'Sarah,' Franz said in a soft voice. But she shook her head, continuing on.

'I screamed at him that everything was fine. I just needed to get back to work. He said he was worried about me, and that he would get his mother to come and stay. I didn't want that – I didn't want to admit defeat. He said we would talk about it more at the weekend. Then he left for another business trip. I was alone with the baby. I felt trapped and panicky. But I took Rowan out for a walk in the pram. That made things better. In fact, as I watched her, asleep, her little lips sucking in her sleep, I loved her so much. I knew that I would make things right. I took her home, determined to make it happen.'

She slumped back, exhausted. 'I made an appointment with the health visitor so I could sort myself out before Victor got home. Rowan was fussy that afternoon, but I rocked her and sang to her. For the first time, I felt like real mum. A good mum. I could do it.' She took a breath. 'When she finally settled, I went to the room next door with the baby monitor. I was going to work on my CV, but I fell asleep.

'I... fell... asleep. Can you believe it?' She asked the question to both of them and no one. 'And when I woke up, I felt great; I felt relieved. So full of love – and hope. I went into the next room to check on Rowan...'

She closed her eyes, steeling herself. Two little words. So small, so devastating.

'Cot death,' she said. 'That was the coroner's verdict. Sudden Infant Death Syndrome. It happens to approximately two hundred babies each year in the UK.' She recited the statistic. 'They tried to reassure me that it was just "one of those things" and "not anybody's fault". But the thing is, I was there. In the next room. Feeling relieved because I'd finally got some sleep.'

Her throat tightened with shame.

'I'll never forget the look on Victor's face. The rage and the blame. The disbelief. "What have you done?" That's what he said to me. I couldn't answer. Instead, I ran away. I went to my mum's house, and stayed there. She handled everything. I didn't go back to the flat to sort through Rowan's things. That's how the giraffe got lost. I didn't even get out of the car at the funeral. I couldn't cry. My baby was gone but I couldn't shed a single tear. I did nothing.' She clenched her fists, furious with herself. 'Nothing. Nothing for my daughter, or my husband. Nothing that benefited anyone. And I'm still doing nothing.' She put her head in her hands. 'I'm just so tired of wasting my life.'

'You are not doing nothing,' Franz said softly. 'You have taken a big step.'

Tomas nodded, his eyes a sea of compassion. Franz put a hand on her shoulder, his warmth a comfort.

Could they be right? Had she moved forward? Her story was told. The words had oiled the door to her mind. Part of her wanted to be alone with her grief, but mostly, she was grateful to her friends for being there. Giving her the space she needed. For making her feel seen and heard.

The first tear tickled her cheek as it rolled down. Then another one came.

Then she couldn't stop.

43

TOMAS

Tomas fought against a tide of emotions as Sarah told her story. They were not the emotions he should be feeling: sympathy, sadness. It was anger, plain and simple. Anger at the husband who had blamed Sarah. Anger at the universe for having dealt her such an unfair hand, taking away the child she'd loved. And underneath it all was anger towards himself.

After what happened at the bookshop, he'd been determined to end things. It had hit home the risk he was taking – not just for himself, but for her. He'd felt weak and ashamed when the urge to text her became too great. The urge to see her. When Franz phoned and asked him to come in and help them with the castle, he'd felt joy again and hadn't hesitated. Now, he knew it was the wrong decision, a selfish decision. Sarah needed a man who could help her learn to love and trust again. He was not that man.

Still, he held her as she cried. Finally letting go, her tears a cleansing relief. He wanted to hold her forever, even after her breathing began to ease, the pain flowing out of her and ebbing away like a tide. But she came to her senses and pulled away, keeping her eyes lowered. Clearly, she was ashamed of her emotions. He knew he should say something – anything – to try and make it better. In the past, heartfelt, meaningful words had come easily to him. In the present, he could usually come up with some sort of witty quip that smoothed things over, lightened the mood, made people laugh. Now, though, he had no words at all. He shook his head.

'I don't know what to say,' was all he could come up with. Stupid, insufficient.

'Don't say anything.' Her smile was like a flower blossoming in a dark place. 'I don't want your pity. The past can't be changed. I want to focus on the future. It's taken me a long time to get to this point.'

'You deserve a great future,' he said. 'I hope you get it.'

Franz looked from him to Sarah. 'With your permission, I will leave now. I have promised Mathilde and Andre a visit.'

At any other time, Tomas might have laughed. Franz was playing matchmaker – it was so obvious. He exchanged a glance with Sarah.

'Sure,' Sarah said to Franz. 'Please give them my regards. I'll stay here for a while, if that's OK. It's good to be busy.'

'Yes,' Franz said. 'In times of strong emotion, it is good to have a job to do.' He got together a bundle of tools and materials to take with him.

'Lock up when you leave,' he said. 'And Sarah, thank you again. You are a remarkable woman. Never forget that.'

Tomas and Sarah both watched without speaking as

Franz shuffled out of the room, weighed down by his heavy bags.

'I should help him carry that stuff,' Tomas said. He worried she'd think he wanted an escape route. Maybe he did.

'OK.'

He couldn't read her expression. Did she want him to stay or go? He remained rooted to the spot.

'You must think I'm a total arse,' he said. 'Taking you around museums, seeing Paris, getting you involved here.' He frowned at the mess around them. 'Like it's somehow important and going to make a difference.'

'But it does make a difference,' she said. 'It's huge. There's more to life besides my job. You're showing me that.'

A flush spread over her cheeks. She was so beautiful.

'You and Franz,' she added. 'And Andre and Mathilde. It may have been an odd set of circumstances that brought us together, but somehow, everything seems to fit. Like clockwork.' She swept her hands around her. 'I can't explain it.'

Clockwork. The gears were winding tighter between them. The tension growing. Now would be the time to take the next step. Give into the desire, the gravity between them. Take her in his arms… never let her go. *She's the one*, the voice called out from his cage inside. Tomas wanted it more than anything. He feared it more than anything. She was looking at him as if expecting an answer.

But the answer was not going to change. Sarah did not need a man like him. Not now and not ever.

'Well, I guess it was just dumb luck. You know – serendipity?'

Light, flippant. He took a step backwards. Retreating…

She held his eyes for a long second. Then, she gave a little laugh. The moment was broken.

'Yes, well, *dumb luck* aside, I'm glad we're friends. Now, shall we have a look at the castle and see what needs to be done? I can get the workmen back in tomorrow.'

Tomas nodded, breathing a sigh of relief. *Shut up*, he commanded the voice inside his head.

44

FRANZ

Franz now understood why he'd been drawn to Sarah. Her story – her personal tragedy and the regrets that still haunted her – were very different from his, but on a deep level of human suffering, they were the same. Her past could not be changed, nor could his own. But Sarah was taking action in her life. She was his inspiration to keep going, step by step, even though his legs ached and his shoulders drooped. He hoped that she and Tomas… well… they were two young people who could figure out such things out for themselves. Could he and Mathilde do the same?

As he knocked on Mathilde's door, his stomach vaulted with nerves and hope. Though he wanted to think of nothing but her and Andre, the excitement and commotion at the shop had left him little time for visiting. It was one of many things he wanted to put right.

Light footsteps reached the door. Franz stood up a little straighter, and when Mathilde opened the door, he felt a rush of warmth. 'Hello, Mathilde,' he said. 'I hope this is not a bad time.'

'No worse than any other.' She gave him an off-handed shrug. 'Andre would love to see you.'

Though she stood aside to let him in, he remained in the hallway. 'And you, Mathilde?' This was risky, dangerous. But he had to know. 'Are you happy to see me? Because I am very happy to see you.'

He looked into her eyes as they flickered with images and memories, then a strange sort of blankness. She blinked rapidly, as if disorientated. His heart felt like it was being squeezed by a powerful hand. She stepped out into the hall. 'I am happy to see you,' she said. 'But I do not want to lead you down a path that goes nowhere.'

It was like walking into a brick wall. Franz took a moment, struggling to compose himself. He'd been so happy – so certain that things could be right between them. He'd been prepared to forgive himself and grab this chance of happiness with both hands. In doing so, he'd made it all about him, when it should have been about her.

'I… would not ask you for what you cannot give,' Franz stammered. 'But at least let me continue to help you with Andre.'

She considered him for a long moment before gesturing for him to come inside. 'Of course,' she said. 'Andre is quite lonely these days. Now that he is making progress, he wants to have visitors all the time. But people are busy.'

'We are busy on the project.' He gave Mathilde a little wink and was pleased to see the lines on her face soften. 'An entire toyshop – for when he is ready.'

'You and your secret project.' A smiled ghosted across her lips. 'It sounds like you've been reading too many of Tomas's stories.'

'Perhaps,' Franz said. 'But stories can be powerful. Especially when they take on a life of their own.'

'As long as one is not too hopeful of a happy ending.'

He set down the bags he was carrying and looked into her eyes. They were deep and expressive. How many people walked by her on the streets – and him too, for that matter – seeing just another old person? Not appreciating their depth of experience and feeling. Not thinking of them as people who might still choose to feel the sensations of wonder and love. Franz had seen himself that way, too, but now, the image had shifted. He longed for those sensations. He wanted to touch her face, to feel the warmth of her skin. He imagined the moment; he knew exactly how it would be.

'I think, Mathilde, that that is exactly what humans are meant to do.'

She laughed – a low, musical sound – and the years melted from her face. All he had to do was step forward and make it happen—

Just then, Andre emerged from his room. He took one look at Franz and rushed towards him. 'Monsieur Franz!'

Franz hugged the boy. 'Ah my lad, you have grown since I saw you last.' He smiled at Mathilde and was grateful when she smiled back. *To be a part of their lives...* that was his dream now. All the hardship and uncertainty of the shop refurbishment would be worth it in the end – if he could pull it off.

'I brought you some things,' he said to the boy, indicating the bags.

'You should not do that,' Mathilde said. 'You will spoil him.'

'Ah. But this is not a gift.' Franz turned to Andre. 'This is work. I need to repair a musical box for a customer. I have taken it apart and must put it back together again. My eyes are not as good as they used to be. And my workshop is – shall we say – in chaos at the moment.'

Andre took his hand and practically dragged him over to the kitchen table. Mathilde gave a theatrical sigh, but it was accompanied by a smile. 'So, you will be taking over my kitchen then?'

Franz sparkled inside. 'With your permission.' He turned back to Andre. 'It will be an experiment – to see if you have what it takes.'

45

SARAH

SUNDAY, OCTOBER 1ST

If she were honest, Sarah didn't believe in the power of stories. The past could not be changed, but it could still hurt. For years she'd resisted going to therapy, terrified of unleashing the feelings inside.

The toyshop was a strange key to that particular lock. Having told her story to Franz and Tomas, she felt lighter and more at peace. She put it down to the beauty of the city, her friends, and some kind of mysterious alchemy brought on by time and perspective. Whatever it was, the weeks flying by were some of the happiest of her life.

To her relief, her work days were largely engaged on Komitov's projects outside of Paris, and for the time being, at least, the spectre of Rouveau's development had faded into the lengthening shadows, along with the summer weather. She knew, however, that it was bound to rear its head eventually, and her best hope was to make Franz's shop as profitable as possible and raise its profile so that any neighbouring development complimented rather than swallowed it.

As autumn drew in, she spent nearly every evening at

La Boutique Fantasque: overseeing the clear-out, managing the workmen, and coddling an understandably stressed-out Franz.

To be fair, they'd unearthed considerably more hidden gems than she'd expected. Antique toys, old musical boxes, and quite a bit of new, modern stock squirrelled away in the warren of rooms at the back of the workshop. She uploaded photos of his most valuable merchandise onto the new website, and enquiries were already coming in. Sarah taught Franz to use a laptop computer to keep his accounts and list items in online auctions. She made him resurrect an old suit and frogmarched him to a bank to fill out forms for a loan. The loan had not yet been approved, but she'd convinced the bank manager to grant him an overdraft to cover his rent and immediate expenses. All in all, the project was going as well as – or better than – expected.

She scheduled much of the work at times when Franz was likely to be away from the shop. He wanted to spend more and more time with Mathilde and Andre, and Sarah was impressed with the quietly confident way he had made himself part of their lives.

Tomas often came by unannounced. Her story had shaken up the dynamic between them. They didn't speak about the past, but it was no longer a barrier. They were making new memories. Laughing together, occasionally having a good-natured argument over new stock or the odd antique. Sarah expected someone as worldly and debonair as Tomas to be a firm believer in 'out with the old', but he could be surprisingly sentimental, often siding with Franz over whether something stayed or went. He took over supervising work on the castle, which, even with Sarah's careful management of the budget, was costing more than expected. When a mysterious package arrived with some expensive parts that she had not authorised, Sarah suspected he'd used his own money to bridge the gap. Even on top of what she already felt, she loved him a little for that.

In her spare time, she made a point of visiting Andre as often as possible – sometimes with Tomas, sometimes on her own. The boy was making visible progress. He was growing more and more talkative and engaged – a far cry from the early days when he'd mostly stayed curled up on the sofa, content to look at the magazines she'd brought him. He changed his clothes and washed his hair, and became fully engaged in learning how to run Franz's website. Gradually, Sarah began to speak of the world outside. The feeling of rain on her skin, the sound of crisp golden leaves underfoot, the lights of cars and cafés, the smell of fresh-baked croissants, the shimmer of cloud reflections on a rain-soaked pavement. The boy was interested, but only in an abstract way. He grew more engaged, however, when she talked of Franz and his shop.

'Would you still like to go there?' she asked him one dreary afternoon. The rain had been falling steadily outside, and she'd arrived soaked through, the sky already darkening to an early night.

'*Oui*.' Andre nodded vigorously. 'I know all about his secret project.'

She laughed. 'I suppose it's no secret. Tomas and I are helping him transform the place – into a magical destination for children and adults. Like his father's shop.'

'Anna loved his father's shop,' Andre said.

The comment was unexpected – of all the things she and Andre talked about, he still seemed very interested in Franz's former sweetheart. 'Yes,' she said. 'I think that was true.'

Andre shrugged and went back to staring at his iPad. 'I have a secret project too,' he said absently.

'Oh?' Sarah said. 'What's that?'

'A *secret*.' He looked up. 'I will tell you when it is done.'

'Fair enough.'

Mathilde set aside her knitting, got up from her chair, and came to stand over the boy. 'Be polite, Andre,' she said. 'And make sure that when Franz has the toyshop ready, you will be ready to leave this flat. Franz is doing it for you. You should be more grateful. His friend Anna never got a chance like that.'

Sarah frowned at Mathilde. 'Andre will be ready,' she said. 'Won't you?'

'*Oui*,' Andre whispered, looking a little terrified.

'Good.' Sarah stood up to leave. 'Remember, Andre, you can rewrite your story. Set a goal and start living it in your mind. And be proud of the progress you're making. We can talk about it more on Sunday. With Tomas. Is that OK?'

Andre responded by giving her a huge bear hug.

'It is more than OK,' Mathilde said. 'Thank you for everything you are doing. For Andre, for Franz, and for Tomas.'

Sarah blushed. 'Oh, it's nothing. I want to help if I can.'

'It is not nothing. You are helping more than you know. And no matter what happens, we are all relying on you. Remember that.'

Her words sounded like a warning.

Of what?

For a second, Mathilde's eyes glazed over. Was she imagining the past? Or the future?

'I will remember,' Sarah said as she went to the door. 'Definitely.'

46

MATHILDE

Things that seem too good to be true usually are.

She doesn't remember where she heard this, but she knows they are words to live by. Time after time, her life has proved it true. She had a fine husband and a beautiful daughter – she lost them both. Now she has a grandson and a quirky old man who makes her feel something again. She is going to lose them too.

But as Sarah leaves the flat, Mathilde is not worried for herself. She is tough, and loss is second nature to her. But Sarah – so beautiful and strong on the outside, but so frail underneath. And Tomas…? In all her years of living across the hall she has not figured him out. It scares her a little. She knows a man with secrets when she sees one.

It is almost time for dinner; she walks to the kitchen – or is it too early? Time is so confusing now…

'*Grand-mère*? Can I have a glass of milk?'

Milk. That should be easy enough. Mathilde goes to the refrigerator. She finds eggs and cold meats, and… strangely… a book that surely doesn't belong there. She removes the book. No milk. Not even a carton past its sell-by date.

She could go out and buy some. The urge to go outside into the world is so strong. For that reason alone, she must resist it. Tomas… she can… what was the phrase… *'Kill two birds with one stone'*?

'Wait a minute,' she says. She goes out of the flat and knocks on the opposite door. By the time Tomas answers, Mathilde has forgotten what she came for. But she knows what she needs from Tomas.

'I had a flat on Rue d'Austerlitz,' she says. 'I lived there with my husband and daughter. The building had an attic. I need you to go there – see if the box is there. The box with the shoes.'

Tomas stares at her, concern on his face. 'Mathilde, are you OK? Do you want to come inside?'

'Milk.' The threads twist themselves back together. 'I need milk.'

'Sure,' Tomas says. 'I'll get it.'

Mathilde looks inside the door. Clean for a bachelor's flat, good natural light, but lacking a woman's touch. Sarah designs shops or hotels or something. She can work wonders. What is Tomas playing at? Why isn't she here now?

Tomas returns with a carton in his hand.

Mathilde frowns – does she need milk? She decides to take it.

'She is a very special woman,' she says. 'I hope you are treating her right.'

For a second Tomas looks confused.

'Sarah.' Mathilde cools her hands on the carton.

Tomas shrugs. 'Sure I am.'

He tells her about the museums and galleries they've visited. Everything they've seen. He is showing her *his*

Paris. The words and images blur together. Focus… she has to focus.

'Yes, you have seen a lot.' Even to her, the tone sounds accusing. 'But what have you done?'

'Well – we've also been working together on the toyshop. That's taking up a lot of time.'

Mathilde shakes her head. 'That is not what I mean, and you know it.'

'Come on, Mathilde.' Tomas's mouth crooks into a smile. 'I'm not one to kiss and tell.'

'No,' she says. 'But make sure you do more than just tell. Be careful, Tomas. Do not let her get away.' Tiny bubbles of condensation form on the milk carton, like tears. Mathilde's chest aches. There is so little she can do. But she wants to do this.

'I don't think she knows where her next project will be.'

'Now you are being obtuse.'

'Look, Mathilde, I'm doing my best, OK?'

She lets out a long sigh. 'That's what I'm afraid of.'

Tomas laughs; Mathilde steps back. The distance across the hall seems as vast as an ocean. Andre is waiting for the milk.

Tomas promises to stop by soon. His door closes. She doesn't allow herself the luxury of another sigh as she goes back into her own flat.

Andre is on the sofa; his iPad is out. '*Grand-mère*,' he says, 'can you help me with something?'

She walks over slowly. 'With what, *ma petit poulet*?' This time she allows the sigh. She puts down the milk and perches on the edge of the sofa.

'With the secret project. For Franz.'

Franz – another gift she has been given. Just thinking of him makes her think about smiling – and she can almost remember how. His patience with Andre, bringing him little projects, teaching him to use his tools. Sometimes when she watches them, her eyes swim with the vision of Renée and Jean-Louis. Franz is nothing like her late husband, but that does not diminish him. For a failed chrysalis, she has managed to attract great love into her life. Is it too late to give something back? But what? She doesn't know. Could Andre hold the answer?

As the boy explains his idea, Mathilde forgets all about the milk, dinner, and even the shoes. This time, it has nothing whatsoever to do with the letter in the drawer.

47

SARAH

THURSDAY, OCTOBER 5TH

'Sarah, can I talk to you for a minute?'

Sarah stopped buttoning her coat and turned to face Jeanette. She'd been on her way to meet Tomas for a late opening at the Rodin Museum – a rare night away from the toyshop. Her body was fizzing with excitement and nerves. But when she saw her friend's face, a premonition of dread swept over her. 'Sure,' she said. 'Shall we get a coffee?'

Outside, a dull and steady rain was falling, the puddles reflecting the menacing grey sky above. They went together to a small café around the corner. 'What's up?' she said.

'I have found out about my new role,' Jeanette said. 'I am to become Komitov's personal assistant.' Her face coloured, and Sarah wondered, uncharitably, exactly what the job description entailed.

'That's… great,' she said.

'Yes,' Jeanette said. 'It will be a big step up for me, and I wish to do my job well and be a loyal employee, you understand?'

'Of course.'

'But we are friends, are we not?' The other woman lowered her voice. 'So I must give you a warning. I overheard something, you see. Mr Komitov was on the phone with Monsieur Rouveau.'

'And—?' Sarah's stomach fell.

'And they have "got wind", as you say, that you are involved in another project. One that involves the toyshop they wish to make part of their development.'

'No – that's incorrect.' Sarah heard the defensiveness in her own voice. 'The toyshop is not part of the development.'

'Ah,' Jeanette said, 'So the other part – your involvement – is right?'

'I can do what I like outside work, can't I? And you know what the regulations say. The independent shops must remain. I'm helping raise the quality of the local area. It will benefit Rouveau's development too. You can tell your new boss…' she practically spat the words, 'that I'm doing him a favour.'

'Sarah,' Jeanette warned, 'he is *our* boss. Please stop to think what you are saying and doing.'

Sarah's chest constricted. Jeanette was right – this was madness. All her hard work, all her ambition – everything was teetering on a knife's edge. And why? For what?

'Yes,' she said, forcing in a breath. 'You're right. Please don't say anything. Give me a chance to put it right.'

'If Komitov decides to invest and wants more space, the toyshop will need to close.'

'Surely, there's another solution.'

Jeanette stood up. 'I must get back to work. Think about what I've said – and more importantly, think about what you want. You can't have it both ways, Sarah.'

The other woman walked off. Sarah put her head in her hands. *You can't have it both ways.* It was painful; it was true.

She was in a bad mood when she met up with Tomas outside the Métro station at Invalides. The rain was falling harder, and even the shimmering golden dome of Napoleon's tomb did nothing to brighten the day. Indecision gnawed at her – should she step back from the project and embrace her old life, or listen to the inner voice telling her she was doing the right thing?

But was she? Her mixed feelings towards Tomas weren't providing any clarity. She'd taken on the project in part to get closer to him, and yet, in all the time they'd been working together, what had she really learned? That he didn't want to be more than friends? That seemed abundantly clear. And yet, there was that spark between them – she was sure it was mutual. He was giving her space, and she appreciated that; but there was something else too – something underlying everything. What was it?

'Guess what,' he said. 'I spoke to my friend, Anne-Marie. She's working on a "save the local shops" publicity campaign for her Facebook page.'

'Great,' Sarah grumbled. *Anne-Marie.* Was she the 'something else'?

'She wants you to be a spokesperson. I said it was unlikely, but that I'd ask. So… I'm asking.'

'You know I can't.' Her anger spiked – along with her jealousy. She forced her mind back to the more immediate concern.

'My involvement with the project is strictly off the

record,' she said. 'In fact, I need to pull back. My boss has discovered that I've been helping Franz. I can't jeopardise my job.'

'OK, OK.' He held up his hands. When he gave her the charismatic grin that usually melted her, it had no effect. 'Sorry – it was stupid to ask.'

'And anyway,' she snapped, 'if you're so "friendly" with Anne-Marie then why don't you do it? You're local, and people know you. It has nothing to do with you as an author – your "international man of mystery" persona will be quite safe.'

Annoyance flickered across his face along with something else she couldn't quite interpret. Fear?

'I don't do publicity. Anne-Marie knows that and respects it. And besides, she doesn't want me – she wants you. I thought it might fit in with the bigger picture – your dream to start your own business and be a voice for local independent shops.'

'That's a pipedream!' She raised her voice. 'I have a career, and it's important to me. The toyshop was a mistake – I see that now. At this point, my job has to be my priority. Is that so wrong?'

'I don't know,' Tomas said. 'I think only you can answer that. I mean, forgive me, but you don't seem very happy working with those people. Lining their pockets, contributing to their schemes.'

'*Those people* believed in me when I didn't believe in myself. They gave me a job. And now a promotion.'

'And you did the job and earned the promotion. You don't owe them anything else.'

'Not loyalty? Not truth?'

'Not your soul,' he said.

'You wouldn't understand.' Turning on her heel, she

walked away, guilt and shame pounding in her head like a second pulse.

'I understand more than you know,' he called out.

Shaking her head, she half-ran down the steps to the Métro, refusing to look back.

48

TOMAS

Stupid. He was so stupid. Stupid to be with her, stupid to let her go. Mathilde was right to warn him – he was going to cause another disaster of epic proportions. *You hurt people.* No one had been more right than Jessie, all those years ago.

Now Andre was involved, and Franz, and Mathilde – vulnerable people caught up like flies in his web of lies. It wasn't just stupid – it was cruel.

He dialled Anne-Marie. She was one person he hadn't hurt. All throughout their dalliance she'd made it clear that he was neither rich nor ambitious enough for her. Hearing her cool, seductive voice was like fingernails on a blackboard. He'd been avoiding her, just like he'd been using the work at the toyshop to avoid Lucinda Clarke and his edits. Just like he'd been using his entire ridiculous life in Paris to avoid the hidden truths he couldn't face.

'She won't do it,' he said. 'Like I told you. Please keep her – and me – out of this.'

'Oh, *chéri*,' she cooed. 'You are truly sleeping with the enemy now.'

'No, I'm not. And anyway, it's nothing to do with you.'

'You are right about that,' she said. 'I have met someone, you see.'

'Good for you.'

She laughed. 'The problem with you, Tomas is that you think you are better than everyone else.'

'That's a crock and you know it.' He didn't even care enough to laugh.

'When, in truth, Tomas Mercier is a nothing more than a little man, with little ambition.'

'You don't know anything about it,' he snapped.

She laughed again. 'I hope you know what you are doing.'

'I know I'm ending this call.'

Tomas Mercier is nothing more than a little man, with little ambition.

God, the truth hurt.

49

SARAH

FRIDAY, OCTOBER 6TH

After a sleepless night, Sarah came to a decision – it stung; it ached. But even so, it was the only real alternative. She had done her best to set Franz on a path to save his shop, but she could no longer stand the duplicity. Her bed was made – she'd been given a promotion and was paid to do a job – it was time to lie in it.

She decided to do it first thing – before work – before she could change her mind. Sarah wound through the tangle of streets, which were empty as usual. But when she rounded the corner to the toyshop, she was surprised to see that the pavement outside was crowded with people. Signs, placards, chanting in French. Even with her lack of fluency in the language, the meaning was clear: 'Big money out; big money out'. A sign board waved in her face; a woman was filming the proceedings on her phone. Instantly, her stomach clenched. It was Anne-Marie. She'd expressly told Tomas that she didn't want to be interviewed. Had he failed to pass on the message? Anger and fear flared inside her. Instinctively, she put her hand up to cover her face, but it was too late.

'Whose side are you on?' The woman pushed through the crowd, waving the camera in her face. 'You work for the consortium, and yet, you seem to be helping the elderly proprietor of this shop. Which is it? Are you a spy?'

'I don't want to be interviewed,' Sarah said. 'Please delete that footage.'

The woman laughed. 'You don't want your bosses to see that you are nothing more than a pretty snake in the grass – am I right?'

'I am doing my best for the people of this community.' Her voice rose desperately. 'I believe that the old and the new can – and should – coexist.'

'A pretty sentiment,' the woman said. 'But it seems to me that you are walking a tightrope. I hope you don't fall down without a— what do you say?— safety net underneath.'

'It's none of your concern,' Sarah shouted. 'And if you post that footage, I'll sue you.' Sarah turned a shoulder to the woman as the chanting raised in volume. 'Big money out; big money out'.

Abandoning her errand, she turned around and walked as quickly as she could away from the shop. Her pulse quickened with panic and the urge to crawl back into her shell, and stay there for a very long time.

50

SARAH

MONDAY, OCTOBER 9TH

When the message came in demanding her presence at an urgent meeting, Sarah knew her race was run. She walked into the plush office with the demeanour of a prisoner marching to the gallows. Jeanette was sitting at her new executive desk outside their boss's huge office.

'Sarah.' Jeanette's voice was flat. 'Mr Komitov will see you now.'

'I'm sorry,' she said to her friend.

She actually meant it.

Feeling sick, she entered the office. The lights were low – almost as if Komitov had planned a romantic occasion. But the dim lighting allowed a better view of the projection screen. She stared at the images that flickered, larger than life. A vlog – a Paris street, a protest. The camera panning to a woman's face. Her face.

'So this is how you repay my trust.'

Komitov's voice, usually so smooth, held a knife-sharp edge. 'Like the journalist said – you are "a pretty snake in the grass" – a liar and a traitor.'

'No,' she said. It sounded like a prayer, a plea. Instantly, she came to her senses. 'That's not true. I did what I thought was right: helping out a friend with his life's work. I've done it all on my own time. I've been very careful to ensure it doesn't interfere with my job.'

'You deliberately interfered with project of interest to the consortium.'

'Rouveau's proposal is not a good fit – you know that! The numbers don't add up, and you have more glamorous, more lucrative projects elsewhere. You don't need the toyshop. You'll be tied up in red tape with the council, and get bad press – I was acting in the best interests of the company.'

He stood up and came round the desk. Though he was an inch or two shorter than she, he was strong. She recalled the night of the gala when he had tried it on with her and she'd been rescued by Tomas.

No one to rescue her now.

'What I do not need, is someone who is not what they seem. I should have known it from the moment I saw you with your author boyfriend.'

'What?'

'It is like I said before – you are clearly the muse for his character. Agent Lucinda Clarke too is a law unto herself. She is cold and calculating, and uses her beauty and charms for intrigue and deceit.'

In straits less dire, Sarah would have laughed. As it was, she looked Komitov in the eye. 'Agent Clarke is out to save the world,' she said. 'I know I can't do that. But in this case – this one small way – I can make a difference. I can help a young boy who can't leave his flat. I can help an old man keep his livelihood. I can help people I care about fulfil their dreams. People on the margins – people who have no one else.'

'Well, *chérie*, if that is how you feel, then I think we –

and you – are finished here. Give me a call if you change your mind. "People on the margins."' He sniffed. 'I think you have just become one of them.'

'Yes.' She swallowed hard. 'And not before time.'

We're finished here.

The words echoed in Sarah's head. Inside, a part of her was screaming: *what are you doing? What the* hell *are you doing?* But another part…

She walked out of the building. The slanted autumn sun warmed her face, the leaves of the plane trees dazzled, copper and bronze. On a whim, she stretched out her arms, half expecting the breeze to lift her into the air.

What was wrong with her? What the hell *was wrong with her?*

She walked to the quayside and looked out over the river. Light scribbled the peaks of the waves; smoke curled from the chimneys of colourful canal boats. A group of school children were taking photos of the Eiffel Tower and Pont Neuf. Instead of the familiar pull of loss, she felt light and airy, ready for the emptiness inside to be filled with possibilities. Her new friends – an old man, a run-down toyshop, an old woman, a shut-in boy. And… Tomas. Last time she'd seen him, it had ended badly. But today felt like a whole new beginning.

Can you meet me? She texted. *We need to talk.*

Butterflies floated in her stomach until the reply came in – less than a minute later.

I'm at the toyshop. Meet me there?

Yes.

The message swooshed away. The toyshop – yes, it was only fitting. She'd fallen off the tightrope, and there was only one place she could possibly land; one person that she wanted to catch her before she hit the ground.

51

TOMAS

Something was different. Sarah was breathing heavily from walking quickly, her hair loose about her shoulders, her eyes as bright as twin stars. When he'd received her text, his anticipation was overshadowed by doubt. He hadn't seen her since the day they'd quarrelled outside the Métro, and he hated the way they'd left things. Seeing her now, he was no closer to knowing whether she'd forgiven him or was here to end their friendship.

'Hi,' she said, as he met her at the door. 'How's the work going?'

'Good,' he said. 'A health and safety inspector dropped by. I think the landlord sent him. Fortunately, I was here and Franz was out – he's visiting Mathilde and Andre.'

'That was lucky.'

'Yeah. I think it went well. We're not out of the woods yet, but I think we'll get there. The builders are looking at the snagging list. But what about you, fair maiden?' He cocked his head as she came inside. 'I didn't know you took a lunch break.'

'As of right now, I'm on a permanent lunch break,' Sarah said. 'I've been sacked.'

'Oh. No—'

Sarah's face gave nothing away, but his emotions spiralled like a whirlpool. 'Please say it wasn't— Oh God— I *did* talk to her. I told her you didn't want any publicity and that she should leave you alone.'

'Well, she didn't listen.'

'God.' He put his hand over his face. *Anne-Marie.* This was her fault – which meant that it was his fault too. 'I can't believe it. I'm so—'

'Don't say it.' She put a finger to his lips, taking him by surprise. 'Don't you dare say it, and don't be it either. I'm not.'

'OK?'

'I couldn't keep living in two worlds. It made a liar of me, a fraud.'

Anger simmered inside him, rising to the surface. He wanted to hit something – like his own reflection. *Liar, fraud* – Sarah was none of those things. *But I am…* he opened his mouth to speak the words; words that finally told the truth. Since the first, Sarah had been open and honest, genuine and compassionate. Surely, she deserved the same. But Sarah needed him now, in this moment. Once again, it wasn't the right time.

'That's not true,' he said. 'Not in any way. You're the most genuine person I know.'

'I don't feel very genuine. Komitov called me a "pretty snake in the grass".'

'Komitov's an idiot.'

Sarah sputtered a laugh. Then, she guffawed. Pretty soon, she was laughing so hard that tears were streaming down her face. 'I'm sorry,' she gasped. 'It's just – I feel so… I don't know. Free? Full of clarity?'

Tomas laughed with her, uncertainly at first, but her levity was infectious. She took his hand and led him through the warren of rooms to the theatre where the workmen had the castle in full operation, the music bright and loud.

'Can we take a ride?' she said.

'Really? You want to?'

'Yes. We've helped create this, and it's magical. If we're the elves, then it's time to try out the shoes.'

'OK.' He signalled to the man to stop the mechanism. He helped Sarah onto a white horse with a gold mane and tail trimmed with ribbons and flowers, and mounted a black horse beside her. With her hair loose, she reminded him more than ever of the Lady and the Unicorn. *À mon seul désir.*

The workman flipped the switch. The carousel started moving, the horses bobbing up and down on their mechanised poles. The music was festive, lively, almost overwhelming. But his attention was drawn fully towards Sarah. Her radiance, her beauty, her unexpected levity and abandon. Her face softened by wonder. The toyshop truly was a place of magic. Here, in this moment, troubles did not exist. Here, it was perfect…

When the carousel stopped, he helped her down and off the platform, but somehow, they were still touching. Joy radiated from her; her cheeks had a warm and rosy glow.

'What do you want to do now?' he said. 'Get something to eat, or plan what's next or—?'

'What do I want?' Without warning, she leaned in. Her breath tickled his ear, sending waves of heat pulsing down his body. 'I want to kiss you,' she said.

He stared at her for a long moment, wondering if he'd misheard. It was everything he desired; but he'd convinced himself it was impossible. *Friends…* from the very first moment, it had been more than that. How could it not be, when they both felt the way they did?

'Then what are you waiting for?' he whispered.

It happened in an instant, their lips coming together. Brushing softly, opening, exploring. Tomas closed his eyes, drowning in the sensations of overwhelming beauty. She was so soft, so vulnerable, like the petals of a flower opening up to the light. Desire rushed like a wave from every cell of his body. It was over in an instant, and when they came apart, he felt like he was still on the carousel; every emotion inside him had begun to shimmer and spin. One of the workmen whistled. Sarah waved glibly; Tomas ignored everything but her. The barriers inside him were wide open. He wanted this more than anything; he wanted *her*.

'Sarah,' he whispered. 'Are you sure?'

'Shh.' She breathed into his ear. 'I've never been more sure of anything in my life.'

He laughed as she kissed him again, playful and light, but with a shared promise that he meant for both of them to keep.

52

SARAH

Kissing Tomas by the castle was beautiful. Kissing him in the taxi, riding in the lift up to his flat, bodies pressed together, hands already loosening shirts and unfastening buttons, was beautiful. And when they made it inside and he carried her to his bed, making love to Tomas was beautiful. She watched his face, memorising his ever-changing ecstasy as they explored each other, immersing all their senses, culminating in a perfect moment, like light sparkling on water. Afterwards, when he held her in his arms, cosy and cocooned, there was no shame or self-doubt. Sarah felt at peace for the first time in years. Whatever her future held, she had this sweetness to cherish: she'd found feelings inside her she'd thought were lost forever. His body was warm against hers, and he nuzzled his lips into her hair.

'I didn't think I could feel this way,' she said. 'It's… so different from…' the shadow flickered at edge of her mind. She pushed it aside, not wanting a *before* or an *after*. This moment was perfect. It was enough.

He caressed her naked thigh under the blanket and nuzzled her neck.

'You're a very special woman,' he said.

'No. I'm really not. Maybe you're the one who's special.'

He grimaced. 'Not me. I'm just normal. I'm ordinary.'

'I thought you were, Tomas. And all along you were lying.'

She said it flippantly, laughed lightly; but he didn't join in.

'OK, OK,' she said, turning a little. 'If you want to be normal and ordinary, then that's fine.'

'Sure.' He swung out of bed and put on his underwear. 'That's me, then.'

She pulled the blanket up to her chin, wondering if the sun had gone behind a cloud.

'Should I make coffee?' he said. 'Or do you want something stronger?'

'Coffee would be great.'

'How about an afternoon breakfast in bed? I've got eggs.'

'Yes, please.' The world was sparkling again. She would have feelings to process later – momentous ones, good and bad. But all that could wait. Right now, *later* didn't exist. 'I've got no other plans.'

'Good,' he said.

She lay in bed listening to the unfamiliar sounds. The traffic noise and city sounds were muted in Tomas's eyrie, high above Paris. His room was simply furnished, with an antique Louis bed, a chest of drawers, and a chair by the window. There was a pile of books on the bedside table. Proust, Milton, Homer's Odyssey. Not books she'd expect a crime writer to be reading, but most of the time Tomas didn't strike her as that kind of writer. She breathed in the scent of him on the pillow. *Happy*. She was so happy…

From the kitchen, Tomas called to her that he was going out to buy some croissants. She stretched languidly and put on the shirt he'd discarded on the floor. It smelled of him and aroused her all over again. This was magic. This was real.

She went out of the bedroom to the main room of the apartment. The view played a starring role. Daydreaming, she wondered what it would be like to live here, standing at the window drinking coffee or a glass of wine. Now that she was without a job, she'd have to move. The thought momentarily darkened her mood, but she pushed it aside, staying in the moment.

The flat itself was a consummate bachelor pad, sparsely furnished with a sofa and dining table that were a little too modern for the otherwise elegant *atelier*. She was relieved to see that there was no evidence of a woman's touch. Tomas's laptop was on the table, and next to the chair, a wastepaper basket was overflowing with balled-up paper. Built-in bookcases covered one entire wall, even going above the lintel to the hall. She perused the titles. There was an eclectic mix of fiction and non-fiction in a number of genres: from romance to military history; philosophy to marketing. Many of the books looked new, their spines unbent. But at one end, she found a collection of well-thumbed classics: even a few first editions of modern classics. Kerouac, Saramago, Ellison, Capote. She picked up one by Ian McEwan and found that it had been signed by the author.

To Tom W. Congratulations on your great success!

Sarah frowned at the initial, closed the book and put it back on the shelf. Perhaps Tomas had bought it second hand, or maybe it was some kind of inside joke where the signatory had written the M upside down.

She continued to scan the books, running her hands over the bindings. She stopped on a large book inserted backwards, spine to wall. A photo album.

Sarah pulled it out halfway, then paused. This was snooping, surely. Not something that friends do – especially not ones who have just become lovers.

Indecision racked her. What happened now? There was no going back, but could they go forward? Her heart answered with a distinct 'yes'. Wherever they were headed, she wanted to follow the path.

Sarah took the album off the shelf. Tomas rarely talked about his past. Maybe the album would spark him to open up. She wanted all of him, and that meant learning everything. Opening the album, she peeked inside. There were photos of Tomas as a boy – at the seaside, playing sports, on a bicycle. His hair was longer and darker. A young man with glasses and a beard. Still, though, with that charismatic smile…

Tomas with a beautiful, dark-haired woman: was this the girlfriend he'd lived with? The one that 'didn't work out'? Sarah felt a stab of jealousy. Of course he would have photos of her – she was part of his history. Flipping the page, she saw photos of a gathering. Tomas stood in the centre of a group of mature women. There was a banner in the background. 'The Buckinghamshire WI welcomes Tom Willowfield.' A newspaper clipping: '*Tom Willowfield's* The Rites of Spring *wins Curtis P. Whitney prize*'. The date was fifteen years ago.

She turned the page. Nothing—

'What are you doing?'

Sarah jolted, almost dropping the album. She slammed it shut and jammed it back on the shelf. 'Nothing.'

Tomas's face was a hard mask of anger. She was catapulted back to the moment when Victor had come inside and heard the news. She blinked hard. He wasn't Victor – she knew that.

But who was he?

'OK,' she said, her cheeks hot. 'I admit it – I was snooping. Looking at your photos. You were such a cute kid.'

His face softened with something akin to relief. Her heart continued to race.

'Freezing holidays at the English seaside, football and rugby at weekends. You know the drill.'

'Yes, I do.'

'It was a long time ago. Now, have a seat and I'll bring you your "breakfast". And then…'

Her mind was in turmoil, but her body responded with a warm surge of anticipation.

'And then?'

'Then, I've got to get back to work,' he said. 'My revisions aren't going well. While I was out, I got another chasing email from my editor.'

'Sure.' Sarah exhaled, deflated and relieved in equal measure. It was a far cry from the heady euphoria she'd experienced earlier. Why had she gone and snooped?

And what exactly had she found?

He brought the food over to the table and they ate in relative silence. Sarah tried to fill it with nothing and anything – how much she admired the view, how the space suited him, how fluffy and delicious the croissants tasted. Coming back to English seaside holidays and Mr Whippy. Tomas responded in his normal fashion, but his air of detachment made everything feel off. And underneath it all, the unspoken question whispered in her mind.

'Who is Tom Willowfield?'

Only as she was putting on her coat to leave and saw the look on his face, did she realise she'd voiced it aloud.

'No one,' he said. 'A distant cousin. I'm afraid... he died.'

'Oh. I'm so sorry.'

'Don't be.' He gave her his melting smile. 'Anyway, take care, Sarah. And thank you for a lovely day. I'll... see you soon.'

He walked her to the door. He kissed her on the cheek. His lips were cold.

PART IV

It is dark – so dark. She floats through time on an ocean of loss, her memories sharpened by each muffled tick of the clock. Once there were others, made by the same skilled hand. Once there was the laughter of a child, the clasp of tiny fingers. Once there was light and warmth, and love. Now, that child is gone. She was there at the moment of its passing. Longing to cry out, to fetch its mother, to do *something. But she is wood and paint and varnish. She has no voice other than what*

others give her. When last she moved, she fell down against a wall, was buried in a box, shrouded in pain, forgotten in grief.

How long will she remain here? A minute, and hour, a day – forever? Will she rot? Will she ever again see light? Perhaps it is cruellest of all that hope has remained – a tiny flame, flickering, guttering, but still there inside her wooden heart.

53

FRANZ

MONDAY, OCTOBER 23RD

Was it something he'd said? Something he'd done? Not done?

Franz thought he had got it right doing the things on Sarah's list. As the leaves had turned golden and begun their gentle fall, he'd dressed up in his only suit and gone back to the bank, signed a number of bewildering forms in French and been told that, magically, he had money in a bank account. He'd signed another form and half the money disappeared – the bank manager assured him it had gone to pay the workmen, plus a healthy chunk to Rouveau. Franz rewarded himself with a visit to Andre and Mathilde. But Andre was agitated and Franz quickly learned the reason for it.

Sarah was gone.

When he asked Mathilde about it, she was matter-of-fact. Sarah had come round to the flat to say goodbye. 'She said she had to go back to London. As that is where she is from, then this is understandable, no?'

No, Franz wanted to say. *That can't be it.*

Deep down, he feared he knew the reason. Because of

her work on the toyshop – because of *his project* – Sarah had lost her job. He saw her only once after it happened; she had waved it off, saying it was for the best. But clearly, it was not.

Now, she was gone. At a time when Andre was starting to make vast improvements and the project was at a critical stage; at a time when she'd become an important part of their lives. She'd abandoned them.

Without realising it, he spoke aloud.

'She said the project is going well – that you are handling things on your own,' Mathilde said. 'She said she will keep in touch by email. I hardly think she has abandoned you.'

Franz thought of the laptop computer that he was still struggling to use. Internet, email. Sarah would continue to be involved. She had not abandoned him…

Even if it felt like it.

'You are right.' He took Mathilde's hand gently. Only then did he notice the tear in her eye.

'Mathilde?'

'I do not think it is because of her job – she would not want you to feel bad about that. In fact, I don't think it is anything we have done.' She gestured with her head, lowering her voice. 'I think it is because of him.'

'Andre?' Franz said. 'No, surely not. Andre is a child. Sarah is very fond of him.'

'Not Andre.'

'Ah.' Franz chided himself for being so stupid. It all made sense. The clockwork figures, dancing, colliding. Tomas and Sarah. He felt a sudden flash of anger.

'What has Tomas done?'

'She said that he is not who he seems.'

'Not who he seems?' Franz considered this. Who amongst them truly was what he seemed? Was that a reason to leave? To turn away from love when one was so close?

'Yes,' Mathilde said. 'And as you can imagine, Andre is taking it very hard. He also feels abandoned. He does not want to come out of his room.'

Franz let go of her hand. The anger gave him a kind of energy he didn't want to feel. He hobbled over to the door of Andre's room and knocked. 'Andre,' he said. 'It's me. I brought some things for us to do. A doll's house to build. Please—'

Mathilde came and stood next to him. He sensed she was about to shout at the boy, but he waved a hand to stop her.

'Please Andre,' he called out again.

A shuffling sound came from inside. As the door opened, Franz smelled unwashed hair and skin. Andre came out of the room, hunched and reluctant. He looked so small.

'*Je suis désolé*,' he said in a barely audible whisper.

Franz pulled the boy into a gentle embrace, gratified when Andre gave in and leaned his head against his chest. He could feel the boy's heartbeat as he stroked his hair and hummed a half-remembered tune from one of his musical boxes. Mathilde gave him a sad smile.

This was the ultimate test – harder than any before. If he did not stand on his own two feet, then he would fall. He would fail. Once, failure meant becoming a pigeon man. Now, it meant much more. Not only for him, but for the people he'd come to love most in the world. He could not let that happen. *Would* not.

'It will all be fine,' Franz said.

It did not feel fine at all.

54

MATHILDE

There is no point in wishing, no point in wondering what might have been. Mathilde feels the familiar tightening in her chest. The cocoon, the cage. Soon none of it will matter. That is all she can cling to now.

It was all a dream. A pretty illusion like a painted backdrop on a stage. She is an old woman, not a butterfly. Franz is an old man. Andre is a boy who needs more than she can give, Tomas is Tomas, and Sarah is gone.

If it was just her, there would be no tragedy. She has her regrets but she's never been one to wallow in dreams. Life is life – best to get on and accept reality. That is her way.

But as Franz leaves the flat, stooped and broken, Mathilde's heart goes out to him. He deserves magic in his life, a sprinkling of enchanted fairy dust, like he has given her. Franz is a man who deserves love, just like Andre. She wants that for both of them. She wants… so much. But all the wanting, all the discontent – these things have kept her small over all the years. Now, her wanting has changed shape. For the first time in a very long while, she wants to give.

But what can she do? What on earth could she do?

Andre has a foolish notion – a foolish dream. Something to give back to Franz. A lost thing. At first, she allowed herself to be swept up in it too. Andre was asking questions – pressing Franz for details about his former sweetheart, Anna – as the two of them worked on their projects together. But since Sarah's departure, Andre has regressed, Franz is weighted down by heavy cares, and the dream has burst like a bubble. It, like everything else, has proved impossible.

She stands at the door watching Franz until he disappears into the lift. The boy is curled up on the sofa cradling his iPad like a pillow. The phantom of a sharp word comes into her mouth but she keeps her lips together. None of this is the boy's fault.

Mathilde walks towards the kitchen. She must have a reason to go there even if she cannot recall what it is. The boy will not eat anyway, so it barely—

'I found her.'

His words, spoken in a low voice, stop her.

'What? Who?'

He raises his head and holds out his iPad. 'Here, look.'

Mathilde goes over. She takes the tablet and holds it close to her face, squinting at the small image. A newspaper article dated from the late '90s. A chilly paralysis overtakes her.

Not a newspaper article.

An obituary.

She reads the opening line, struggling to make sense of the English: *Anna Steinbauer was an activist and civil servant. She was instrumental in the reunification of Germany following the fall of the Berlin Wall.*

Mathilde takes a breath. 'Do you know what this means?' She points to the word 'obituary'.

Andre's eyes are as wide as moons. 'It means Anna is dead.'

Mathilde braces herself for a reaction. Andre can't handle television news, or sad books, or anything that reminds him of death. He chooses to stay wrapped in grief – in safety – and Mathilde fears anything that might trigger one of his states. At this moment, however, Andre does not seem bereft. If anything, he looks proud, even a little smug.

'Yes, Andre.' She speaks cautiously. 'If this is the same Anna that Franz knew, then she is dead. Just as he thought.'

'No.' Andre takes back the iPad. 'Not like he thought. She did not die in prison.'

'Well, so what?'

Andre shrugs and points to another line.

She is survived by her husband, Philip, and her daughter, Sofia.

Could Andre be right? Is Franz wrong about the fate of his sweetheart? Did Anna survive prison? Did she go on to have a husband, a daughter – a full and worthwhile life?

And what difference will it make? Mathilde can't answer that question for herself, let alone another person. She'd had those things too. Renée is gone, but Andre is alive. Anna is dead, but her daughter is alive… Sofia.

Franz has not allowed himself to have a full and worthwhile life. It is his own fault – not because of his silence but because of the choices he made afterwards. Anna was lost, and that cannot be changed. But would it help to unite Franz with the truth?

'I'm not sure what to do next,' Andre says. 'How to find Sofia.'

'Have you searched for the two names together?' she

offers. 'I know nothing of your precious internet, but it is a place to start.'

She expects Andre to look dismissive – after all, when it comes to such matters she is a silly old fossil – but, to her surprise, he nods. '*Oui*,' he says. 'You are right. That is a good place to start. And when I find her, we will call her on the phone.'

Mathilde shakes her head as reality sets in. She is an old woman. Anna is long dead.

'Do not get your hopes up,' she says. 'And do not tell Franz – best not to get his hopes up either.'

'I will find her.' Andre crosses his arms. 'You will see.'

55

SARAH

Every step of Sarah's journey felt wrong. Packing her bags, stopping off to say goodbye to Andre and Mathilde, emailing Franz, going to the station, buying a ticket, boarding the train. Leaving behind this beautiful city, and the people she had grown to—

No.

It had all been a dream. A beautiful dream that had touched her heart and mind like sunlight dancing on water. But clouds had stolen the sun. The dream twisted itself into a nightmare.

She had come to Paris to do a job; take the next step on a career path. Now, that was gone. She had come here with no intention of losing her head or her heart, and she had lost those too. Gone; left with nothing. Nothing but an incomplete set of wooden animals, and a whole new catalogue of regrets.

As the train pulled out of the station, Sarah opened the internet browser and the research she'd done. Uncovering the ugly, undeniable truth about a man she thought she'd known. A man she'd never heard of…

Tom Willowfield.

The photos online matched those in the album. A gangly young man with unruly dark hair, a beard, and thick-framed glasses. The scandal was over fifteen years old, but there were still a number of articles detailing the whole sordid tragedy.

Sarah felt sick from the churning emotions in her stomach. The last piece of the jigsaw slotted into place, and suddenly, every moment of her relationship with Tomas made sense. He had duped her – and the entire world. Living a lie, living a false identity. He was one thing on the surface and something else underneath. Tomas Mercier was Tom Willowfield. And Tom Willowfield was…

What exactly?

An article from *The Times* summed it up.

Tom Willowfield, prize-winning author, was part-genius and part-narcissist. Coming from unremarkable beginnings, he had managed to create a masterpiece that had been published to great acclaim when he was only twenty-four. He was lauded as a rising star by the literary world and showered with accolades and attention. He was interviewed for newspapers and magazines and appeared on television talk shows. The boy from Beaconsfield became the toast of London. By day, he played the serious author. By night, however, he embarked upon a rock-and-roll lifestyle. Parties, expensive restaurants, women, alcohol. Gradually the tone of the articles began to change, becoming less about his book and more about his antics. Tom turned up drunk at a television studio, Tom was photographed at a bar the night it was raided for drugs. Tom was caught on video rowing with his girlfriend, a young journalism student at UCL called Jessie Ripon. Finally, less than a year after his book was published, a new headline appeared: '*The Decline and Fall of Tom Willowfield:*

Author's Story Ends in Tragedy'. Following one of their legendary rows, Jessie Ripon was left with life-changing injuries. She blamed Tom Willowfield, painting a picture of him as cruel, arrogant, and corrupt.

Like Icarus flying too close to the sun, Tom Willowfield fell from the sky and spiralled back down to earth. As the world denounced him, Tom Willowfield retreated. He disappeared from the public eye and never wrote another book. Tom Willowfield's star faded into the firmament, as if it had never been.

Some of the articles lamented the self-destruction of a young talent, others lambasted him as a one-hit wonder who didn't deserve success or attention. In more recent years, there were a few posts on social media of the 'Whatever happened to Tom Willowfield?' sort. No comments had been made, the threads closed, the question unanswered.

Tomas Mercier was no longer flying too close to the sun, but underneath the radar. He had no social media presence and his Amazon bio was exceptionally brief: 'Tomas Mercier lives and works in Paris.'

Sarah closed the browser, fighting the urge to throw the phone across the train carriage. Tomas had come up with the perfect disguise. A confirmed bachelor living in a huge, anonymous city. Hiding behind his identity as an 'international man of mystery'. Reluctant to talk about his books – even a bit defensive. Convincing his beautiful blogger friend, Anne-Marie, that he 'didn't do publicity'.

It was the perfect cover.

But who was the man she'd met? Spent time with and got to know? Who was the man she'd allowed in through the cracks in her heart: the man who had curled up inside her and given her back her appreciation of beauty and the possibilities of her life? On one side of the coin was suave and debonair Tomas, with his devil-may-care confidence and easy laughter. But it was the other man, the man who was lonely and vulnerable, that had resonated with her. The man who had worked alongside her at the toyshop, giving his time and attention to help an old man and a vulnerable boy. Each moment flashed before her eyes: the poem in the bar, the kiss by the carousel, the tenderness and reverence with which he'd made love to her. That man had looked inside her and seen something worth saving.

That man was a liar and a fraud.

She leaned back in the seat and closed her eyes. She wanted to sleep; she wanted to forget. Forget the feelings Tomas had awakened in her; forget the shame of losing her job; forget her guilt at leaving Franz, Mathilde, and Andre. She would keep managing the project from afar, and stay in touch by email – she might be heartbroken, but she would not be irresponsible. When the toyshop was finished, she would gradually taper off the connection. A fresh wave of pain engulfed her. She would miss the grand opening that they'd all worked so hard to achieve. She would miss Andre leaving the flat – it was only a matter of time. She would miss… Tomas. Oh God, would she miss him.

She held her breath until the anguish passed. Sleep was not possible. Forgetting was not possible. Luckily, though it stemmed from ill fortune and her own bad choices, there was one thing of paramount importance to occupy her attention: finding a new job. She wrestled her emotions back into their box and opened up her contacts. Komitov was amongst them – if she returned with her tail between her legs would he have her back? Maybe. Did she want that—?

There was no need to decide now. She would explore all the other options, all the possibilities beyond Paris. Choose the next best one.

And eventually, when enough time had passed, she would forget.

56

TOMAS

WEDNESDAY, NOVEMBER 1ST

It was all his own damn fault. Dominoes falling in a cascade of stupid, unforgivable mistakes. Everything he'd tried to create, everything he'd tried to forget, everything he'd tried to become – and *un*become. The foundations had started to erode the moment he'd glimpsed Sarah in the toyshop. And every minute spent with her after that.

Tomas closed his eyes and tried to imprint her on his memory. The sound of her voice, the light in her eyes, the music of her laughter, the softness of her lips, the way she melted into his arms, the way her body responded when he made love to her…

No. He had to stop. This was a one-way trip to despair. He had to forget her – right here, right now.

Luckily, he had Lucinda Clarke. The one constant in his life – the woman who could be whatever he wished. Strong and sexy, cold and distant. Those were the things that Tomas Mercier valued in a woman. And if that idiot Tom kept shaking the bars of his cage – well, he could deal with him too. He'd put him on a starvation diet. No more magical afternoons in Paris, no more meaningful conversations, no more lamenting what might have been. No hope of anything different.

He sat down at his computer intending to get to work. Instead, he opened up Facebook. It was the ultimate reminder, the ultimate torture.

Jessie's Facebook page showcased her charity work helping disabled women reintegrate into the workplace. The header showed her giving a presentation to a group of women from her wheelchair. She was smiling, but the smile didn't reach her eyes. In an instant, he was sucked into a pit of blame and guilt. *You hurt people, Tom.* Words echoing through a vortex of space and time, as if he was hearing them again, right here, right now.

First Jessie, now Sarah. Once again he'd proved them right.

His hands shook as he powered off the laptop. On the black screen, the hazy reflection of Tom took shape. Tom as he'd been back then: straggly hair, heavy glasses, an untidy attempt at a beard. Interviewers had described him as shy and erudite, but with a streak of arrogance underneath. Arrogance – was that what it was? It had felt more like terror and shame.

When his dream came true, he wasn't ready. Overnight, he'd gone from lowly bookstore clerk to the toast of the literary world. People were suddenly interested in him. His face appeared in all the major newspapers, and he was interviewed on breakfast TV. Before, he'd done a lot of his living from his tiny bedsit and his parents' garden shed, experiencing the world through his characters' eyes. The newfound attention was overwhelming, but exciting too. He decided to embrace it and live into his fame.

Jessie Ripon was the daughter of an executive at Tom's publishing house. When Mr Ripon asked Tom if his daughter could interview him for her journalism course, he didn't even think of saying no. They met at a café near her flat in leafy Belsize Park. She was beautiful, intelligent, and clearly a big fan of his work. She flirted and flattered; Tom was instantly charmed, instantly insecure. He bumbled the conversation, hating himself for his awkwardness, and left the interview feeling weak and ashamed. An imposter not only as a writer, but as a man.

When her article came out, however, even he got the hint. Jessie wrote that:

'Tom Willowfield denies that that The Rites of Spring *is in any way autobiographical. But his quiet charisma speaks of hidden secrets and fathomless depths. It's impossible not to wonder whether he has cast himself as the main character, Sam O'Rourke, who goes on a journey of sexual awakening following his brother's death. Who is the nameless siren who seduces Sam at dawn on a desert morning? The dancer Sam meets in a remote mountain village? The virgin/whore from a Texas bar that takes Sam to unimaginable heights of pleasure? Are they fictional, or real? Either way, they are graphically and lovingly imagined in Willowfield's celebrated prose.'*

It was the way she wrote about his book that lit the fire inside him. Clearly she had cast herself in the role of muse, so why not go along with it? When he was invited to a soiree at his publishing house, it was inevitable that she would be there. After a few minutes of awkward small talk, he took her hand and they left the party. They went to a bar and had a few drinks. Went to another party. Eventually, when they returned to her expensive, well-furnished flat, he was too drunk to do anything other than pass out.

Inevitable. So things had seemed at the time. Tom was swept away by a force greater than his own free will. But it was not the power of love, or even lust. Not by a long way.

Then and now, the time seemed hazy and unreal. Instead of a simple love story between two people, theirs had turned complicated and destructive. He moved into her flat and lost himself in her lifestyle. Jessie had rich friends with expensive tastes and the best of everything. They moved in stratospheric circles, congregating in country houses, penthouse flats, private clubs. He was the outsider, Jessie's 'bit of rough'. None of her friends cared about his fame or his craft. He hid his awkwardness by drowning in whisky and vodka.

Pills, cigarettes… most of the time was a blur. Rarely were he and Jessie sober at the same time, but when they were, it was as confusing as when they were off their heads. She would get angry, then fawn over him. They would row, then make love. The cycle repeated. People started to notice. A neighbour heard shouting and threatened to call the police. Jessie laughed it off. A photographer caught them kissing. Rowing. Another party, and another. A missed media interview, a chasing email from his editor. A friendly reminder from his literary agent of the deadline for his next book. How was it coming? Wonderful. He hadn't started. Had no idea where to start. The words had fled, Tom's voice silenced by decadence and destruction.

He had chosen it – created it. Over the years, he'd come to accept that it was no one's fault but his own. He'd been weak. And Jessie – both of them had been so young. It had needed to end, but it shouldn't have ended as it did.

Tomas stood up, pacing back and forth by the window. The lights of Paris that had recently shone so bright dimmed and fragmented before his eyes.

'Get a grip,' he said aloud to his own reflection. He fought the urge to punch the man in the glass. Selfish, arrogant Tom. Unforgivably stupid Tom.

There was only one thing for it. Go back to being Tomas Mercier. Find a distraction: something – or someone – to remind him that he wasn't worthy of love, and any voice inside his head that said otherwise needed to be silenced immediately. Find a bar – find another woman – ten other women. Get over Sarah, move on. He'd spent years curating his new identity. One he lived every day and believed in.

He put on his coat and went out into the gathering twilight. The leaves had turned and the days were growing shorter and darker. The city seemed to be holding its breath, hibernating before the run-up to the holiday season. He walked towards the wine bar, paused at the corner, kept walking. He passed bustling cafés and brightly lit shop windows. He passed the supermarket – he should stop in and get some provisions. Hole up for a few days and settle back into the old routine. Put away his feelings – his desire – for something different. He kept walking.

He passed the bookshop and soon came to the edge of the dark passageway that led to the warren of back streets. He practically tripped over a signboard that read: *La Boutique Fantasque*. Grand reopening – coming soon!

Damn Tom Willowfield – he was disgraced, dead – and yet here he was, at it again, trying to take control. Taking advantage of the turmoil in his mind, directing his feet exactly where they needed to go.

The window at the back of the shop which had been dark for almost three months lit up automatically as Tomas drew closer. There was a brand-new display. A magical dance theatre with ballerinas whirling around, pirouetting on their toes, performing scenes from *The Nutcracker*. Clara was fighting giant mice with her slipper; a Christmas tree expanded and grew taller; a nutcracker directed a troupe of toy soldiers. Snowflake dancers swirled out, and Clara and her prince were whisked away in a magical sleigh. The mechanical toy train trundled on its track laden with sweets, and at the front of the window, dancers whirled in the Land of Sweets: Russian, Chinese, Arabian, the Sugar

Plum Fairy. At regular intervals, a puff of glittery snow drifted over the scene. It was a wonder of mechanical design, artistry, and craftsmanship. It didn't belong to this century, but to an older, more innocent time.

He went to the door and waited for Franz to buzz him in. The shop was a construction site, but he was glad to see progress. New shelves and display cabinets had been installed and dustsheets were spread everywhere. The ceiling was freshly painted with a mural of clouds and stars, and the walls had become an enchanted forest of trees and animals.

He should be happy for Franz – he *was* happy for him. But the care, dedication, and love that had gone into the work made him ache for Sarah all the more. She had lost her job to make it possible, and how had she been repaid? He recalled the night they had painted the workshop together, the white heart on her cheek. A moment lost forever. *She* was lost forever.

'Tomas?'

Tomas slumped against the archway. When he looked up, Franz's face was a mask of misery.

'She is gone,' Franz said.

'Yes.'

'It is a strange thing,' Franz said, glancing around them. 'For years I have been on my own. I had my big dreams and small ones, and I never believed that I could achieve any of them. But recently, I had been learning to believe. And what's more, I am no longer on my own. I have made promises. To Mathilde, to Andre. To my landlord. To the bank.' He shook his head. 'I don't know if I can keep those promises.'

'You will.' Tomas tried to muster some conviction. 'Just keep moving forward. One step at a time. In the end, it's all down to you.'

'No, my friend.' Franz's eyes flashed with an anger Tomas had not seen before. 'I think it is down to you.'

Tomas sighed. Once again he'd acted selfishly, without stopping to consider how his actions might affect others. Vulnerable others – like Franz, Mathilde, and Andre.

'I didn't tell her to go away,' he said. 'I didn't want that.'

'No,' Franz said. 'I am sure you did not. Still, I am feeling much guilt over Sarah losing her job to help me. I assumed that was why she left, but Mathilde says otherwise. So I am asking you to tell me what happened between you to cause this. We are friends, you and I – are we not? I am only a toymaker, but I am good at fixing things that are broken.'

'You can't fix this. It's beyond repair.'

'Maybe. But I think I deserve to know.'

Tomas stared at his friend's face. Franz looked tired and haggard – the project must be taking its toll. 'How long have you been working?' he asked Franz.

'All day, of course. There is so much to do.'

'And when's the last time you ate something?'

Franz shrugged. 'I may be good with clockwork, but I do not keep track of such things.'

'Why don't we go out and get a bite to eat? At that pizzeria you like?'

'And then?' Franz raised a bushy eyebrow.

'And then you'd better order a very large beer. It's kind of a long story.'

57

FRANZ

The beer was cold and bitter. Much like the story Tomas had begun to weave. Franz believed in the power of stories, but he was not sure he wanted to hear this one. Like all stories, it began with once upon a time. It began with a man who had been on top of the world. A man living his dream… until the dream became a nightmare.

'I was young, stupid, and insecure,' Tomas said. 'I took it all for granted.'

Franz could understand all of those things. In his youth, he had hurt people over and over and got away with it. But for Tomas, a single incident had resulted in him losing everything. He'd run away from his own life and become another person – the person that Franz knew. As Tomas recounted the ugly events, Franz stared into his glass. He did not wish to stay silent, and yet no words came. He did not wish to judge, and yet… how could he not?

'I can still remember her lying there, bleeding. Voices around me, the flashing lights of the police cars and ambulance. I wanted to rewind the clock – turn back time and do things differently. But it was too late for that.'

He pushed his beer away. 'I wanted to face up to things – really, I did. But the media was relentless. She was rich and beautiful. I was newly famous and living a ridiculous lifestyle. The "decline and fall" of Tom Willowfield was temporarily interesting.

'But none of that mattered – not really. When I tried to visit her in hospital, they told me she might never walk again. She told me she never wanted to see me again – and who could blame her? *You hurt people* – that's what she said. How could I ever put things right?'

Franz had no answer.

'The whole thing pushed me into a deep depression. Before Jessie, my writing was everything. Afterwards, it all seemed pointless. I didn't deliver my second book, and the publisher cancelled my contract. The man who could "paint pictures with words" was gone. In the end, I could only see one way forward. Tom Willowfield had to disappear.'

Franz felt unaccountably sad. He knew all too well what it felt like to leave one's life's work unfinished. He, however, was trying to make amends. That was the difference between them.

'I moved to Paris where no one would recognise me. I changed my name and got a job at a bookstore – my life gone full circle. At night, I tried crime writing. I felt like a criminal, so who better to have a go? It's just genre drivel – but it pays the bills.' He sighed. 'So in the end, things turned out all right – for me, at least. I was happy enough. Happy that Tom Willowfield is dead.'

'But are you really?' Franz finally found his voice. 'Don't you want to go back to being who you really are?'

'I didn't mean to hurt Sarah. That's why I tried to keep

my distance. I failed at that too. The moment came and went to tell her the truth – many moments, in fact. In the end, Tomas Mercier wasn't brave enough. I'm him now, through and through. I don't deserve to be anyone else.'

'Then I am sorry, my friend,' Franz said quietly. The words were empty to the point of being insulting. But they were all he had to offer.

'I'm sorry too.'

58

SARAH

MONDAY, NOVEMBER 6TH

Sarah sat on the sofa with a large globe of wine. Her mum was out at her book club, and she had the house to herself. Her hands shook as she turned the pages of the book on her lap. *The Rites of Spring*. They were right about it, all those critics who had written glowing reviews; every reader who'd been touched by the words, the images, the feelings. Shimmering and ephemeral, like light on water. Leaving no mark on the surface but a deep impression on the soul.

She'd found the book at the village bookshop. Since arriving at her mum's house, she'd gone out only twice: once to take the dog for a walk and once to buy a pint of milk and go to the bookshop. Each time she'd had to consciously remind herself how to breathe as panic gripped her body. At home, she kept mainly to her room, only vaguely aware of how she spent her days. Thinking, grieving, occasionally putting out feelers for jobs. Her mum was worried. Sarah just felt numb.

The novel's cover was very simple: a pale, faded-blue sea meeting a watercolour sky and the silhouette of a boy on a beach. In the left corner there was a printed sticker – 'Winner of the Curtis P. Whitney Prize for Literature.' Inside the cover was a list of quotes from top newspapers and authors. At the time of its publication, it had created a perfect storm in the literary world. Just like its author had done in her life.

The bookseller had approved of her choice. 'That's one of my all-time favourites,' he'd said, when she'd brought the book to the till. 'It's a brilliant novel – the main character is like a modern-day Odysseus. Such a shame that Tom Willowfield never wrote another book.'

'Is it really? I mean, he sounds like a complete fraud. A bad person.'

The bookseller shrugged. 'Maybe, maybe not. They say that artists live in a different moral universe to the rest of us. But in my view, it's still a great book.'

'I'll keep that in mind.'

She had tried to do it. From the first page, she'd been transported. The premise was simple: a teenage boy walks into the sea and drowns, leaving his older brother, Sam, behind. Sam then spends the next seven years on a quest to find meaning in this one act. He leaves behind his family and friends and goes off to see the world that his brother would never experience. He encounters many people along the way, some good, some bad. All written with an unfathomable depth of human understanding as Sam, now a man, tries to make sense of the beauty and pain of a world that was too much for his brother to bear.

The boy who walked into the sea had synaesthesia, which meant that he experienced the colours as sounds, and the sounds as colours. He reminded Sarah a little of Andre. The boy's story was told in reverse, from the moment of his death, going backwards to his halcyon childhood days.

Sarah had the distinct feeling that the book had been written quickly, like a painting done with swift brush strokes, giving the impression of a scene but allowing the viewer – or in this case, the reader – to fill in the details. '*Magical, heart-breaking, and an important insight into the human spirit,*' one reviewer had said. Had Sarah picked it up at a bookshop without knowing more, she would have agreed wholeheartedly. If she'd read the book without ever having heard of the author, she would have felt a deep admiration, a reverence, almost. She would have put it up there amongst the best books she'd ever read.

But in her view, the bookseller was wrong. It *did* matter who wrote the book. All that beauty and wonder – it seemed a lie.

She drank the wine down quickly. Tomorrow she'd take the book to the charity shop. Stop wallowing and get on with her life. Make another new start. Find a way to be happy again.

Already, she had a few leads on potential projects in London. And as she'd walked past the empty shops on the village high street, the idea of helping struggling shopkeepers restore their livelihoods had occurred to her again. If she couldn't be happy herself, maybe she could still make a difference to real people.

She looked up at the photo collage of Rowan as a baby on the wall opposite the sofa. God – she'd trusted Tomas. Told him things she'd never told anyone else. And how did he return the favour? With lies and deceit. She'd allowed herself to be swayed by his silver words and golden touch. She'd allowed him to change her and her feelings about Rowan. The loss that had been everything for so many years had now shifted and changed shape. The sharpness was gone. In its place was a dull ache and the sting of betrayal. In opening herself up to the possibility of feeling again, she'd exchanged an old pain for a new one.

How could she have been so stupid and gullible?

'I'm sorry,' she said aloud to Rowan's photo. 'I've let you down again.'

The silence was overwhelming.

59

FRANZ

WEDNESDAY, NOVEMBER 15TH

The days were shortening; the city was preparing for a glittering festive season. Despite the shiny lights and sparkling decorations in the streets, a permanent twilight had taken up residence in Franz's soul. Now, more than ever, he longed to be connected to people.

He could not remember ever feeling more alone.

Standing on his own two feet was hard – harder even than he'd imagined. Without Sarah's calming presence, progress on the shop had slowed drastically. The workmen had questions he couldn't answer. They needed more time; they wanted more money. Rouveau came around much too often and when Franz let it slip that Sarah had left Paris, his face screwed into its signature frown.

'Ah, so the snake in the grass has bitten you too.'

'That is not true,' Franz said.

'Nonetheless, she has deserted you in your hour of need. How will you finish on your own?' Rouveau voiced the question that Franz had tried to banish from his mind.

'I will manage.' He turned away. Since Sarah's departure, Andre had regressed, and Mathilde needed him more than ever. But instead of being there for her, he was spending every waking hour at the shop. He was doing it for Andre, he reminded himself. The thought kept him going – but only just.

'I hope you do,' Rouveau said. 'The investment consortium is still interested in my premises. I must make a decision very soon.'

'What decision?' Anger replaced sadness; Franz stared his landlord down. 'We have an agreement.'

'Yes…' Rouveau held up a hand, 'we do. And if you honour your side, I will honour mine. But consider carefully Monsieur Himmelberg. It may not be too late to include your premises in my development. I can still offer you a lifeline. I suggest you take it.'

'You know I do not want it.'

Rouveau's frown softened a little. 'Frankly, I did not think you had it in you to get this far. I spoke to my son. He remembers this place well. When the divorce is final, he will have part-time custody of his boy. Perhaps one day he too can come here.'

'You have a grandson?' Franz considered his nemesis in this new light.

'His name is Marc.'

'You must bring him – to the grand reopening of *La Boutique Fantasque*.'

Rouveau laughed. 'Perhaps I will, if you continue to prove me wrong.'

'I will prove you wrong.'

'Good luck,' Rouveau said, as he turned to leave. 'For I think you are still going to need it. Though I suppose it is always darkest before the dawn.'

That was a cliché, Franz knew. But he'd been living in darkness for so many years… He deserved his dawn.

He was his own last chance. He had to make it happen.

With new resolve, Franz put all of his energy into ticking off items that Sarah had left – ordering Christmas decorations, replenishing shelves, putting the finishing touches to his castle and his *pièce de résistance* – the dragon that would swoop down from the fly space high up in the theatre to delight children at the top of the castle. Slowly, as the end of November approached, he began to make progress again. But the excitement was gone, his enthusiasm smothered by the sense of abandonment. He wished he could blame Sarah – be angry at her for leaving. But how could he be angry when she had lost so much as a result of trying to help him? When he understood all too well why she had left?

Franz had turned Tomas's story over and over in his mind, sideways and every which way. The story explained a lot – it fact, it explained everything he knew about Tomas – still, it made no sense.

Now, as Franz made his way up the lift to visit Andre and Mathilde, he thought again of his friend only metres away, closeted in his own flat across the hall. Franz was tempted to knock on the door. Voice his opinion of the things Tomas should have done at the time and should now be doing differently. Tomas had once asked him a question – Franz wanted to turn it back on him: *How long are you going to punish yourself?* As he knocked on Mathilde's door, he let out a long sigh. He knew the answer only too well.

When the door opened, he felt a rush of warmth. 'Hello Mathilde,' he said. 'I hope this is not a bad time.'

For a second, she looked at him blankly, as if she'd forgotten who he was. His spirits sank – she looked so tired and worn out. She blinked hard, as if waking from an unpleasant dream.

'Andre had another bad night,' she said. 'He will be happy to see you.'

She stood aside and Franz came inside the flat. He set down the heavy bag he was carrying with the pieces of a doll's house to assemble.

'Can I make you a cup of tea?' he said. 'Or I could go out and bring you some pastries? Anything you like.'

'Anything I like?' Her laugh was brittle. 'Can you make Andre forget Sarah? I had hoped that time would help, but it has not. And Tomas too is making himself scarce. He says he is working – or trying to. But whatever he is doing, it has been difficult.' Her thin shoulders drooped. 'I know he is just a friend, and I should have no expectations. It is wrong for me to rely on Sarah or Tomas, or… you.'

'But you must rely on me, Mathilde. The shop, the project – it is all for you and Andre.'

'I know,' she said. 'But you are always busy. And I…I have not been feeling myself lately.'

'Oh Mathilde! I am sorry—' he began to say, but she raised her hand.

'Do not be sorry. Please, Franz. I am so tired of people who are sorry.'

'Mathilde?' He was taken aback by her eyes – darkening like a stormy sky, flashing with sudden anger.

With a sigh, she lowered her hand. 'I am tired of myself and this life. Tired of being in this flat. I too have suffered a loss – my daughter, my Renée. Every day the grief cuts me. Knowing that I will never see her face or hear her voice again. I love Andre – of course I do. But when I look at him, I see her eyes. Sometimes… it is all too much.'

Franz had the strong urge to take her in his arms.

Engulf her in love and care for her like a fragile bird with a broken wing. But then it struck him – she was not a fragile creature to be kept in a cage. She was a strong woman who'd got on with her life even in the wake of her own grief. Perhaps she was stronger than any of them, and they should all learn from her example. There was only one thing for it – one gift he could give her beyond all others.

'I will look after Andre,' he said. 'I have a project for us to work on. Go out, Mathilde. Go shopping, go to a park, a gallery, the cinema. Whatever you would like to do. Take this time and be free.'

She looked at him, her eyes as big as oceans beneath long lashes.

'Are you sure?' she said.

'Yes.'

'Then I will do it. Thank you.' She took a breath. 'You are a good man, Franz. Better than you know.'

'I would not pretend to be that,' he said. 'I am just a man who has made many mistakes that I wish to put right. And maybe I am making more mistakes along the way, but I want to put those right too.'

'That is more than most people have the courage to do.'

He brought his things to the kitchen table as Mathilde put on her hat and coat, draping a shopping bag over her arm. She went to tell Andre she was going out, and a moment later, the boy came bounding out of his bedroom and rushed towards him. Franz smiled and opened his arms.

60

TOMAS

FRIDAY, NOVEMBER 24TH

It hadn't worked. Telling his story to Franz, looking for the catharsis that others seemed to experience from unburdening themselves of their past and their mistakes. Sarah was still gone. He missed her.

Working hadn't improved things either – not that he'd done much. He had a looming deadline: a manuscript to deliver, a publication date – he couldn't afford to screw up now. Yet he'd spent most of his time pacing and brooding. Nothing had changed in all the years since he'd become Tomas Mercier. He was still a hack, still an imposter. Sarah was still gone. He still missed her.

Tonight, he decided to try a different tactic to forget Sarah. One that surely couldn't fail. This was Paris – *his* Paris. A city full of distractions and adventures, and Tomas Mercier was surely the man to find them. As he sat at the candlelit table in the bar and the red-haired woman suggested that they finish the bottle of wine up in her room, he felt nothing other than a sick revulsion. This was wrong – all wrong. He'd expected to feel physical desire, some sort of anticipation – or failing that, nothing at all.

Instead, something unexpected began to rise up inside him: panic and shame.

'That sounds nice,' he said. 'But let's have another glass here.'

The woman's eyes flickered with doubt. She was probably beginning to wonder if he was stringing her along. Maybe he should suggest a romantic date up the Eiffel Tower – so he could throw himself off.

Or, he could text Sarah. Reach out to her. Try to explain the unexplainable, justify the unjustifiable. The idea was ludicrous as well as pointless. He flagged down a waiter and paid the bill. 'Actually, you have the rest,' he said, standing up. 'I find that white wine gives me a headache.'

He left the woman sitting there looking dumbfounded. It was probably the first time she'd been rejected. He hated himself as he walked out of the bar. Hated Tom Willowfield and Tomas Mercier; hated the whole damn world. All he wanted to do right now was turn back the clock. Three months would do it – to the time before he'd met Sarah. He would give anything to be indifferent again, anything to be numb.

He imagined bringing the woman from the bar back to meet Andre. Andre would be equally enchanted with anyone: fat, slim, old, young, ugly, supermodel. He'd ask Tomas if the woman was his girlfriend and if he was going to sleep with her. Tomas would say that a gentleman didn't ask questions like that. Then, he'd be bright enough to take whoever it was across the hall and make it happen.

The twilight sky was streaked with pink and orange. He wandered through the streets, taking the long way home. Most of the shops had already dressed their windows for the holiday season, and in his current mood, the sparkle of lights and glittery things hurt his eyes. The weather had turned cold, but even so, the streets were crowded with families, couples, people in cafés – talking, laughing. Living for the moment, getting on with their lives. A sudden kamikaze idea struck him. What if he contacted Jessie? He could message her through her charity or on Facebook – surely, that sort of thing was possible. Was there anything to say after all these years to make things better? Anything beyond 'I'm sorry'?

He clenched his fists, angry at his own stupidity. 'Sorry' was completely pointless under the circumstances. Jessie had suffered because of him, and Sarah had too. There could be no closure for the people he'd hurt, so none for him either.

Closure. As he was about to cross the river, Tomas remembered another task he'd left unfinished. He took a detour, winding his way through a maze of side streets on the Right Bank. He knew vaguely where he was heading, but he took a few wrong turns before finally locating Rue d'Austerlitz. There were no lights or decorated shop windows here. The street might have been nice enough thirty years ago, but now the cheap hotels and apartment buildings were run-down and unloved.

Perhaps he and Sarah would have come here together if events had taken a different turn. His chest tightened as he imagined once again the ghost of her laughter, the feel of her skin, the taste of her mouth. What if he emailed her? Tried to explain. Tell her he was sorry – for his lies, for everything. Ask her if she might be able to find some way to—

No and no. He'd lied his way into her life and heart. Even if Sarah made the conscious decision to trust him, there would always be a kernel of doubt in her mind about what kind of man he was – because what kind of man was he? A fraud? A coward? She'd been through too much to inflict that on her.

He reached the building where Mathilde had once lived. A rough sleeper was camped on the steps in a dirty sleeping bag, a dog tethered to the railing. 'Can you spare some change?' the man asked. In the cold air of early evening, his breath came out in a thin white puff.

Tomas shook his head and went to the door. The names were worn off the buzzers, but he pressed all the buttons until an annoyed-sounding woman responded.

'Is there an attic in this building?' he said through the speaker. 'I'm looking for a box.'

The woman let him have it in a loud torrent: how dare he disturb her, of course there was no attic. No box. Nothing.

Tomas sighed. He'd failed at so much – what was one more thing?

The heavy weight that never left him felt even more unendurable as he apologised to the woman and returned to the street.

The rough sleeper eyed him through a curtain of unwashed hair. 'Maybe there's a cellar,' he said.

Tomas shook his head. He dug in his pocket and gave the man all the coins he had plus his last twenty euro note. As if that would somehow atone for all of his acts and omissions.

'Have a nice life,' the sleeper said.

'You too.'

With a deep sigh, Tomas turned and walked towards home.

61

MATHILDE

For a few precious hours, she is free. Free to wander around the city, go to the shops, sit in the park. Whatever she wants. So what shall she do? What does she want?

Mathilde takes the Métro to Tuileries and walks to Place Vendôme. The central space has been transformed into a winter wonderland of fir trees, each one flocked with snow and decorated with icicle lights that flash from blue to pink, to green, to white, with spotlights projecting the colours onto nearby buildings.

Even after many years, she feels a thrill as she approaches the colonnade of shops, windows lit up, the jewellery and luxury goods elegant, beautiful, and expensive. For a brief time she came close to inhabiting this world. While Jean-Louis worked at the shoe store, she had a glimpse of luxury, even though their flat was poky and noisy. When his mother died and he'd inherited the current flat and a sum of money, it seemed like a godsend. Mathilde's life was on the rise. But soon afterwards, things began to go wrong. Jean-Louis got sick. Renée got pregnant and struggled to support herself and the child. Eventually, she succumbed to the same illness as her father. Mathilde hung onto the tattered threads of her life by her fingernails. To this day, she is still barely hanging on.

The shops are different. The shoe shop has long ago become a boutique selling expensive handbags and watches to tourists. Mathilde waits for the ache as she passes the window where the shoes once sparkled from their plinth. Longing, want, regret. She waits and waits. The ache comes, but not in the way she expects. What are Franz and Andre getting up to? A clever man, a clever boy – and somehow, against the odds, she is central to both of them.

Mathilde turns away from the shop and walks back to the Métro. She'll pick up a few things at the grocery store, and then, go home…

Where she already has everything she needs.

62

FRANZ

Franz watched the boy gluing wooden tiles onto the roof of the doll's house. Painstaking, accurate. It made him aware of how shaky his hands had become. It had gone faster than if he'd done it alone, though it would have helped to have been in the workshop with his tools. The workmen, however, had implied that he was getting underfoot. It had seemed best just to leave them to it.

As he and Andre worked, he wondered about Mathilde. Had she taken his suggestion and done something for herself? Or, like him, was she too long out of the habit? He dreamed of her breaking free – rediscovering the great city of Paris and all the things it had to offer. He could take her to the opera or the ballet; she used to be a dancer – surely she would love that. They could go to museums and galleries, all the places Tomas talked about. In the early days, Franz had tried to go alone to such places but found them crowded and bewildering. But with Mathilde, anything seemed possible. His mood shifted from dark to light and back again, like clouds passing in front of the sun. Possibilities, yes, but what if she did not feel the same?

Working with Andre was calming. Franz spoke quietly, explaining everything. He showed Andre how to sand the wood and slot the pieces into place, making a perfect fit. Even without a diagram, Andre seemed to know intuitively how to construct the little house. Time marched forward like a well-wound clock, and in those magic hours, Franz forgot his troubles and loneliness. They were still working when Mathilde returned, her cheeks flushed, her arms laden with bags of groceries – once again she had looked after others rather than herself. Franz left Andre to the gluing and helped her unload the groceries.

'I am sorry for the mess,' he said.

To his relief, Mathilde smiled. 'It is a gift you have given me…' she said.

Franz felt a burst of colour and light inside his heart.

'… Free babysitting.'

His elation dipped.

'I understand, Mathilde,' he said. 'For a long time, I have made myself a prisoner in my shop. But now…' He had to know. 'Since meeting you, I have wanted to change. I have wanted something different – something more. Please tell me if I am wrong in this.'

She did not answer for a long moment. Instead of putting away the milk and eggs, she opened a drawer and took out a folded piece of paper. She did not look at it, but turned it over in her hands. Franz could not tell what she was thinking. She put the letter in the pocket of her dress and turned to face him.

'You are not wrong,' she said. 'And I am sorry for how I spoke earlier. Do not think me ungrateful or discontented. It's just that sometimes…' she trailed off, looking momentarily confused. 'Things seem very hard.'

'I understand.' Franz's pulse was racing. He couldn't process the words or his feelings. 'And you must rely on me to help you. I am happy to stay with Andre. I think our time together has been very positive. For him and for me. If you wish to go out alone, if you wish for… free babysitting… then that is fine too.'

She looked mildly amused. 'When your shop is finished, I am hopeful that Andre will be able to babysit you.'

'That would be nice.'

'It is strange to think of the paths our lives take,' she said. 'Had your friend Anna lived, then perhaps you would have been married with children. Perhaps you never would have come to Paris. It would have been a very different life, no?'

The flash of pain momentarily blindsided him.

'Yes,' he managed.

'And if my daughter had lived, I would be an old woman alone in the flat – perhaps with a cat or a bird for company. My life would be over. Instead…'

'Instead?' he whispered.

The moment shimmered between them.

'We cannot change the past,' she said. 'But maybe… I don't know.'

He looked deeply into her eyes. And in that instant, he did know – everything was so clear. He could change the future – their future. He reached out and brushed a strand of hair back from her cheek. Her skin was faintly lined, but soft and warm. Electricity tingled between them, like a child's experiment with making a circuit.

Her eyes lowered, and he dropped his hand. He wanted so badly to kiss her—

'Monsieur Franz – I need help.'

He turned away and went over to the table where Andre was struggling to get the last of the glue out of the tube.

'I think we will have to finish another day,' Franz said. 'It is time to clean up. When my workshop is finished and you come there, I can show you how to use all my tools. The work is progressing well. It will be finished very soon.'

It was a gamble, just like reaching out to Mathilde had been. Franz judged Andre's reaction. The boy had been excited and energetic all day, speaking in garbled, rapid French that Franz had had difficulty understanding. Now, Andre's excitement had given way to frustration. He voiced the question in the back of all their minds.

'When is Sarah coming back?'

Franz shook his head. 'I don't know.'

Andre crossed his arms in defiance, but Franz sensed the boy's doubt and worry. Without Sarah, the circle of their lives felt incomplete.

'And Tomas?'

Franz sighed. 'If I could wave a magic wand, Andre, I would bring Sarah back again – and Tomas. We could all go out into the world together.' He glanced at Mathilde. 'Think of the things we could do. Go to the top of the Eiffel Tower – an amazing feat of engineering. Or the Pompidou Centre – a great modern building. We could see the Rodin sculptures, and take a *bateau mouche* on the river. We could do it together. If only we can take the first step. Do you see?'

But he'd gone too far. Andre was shaking his head – the haunted, frightened look was back on his face. Mathilde came over and rested a hand on Andre's shoulder. 'I think the boy is tired.'

Franz took the hint. 'I will leave now,' he said. 'Thank

you for the expert help.' He smiled at Andre and began packing up his things. 'Can I leave the doll's house here so that the glue can dry?'

'Of course.' Mathilde seemed eager for him to go. His stomach tightened into a knot. This feeling – this being in love – was such hard work!

He finished tidying up the workspace. It would be so much easier if Andre came to his workshop. He had his own reasons for wishing that Sarah was still here, but most of all, she'd been the one who was helping Andre with his anxiety. It was like that old myth about Sisyphus: Sarah was the lever helping them push the rock up the mountain. Now that she was gone, everything was in freefall.

On his way out, he patted Andre's arm. 'Great job today,' he said. 'You have the knack for making things. When I come back, we can paint it together if you like.'

Andre nodded almost violently. '*Oui, oui*. I want to.'

Franz picked up his cane and walked to the door. Mathilde followed him. There was so much he wanted to say! But cowardice won out. It was easiest to leave things as they were. Resume his own path: let his clockwork heart tick down, beat by beat, until the end.

As he reached the corridor, Mathilde grabbed his arm. 'Franz,' she said. *Brave, strong*. In an instant, she was in his arms. He held her small, delicate body against his and breathed her in, wanting never to let her go. Feelings he'd stifled since he was a young man now rushed to the surface. As she lifted her face, he closed his eyes and followed her lead as she parted his lips, kissing him deeply. He ran his rough fingers down the velvet skin of her face. Every cell of his body was bursting with life.

'This will never work,' Mathilde said, breathless as they came apart. 'We are much too old to be acting like teenagers.'

'You are absolutely right.' Franz bent down and kissed her again with all his being, all his soul. Even though their lips were locked together, he could sense that she was smiling, just like he was.

63

TOMAS

It was ludicrous. Tomas was out of breath as he climbed the stairs to his flat. Was this what it felt like to get old? To come home to nothing and no one?

Well, not quite no one. Maybe tonight he'd have a date with Lucinda Clarke. He had to stop feeling sorry for himself, knuckle down, and work harder.

Maybe that was the cause of his catastrophic failure with the woman at the bar. Maybe he was being faithful, not to Sarah, whom he had known for only a short time, but to Lucinda, whom he'd been involved with for years. Lucinda Clarke had no hang-ups about physical intimacy, be it with another agent, a clandestine criminal, or just an ordinary bloke like the ill-fated Dr Clint. Until now, she'd never had any actual feelings about her encounters other than whether the sex was good or bad or her partner ended up trying to kill her or not. In all the years he'd written her, she'd never had a long-term relationship. Writing Lucinda was like looking in a mirror. Maybe this maelstrom of negative emotions meant that he was finally on the edge of a breakthrough. The idea was so laughable that he felt like crying.

As he reached the top floor, he was greeted by a strange scene down the corridor, like an old-time photograph of a couple kissing. A couple *was* kissing. The light flickered, and for a split second, he thought they were kids. But then, he realised who it was.

'Christ,' he muttered.

Mathilde pulled abruptly away from Franz, her cheeks flushed.

'Don't mind me,' Tomas said.

'Tomas.' Franz was breathing hard. 'I'm sorry. Andre, you see…'

'No, old chap, I don't see Andre,' Tomas said. 'And if I can just get to my flat, I'll leave you two in peace.'

'*Mon Dieu*,' Mathilde said. 'I am too old for this.' She smiled at Franz, her eyes shiny.

'No, I don't think so.' Tomas paused for a second. 'In fact, why don't I stay with Andre? You two go out, have dinner. See a show. Or… get a room.'

'Oh, no, Tomas.' Mathilde looked shocked. 'We could not.'

'Well, suit yourself. Sort out what you want to do and let me know.'

Tomas went inside his flat, his heart thudding. Not from seeing two old friends in the first blooms of love, but from his own anguish. Sarah. God damn it. He took out his phone. He would text her – right away. But what on earth could he possibly say?

64

FRANZ

'Mathilde,' Franz whispered, as soon as Tomas was gone. Had he lost her? That frightened, distant look was back in her eyes. But he couldn't lose her, wouldn't. He wrapped her in his arms. She seemed to weigh nothing. Made of the purest light.

'It must be so difficult for you.' He stroked her hair. 'Coping for so long on your own. I can see how much you love the boy. But maybe, in doing so, you have lost yourself. You forget that you too are important. That you are the brave and courageous one.'

She shuddered in his arms but didn't pull away.

'I would like to help you, Matilde, with Andre. I would like to be part of your life. I know we are not teenagers, to say such things lightly. But I can't help the way I feel. My whole life has been leading up to this.' His voice broke under the tide of emotion. 'Please give me a chance, Mathilde. Please, say there is hope.'

Her thin frame began to shake. She was crying – he had made her cry! But could not tears be a good thing at times? Cleansing, purifying. Unlocking the door to feelings kept hidden away for so long?

She pulled away and reached up to touch his face, tracing the line of his cheek.

'You are a good man, Franz Himmelberg.' Her sad smile was like the sun breaking through a cloud. 'I don't want to take away your hope. So, if Tomas is serious about his offer to stay with Andre, then what shall we do?'

Franz lifted her. Whirled her around. She laughed and kissed him. In the blink of an eye, he was young again, and she was as light as a butterfly's wing.

'I think, Mathilde,' he said, 'that you should get your coat.'

65

TOMAS

Sarah, I'm so sorry I lied. Can we please talk? T

It was all wrong. He deleted the words from the screen.

Sarah – Please don't hate me. I didn't mean to lie to you. It's just… complicated.

Delete.

Tomas leaned against the kitchen worktop. It was a good thing he no longer had a reputation as a famous – or even a good – writer, because he couldn't draft a simple text message.

He tried to stop thinking. Let the words come from the heart. He'd written most of *The Rites of Spring* without thinking. Allowing the words, the images, the emotions to flow out onto the page. In those days, the physical act of writing had been almost hypnotic. The book had a child-like quality, because back then, he hadn't yet grown up. Dreaming was easy when success was remote. But its arrival had changed him for the worst. Instead of expanding his life, he allowed it to make him feel unworthy and small. He'd been so eager for acceptance by others that he'd lost the core of his identity and self-respect. Without that, he was doomed to be alone.

Outside the flat, voices came from the corridor. Franz and Mathilde. At least he could do something kind for these two people who deserved happiness.

He tried one more time to type a text message:

> *Sarah, I'm thinking of you. I am so sorry about everything. I'd like to explain. Are you coming to Paris again? Can we talk?*

Without even reading the words, he pressed send. It was done. Tomas gathered a few things to take over to Andre's. When he left the flat, Mathilde and Franz were holding hands, their faces bright and youthful. He was on the outside of a bubble that held just the two of them.

'Have fun.' Tomas forced a smile.

Franz grinned like a happy cherub. 'You are a good man, Tomas, whatever you may think of yourself.'

'Thank you, Tomas.' Mathilde patted his cheek. 'We will not be too late.' She shot Franz a stern glance.

'Stay out as long as you like,' Tomas said. 'Stay out all night. I can sleep on the sofa in your flat.'

'I do not stay out all night on a first date.' She gave Franz a teasing little glance. 'I am not that kind of girl.'

Tomas groaned. 'Then should I tell you to be back by midnight? Or you'll turn into a pumpkin?'

'Yes,' Mathilde said. 'It is like being young again.'

'But let us not waste another moment.' Franz offered his arm and Mathilde took it. The bubble closed around them again as they walked together to the lift.

As Tomas was about to enter Mathilde's flat, his phone

buzzed in his pocket. A text message. His hands jittered as he took out the phone and read the words.

You're a liar and a fraud. Don't contact me again. Sarah.

66

SARAH

When his text came in, her body betrayed her. Primeval desire surged to the fore. She remembered every moment they'd spent together: every word, every kiss, every shared laugh, every touch. But reality descended like the blade of a guillotine. She'd been taken in by Tomas's handsome face, practised words, manufactured empathy, and undernote of vulnerability that didn't exist.

Liar, fraud. God, what an easy mark she'd been. Why did she always choose the wrong sort of men? She'd had a good childhood and been raised by loving parents. Before her marriage, Sarah had been happy and confident. She'd always looked for the best in people.

She wouldn't be making that mistake again.

So why, when the text swooshed off into cyberspace, did she feel so empty and alone? Was she doing the wrong thing? No. The man she'd fallen for was not real – he was a chimera, a charlatan.

She gazed at the photo of Rowan by her bedside. Her

baby daughter was like a beautiful rose that pricked her heart and made her bleed every time she looked at the photo. She'd set up the animals in a circle on the bureau – a further reminder of her never-ending guilt – leaving a little space for the giraffe. Stupidly, she still held out some hope that it would be found. The set of memories would be complete.

She closed her eyes waiting for the familiar grief to pass. Grief for Rowan, grief for the loss of her new friends in Paris. Andre, Franz, Mathilde. She hadn't known them long, and yet each had resonated with a part of her. Each had been instrumental in helping her begin to heal. And vice versa, she hoped. And the little toyshop, with its particular quirky magic – she had lost that too.

What could she do to fill the space? Surely, she could meet other people – even find a lover – who was more than a liar. In the meantime, maybe now was a good time to reconnect with old friends. Did she have any? Why didn't she know?

Steeling herself, she opened up Facebook. She hadn't been on it since well before Rowan's death. She winced at her profile photo taken just after her marriage. She looked fun and happy – a woman with a great life ahead of her. Would she use it to create something brilliant? Or not… the clockwork of fate certainly was cruel.

She clicked on the search button and found Jessie's charity page. She was a beautiful woman with dark hair and liquid eyes. Sarah scrolled through the photos, trying to get a sense of the woman. Unlike Tom Willowfield, she had clearly faced up to her ordeal and made something of her life. How did the saying go? 'That which does not destroy me makes me stronger'?

Sarah sat back in her chair. What was Jessie's secret for

creating a good life from the seeds of adversity? Was it as simple as not allowing the past to define her?

There was no reason to waste another thought on Tomas. A distraction – that was what she needed to break the spell he'd woven around her. She was still young, still attractive. She *would* go out and meet someone else. Surely, that was what a man would do – what Tomas himself would do. Something Lucinda Clarke would do. Sarah recalled Komitov's laughable assumption that she was Tomas's inspiration for his cold, fantasy woman. For tonight, at least, Sarah wanted to be her.

With a thrilling sense of recklessness, she went to her room and chose a dress: black, low-cut, and form-fitting, and a pair of black patent shoes with sharp stiletto heels. When she finished her hair and make-up, the woman in the mirror was barely recognisable. A woman that men would want. That *he* would want.

Liar. Fraud. She had to break the pattern. She told her mum that she was going out and called for an Uber. Ten minutes later, the car was at her doorstep. She got the train into London and another taxi from the station, directing the driver to drop her at Leicester Square. The thousands of sparkling Christmas lights strung between lampposts and across the city streets blurred before her eyes, as rain streaked down the window like tears.

What was she planning to do? Wander around bars in Soho until she found a man? Go to his place and have sex? She'd never found it easy to meet men casually. In fact, she couldn't remember ever picking up a man in a bar except for… Tomas.

Damn it. Yes, it figured. He was out prowling the night of the gala and she was an easy mark. The shame of it sickened her.

The cab stalled in traffic. There had to be a better way. *Facebook.* She still had the tab open on her phone – the list of friends that she hadn't connected with in years. Clicking on the notifications icon, she found a long list of unread status updates. The top notification, however, made her stomach lurch. *Victor.*

In the five years since she'd left him, she'd managed to survive the funeral, sign divorce papers, and avoid his calls, which had at first been frequent but had tapered off over time. It seemed, however, that she hadn't managed to unfriend him on Facebook.

She clicked on his profile. The shock of seeing his photo – handsome and laughing on a beach with a thin brunette she didn't recognise – was like a slap in the face. Her phantom anger took shape. For so long, the spectre of Victor had haunted her. He'd clearly moved on, but she had not. Instead, she'd summoned another ghost – another man – who could hurt her. Why had she let it go on for so long? More importantly, what could she do?

As the cab began to move again, she scrolled down Victor's page, reading all his posts and updates. He was apparently 'in a relationship' and worked for a FinTech start-up called Xcite! as a manager in the accounting department. There were a number of new messages arriving even as she stalked the page. Right now, Victor was on his way to some sort of fancy event – the Xcite! holiday party.

Sarah held her breath as the messages confirmed the location. 'Change of plan,' she said to the driver.

No. She should not be doing this – she *could not* do it. Except a voice kept screaming inside her head that enough was enough. She'd spent years of her life unable to bear the thought of the outside world; even longer trying to drown herself in work so she wouldn't *feel* anything. She'd told herself she was honouring Rowan, but in reality, she'd been too scared to live her life. Meeting Tomas – as ill-fated as that had been – had kindled a new fire inside her. If she didn't take action now, she never would.

'Take me to the Strand,' she said. 'The Saville Hotel.'

67

TOMAS

L*iar. Fraud.* Tomas stood in the hall staring at the words on the screen as Andre came to the door and stuck his head out. Another positive and unusual step. Tomas barely noticed.

'Why are you sad?' Andre said.

'Am I?' Tomas put the phone away and forced a smile. 'I'm fine.'

'You are not fine. You miss Sarah.'

Tomas came inside the flat. 'Yeah, mate. I do.'

'Why won't she come back? Franz and Grandma say it's because of you.'

Tomas stared at him for a long moment before responding. 'Yeah, that's right.'

Andre slouched against the bookcase 'So… tell her you are sorry for whatever you did. Then, she will come back.'

'I wish it were that simple.'

'It is simple. Sarah said she would help me go to the magic toyshop. It is a special project for Franz, and I want to help. To be like…' he struggled with the English word '… like a grandson. That is what I want to be.'

'That's great, Andre.' Tomas was touched by the boy's strength of feeling.

'Look. We made this.' Andre beckoned Tomas to follow him over to the dining table where a wooden doll's house had been placed on the floor to dry. Tomas knelt down and looked at the structure.

'Don't touch it,' Andre warned. 'The glue is not dry.'

'I won't,' Tomas said. 'It's amazing. Did you enjoy it?'

'Monsieur Franz says we can paint it together. In his workshop.'

'Good. So when will you go there?'

Panic blazed across the boy's face. 'When Sarah comes back.'

'You're going to have to forget her.'

'But why?' Andre gestured emphatically. 'She likes you. You like her.'

'Yes, Andre, I do.' The boy was starting to access his feelings for other people – an important step. Tomas hated to disappoint him.

'You two can live together in your flat,' Andre continued. 'When I'm older, I'll have my own flat, but I'll come and visit you and *Grand-mère*.'

Tomas shook his head. 'I can see you've got it all figured out. But sadly, things don't always go to plan. Adults are boring – they have things like jobs and problems. There's no guarantee of a happily ever after. Not in this lifetime.'

Andre crossed his arms stubbornly. 'You are wrong.'

'OK, OK.' Tomas held up his hand. 'Keep your big dreams for now.'

'You must send Sarah a message.'

'What? No. I tried. She doesn't want to hear from me. It's over.'

'But… why?'

Tomas took a long breath. 'Because she found out something about me. The truth about something that happened a long time ago. Before you were born.'

Andre shrugged, clearly confused. The boy deserved an explanation, but what could he possibly say?

'A bad thing happened,' he began. 'A woman I knew… she got hurt.'

'What?' Andre's face shrivelled.

'It was a really bad time. A terrible accident. I came here to get away from it.'

'You came to Paris to hide?'

'Yes, that's right.' Tomas realised why he felt such empathy for Andre and Franz. Prisoners of the past – and he was just like them. Andre's prison was a flat; Franz's prison was a toyshop. But his own prison was an entire city.

'I've been hiding who I was back then. Who I still am. Sarah found out. She – rightly – doesn't want anything to do with a man like me.'

Andre straightened up. 'Are you sure? Have you talked to her?' The tables were turned. Andre was the adult and Tomas the boy.

'No,' Tomas said. 'There's no point. Now, let's think about something else. How about I teach you a new game?' He took a pack of cards out of his bag. 'Blackjack. Do you know that one?'

Andre shook his head.

'It's fun – you'll like it. And someday when you're at school, you can teach it to your mates.'

Tomas did a fancy shuffle of the deck and dealt out a practise hand. 'The object of the game is to get as close as you can to twenty-one without going over. An ace is worth one or eleven…'

Andre looked down at the cards, then at Tomas. 'You

should speak to Sarah. Do not stay silent. Franz says it is bad to stay silent. That is why he lost his friend Anna.' He turned over a card thoughtfully. 'That is what he thinks anyway. *Grand-mère* says he lost her because he did not try to find her again.'

'What do you mean?'

'Franz. He left Germany and did not go back. That is why he lost her.'

Tomas shook his head. Sarah and Mathilde were both seeking memories of an earlier time – a better time. But even if the memories were found, the past could not be recreated.

'I don't think it would have helped if Franz had stayed.'

Andre shrugged. 'He could have said goodbye before she died. And he could have met Sofia.'

'Who?'

'Anna's daughter. She is alive. *Grand-mère* and I are going to find her.'

Tomas shook his head. 'I don't know what you're talking about. Franz's sweetheart died in prison. Sometimes, we have to accept the truth even when it's hard.'

He dealt a new hand.

Andre pouted. 'What if the truth is wrong?'

'The truth is the truth.'

The words hung in the air as Tomas dealt another hand. 'Now, let's finish this game,' he said to break the tension. 'I'm the babysitter, remember?'

Andre sulked as Tomas dealt a new hand. Andre had two jacks. Tomas got a five of clubs and a king of diamonds. He took another card: a ten of spades. Bust.

'Right then, you win.' He took some coins out of his pocket and pushed them across the table. 'Lucky bugger.' He dealt another hand. Another win for Andre.

'Please send Sarah a message.' Andre stacked the coins.

'Tell her that Franz needs her. Tell her that *you* need her and want her to come back.'

Tomas sighed. 'Look, Andre. It isn't going to happen. She won't be coming back on my account.'

'But she can't miss the grand opening.'

'I hope not.' Tomas reshuffled the cards. 'But either way, Franz wants *you* to be there.'

Andre shook his head. '*I* need her too.'

'Sarah cares about you,' Tomas said. 'I'm sure of that. I could send her a message – strictly on your behalf. But if I contact her against her wishes, then you'd better not change your mind.'

'I will not change my mind,' Andre said. 'I want to go to the magic toyshop. I want to go outside. To a real school. To meet… friends.'

Tomas reached over and ruffled his hair. 'That's great. I can't wait for you to do that. Your whole life is ahead of you, and you're going to make it really special. You're going to create things and meet people, and someday you're going to fall in love…' He stared at the cards. 'There's no better feeling in the whole world.'

He closed his eyes and pictured her face. *Sarah.* Their lives had come together and she'd drawn him like a magnet. An irrepressible, irresistible force. Loving her would be so natural, something he was born to do. For a brief, mad moment, he allowed himself to dream. A house, a child, a normal life.

Was that too much to ask? Was it too damned much?

Suddenly, Tomas felt light-headed. Deep inside him, something twisted and broke. Collapsing, crumbling, struggling to be free. All of a sudden, he understood. He had been the ultimate coward. It was not Jessie and her tragedy that had got him here. He was the one who had ended Tom Willowfield's life. Locked him away in a tiny box, deprived him of air, light, and feelings. In his mind he'd been an imposter. That was exactly what he'd become.

But now, as the prisoner exploded through the bars of his cage, he realised that the truth was a moral responsibility. Franz was living proof of the importance of stories. Of speaking out even when it's hardest. Franz had stayed silent and regretted it all his life. Tom, too, had allowed his own story to be written by other people. That was the most unforgivable thing of all.

A tap on the shoulder made him jump, startling him back to reality. 'Tomas?' Andre looked concerned.

'Sorry, mate. I got a little distracted.' He dealt another hand and peeked at his own cards. The queen of hearts. The queen of spades. Throwing caution to the wind, he took another. The ace of clubs. *Blackjack.* He left the cards face down. 'You win,' he said to Andre, pushing the rest of his money across the table. He stood up and took his laptop out of this bag. 'It's time for you to go to bed. There's something I need to do.'

68

SARAH

The taxi pulled into the brightly lit alley. Sarah paid the driver as a doorman in a red coat and black top hat held the door open for her. She tried to channel Lucinda Clarke and act confident and self-possessed, like she belonged there. Like she knew what the hell she was going to do next.

The hotel was decorated to the nines for Christmas. Swathes of white lights hung from the ceiling, and a tall Cinderella-themed tree trimmed with blue and silver bows, life-like doves, candle bulbs, and sparkling glass slippers dominated the centre of the space. Her heels sank into the plush carpet as she walked through the lobby to the American Bar, famous for showcasing jazz acts in the 1920s.

Couples and groups of businesspeople were scattered about the bar. Soft jazz music played in the background. She didn't see any sign of the Xcite! party. Either her information was faulty, or it was taking place in one of the function rooms.

Just as well. She made her way to the bar trying to recover her rapidly failing nerves. Last time she'd gone to a hotel bar – the night of the gala – she'd been rescued by a perfect stranger. A stranger who seemed like the person she'd been searching for all her life.

A glass of Burgundy set her back almost twenty quid. A man eyed her from down the other end of the bar. Clean-cut, handsome features, brown hair greying at the temples. She should take another leaf out of Lucinda's book – flirt a little and get her confidence up. This man would be perfect. No spark, no animal magnetism. No danger whatsoever. He picked up his glass and came towards her…

And walked right past her, greeting another man who had just come in the door with a kiss on the lips.

So much for that. Sarah took a long sip of wine, feeling no calmer. Was Victor here – in the same building, on the same floor? Her stomach began its familiar churning. Fear of his moods, shame that she wasn't good enough. She drank the rest of the wine. It had been *five years*. These sensations were phantoms, nothing more. She had the power to walk out right now. Maybe that's what she would do.

Another man came to the bar: hip and edgy, expensive leather jacket, blond hair cropped short. He looked at her, and she sensed his interest. What was it that moths secreted? Pheromones. She gazed levelly back at him. Not her usual type, but then, she didn't have one.

He ordered a beer and came over to her. 'Hello, is it me you're looking for?' he said in a sing-song voice.

'I don't know.' Sarah met his eyes. 'Maybe.'

'Great.' He leaned on the bar, standing too close. His breath stank of beer. This time, Sarah did have a physical response. Revulsion.

'So, what's a hot babe like you doing in a place like this?' He pulled back a little. His smile was nice enough.

'What's a man in a leather jacket drinking a beer from a bottle doing in a place like this?' she countered.

'Good question. Simple answer. It's the Xcite! awards party. I'm the regional manager for Greater Manchester.'

A tremor went through her. This was the right place. But for what?

'So, would you like another glass of wine?'

Sarah looked down at her empty glass and weighed up the options. Let this man buy her a drink and feel under some obligation or switch to water? What would Lucinda do?

The man had already flagged down the bartender and was ordering her a second glass.

'So that's me then, what about you?' He handed her the glass.

'Facebook is a crazy thing, isn't it?' she said breezily. 'I wanted to come out tonight, but I didn't have any plans. Then I saw that someone I knew… once… was coming here. Maybe you know him? Victor Bertrand?'

The man frowned, his face a mixture of disappointment and annoyance. 'Yeah, he's here. If it's the guy I'm thinking of. He's in accounting, or tax, or something.'

'That sounds right.' *Leave*, the voice shouted in her head.

'Anyway. I'd better get back.' The man's eyes gravitated to the door.

Sarah sighed. She would never be Lucinda Clarke nor did she want to be. Flirtation practise was well and truly over.

'It was nice to meet you,' she said. 'Thanks for the drink.'

'No worries. Should I tell Victor you're here?'

'No!' Sarah said. 'I'll wander over.'

The man left and she stayed at the bar, finishing the

wine, gathering her courage. Two glasses in and she was feeling decidedly unsteady on her feet. If she was going to do this… thing… it was now or never.

Her heart raced as she followed the noise down the corridor to a function room that had 'Xcite!' posted on a signboard outside. She poked her head inside. The room was crowded – a party in full swing. A woman was handing out lanyards with name badges. Sarah hovered, trying to spot Victor.

'Can I help you?' the woman said.

'I'm looking for Victor Bertrand.'

The woman gave her a once-over as if measuring her up against Victor. 'He's not here.'

'Not here? But I thought…' Sarah felt like she'd been slapped. It had been hard enough coming this far.

'He just left. He might have gone to the other bar. I'm not sure.'

'Thanks.'

Sarah retraced her steps, feeling like she was marching to the gallows. A big man in a blazer was standing at the bar talking and laughing with a woman. Sarah's heart ticked out of time. *Five years*. He was still handsome. He was still… the same.

She walked up behind him: caught the scent of Hugo Boss. A sinking fear settled in her stomach.

Rowan would want you to live your life…

Her hand shook as she tapped him on the shoulder.

He turned.

'Hello, Victor,' Sarah said.

69

FRANZ

It was like being a boy again. A boy he'd never been in real life. Now, with most of his life behind him, he was finally discovering what living was all about. It was about moments like this that couldn't last: perfect and unrepeatable, like the unique crystalline structure of a snowflake.

Franz held Mathilde's hand as they went out into the night. The great city was before them. Their futures were ahead of them. Not as many years as might once have been, but whatever was left, the clock started now.

'What would you like to do, my Mathilde?' Franz turned to smile at her. 'Shall we get something to eat? Or go to a show? This is your evening. Anything you like.'

She looked pensive, not quite meeting his eyes.

'If it is OK with you, I would like to walk for a while.'

'Yes, of course.' Walking was the one thing he'd been hoping to avoid; the arthritis in his knees was playing up. But whatever she wanted. The joy of being with her was worth any amount of pain.

They turned onto the main boulevard. Mathilde stared at the well-lit windows of the shops. Several times she drew a breath like she was going to speak but remained silent. Franz kept talking – about Paris and all the places he would like to take her. The quieter she became, the more he tried to fill the silence. She walked quickly; Franz struggled to keep up. Finally, she stopped and turned to him.

'I'm sorry, but I cannot do this.'

The words exploded in his ear. The bubble he imagined around them burst into nothingness.

'Please, Mathilde,' he said. Was this how it was going to be? This beautiful feeling that they were moving forward and then sliding backwards into despair?

She grabbed his arm to steady herself. From her pocket she took a folded piece of paper – the one he'd seen earlier – and handed it to him. A letter from a doctor; the French words swam before his eyes.

'What is this?' he said.

'I'm ill,' she said. 'The letter confirms it. Not in my body – I don't have cancer. It's worse than that.'

'Worse?'

'I have dementia. Alzheimer's. Truly, I am losing my mind.'

'Oh Mathilde.' Flooded by fear and compassion, Franz let his cane fall to the ground and reached for her. Once again, he crushed her to his chest. Where she belonged.

'I have to think of Andre.' She pulled away. 'What I'm going to do about him. I have to focus everything on that. You understand?'

'No,' Franz said. Now was the moment to step up. Once before he had been silent and let life – and death – take its course. Never again.

He held onto her shoulders and looked into her eyes. 'Mathilde – I promise you this. We will sort out Andre,' he said. 'Tomas and me. We will help him and take care of him. You do not need to worry about that. Or about anything. Just yourself. Just being happy. In whatever time we have. Please Mathilde, let us both be happy.'

'I… don't know.'

He put his hand under her chin and lifted it. Kissed her deeply, passionately, there in the street. It seemed even more urgent now. He looked around, trying to get his bearings. His flat was half a mile away. Too far even to contemplate walking. There was a small hotel down a side street.

'Let me love you, Mathilde. Please. Not just for me, but for you.'

She gave a little laugh. He bent down and picked up his cane. She put the letter back in her pocket and took his arm. As they walked towards the hotel, she shook her head and tsked. 'Really, at our age…'

Franz smiled. 'There is no better time in life than right now.'

70

SARAH

She'd taken him by surprise, that much was clear. Victor's face flashed first with confusion, then recognition. Half-remembered strangers – that was all they were to each other now.

'Sarah?'

'I saw your Facebook post,' she said. 'I was in the neighbourhood, so I thought I'd drop by.'

Victor said nothing. The woman moved away and left the bar, as if repelled by the tension.

'Can I buy you a drink?' Sarah was losing courage fast.

'What are you doing here?'

'I thought we should talk.'

'Talk?' His voice rose. 'It's been five years. I reached out to you so many times, and you made it clear you wanted nothing to do with me. So, why now?'

Sarah shrank into herself. The urge to hide, to retreat, to... *pretend*... was overwhelming.

'I'm sorry.' The words came out automatically. 'I wasn't ready to talk before. And I don't know if there's anything to say now. But I wanted to see you.'

'This is my company Christmas party,' he said. 'It's not exactly a good time.'

'So, let me buy you a drink. Just one.' She flagged down the bartender. Before Victor could accept or refuse, she ordered two more glasses of Burgundy. In the old days he'd been the one who had ordered the wine. She braced herself for the familiar rush of shame and uncertainty – and was surprised when it didn't come.

'You seem different,' he said as if confirming her thoughts.

'Five years is a long time. It took me that long to find myself again.'

'Find yourself? Is that what you call it?'

The bartender put the two glasses on the bar, and Sarah parted with forty quid on her card. She turned to Victor, ready to face his anger and deflect it back.

'I was your husband,' Victor said. 'You walked out on me without a word. And I tried to understand – really, I did. I knew you were suffering; I was too. I wanted to be there for you to help you through it. We could have helped each other.'

'Could we?' Sarah gripped the stem of her glass. 'Does that really work? We lost our child.'

'Yes, we did. And that was devastating. But I still loved you. Even if at the time—'

'You blamed me,' she finished for him. 'Don't deny it. I know you did.'

His nostrils flared. 'You were there – I wasn't. It was only after it happened that I realised how little I knew you. That scared me.'

'I didn't do anything to hurt Rowan,' Sarah said. 'I hope you know that. I loved her, but I was struggling. I was afraid to show that. Afraid to reveal myself to you. I felt like nothing I did was good enough.'

'I just wish you'd been honest,' he said. 'Trusted me enough so I could love you.'

'I was depressed.' She sighed. 'I lost myself in that. I couldn't trust myself, let alone anyone else.'

He stared into his glass. 'After it happened and you left, I got depressed too. I didn't know what to do or how to go on. I blamed myself too.'

Sarah looked into his eyes, shiny with unshed tears. Guilt pooled inside her, but guilt wasn't going to do either of them any good.

'I'm sorry for what happened,' she said. 'Sorry for the way I treated you. I wish I could have pulled myself together. But it was all just too painful.'

'I think the pain will always be there,' he said. 'But one thing's for sure, the past can't be changed. It's taken me a while to accept that. I've been seeing a therapist off and on ever since it happened. She's helped me focus on the future again.'

'I saw from your post that you're in a relationship. The woman in the photos – does she make you happy?'

'I've learned that you can't rely on someone else to make you happy,' he said. 'But I am seeing someone.' He smiled. 'In fact, we're hoping to start a family in the near future.'

'That's—' Sarah struggled to process the maelstrom of emotions. But one feeling floated above all the others. *Relief.* 'Really great. I'm happy for you.'

'Thank you. It helps to know that.'

The words shifted something inside her, a frozen place beginning to thaw. 'Actually, it's just what I needed to hear,' she said. 'I've felt so guilty, you see.'

He reached out and brushed a strand of hair back from her face. 'Going forward, I want to be happy. I hope you can be happy too.' He lowered his hand. 'Isn't that what *she* would have wanted?'

'Yes,' Sarah said. 'You're right.'

Victor took a step back, his eyes on her face. It was a strange sensation – almost like he was seeing her for the first time.

'I hope you can get there, Sarah,' he said. 'Really, I do.'

A face came into her mind like a half-remembered dream. A man she was born to love. If only she could trust again.

'Me too,' she said.

Victor nodded and turned to leave. A thought jumped into her head. 'Wait, Victor,' she said. 'Can I ask you something?'

He stopped. 'What is it?'

'What happened to Rowan's little giraffe? You know, the one she used for teething? It was in her room that night.'

His face darkened. 'I don't know.'

'It's just that I found something in a toyshop in Paris. A set of circus animals just like the ones she had. But the giraffe was missing.' She hung her head. 'It's stupid, I know. I was hoping to find it.'

'That set was a family heirloom.' The accusing tone was back. 'After you left, my mother helped clear the flat. Almost everything got moved to her house in Chantilly, because that's where I was living for a while. I suppose it was there.'

Chantilly. Franz said that the animals came from there.

'Are there other things?'

He shook his head. 'No. Mum died last year. I've got a box or two of keepsakes, but most of her things went to an estate clearance firm.'

'Oh. I'm so sorry.'

'Thanks.'

Sarah felt a new wave of sadness. Getting even some of the animals back was more than she'd had reason to hope for. But she'd wanted to find the giraffe. If it wasn't with the others, then mostly likely it had got lost or thrown away. All the pain, joy, and loss it held… *gone.*

'With everything that happened, I just wanted to forget,' Victor said. 'I didn't want those things around to remind me. But if you wanted it, then I'm sorry.'

'It's fine,' Sarah said. 'I understand.'

'Good.' Victor gave her a kiss on both cheeks, then he turned and walked away.

Sarah went out of the bar. The evening had left her drained, exhausted, sad, and a little drunk. And yet, she'd achieved something important. She had to keep holding onto that.

In the taxi, she collapsed against the seat and stared out the window at the too-bright lights and the crowds of people rushing to make the last Tube. Eventually, she took out her phone and opened up her messages. There was a new one from a promising contact who wanted to discuss a high-rise hotel project in Malaga. Spain… sea, sand, sun – bright enough to dull even the sharpest of memories.

But just below, the message from Tomas was still there. *I miss you… Can we talk?*

She was struck by a sudden, visceral longing to be in Paris. In his arms, in his bed, his warmth engulfing her. He had charmed her, made her laugh. He had seen and accepted her for who she was. That was the most painful thing of all.

In the bubble below was her reply. *Liar. Fraud.*

Had she done the right thing? For many years, she'd let her own anger and guilt poison her life. She'd assumed that Victor still blamed her without ever having asked. Used him as an excuse to stay stuck in a half-life that didn't involve risking her heart. Now, all that was changing. If she talked to Tomas and got his side of the story, would that make a difference?

No.

Maybe someday she would learn to trust again. Maybe someday she would meet someone else. For now, though, she had to focus on her own new start. A clean slate, one free from shadows and doubts. As the taxi reached the train station, Sarah responded to the contact about the Spain project. She'd be happy to schedule a Teams meeting, or even fly there and discuss the project on the ground. When the message zoomed off, she deleted Tomas's text and his details. She would delete the man, too, from her head and from her heart.

71

TOMAS

It was a battle to get Andre to bed. Franz and Mathilde clearly weren't coming back, and Tomas was glad for them. When the boy finally sulked off to his room, Tomas sat down at Mathilde's kitchen table. He turned over the cards: the red queen, the black queen. He moved the ace of clubs between them.

Meeting Sarah had been a watershed, a tipping point. For the first time in years, he wanted something – someone – enough to take action. But what could he do? What the *hell* could he do?

Andre wanted him to contact Sarah. If he did, then what exactly would he say?

Well, he was a writer, wasn't he? Perhaps that was why Tom Willowfield had been whispering to him lately, the half-formed words a sign that it was time to tell his side of the story. Sarah and the world might look upon him with contempt, but at least he'd be able to look in the mirror and see something other than a ghost – something other than a lie.

He turned on his laptop and created a new document.

As he stared at the blank page, the old fears welled up. He was an imposter, then and now. He'd never again be able to write as he once had – it was pointless to try. Yet, over the last few months, words had been weaving themselves in his mind in ways that had eluded him for years. Images, pictures, feelings. The vague idea of a story he needed to tell. A story of a man who'd been full of self-doubt and allowed his self-worth to be determined by others. A man who had let the world act as judge and jury over his own life, and run away from the verdict of guilty-as-charged.

He started to type, his fingers moving automatically. Spinning words out of the ether, giving shape to images and emotions. The lights of Paris disappeared. The screen in front of him disappeared. Reality was the world he had created in his mind. Created… and remembered.

My second book was late. Readers and fans were eagerly awaiting the follow-up to The Rites of Spring. *The publisher had a huge publicity campaign scheduled. My agent was gently checking in every other day. I assured all of them that the draft was on track – I'd deliver it on time, and it would be amazing.*

I was lying.

There was no draft – nothing worthy of the name. I had a working title: The End of Us. *A brief outline. A few pages of snippets and notes. I'd shown some of it to my agent. She worried the main character was 'a bit self-indulgent'. I laughed – it had seemed expected. Secretly, the tiny seed of belief I'd been nurturing was crushed underfoot. Drowned out by the voices inside my head whispering that I was an imposter. My first book had been a fluke. I had nothing else to say to the world. It was easiest to silence those voices with alcohol, parties, and distractions. Easiest to have Jessie around: fawning over me, feeding my ego, introducing me to 'all the right people'.*

I wanted to blame Jessie. Before we'd met, my fame had bewildered, but not changed, me. Meeting her was a watershed. Her hero-

worship flattered me; her glittering lifestyle tantalised me. But deep down, I knew it wasn't her fault.

The fault didn't lie with fame and success, either. In The Rites of Spring *– God, I hated that book now – my main character, Sam O'Rourke, went on a journey to lose his innocence, only to end up finding it. What had I found? It didn't bear thinking about. One by one, I balled up the pages of notes and threw them in the bin.*

The time had come – I needed to clean up my life and start again without pleasure and distractions. Write my next book the way I had written the first – with hard work, energy, and belief. The idea of it… why was it so hard? My throat burned for whisky, my fingers restless without a cigarette. I'd become a living, breathing cliché. An artist burning the candle at both ends, drowning the flame in its own wax. It had to end. Right here, right now.

When the last piece of paper was crumpled beyond all recognition, I went to the kitchen and got out all the bottles of whisky and vodka. One by one, I poured them down the sink. Then I went to the medicine cabinet. Threw the pills into the toilet, watching them swirl away out of sight. I didn't want them, and Jessie could always buy more. It would go on and on…

No. Getting rid of the alcohol and pills would not be enough. Sam had found his sanctuary only on returning home. I needed to do the same. My old life that had once seemed so small, was in fact rich with love and meaning. Suddenly, I longed for the shed at the bottom of the garden where dreams and ideas had flitted around my head like butterflies. I packed a suitcase with all my things. Jessie was out, but she'd be back soon. I'd leave her a note. She'd be upset, but ultimately this was best—

A key turned in the front door. My epiphany interrupted—

Jessie came inside carrying a rainbow of shopping bags. I felt a surge of desire, a shower of loathing. Why was it so hard to be strong?

'Hi,' she said. 'Let me just get changed. Then we'll go.'

'Go?' I had a vague recollection that we'd made plans. A party, a

date? I'd been drunk at the time. The shame of it crashed over me like a wave. Lost hours, lost time. Lost innocence. I needed a drink. And when I looked at Jessie, my body reacted. She was beautiful. The kind of woman who knew that men wanted her. I wanted her. Loved her… my resolve began to crumble, hanging suspended in mid-air.

'Yeah.' She seemed confused by my confusion. 'We're meeting my parents. Daddy's sixtieth – don't tell me you've forgotten.' Her frown deepened. 'I thought you were going to shave.'

Loathing and annoyance won out. She'd been on me to shave. On me to do a lot of things. Whenever I sat down to work, she'd pout. We should go out for a walk, go shopping, meet with her friends – I wasn't paying enough attention to her. She'd pour me a shot, then another. All would be forgiven and forgotten. But the idea of seeing 'Mummy' and 'Daddy' brought on anger and panic. This could only go one way – another row with things getting broken. I didn't want to do this anymore.

'No.' I dragged my suitcase forward.

She stared down at it. 'What are you doing?'

'I'm leaving, Jessie.'

She laughed. 'Come on, Tom. I was joking – you don't have to shave.'

'God will you stop!' I clenched my fist around the handle of the suitcase. 'It's not about that. Obviously.' I turned away. She would have something in her handbag – I could take the edge off. But no. I had to stay strong.

'Tom…?' She came to me. Threw her arms around my neck and tried to kiss me. Her hair smelled of shampoo, her breath of alcohol. Three o'clock in the afternoon, and she was already drunk.

'Don't, Jessie. Please.' I unwrapped her arms and went towards the door. 'I love you, but I need to get some space and perspective. I need to find my voice again.'

I, I, I… *Her face morphed into something ugly and unfamiliar as the words sank in. She was right – it was always all about me. My useless, non-existent craft.*

'No, Tom…' Her voice trembled. 'You can't leave. I love you. We're meant to be together. Like the characters in your beautiful book.'

'No,' I said firmly. 'We aren't. We're wrong for each other. This whole thing is wrong. This isn't my life. Not the one I want.'

'You bastard,' she hissed. 'What about my life? The life you promised me?'

'I never—' I started to protest. Memories trickled like an underground stream. What had I promised her?

'You said you loved me. That you wanted a life with me. That once I graduated, we would get married.'

'No—'

'Yes. You did.' She stepped forward. The sound of the slap preceded the sting. I lifted my hand to my cheek, stunned. 'You hurt people, Tom. I let you hurt me over and over.' She yelled the words into my ear.

'You're drunk.' I went out the door. It was time to get away, once and for all.

'Tom!' she yelled. A person walking by on the pavement stopped and turned at her frantic cry. I didn't turn around; I kept walking to the kerb. The bus stop was on the other side of the street. The bus was stopped at the light just up the hill. If I missed it, then it would be a twenty-minute wait. I didn't trust myself to stay strong. Anything could happen in that time.

I stepped out into the street, walking quickly. The light changed, the cars coming forward as I reached the opposite side. I turned towards the bus as a cry rang out, reaching my ears slowly, like sound through water. 'Tom—'

Time hung suspended in mid-air. The blur of the cars, a figure darting out after me. The squeal of brakes and then a sickening thud. A scream – mine – as the car skidded. Someone lying in the road. The world around me began to crumble.

Tomas pushed the laptop away, his hands shaking. 'Jessie,' he moaned. Now or in his memories – he couldn't be certain. *Sirens, flashing lights. Hunched over her body, lifting his hands to his face. Finding them covered with blood.*

He covered his eyes, his pulse thundering in his head. Willing the images to go away. Slowly, he lowered his hands. The memories devolved into reality. A Paris apartment. The lights of the city spangled below. The years spun forward. He was here, not there. The memories shaken up like a snow globe – unstoppable, unbearably painful.

Those awful moments had slipped away like sand through an hourglass. So short, so swift. Changing the course of his entire life.

He didn't blame the driver of the car. He didn't blame the reporters who came round, or the neighbours who had a field day talking about the noises from the flat: 'It sounded like they were always drinking, fighting, or screwing.' He didn't blame Jessie – she'd loved him in her way.

Afterwards, she had been very clear where the blame lay. When he went to visit her in hospital, she hadn't let him apologise. 'I have a spinal injury,' she said. 'The doctors say I may never walk again.' Tears welled up in her eyes. 'I loved you, Tom. I didn't want you to leave. I tried to follow you. But now… just go. You hurt people. I never want to see you again.'

You hurt people… you hurt people…

He could have stayed; surely that had been an option. Refused to take no for an answer and stood by her. Instead, he had chosen to disappear.

He swept the two queens onto the floor and stood up to massage his aching wrists. The city was growing darker, the lights winking out. He went to check on Andre. The boy was asleep, the iPad fallen onto his chest. Tomas tucked the blanket around him and turned out the light.

Returning to the table, he read over what he had written, reliving every painful moment, every painful emotion, trapped forever in his words like a fly in a bubble of amber.

But as the words swam before his eyes, it dawned on him that he was not the words on the page – he was not his story. He was a man with a past he'd run away from. He'd given away all his power to something that could never be changed. Guilt, shame. He'd let himself be defined by those things.

But he was also a man with a present and a future. He couldn't turn back the clock, but surely, he could make better use of each moment that was ticking away. Franz was living proof of that. *How long are you going to punish yourself?* Tomas had asked him once. Maybe this was the wrong question. By punishing himself for all these years, Tomas had a great excuse to do absolutely nothing. *What right do you have to keep punishing yourself?* was more apt. The world had given him so many gifts – fame, talent, a chance at love. Wasn't it time to stop squandering them?

He opened up a new message and typed in Sarah's email address. He attached the file of what he'd written. This so-called 'story' would never see the light of day. Writing it had been agony; editing it would be excruciating. The writing was laughably bad – unfinished, full of typos, mixed metaphors, and bad prose. But he'd written it from the heart. The first such writing he'd done for years. He'd written it for her.

He typed the words 'Draft Story' in the subject heading line. Then, he pressed send. Would Sarah delete it without reading it? Or… he couldn't bear even to hope. In any case, it was done and gone.

72

FRANZ

It hadn't been quite like in the movies. The first time had been a little awkward. Two bodies, painful and arthritic, trying to find that youthful spark. And they'd found it. Franz smiled as he stared up at the ceiling of the hotel room. They'd found it. But not before they'd had a laugh.

Beside him, Mathilde was asleep. She was his, but she was slipping away. Soon she would be no one's, not even her own. He tried not to lament the unfairness of life. For now, they had each other. It would not be long enough, and yet it was more than he'd ever hoped for.

In his old age, he would become a grandfather to a young boy. He had promised to give Mathilde all the help she needed, and it was a promise he meant to keep. They say it takes a village to raise a child. He and Tomas would have to do.

After they'd made love, Mathilde had lain in his arms, smiling and sobbing. He had forced himself to be strong. When the dementia fully took hold of her, she would forget the names and faces of people she knew. For her, it would be confusing. For those left behind, it would be devastating. But he wanted to be with her the whole way.

He'd kissed away her tears and swung out of bed, opening the bottle of champagne. Like the hotel, the bottle was cheap and far from the best. But the night was a cause for celebration, and he intended to make the most of it. He poured two glasses and made a toast, brimming with emotion as they clinked glasses together.

The second time (who knew at his age there could be a second time so quickly!) things went more smoothly. Already, he was getting to know the intricacies of her body, much more complicated than any clockwork mechanism. And more beautiful. Nicest of all was the way she melted into his arms. Her warmth flowed into him, smoothing out the rough barbs of his soul. This was love. Not a lifelong thing but a series of moments like this. Someday Mathilde would forget this moment. He would hold on to the memory for both of them.

As the grey light of dawn peeked through the curtains, he was itching to get up, like the shoemaker visited by elves in the night. He wished he was at his workshop and could make her something. Something to help her remember this night. Not a ring or a piece of jewellery – something even more special. A musical box? With a beautiful dancer inside? Anna's had got broken, but now, years later, he had a second chance. He thought of the two clockwork dancers that always seemed to collide. They were prophetic, almost magical. He'd once thought they represented Tomas and Sarah. Not for a moment had he imagined himself as a player in a pantomime of the human heart.

Mathilde stirred in her sleep. Under the covers, her body was so thin. He rolled over and pressed himself along the length of her. He was a little afraid of the moment when she woke up. Would she remember where she was and who she was with? Would she regret what had happened?

'Franz.' His name came sleepily from her mouth. His heart danced in his chest; she remembered! If she regretted anything, she wasn't showing it. He turned her around to face him. Though he couldn't see the details of her face, his lips found hers, and he kissed them gently. 'I love you, Mathilde.'

73

MATHILDE

Mathilde gives herself to the thrill of it. To this man who has appeared when she thought her life was over. She can give him this. She can give it to herself.

Her life has spiralled around in a full circle – a perfect storm. She knew it the moment she'd come home from the shops and seen the magic in Franz's eyes. Eyes that were only beamed at her.

But she had hesitated. In the flat when she'd put the letter in her pocket. In the street when Franz's own excitement and freedom had seemed overwhelming. He was the only person she'd shown the letter to. Her secret revealed between them.

And still he wants this. Still he wants her. When he kisses her, she knows she wants it too.

When it is over, she cries. Because she wants to remember everything. She's shown him the letter – hasn't she? Yes, she must have – because she feels less afraid of what is coming. He knows. He wants her anyway.

As much as it feels strange to not be alone, the togetherness slips on easily like a beloved dress or a favourite pair of shoes. Her silver shoes. It is easy to let their loss diminish her as so many other losses have. But ultimately, it is a choice. Before, she made one choice: now, she can make another.

And when Franz tells her he loves her, the choice is clear.

'You are an old fool,' she says, teasing the soft whiskers on his cheek with her fingers. 'But I am beginning to think that I love you too.'

74

TOMAS

SATURDAY, NOVEMBER 25TH

Tomas awoke the next morning on Mathilde's sofa. His mind was racing. His story… Jessie… Sarah. All he wanted was oblivion: an escape from his own thoughts. Once upon a time, Tom had been obsessed with the idea of consciousness – the fact that a person could only ever have one inescapable voice in their head. Tomas Mercier had tried very hard to prove that wrong. One more way in which he'd failed—

A noise from Andre's room startled him. He sat up. The last thing he needed was for the boy to have one of his meltdowns. Should he call Franz on his new mobile? Try to reach Mathilde and tell her to come back?

No. If two people were happy in the world, then he wasn't going to spoil it. Surely, he could deal with an eleven-year-old boy for a while longer.

Andre came out of his room, waving his iPad in Tomas's face. 'Look,' he said. 'See – I told you I was right.'

'What?' Tomas had a sudden stab of panic. All that talk last night about contacting Sarah – was Andre interfering? Making things worse—

'Sofia. I have found Sofia. Anna's daughter.'

Tomas took the screen. It was a website for a German university. A woman was pictured giving a talk on cross-border economics. Andre switched tabs, bringing up a loose translation of the scholarly article. Tomas skimmed a few words. Sofia Weber, daughter of the late Anna Steinbauer, speaks of her mother's contribution to the reunification effort…

Tomas handed back the iPad. 'That's interesting, Andre. But you have no reason to believe it's Franz's Anna.'

'It is!' Andre looked scandalised. 'How can you not see?'

'So, let me get this straight. You think that Franz's former sweetheart – the one who supposedly disappeared into a prison camp – didn't die but was released after the fall of the Berlin Wall? She went on to get married and have a daughter who's still alive?'

Andre nodded vigorously. 'We must find her.'

'What? No. It's impossible. You shouldn't get your hopes up, OK?'

'I want to do this for Franz.'

Tomas felt a rush of warmth towards the boy. 'That's great. But seriously, it's best if you don't mention it. You don't want to get *his* hopes up.'

Andre looked at him like he was very stupid. He waved a dismissive hand. 'There is nothing wrong with hope. Sarah would understand.'

'Maybe,' Tomas said. 'But Sarah's not here. Anyway, it's good work. But it's still early. Go back to bed – please.'

Andre hugged the iPad to his chest and stomped back to his room.

Tomas lay back, elbows splayed behind his head. Franz had lived his whole life plagued by guilt over Anna. But what if he'd had the facts wrong all these years, and his so-called memories were nothing more than untested assumptions? Would exposing the truth and rewriting history make any difference?

Yes, of course it would. Franz was a man with a huge, kind heart. He would be genuinely happy to know that the girl he'd once loved went on to have a good life and a purpose in the world. He could imagine the old man's face, the emotions projected on it like a screen in an old-time theatre. Joy and sadness, loss and hope. The human condition personified.

In contrast, his situation was the flip side of the same coin. If he didn't take action to own his mistakes, his life would continue to shrink until it wasted away to nothing. A future unrealised, all the love in his heart squandered like dandelion seeds on the wind.

He swung out of bed and checked his messages. No response from Sarah. He hadn't expected one.

Writing his story had been cathartic, but it wasn't enough. Fifteen years ago, history had been created by two people and one series of events. One sequence of facts that created the truth. He'd tried to run – tried to escape that truth. He'd outrun events, but he could never outrun himself. Now, one way or the other, it was time to stop running.

He pulled up Facebook. Jessie's picture stared back at him. Those eyes. She wouldn't be smiling if she knew who was looking at her profile. What was her life really like? Suddenly, he was seized by a burning curiosity to know.

He pulled up a new window. If Andre could track down someone who disappeared years ago in East Germany, then he could take action too. He typed in the details to make a booking on the Eurostar.

Leaving tomorrow.

75

SARAH

Sarah's head felt like a cement block. She had no recollection of getting home the previous night, which was a little scary. Memories of the bar; memories of *Victor* exploded in her head. All because of Facebook. She should delete her account. Right away.

A wave of nausea blindsided her; she closed her eyes until it passed. Had she really gone to a bar alone and ended up crashing the Xcite! holiday party? The look on Victor's face – it still gave her shivers knowing she'd actually done it! She wanted to tell someone how she'd ended the silence and confronted her fears. She wanted to tell… Tomas.

Tomas. She didn't feel angry with him anymore. If anything, she felt sorry for him. If he continued to run from his guilt, he would never be free. Whereas she was finally accepting her past and moving beyond it. For all these years, she'd been afraid to confront Victor for fear of rekindling her pain. Fear of her own emotions was worse than the emotions themselves. She'd kept the darkness locked inside, feeding it until it grew into something monstrous. Now, however, the door was wide open. The light was shining in.

'Things are going to change, Rowan,' Sarah said to her daughter's photo. 'I'm done making excuses. I'm going to start living my life – like you would have wanted. And in a way, it's Tomas we have to thank for that. He and I can't be together,' she swallowed back a rogue sob, 'but I'll always be grateful that he helped me see myself in a new way.'

Levering herself out of bed, she got dressed and went to the kitchen. Her mum had already left for work. Sarah's stomach roiled as she drank down a cup of strong coffee and ate a piece of toast. As the wine haze began to ease, she recalled what Victor had said about Rowan's little giraffe. The animals had ended up in Paris, which was where she needed to look. Paris – there were so many reasons to return. Andre, Franz – despite her best efforts to keep in touch remotely, the toyshop project was languishing – she'd been horribly irresponsible not to see it through. People needed her. This was about so much more than Tomas.

But without him in her life, could she bear to return to Paris?

Sarah poured a second cup of coffee and turned on her laptop. She skimmed over the new messages. One of them caught her eye:

Sender: Tomas Mercier

Subject: Draft story

Sarah stifled a shiver of desire. She would not let herself give in. He had lied to her – deliberately deceived her. The betrayal sat heavy in her chest and it wasn't going away.

She opened the message. No text at all, just a Word document attached. *Delete it!* her head screamed. But the recently awakened voice inside her took control. She clicked the icon. There was no title, but it started right in with chapter one.

A figure running out into the street – the dull thud of impact. 'No!' I screamed. But it was already too late.

Sarah's heart beat wildly. After last night, she'd thought herself incapable of feeling any more strong emotions. But this untitled story by a stranger called Tom Willowfield had toppled another wall of dominoes inside her, falling one by one towards her dark place. In some books the characters seemed like friends or acquaintances. But Tom Willowfield had a different gift altogether. His words flowed almost like they were a facet of her own personality, her own soul. Tom was flawed and human and possessed a number of unadmirable traits. But the story painted a picture, capturing emotion in words that held their own truth. It was beautiful; it was chilling.

Did it change anything?

Sarah closed the file. Everything in her life was pointing in one direction. Should she resist it? Give in to the doubts whispering in the background? Tom's story didn't justify Tomas lying to her and deceiving the world. On the other hand, she of all people knew how easy it was to use the past to justify the present. For years, she'd convinced herself that she didn't deserve love or happiness because of what had happened to Rowan. When you told yourself a story for long enough, you began to believe it was fact. For her, it had taken meeting Tomas – and her other friends in Paris – to make her want to challenge that belief. Maybe Tomas hadn't got there yet when she'd discovered his secret. Would he have eventually told her the truth? Was that what he was trying to do now? She

sighed. Last night, she'd made a promise to herself to forget him, and surely that was still the best strategy. Her feelings were too muddled – all over the place. Whether or not she could trust him, she definitely couldn't trust herself.

As she was debating what to do next, an email came in from her contact. He would be happy to meet with her in Malaga the following week to discuss the project. If she contacted his assistant, they would book the ticket. A knot formed in her stomach as she responded: *Yes, sounds great. Send me the prospectus and I'll see you soon.*

Gone. Done. Other projects… other possibilities beyond Paris.

But while she'd typed her response, another email had come in. This one was from Andre. It began with a heartfelt plea for her to return. Her guilt spiked as she realised how much she missed him and vice versa. She'd promised to help him leave the flat and go to the toyshop. Although she'd been sending him regular emails to encourage him, she knew she had failed him. His clear need for someone to champion his progress filled her with shame, but it was the final paragraph of his email that she read twice.

I know it is her, but Tomas does not believe me.

Anna. Andre had found her. He'd attached an obituary – Franz's one-time sweetheart was dead, as he'd thought. But Franz hadn't known about Anna's daughter, Sofia. Andre had looked her up too. She was a university professor who lived in Berlin.

Tomas told me not to tell Franz. But I want him to be happy and you too. Please come back. Tomas needs you. Love, Andre

Emotions overwhelmed her. Somehow, she had entered the life of this boy and the people he cared about. A boy who was close to the man she wanted to love. But could she allow herself to do so? Surely, it would be easiest just to go about her life, abandoning them all to their fate. Or…

she could make a different choice. A riskier choice that involved opening her heart to the possibility of even more pain. But wasn't that the braver option? Wasn't that the essence of being human?

She stared up at Rowan's photo. 'I want you to be proud of me,' she said.

Sarah reread what Andre had sent and did some research of her own. She pulled up the website of the university, wrote down the contact number, and picked up the phone.

76

TOMAS

SUNDAY, NOVEMBER 26TH

He had well and truly lost the plot. The train pulled in to St Pancras station. What was he doing here? What was he hoping to achieve? His story was not destined to have a happy ending – it was stupid to think it could.

And yet, last night – was it really only last night? – he'd let Tom's words fill his mind and the page. It had felt wonderful to write in that voice again. His true voice. He couldn't remember the words, but it was enough to know that the flame inside him was still flickering. But had he been wrong to send the story to Sarah? It was so painful knowing that she thought the worst of him – and with good reason. Would telling the story in his own words change that? Would she understand? For a moment, he allowed himself to imagine a different outcome. With Sarah in his life, anything might be possible. But without her…

He'd be stuck with Lucinda Clarke and the ticking clock.

It was strange to be in London; the once-familiar sights and sounds now belonged to someone else's memories. He had forgotten the winter greyness, the slanted light and muted colours. He got a taxi from the station, the traffic heavy as they made their way north towards Camden. He'd see this through, fail at it, and go home. Once upon a time he'd thrown everything away and had to reinvent his entire life. He no longer had the strength to do it again.

With a sinking sense of dread, he exited the taxi outside the Tube station at Belsize Park. An online search had revealed that Jessie's charity was registered at her parent's address. Had she really stayed in the same location, just around the corner from where the accident had occurred?

He walked up the hill, trudging through soggy orange and yellow leaves. At the end of the block he stopped just opposite the bus stop. At the exact place where it had happened. The light changed and traffic sped forward like racehorses from the gate, oblivious to the tragedy that had once unfolded here. Tomas felt sick as the images played out in his head. He turned onto the smaller street and came to the front of the substantial double-fronted Victorian House. It was the same as he remembered it – except for the wheelchair ramp that zigzagged beside the steps to the front door. Walking up those steps – it was the hardest thing he'd ever done.

An evergreen wreath hung on the shiny black door. His hand shook as he rapped the brass knocker. No one came. It was mid-day – Jessie probably wasn't even home. This was nothing more than a waste of—

The door swung open. Time spiralled backwards. Reality crumbled like a sandcastle taken by the tide.

She was standing there.

Standing. There.

No wheelchair.

The dark pools of her eyes pulled him in, just like

they'd done so many years ago. She was older now: thinner, with a few streaks of grey in her shoulder-length hair. If anything, she was even more beautiful now than then. Her face mirrored his own shock. Recognition, remembrance. She blinked rapidly as if to dispel a vision.

'Tom? Is that really you?'

'You can walk!' he said. 'You… you're not…' He looked heavenward. Emotion bubbled in his chest, overflowing.

'Disabled?' she said. 'Or shall we drop the political correctness and say "crippled"?' Her face gave nothing away. 'No. Not now.'

'Oh my God,' he said. 'I'm so—' Words failed him.

She, on the other hand, seemed utterly unfazed. 'You'd better come in.'

He followed her inside. She walked with a limp, he noticed, but her back was straight and upright.

She led him into the living room. A tall Christmas tree stood by the fireplace, its branches trimmed with tasteful cream ribbons, twinkling white lights, silver baubles, and a Victorian angel on top. The lid of the grand piano was covered with framed photos. A man, a boy. A husband? A son? For so many years, he'd imagined her life in the worst possible way. Told her story in a way that let him stay stuck. Told himself that he didn't deserve to be happy because of what had happened.

Had he been wrong all along?

He felt her watching him as he stared at the photos. Some showed her using a wheelchair. One photo showed her gritting her teeth on a treadmill as she relearned to walk. Photos of other wheelchair users – adults and children – a photo of her accepting a cheque at a charity function. A life of service, full and abundant.

Other than the photos, the room was just as he remembered. He experienced another powerful flash of déjà vu: time unstuck, the past spinning forever in an endless loop. But it was not the past or the present that he'd imagined – the one that had haunted him all these years. He caught a glimpse of his reflection in the mirror above the mantel. He was older now too. The glasses and scruffy hair were long gone. Was she wondering what happened to the young man she'd known back then? What had she imagined about his life?

'Would you like to sit down?'

Even her voice sounded different. He perched on the edge of the sofa and she sat in the wing chair opposite. Everything he wanted to say – or thought he might say in this moment – went out of his head.

'I saw your photos on Facebook,' he said. 'The ones for your charity. But I didn't know you could walk again.'

She arched an eyebrow. 'I guess you never know who's looking at your profile.'

'I guess not.'

'Whereas you don't have a Facebook page, do you, Tom?'

He shook his head.

'You chose to fall off the face of the earth. Left me – just when I needed you most. And wherever you landed, you've stayed there all these years. And yet… here you are. Why?'

A car sped by in the street. The familiar nausea rose in his stomach. But this time, it was more of a phantom response. A ghostly neural pathway that served no purpose whatsoever. One moment could change the course of a lifetime. What would he do with this one?

'I came here to say I'm sorry, Jessie,' he said. 'For everything. Who I was back then. What I did – and didn't do.'

Her eyes narrowed. 'I was in love with you, Tom. You left me and I was upset. And then, I ended up in hospital. You didn't stand by me.'

'But you told me to go.' His mind reeled. 'You said that I hurt you, over and over again. That I hurt people. That's what I've thought about myself all these years. The sentence I've repeated over and over in my mind.'

'I was angry and in pain. Drugged up, bruised, broken. I'd just been told I might never walk again. I was scared! I had to blame someone, and you were in the frame.' She laughed bitterly. 'But even so, that isn't why you left.'

'No,' he admitted. 'I left because I was weak and unforgivably self-absorbed. I couldn't handle any of it. Not the fame, or the pressure, or our relationship. Then, I couldn't come to terms with what happened.'

Her dark eyes bored into him. 'Did you ever love me, Tom?'

Memories ghosted through his head of their early days together. Her beauty and laughter, her youth, her vibrancy. Afternoons in the park, cafés, and kisses. Talking about his novel long into the night. And then… the darker things they had done together. They were both so young. They had grown up too quickly.

'Yes, I did love you,' he said. 'But we weren't good for each other. Surely, you can see that.'

'Of course.' She grimaced. 'We followed each other down the rabbit hole. It was only going to end one way.' She indicated her lower body. 'The tortured artist kills his muse.'

'You make it sound like a cliché,' he said.

'Because it was.' She turned to stare out the window. '*The End of Us*. That was the name of your book, right? Did you ever finish it?'

'No, of course not. After what happened, do you really think I could write in the same way as before?'

'I don't know,' she said. 'I don't know how you wrote the first one. So powerful and imaginative. So… perfect.' Her face softened. 'I still remember every word. I wanted to be part of it, but I ended up destroying it. You were right to leave. The accident was horrific – painful and life changing. But ultimately, it made me get clean. I found a purpose in life. I met someone older and more settled. I grew up. I'm not a victim of anything. Not anymore.'

'I'm so glad.'

'I did try to find you, Tom. I thought closure might help – for both of us. I tried to find out where you were living, what you were up to. But you did a very good disappearing act.'

He told her the bare bones of it. Living in Paris, writing spy novels. She raised an eyebrow. 'Do you enjoy that?'

He took a second to answer. 'Yes and no. Deep down, it's still my dream to write something beautiful. Something meaningful. But, given what happened, I haven't earned the right. Not even to try.'

He sensed a new current of anger rising from her.

'So in other words, you didn't come here to apologise. You came to blame me. Not for what happened back then, but because you couldn't pull yourself together afterwards – and still can't from the sounds of it.'

'No, absolutely not,' he said. Jessie was twisting his words into a noose around his neck.

'Good, because if there's one thing I've learned, it's that we've all got to take responsibility. I was the one who ran out in front of that car. I'm the one who's walked the road to recovery, step by painful step. I'm stronger and braver for it.'

'I can't tell you how glad I am to see you're OK,' he managed.

'I still have pain. I'll have it for the rest of my life. But I can forgive what happened. There's only one thing I can't forgive, Tom.'

His stomach lurched. 'What's that?'

She sat forward in the chair. 'The fact that you gave up. That you were too scared to follow your dream.'

Jessie: his shadow, his tormentor. Shining a blinding light on the real truth he'd been denying all this time.

'I spent years relearning how to walk,' she continued. 'Trying, falling, failing, gritting my teeth, getting up again. Because that's what it takes. It takes showing up every day. Have you done that, Tom?'

He stood up and went to the window. The trees outside were bare and stark, but in a few months, green shoots would sprout again. A season… fifteen years. Time curved in and back on itself. One thought rose above the others.

'No. But maybe it's not too late.'

Jessie smiled then, easing the tension. '*Maybe* is a start. The first step. 'Now what's prompted this. Why after all these years?'

'Because I met someone,' he said. 'Someone who's made me want to come out of hiding.'

'That's great.' Jessie said. 'What's her name?'

'Sarah.' Saying it out loud gave him a powerful surge of hope. 'Sarah Williams.'

'And where did you meet this Sarah Williams?'

'At a little toyshop in Paris.' He told her briefly about Sarah, Andre, and Franz's project. The time seemed beautiful and remote, almost like a dream. But the dream began to slip away as he spoke of the lies and deception. He needed to grab it with both hands before it dissolved into thin air.

'I want to put everything right,' he said. 'Once and for all.'

'So what are you going to do?'

'I don't know yet.'

Could he really do something? Something big… something momentous?

'Yes, you do.' Jessie stood up. 'You do know what to do, Tom. You have everything you need inside you already.' She smiled wistfully. 'All this time, Tom Willowfield was never dead to me. I've always felt the pull of his gravity. Our story didn't end well, but it's not too late. Someday, my son will read your book. Maybe I'll tell him that I once knew the author. But what I'd really like is to tell him a different story. Write another book, Tom. Another beautiful, life-affirming work of art. A happily ever after for both of us.'

He stared at her. His head exploded with a kaleidoscope of colour and possibilities. Jessie was giving him permission to move on. Permission to become Tom Willowfield again – not that he was sure he wanted to. He gripped the window frame as the glacial shift inside him made him unsteady on his feet. The possibilities… the swirling began to slow. One image formed in his mind. A face. *Sarah*…

'Do it for her,' Jessie said. 'For Sarah. She's a lucky woman. I hope you and she will be very happy.'

She walked him to the door. He moved slowly, as if in a trance.

'Are you happy, Jessie?'

'Yes, Tom,' she said instantly. 'I am.'

'Good,' he said. 'I'm so glad.'

'Goodbye, Tom.' She opened the door. Her voice caught as she said his name, and he felt tears welling up in his eyes. Jessie had been a part of his life for a long time. A painful, unwelcome part, like the thorn of a rose digging into his skin; but a part, nonetheless. He pictured the young girl she'd been when they first met – full of life and her own potential. But now, superimposed on that image was the woman she'd become. A woman who was strong, empowered, self-actualised. Shaped by grief but not defined by it. A woman like Sarah. He opened his arms, and she went into them. He breathed in the scent of her that brought back the long shadows of memories and desire. He held her tightly for a long second. And then, he let her go.

PART V

Once again the seasons change; there are births and deaths, new hopes, fading memories. A new day dawns, the animals are on the move again. They carry with them the space; they carry with them the loss. They carry with them stories, many of which will never be told. But some will be told, and there will be both truths and twists in the telling. Each tick of the clock, each beating of a heart, every thought, every breath is a story in itself.

And if the story can touch the heart of even one person, that story is magic. If the story can change the mind of one person, it will have reached a worthwhile end.

77

SARAH

SUNDAY, DECEMBER 3RD

Sarah stared out the window of the taxi. Paris had changed. The city was decked out in its Christmas best. Every shop window, from the *grands magasins* to tiny boutiques, held a confection of light and sparkle. The winter-bare trees along the Champs-Élysées had been decorated with a million miniature lights, and outdoor skating rinks and Christmas markets proliferated in the plazas. Despite the chill in the air, people were moving in the streets with energy and purpose. Along the river, pale winter sun bathed the buildings in gold, giving their architecture a muted majesty.

She had changed.

When she'd come to Paris many months ago, she'd been trapped inside her own grief, shackled by pain and guilt. She had fortified herself against the world, against her own feelings and desires. Now, she had broken free. Grown strong enough to forgive herself, strong enough to allow the possibility of happiness. Even if she wasn't meant to find that happiness with Tomas, she would forever be grateful to him for the role he'd played in her metamorphosis.

Her first stop was to see Andre. When the door opened, a hurricane bombarded her. Andre flung his arms around her and somehow managed to lift her up and swing her around.

An attempt had been made to brighten the flat: next to the table, a little evergreen tree was decorated with a string of white lights, a paper chain, and some red and gold baubles. But as Andre let her go and ran over to get his latest sketches, she saw that her absence had affected him for the worse. He was back to wearing his old clothes; his hair was unwashed, his skin pasty. She felt guilty all over again. But she was determined to be done with guilt.

'You came back.' Mathilde's tone was a shade off accusing.

'I'm…' Sarah stopped herself from apologising. 'Yes. I needed time to think. But now I'm back to help with the final push. The grand opening is coming up.'

'And then you will go away again?'

'Yes. Probably.' Though she'd postponed the Spain meeting for now, she was not going to lie.

Sarah waited for the recriminations. Instead, Mathilde bowed her head. 'I am sorry to hear that. But I understand. Tomas is… well… I am very sorry.'

'Don't be. He's a good neighbour to you, and he really cares about Andre. You are very lucky.'

'Yes.' Mathilde set her lips in a line. 'He *was* a good neighbour. But now, he is gone. That too has affected the boy.'

'Gone?' A hole opened up inside her. 'Gone where?'

'I do not know.' Mathilde shook her head. 'It is strange, is it not? Our lives were like a balloon – getting bigger and brighter and ready to float free. But now, the balloon has burst.'

'I don't think that's true,' Sarah said. 'Or it doesn't have to be.'

Mathilde sniffed. 'I will make coffee. That is one thing we can count on.'

As Mathilde left the room, Sarah sat down on the sofa next to Andre. Her mind was reeling. Where was Tomas? Had he really gone away? For good? Disappeared into another false identity, living a brand-new lie? A part of her had hoped that maybe they could talk. But it was hopeless. She needed to let it go.

Besides, she had other, more positive things to focus on. Andre sat close to her on the sofa, telling her his news in rapid-fire French. She concentrated hard to follow along, and when Mathilde returned with a cup of tea, not coffee, she took it gratefully.

'I've got news for you too.' She gazed fondly at the boy. 'If you decide not to be a toymaker or architect, you can be a detective. Because it turns out, you were right. One hundred per cent.'

'Right, how?' Mathilde said.

'Andre told me what he discovered about Anna,' she said. 'He did some searches and found out Sofia's name and where she worked. I helped with the final piece – making the phone call.'

'You did this? It is all true?' Mathilde looked at Andre, her eyes wide with wonder and disbelief.

'I did what you said, *Grand-mère*,' he said. 'I searched for the two names together. So you helped too. *We* found her.' The boy's proud smile beamed like a spotlight.

Mathilde's eyes filled with tears.

'Well, congratulations to the both of you,' Sarah said. 'It's a great result. And in fact, I'd better leave soon to go see Franz.' She checked her watch. 'His special visitor is arriving later today.'

As she stood to leave, Andre jumped up from the sofa. He gripped her arm hard enough to hurt. Was he afraid she might abandon him again? 'It's fine, Andre,' she started to say, 'I won't be going until—'

'I want to go to the toyshop now! Take me with you – don't leave me!'

'Andre – let go of her.' Mathilde was firm, but her brow creased with worry – but not as worried as Sarah felt. She'd hoped that when Andre did finally leave the flat, Tomas or Franz would be there to help. She knew from experience that the first time would be the hardest. None of the holiday energy outside had found its way into Mathilde's flat. All the noise, all the colours, all the stimulation. Sometimes she still found it too much.

'Are you sure?'

'I want to go now!' Andre moved swiftly to the door.

Mathilde started to follow him, but Sarah held her back. 'If he's ready, then he'll do it on his own. If not—'

Andre flung open the door and took a step out into the hall. Sarah stood behind him as his body began to shake and shudder. He grabbed the doorframe as if trying to force himself out. She could hear the quickening of his breath. The boy's will was strong.

But the panic was stronger.

'Andre!' Mathilde's voice was frantic.

Sweat beaded on Andre's brow. Sarah tried to take his arm to steady him but he threw her off. Then, he opened his mouth. He let out a long, thin wail.

With Mathilde's help, Sarah managed to pull him back inside the flat.

'*Mon Dieu*!' Mathilde said as they took him to the sofa.

Sarah sat next to him, handing him a cushion to put

over his face to block out the light and steady his breathing. She rubbed his back with slow circles. 'It's OK, Andre. It's OK.'

'*Non*!' he gasped.

Mathilde went to the kitchen and returned with some juice and a plate of madeleines. Andre's breathing began to ease. Sarah, however, felt on the verge of panic. What business did she have acting like some kind of saviour to this boy?

'*Je suis désolé*.' Andre hung his head.

'It's OK.' She lifted his chin with her finger. The best thing she could do was stay strong and continue to encourage him. 'That was a great first attempt. Next time you'll get further.'

Mathilde crossed herself. 'I do not think I can handle a next time.'

Sarah gave her a stern look. 'Andre will do it.' She glanced at the boy. 'Just not today.'

Andre's eyes were wide and haunted as he nodded.

'Good,' Sarah said. 'Next time, I'll come better prepared. I'll see you very soon.'

Sarah hated the look of despair on Mathilde's face, but she needed to get to the toyshop. She laid a hand on Andre's arm. 'Don't you ever give up,' she said. 'You'll get there in the end and be stronger for it.'

Andre crossed his hands over his heart. 'You promise?'

She felt a surge of love for this vulnerable boy.

'Absolutely.'

78

FRANZ

Franz wiped the sweat from his brow. He was tired; his back and knees were aching. It was a 'good' tired but also an 'old' tired. The painting was finished, the new shelves and fittings were in, and the rooms looked bigger and brighter. All good. But he still needed to finish restocking the shelves and put up Christmas decorations. It all required effort and energy, and in truth, he didn't feel up to it. Not on his own.

He'd been hoping that Tomas would help him. After Sarah left, Tomas came in a few times to help with odd jobs and heavy lifting. On those occasions, Franz had felt a little awkward around him. As much as he wanted to be understanding and accepting of Tomas's long-practised deception – he, of all people, knew the value of forgiveness – he still found it difficult to reconcile the man he thought he knew with the one that was hidden underneath. He regretted his own reaction and wished for a chance to make things better. But Tomas had disappeared. No one knew where he'd gone or when he would return.

The workmen were talking as they took down their

scaffolding in the old theatre. The new door off the main street was propped open for fresh air. He was almost used to the idea now of being so close to the world. Soon, he hoped, the shop would be a haven – a *destination* – where people from all walks of life would come to see the wonders and treasures within. He was looking forward to that day… or… he should be. Why was change still so hard?

In truth, there was another option – one he couldn't quite get out of his mind. He could call Rouveau and accept the offer to buy him out. Spend all his days with Mathilde. They could sit in the park and feed the pigeons together. Fade away together; stay the same together.

But would she want that? He sat down on the new stool behind his workbench and took out the small wooden box inlaid with gold marquetry. He'd been working on it at night after the workmen left. A musical box. The most beautiful object he'd ever made. He opened the lid and watched, transfixed, as the two enamelled dancers spun on their tracks to *Swan Lake*. He closed his eyes and pictured Mathilde unwrapping it. The joy and wonder on her face. The love in her eyes. He would give it to her on her birthday and then he would ask her… the biggest question of his life. But what would she say—

'Franz?'

A woman's voice. He looked up, his heart taking flight. 'Sarah?' He peered at her as if she were a vision come to life. 'It is really you?'

'Yes, Franz. I'm back. I see you've done wonders without me.'

'It is because of you.' He went to her and clasped her hands. 'It is so good to see you. Does this mean that you and Tomas are—?'

'No.' She drew back. 'This is not about Tomas.

Besides, no one's seen him. This is about you and Andre and Mathilde. I want to see the project through. I'll help you with the final push and stay through the grand opening – make sure you're up and running and taking full advantage of the Christmas trade.'

'That is very good.' On one level, it was. But another part of him could not help thinking it was a tragedy. In his clockmaker's brain – his child's brain – he had imagined a happy ending for Sarah and Tomas. Together. But in real life, they seemed determined to stay apart.

'And most importantly, I'll help Andre come to the shop. He wants it so desperately. In fact, when I visited him earlier, he was so eager to help that he tried to come with me.' Her smile faded. 'Sadly, he wasn't quite ready.'

'The boy will come when it is right for him.'

'Yes,' she said. 'It's just that Mathilde and Andre have been on the hunt for a lost person. They have found someone they want you to meet.' She checked her watch. 'Any minute now.'

'A lost person? Who could it be—?'

He stopped talking as footsteps came from the direction of the street door. The music of children's laughter and voices. A woman telling them not to run: not to touch anything. Franz's ears had to adjust to the sound. She was speaking German.

Sarah popped her head out and gestured. A second later, a woman came to the workshop door. She was about Sarah's age, but shorter with wispy blonde hair and huge brown eyes. A lightning bolt shot through him. She looked… familiar.

As Sarah greeted the woman in English – he gathered they had not met in person, but had spoken over the phone – Franz had a strange sensation in his stomach. His old life blending and swirling into his new one. But no…it could not be—

Two children ran past: a boy and a girl, both about nine or ten. As swiftly as his joints would allow, he hobbled to the door. The castle was roped off. Although it had passed its final safety checks, there were still many tools lying around to create a hazard.

'Hello!' he said, trying out words he'd not spoken in years. '*Guten tag*?'

The boy went over the rope. Franz held his breath as the girl followed him. This was all very unexpected, but also an opportunity. He went over to the bank of switches on the wall. He flipped them one by one. Lights flashed, music played, and the entire structure began to rotate. The two children ran up the ramps, shrieking in delight.

Sarah stood to one side. The other woman's face when she saw the castle was one of pure delight. At that moment, Franz *knew*. It was not possible; but still, he knew.

'Franz,' Sarah said. 'This is Sofia. She's—'

'Anna,' Franz whispered. 'But… how?'

'Hello, Franz,' the newcomer said. 'I have heard a lot about you. From Sarah, but also from your grandson. Andre.'

'My—'

Sarah took his arm and helped him over to one of the benches.

'Who are you?'

Sofia smiled gently. 'I am the daughter of Anna.'

'Her daughter! But that is not possible.' The castle circled slowly, the music danced brightly. The whole world tipped and swayed. The woman, Sofia, told him a story. One he could not believe. Anna surviving her arrest and imprisonment; released when the wall came down. Living her life; having a husband and a child.

'She always spoke fondly of you,' Sofia said. 'She said you made beautiful things. Musical boxes and toys that were full of magic. She would have loved this place.'

'You speak of her in the past,' Franz said.

'She died a few years ago,' she said. 'But she'd lived a good life.'

'A good life.' Franz struggled to absorb what this woman was saying. The two children were on the balcony at the very top of the castle now. One of them began to sing, then the other joined in. An old song that Franz recognised from his childhood.

'And she was happy?'

The children ran down and went to the box of foam swords and knight helmets to have a battle.

'Yes,' Sofia said. 'Happy and fulfilled. She got a job as a civil servant after the wall fell. She worked on reunification. Later on, she and my papa worked for UNICEF. We lived in places like Africa and the Middle East. They did good things. Worthwhile things.'

'And your children?'

'Twins. The girl is Mia. The boy is…' she coloured a little, 'Franz.'

'Franz!'

Sarah put her hands comfortingly on his shoulders. His hand shook as he gripped his cane, looking up at her.

'You did this?'

'Actually, it was Andre who found her.' Sarah said. 'He's quite the computer whiz – as you know from what he's done on the website. But actually, it was Mathilde who suggested he start with a simple Google search.' She exchanged a look with Sofia; Franz felt very old and very stupid. But no matter. No matter.

'Andre and Mathilde.' He sparkled inside like moonlight on water. 'They did this for me?'

'Yes,' Sarah said.

'I don't know what to say.' He turned back to Sofia. 'But did Anna tell you what I did?' He had to know. 'That I kept silent? That I did not stand up and fight for her?'

'She told me that you had a good heart. There was nothing you could have done. But her brother – he was a different story.' Her face darkened. 'My mother said that oppressive regimes bring out the worst in people. Men who are cruel can find a state-sanctioned outlet to prey on the weak.'

'Yes.' Franz recalled that awful day. The self-satisfied, almost gleeful look on Heinrich's face when he was commended for informing on his sister. 'That is true.'

'He died young,' Anna said. 'Not long after reunification. I never met him.'

Divine clockwork. Divine retribution.

'I wish I'd known your mother was alive,' Franz said. 'I wish… many things. But you are here now.' He turned to Sarah. 'I am very grateful.'

Sarah squeezed his hand. 'You've already done the hard work to change. You deserved to know the truth.'

As she spoke the words, tears flooded his eyes. Washing away the past once and for all. Healing the regret. Clearing his eyes so he could focus on what was in front of him. The future. Not as many years as he would have wished. But every moment precious.

'I would like to see Mathilde and Andre,' he said.

'Of course.' Sarah turned to Sofia. 'You'll be back for the grand opening?'

'Yes,' she said. 'We would not miss it for the world.'

79

TOMAS

TUESDAY, DECEMBER 12TH

Tomas wondered if he'd dreamed the whole thing. Had he really gone to see Jessie? Had she really become stronger for what happened and turned her life around? Could he do the same and somehow make things right with Sarah? It all seemed like a strange, impossible dream.

The time for his return to Paris came and went. Like his one-time character Sam O'Rourke, he was hardly aware of time passing, of his brain trying to process his emotions. He took a train north to a seaside town on the Suffolk coast. Holing up in a small B&B on the front, he wrote and wrote, page after page, draft after draft. Sometimes as Tom, sometimes as Tomas. Capturing moments and feelings in words, the way a painter captures sunlight on water. The words flowed in a way they'd not done for years. The joy of it astounded him.

Late at night, he wrote emails to Sarah, attaching his new work. Pouring out the deepest feelings of his heart. He didn't send them, but composing them was enough. The man he'd kept under lock and key for fifteen years had exploded from the cage.

Overnight, Lucinda Clarke developed feelings. Ones she couldn't fathom, couldn't control. She threw away the four-inch stilettos; she tossed her SIM card into a bin at Charing Cross. She took a train home at Christmas and told her family everything – about the killings, the blood, the terrible things she had done and had been done to her.

In fact, Tomas was getting to know Lucinda so well that even though he'd written five earlier books about her, it was like they had just met. His manuscript was starting to read less like a crime thriller and more like chick lit. Whether it was good or bad – or would all be edited out – he didn't care. He realised how much he appreciated Lucinda, loved her, even. She had kept him going over the years, kept him creating. He threw out the notions of whether or not she embodied his 'best work' and just kept writing.

He barely stopped to eat or drink. His wrist ached and his eyes grew tired. In the back of his mind, he was aware of the problems he was not facing up to. Andre, Franz, Mathilde – they needed him more than ever and he wasn't there for them. And Sarah… she was still gone. Not even words were a balm for the deep gash of regret. If he ever published another book, he would dedicate it to her and Rowan. She might not be part of his life, but she was the catalyst for the change inside him. His Ariadne, spooling out golden thread to lead him from the labyrinth. She wouldn't be waiting on the other side, but she'd unlocked the door that let in the light.

As the days went by, a decision came to him. In the new year he would make a statement – come out of hiding. It was the only way. He began making notes, trying to find the right words. The idea filled him with terror, elation, and hope all at the same time. Could he do it? Was he really brave enough? Could he really move on with his life and find happiness?

And if so, which man would emerge from the cage – Tom or Tomas? He didn't know. There were many questions and many unknowns. But for all the uncertainty, a line was drawn in the sand and there was no going back. For the first time in fifteen years, he had the rest of his life to plan.

One morning, he took a long walk on the beach. Frost sparkled on the shingle, his breath a white cloud of vapour. He studied the colours of the sea as the clouds shifted and the light changed. The beauty was astonishing, and he wished Sarah was there to share it with him. In the vast kaleidoscope of sky, he caught glimpses of the man he wanted to be: reborn, new, as yet unformed.

His reverie was startled by a text message coming in. It was from the concierge of his building advising all the tenants of upcoming building works in the lobby and lower-ground floor laundry and storage area. He skimmed over it, his thumb on the delete key. But something in the message caught his eye. Brought back a memory. A run-down building. A homeless man outside. What had the man said? Not an attic… a cellar? An idea… was it possible?

In that instant, time came unstuck, the hands of the clock racing forward. He'd neglected everything and everyone for too long. Had he missed the grand opening? Missed Christmas? Why didn't he know? Tomas realised that he could never be the new man if he let down the people he loved. He had to pull himself together. Take another risk – the hardest one yet.

It was time to go back to Paris.

80

SARAH

THURSDAY, DECEMBER 14TH

It was almost time, and they weren't ready.

Sarah woke up early the day before the grand opening with a churning sensation in her stomach. Although they'd made a monumental effort to finish everything in the last week, there were still caterers to coordinate, temporary assistants to train up, and crates of wine and champagne to be unpacked. Franz had a meeting set with Rouveau – she'd forgotten to remind him to wear his suit.

When she checked her phone, the first thing she saw was an email from Andre.

Please, Sarah. I am sorry. I want to try again. Today.

If she wasn't already stressed, she would have found the boy's apology touching. She wanted him to succeed so much – they all did – but really, the timing could not be worse.

But Andre and Mathilde were the very people who had prompted Franz to change. He was doing it for them. They were the most important thing here.

She showered, dressed, and got ready to leave the flat.

She'd go to the toyshop first and make sure the work was being done, but at some point, she'd pop out and see Andre. After his failed attempt to leave the flat, she'd gone shopping for a few provisions: noise- cancelling headphones, a galaxy print rucksack, dark sunglasses, a hoodie with graphic splashes of paint, a thick puffer jacket. She hoped it would be enough.

Just as she was leaving, the concierge called to say she had a delivery. She waited until the courier came up and handed her a small box. Posted from London. Who could have sent it? Her mum? No.

Curious, she opened the box. Inside, there was a single compliments slip and a nest of red and green tissue paper. Sarah read over the note:

I found this in a box and thought you should have it. Vx

Sarah's hand shook as she drew out the small wooden giraffe, just the right size for a baby's tiny hands. Its spots were faded, nearly loved off, and there were tiny chew marks on its horns. Its painted expression was gentle, almost tender. An object passed down the generations and made with love. She put the giraffe with the other animals. The set was now reunited, complete. Sarah felt an overwhelming rush of love, a life-affirming sense of grief. Life was full of both, and she wanted to experience it all. She smiled through her tears, as just for a second, her daughter's face was clear in her mind. Gurgling, smiling, shining down upon her, like a star whose light would never fade.

81

FRANZ

Franz had felt sick before – of course he had. The sickness of flu that swept through the tenement blocks, the sickness of hunger hollowing out his stomach. But the sickness he felt when he woke up the morning before the grand opening eclipsed all others. The hour was nearly upon him. Tomorrow, his dreams would either come true or shrivel up and die forever.

But when he went downstairs to the shop and looked around, his sickness miraculously vanished. It was a new day – the first day of the rest of his life. Tomorrow would be even better! In the last week, he and Sarah had worked round the clock on the finishing touches. They had created a true Christmas wonderland, with real fir trees, wreathes, bows and ribbons, shining glass stars, and thousands upon thousands of fairy lights. The shop was transformed. He was transformed. But there was still one more thing that needed to happen before everything would be complete.

Andre. He had done all of this for Andre. But would it be enough?

Franz left the shop through the new front door with an

unusual spring in his step. He went to a patisserie and bought a box of fresh croissants and a dozen macarons iced like angels and plum puddings. He rode the lift up to Mathilde's flat, a delicious bubbling inside his belly. The joy of being in love.

But when he got to the flat, he was dismayed to see that things were not going according to plan. Andre had had another one of his fits. The little Christmas tree was listing in its stand, a string of lights hanging limply from the top, most of the glass baubles shattered on the floor below.

Mathilde took him aside and told him that it had been happening all week – ever since Andre's failed attempt to leave the flat. Franz hated to see her so agitated. When he returned to the living room where Andre was curled up on the sofa, he was tempted to get angry with the boy. He managed – barely – to hold his tongue.

'You must pull yourself together,' was all he said.

Andre lifted his head. Muttered that he was sorry. He even went so far as to get up off the sofa and help sweep up the glass, cutting his bare foot in the process. Franz was glad to see him up and about, but he still felt pent up and anxious. Change was hard – was Andre ready?

Mathilde took his arm and led him to the kitchen. 'I think you should go back to your shop,' she said, her lips tight. 'You must have many things to do.'

'Of course I do.' Franz touched her cheek tenderly. 'But nothing is as important as you and the boy. In fact, I was thinking…' He hesitated, faltered. But he had to know. 'If you think it best, I could sell the shop. There is always that option. The landlord, you see—'

The look on her face – once again so similar to Anna's – told him all he needed to know. 'Stop.' Mathilde put a hand to his lips. 'Do not say any more – or *think* any more. You must not give up, Franz. I would never ask that of you.

And Andre – he needs your example. You have done the impossible. You must not go back again.'

Franz took her in his arms. 'Thank you,' he said. 'With your permission, I will carry on.'

'Good.' Her smile was like sun sparking on snow. 'In the meantime, I will take care of my grandson. And keep hoping for a miracle—'

A knock at the door. They came out of the kitchen, as Andre bounded over to answer it. Sarah was standing outside with a large carrier bag. 'Maybe your miracle has arrived,' Franz said quietly.

Mathilde took his hand and squeezed it. '*Our* miracle.'

Sarah came inside the flat and declined an offer of tea or coffee. She went straight to Andre and began to speak to him.

'I'm not going to tell you that it will be easy,' she said. 'It's going to be the hardest thing you've ever done. Just know that you can go to the shop anytime – it's all ready for you. It doesn't have to be today. There's no rush or pressure – none at all.'

Franz sat next to Mathilde at the kitchen table. Sarah's words spread magic about the room. Her patience and empathy: the fact that she knew from experience what Andre was going through. After a few minutes, the boy uncurled and sat up. Sarah handed him the carrier bag. 'Consider it an early Christmas present,' she said.

'What is she doing?' Mathilde whispered loudly.

Franz smiled and put a finger to his lips. The spell was woven in the room like a shimmering web. He did not want to break it.

'For me?'

Andre's face was pure wonder. One by one, he unpacked the items and put them on: hoodie, shades, earphones, trainers, coat. Mathilde put her hand over her mouth as Andre was transformed from shut-in boy to edgy Parisian youth. He strutted up and down the front room of the apartment, grooving to imaginary music. He came over to Franz and his grandmother and bowed.

Franz clapped his hands. 'Fantastic! You look great.'

'*Mon Dieu*,' Mathilde muttered under her breath.

Andre beamed. Then, he walked to the door.

'There's no rush,' Sarah said. 'You don't have to—'

Andre opened the door.

He stepped out into the hall.

82

TOMAS

In the end, the box was surprisingly light. With a little persuasion, the concierge had given him the key – to the storage locker in the cellar that was assigned to Mathilde's flat. He found a few suitcases filled with old clothing, a bicycle with a flat tyre, and one box. If his hunch was right and this was box she'd been looking for, then Tomas hoped it would serve as an apology for his absence.

He brought the box to his flat and set it on the table. He'd take it over later and see Andre, but first he needed to order a crate of champagne to try and make amends to Franz. Luckily, he hadn't missed the grand opening; he'd managed to return with one day to spare. Enough time to go to the toyshop and see if Franz needed any last minute help. On his way back, he'd buy groceries – there was no use trying to plan a new life on a diet of tuna and fuzzy mayonnaise.

But before he did any of those things, Tomas wanted to take the next step towards making amends to the world.

He sat down at the table and reread the words on the screen:

I am deeply sorry for any hurt I have caused through my actions and inactions. I do not ask for forgiveness or understanding, and the world can judge me as it wishes. But from now on, when I look in the mirror, I will see a man who told the truth.

He was tempted to delete it, as he had so many previous drafts. But that was the coward's way out, and he was done with that, he reminded himself. Now, he just needed to finish it. He'd ask Anne-Marie if she had a contact at a newspaper to send it to.

Tomas sent the document to the printer, took a sip of coffee, and stared out at the view. Paris was hazy; the future was hazy. Could he really merge his two identities? Could he really allow Tom Willowfield's writing – his beautiful, desperate, from-the-heart writing that was building and cresting again like a wave – back out into the world? Those were questions he couldn't answer yet.

A noise came from outside in the corridor. A door opening and closing. Voices. A thump. What was going on?

He got up and went to the door. Outside, he was greeted by a strange sight. Andre was standing in the hall with dark glasses and earphones. Franz was at his side along with Mathilde. And—

His body registered Sarah's presence before his mind did. Her eyes met his. The corridor crackled with electricity—

She looked away.

'Do you want to go any further?' she said to Andre. The boy was gripping her arm tightly. 'You don't have to. But look, here's Tomas.'

Andre turned. Tomas focused on the boy and his brilliant achievement. He felt like a planet forced out of orbit by an exploding star. 'Well done, Andre,' he said. 'This is brilliant.'

A storm of emotions crossed the boy's face. Abandonment, fear. Self-doubt. His breathing was shallow, and sweat glistened on his forehead. Tomas came forward and put a steadying hand on the boy's shoulder. Andre froze. Tomas held his breath. Had he just done the worst possible thing?

'Andre, what do you want to do?' Sarah's voice was steady and focused. 'Have you had enough, or do you want to go down the lift?'

The boy pointed to the lift.

'OK,' she said calmly. 'Let's do it.'

Tomas grabbed his coat and locked the door to his flat. Together, he and Sarah helped Andre walk step by step down the corridor. There was barely room in the lift for three people, but Tomas squeezed in alongside Andre. Franz and Mathilde agreed to get the next lift. 'We're right behind you,' Franz assured Andre.

The lift rumbled downwards. All the while, Sarah talked soothingly. 'You're doing so well. You're very brave.' Tomas felt dizzy with the proximity of her, but she hadn't spoken to him – she'd barely even looked at him. Clearly, she was only here to help Andre and attend the grand opening – the transformation of Franz's shop was in large part down to her. But would she walk away without acknowledging him? Surely not – she was not a cruel person. Her silence, however, held a clear resolve. She would see to Franz and Andre, and then she would leave. His deception had proved unforgivable. She did not feel what he felt. How could he go on knowing that?

Andre's face was rigid with tension as they reached the

ground floor. The door opened onto the lobby with its riot of black and white tiles. 'Close your eyes if you need to,' Sarah said. 'Imagine your peaceful place, like we talked about.'

Each step Andre took seemed like a monumental effort. Franz and Mathilde came down the next lift, clinging to each other for support. The door to the building was propped open for a delivery. The street outside was busy with traffic and shoppers hurrying past on the pavement. Motorbikes and electric scooters whizzed by. Overhead, the sky was a bruised purplish brown, hinting at snow. Just before the door, Andre came to a dead stop, his eyes widening with fear.

'The outside world is very busy, Andre,' Sarah said. 'There are lots of people, and noise, and commotion. There's no changing that. Do you understand?'

'I wish… my mum… was here.'

Sarah's heart went out to the boy. 'It was very tragic that your mum died,' she said. 'I know how it feels to lose someone you love. I know that clawing sensation in the pit of your stomach – every day, every moment. It feels like the worst thing in the world to be left behind. But your mum would want you to be happy. To experience life and take risks. Does that make sense?'

And then, she looked directly at Tomas. Though her eyes were shadowed, for a fleeting second they were lit by an electric spark that arced between them. He remembered so clearly every moment they'd spent together. Her laughter… her anger… her wonder… her body one with his.

'Bad things happen,' Tomas said. 'That's part of life. But beautiful things happen too – and hope is our birthright as human beings. It's our gift to know that things are always changing and each moment is precious. To know that we will suffer – maybe even lose everything – and still believe we can be happy again.'

'Yes,' Sarah said. The single word contained a universe of possibilities.

'I'm going to let go of your arm, now, Andre,' Sarah said. 'You need to make a decision: go forward, stay here, or go back. It's up to you.'

She released his arm and nodded at Tomas to do the same. The boy staggered a few steps, then straightened up. He walked forward to the door and into the street.

'I want to go to the magic toyshop,' he said. 'I am ready.'

83

SARAH

The moment she saw him, all of her resolve to stay detached – to stay *safe* – melted away. Sarah thought of the story he'd written and the pain and guilt he must have felt over the years. It was similar to hers, and yet so personal. She remembered the joy they had discovered together: the laughs they'd shared, the sparkle in his eyes when he looked at her, his hands reverent as he explored her body.

And now, his words spoken on a Paris street seduced her all over again: *'To still believe we can be happy again.'* She longed to be happy; ached for it. But for now, she had to focus on Andre. It was paramount not to show even a flicker of doubt.

She stood close to the boy whispering encouragement with every step. A few times, he cringed at a loud noise or fast-moving vehicle. Still, he kept going.

Eventually, Andre would be interested in the sights and sounds around him. The sparkly lights and Christmas decorations, the sumptuous window displays, and all the delights that Paris had to offer. This first time, however, she tried to keep distractions and stimuli to a minimum. The journey seemed to take forever. Behind them, Mathilde and Franz spoke in hushed voices. Tomas mostly stayed silent, but Sarah was as aware of him as if his heart was beating inside her body. She tried not to look at him, but when their eyes did meet, she felt a breathless, intense longing; but at the same time her mind whispered to take care. This man had lied to her and the world. Why were her feelings for him still so strong? Could she dare risking her heart?

The new door to the shop fronted the main street, but to keep things quieter they went the back way; walking through the tangle of streets that Sarah had finally learned to navigate. Gentle snowflakes began to fall. They rounded the corner where a new signboard pointed the way to *La Boutique Fantasque* – the doorway to an enchanted world. 'Almost there,' she said.

Andre's face was ghostly pale. Sarah hung back and whispered to Tomas, 'He's going to need a hot drink and something sweet.'

'I'll get some food,' he said quickly. Clearly, he was eager to be away from her.

Tomas went off as Franz and Mathilde caught up. Mathilde's face was as pale as Andre's. 'He's doing great,' Sarah reassured her. Mathilde gave her a rictus grin.

Franz took out his keys and gestured to Andre. 'Welcome to the Fantastic Toyshop.'

Andre stood in front of the window, transfixed by the Nutcracker display: a magical land of sweets and dancing clockwork figures. Franz had added white-flocked Christmas trees decorated with stars and swans, and a sleigh on a model train track that transported Clara and her prince around the enchanted land.

'It is amazing!' Andre whispered, wonder shining in his eyes.

Franz ruffled his hair. 'Wait until you see inside.'

The door was hung with a pine wreath trimmed with twinkling white icicle lights and a red velvet bow. Franz unlocked the door; Andre went inside. It was as if the last few years of his life had been erased, and he was a small boy of four or five again. He let out little cries of wonder at the toys on the shelves as Franz turned on the lights. Mathilde too seemed fascinated, the blankness and stress vanishing from her face. Together, she and Andre explored the wonders of the Fantastic Toyshop, decked out in Christmas splendour.

Sarah went with Franz to the theatre. The old man flipped the switches to activate the castle. 'Do you think he's cured?' he whispered.

'I don't know.' In truth, she hadn't expected Andre to get this far. 'I think it will be a long road back to leading a normal life.'

'Ah. But the hardest roads always lead to the best places, no?'

She laughed. 'You're right. But are you ready to be a grandfather?'

The old man had a twinkle in his eye. 'I may be an old man, but I also own a toyshop. What more could a boy want?'

They stood together watching the castle rotate, the figures moving in their intricate mechanical dance. The castle too had been decorated for Christmas, with a huge tree turning at the top. Sarah marvelled at the sight. Once upon a time, the toyshop was run-down and sinister, glimpsed through the veil of her own guilt, grief, and loss. Now, however, the transformation was complete.

'I have something to show you.' Sarah opened her bag

and took out the small bundle wrapped in tissue paper. 'I got it back. From Victor.'

Franz unwrapped the giraffe. He traced the spots and little horns with his gnarled finger.

'It found you at last,' he said. 'At exactly the time when you were ready. I am very happy for you. Now I hope you can have both an ending and a new beginning – like I have found. You have so much love to give. That is the true magic.'

'Thank you,' she said. Images of Rowan flashed into her mind. She let the memories flow through her, welcoming them. Being alive meant sadness, but happiness as well. It meant suffering, but also the possibility of joy.

'Yes, it is this way, I think.' She heard Mathilde's voice in the next room and Andre's footsteps.

'Sarah,' Franz leaned in, his voice low, 'we have all suffered so much. Too much. You, Andre, Mathilde, me—and Tomas. Please, do not take away this chance to find happiness together.'

He handed her the giraffe, and Sarah held it close to her chest. 'How can I trust that I'm making the right decision?'

Franz tapped his chest. 'Because you know you can trust in here.'

They turned and watched as Andre ran to the castle, his face aglow with amazement. Mathilde followed him, breathless. 'I think Andre will never want to leave,' she said. 'He is happy. And it is thanks to you—' she looked at Sarah, then Franz '—and you. How can I ever repay you?'

'Oh, Mathilde.' Franz took her in his arms. Sarah left the workshop to give them space. Andre was the only one who seemed totally oblivious to the strong currents of emotion around him. He gestured wildly to Sarah to come over to him, holding out a foam sword. But before she could go over, Tomas came in carrying two bags. He set them down and went over to Andre. He gave the boy a mercurial frown and took the sword. '*En garde*,' he said.

Sarah laughed as the two of them went at it. Despite being unaccustomed to exercise, Andre had the vigour of youth, and it was Tomas who seemed winded from the exertion. Watching them, Sarah felt light and happy and overwhelmed all at the same time. She tucked the little giraffe back into her handbag. Rowan never got the chance to play like this, which was tragic and sad. But Sarah was determined to experience joy for both of them. To put aside her regrets and keep moving forward. Whatever happened, there was no going back.

84

TOMAS

His joy was tempered by fear. Tomas sensed Sarah's turmoil; her feelings saying one thing, her head another. He needed to get her alone. But would she want to be alone with him?

Andre's departure from the flat had been momentous, and Tomas was glad to have been part of it. It was brilliant to see the boy's transformation. But as Andre whacked him with the sword and they explored the ramps of the castle, his anxiety increased. Sarah might leave at any minute. They needed to talk. He dropped to the ground and let Andre slay him. 'That's enough,' he panted. 'You win.'

Andre beamed and put his trainer on Tomas's chest to enforce his victory. Sarah laughed. Tomas thought she was enjoying herself. But once again, when she caught him looking at her, the smile faded. Enough was enough. Tomas got up. 'We should take you home, Andre. It's been a lot of excitement for one day.'

Andre shook his head vigorously in protest.

'Tomas is right,' Sarah said.

'Please can I stay for a bit longer?' Andre pleaded.

'Go see the workshop,' Tomas said. 'Have something to eat. Then, we'll see.'

The boy nodded and went off. Tomas was left facing Sarah. Her eyes were clear as they met his. She had never looked more beautiful, a pure and radiant light shining from within her. In contrast, he felt like an awkward teenager. 'Would you like some food?' he said. 'I bought sablés – the tastiest iced biscuits you're ever likely to find. Little stars and angels.' He rambled on. 'Or… I could make cocoa?'

'I'd like to talk.'

'All right,' he said. 'Should we go for a walk? We can come back later to help get Andre home.'

'That's why I'm here,' she said.

That didn't sound too promising. Before she could change her mind, Tomas went to the workshop where Franz and Andre were deep in conversation over some sort of gears and clockwork mechanism. Mathilde was sitting at the end of the bench sipping a cup of tea. When he told her they were going out, Mathilde gave him a teasing look. 'You should go and not come back.'

'No. We'll come back,' he said. 'We both want this day to go well for Andre. That's what's most important now. You'll need help to get him home safely.'

'We do not deserve you,' Mathilde said. 'But *she* does.' She indicated her head towards the main room. 'I hope you two can work things out.'

'Me too.'

85

SARAH

Snow fell from the sky, the delicate flakes swirling in the wind like feathers shaken from a pillow. The chill air bit at her cheeks and rushed in her ears as they walked to the bridge. The sky above the river was a dark twilit blue, the yellow pools of light from the streetlamps alive with movement as the snowflakes floated onto the stonework of the bridge.

It was beautiful and magical.

Or – it should have been.

The conversation did not flow. How could it? There was so much that needed to be said, but so many potential pitfalls and misunderstandings. Being with Tomas had changed her life – no denying that. But was that change for better or for worse? She would listen to what he had to say. That was all she could promise.

'So, you came back?' Tomas said.

'Yes.' She pulled her pink cashmere scarf closer around her chin. 'For now. Franz still needs my help. He needs to learn how to run a business, and he needs to hire an assistant – maybe more than one. It's going to take time.

And I know he wants to prioritise Andre and Mathilde. I've got other opportunities elsewhere – including a promising one in Spain – but I've decided to stay until I know he's up to the job.'

'It's amazing what you've done for Andre,' Tomas said. 'Somehow, you've accomplished singlehandedly what the rest of us have failed to do for years.'

'It was the right time for him.' She hated the awkwardness in her own voice. 'And he found the right place to go. It was his decision – all his own doing.'

'But you were his role model. His inspiration.'

'Well, Franz had a lot to do with it. You know what Andre did for him, right?'

As they crossed the street and walked onto the bridge, Sarah filled him in on Sofia and the twins. Tomas was dumbfounded. 'So it was true? He really did find Anna's daughter?'

'Not only found, but she's here in Paris. She came to the shop.'

Tomas smacked himself on the head. 'He told me about the search, but I didn't give it any credit. I was too wrapped up in my own problems. Once again, kudos to you.'

Sarah reached the middle of the bridge and stopped walking. Tomas stood next to her; the white clouds of their breath twined together in the air. Every precious moment they'd spent together reformed itself and dissolved. The poem he'd composed about Rowan... waterlilies... laughing together at the toyshop, the way he'd kissed her so reverently. *No.* Sarah shook her head. 'I think we should go back, Tomas – or should I say Tom? I can't do this; it all feels wrong. I don't know you. Not really—'

'Yes you do,' he said emphatically. 'You know me better than anyone. I could never hide from you.'

'But that's exactly what you did!' She spun towards him. 'You hid your true identity. Not the name you go by or what kind of books you write – but who you truly are. I told you everything – things I'd never told anyone else. And you didn't trust me enough to do the same. You repaid me with lies! That's the part I can't forgive.'

His whole body slumped as he leaned onto the railing, snow dusting his coat and hair. 'You're right,' he said. 'It is unforgivable. And I guess that means it's hopeless too. We can't be together – not if you genuinely believe that I wanted to deceive you. I didn't want that at all. The moment came and went – and then it was too late.'

'I just wish you'd told me the truth.'

'Do you?' His laugh had a bitter edge. 'What was I supposed to say? "Oh, by the way, you think I'm Tomas Mercier – a small-time but perfectly respectable crime writer; but really, I'm a much-hated pariah, Tom Willowfield: a fallen man, a narcissistic hedonist." How would that have worked exactly?'

Sarah hesitated. 'I don't know.'

'What would you have done? Walked away? Run?'

'Yes. Probably.'

'There's no "probably" about it.'

Sarah stared down at the dark serpentine water of the river. The snowflakes speckled the surface before dissolving into the murk. Constantly moving. Constantly changing. Beautiful and complex. Like life itself.

'Maybe I would have done,' she said. 'But you didn't give me the chance to decide for myself. As it is, I'd like to understand. I mean, that story you wrote – the one you sent me – it was just so… awful.'

'Um… thanks.'

'Not the writing.' She nudged him with her elbow. 'I mean, what happened. I'm not going to play judge and jury. But why do you think it was all your fault? You might not have stuck around or taken responsibility – but then again, neither did Jessie.'

Tomas kneaded his temples with his fingers. 'It didn't matter who was responsible. It all happened so quickly. One minute I was a struggling writer, the next I was a "fallen man". I just wanted to be happy and settled, living a creative life. But fame was harder than I thought. It was a house of cards, and because of the choices I made, I couldn't stop it tumbling down around me. I couldn't make my relationship work with Jessie. I couldn't write. I lost my way. But Jessie lost a lot more than that. I can still see the look on her face when I visited her in hospital. I heard her voice over and over in my head: *"You hurt people…"* That was what I believed about myself.' He glanced at her. 'You know how that is.'

'Of course,' Sarah said. 'I understand the guilt and self-loathing – probably better than anyone.'

'Yes. That's what it was. And the fact that I was scared witless. Scared of success, terrified of failure. After what happened, I couldn't go on being Tom Willowfield – the man who had everything and threw it all away.' He spread his hands. 'The only thing I could create was a new life. It was the best I could do.'

'And now?' she said.

'I could have been Tomas Mercier forever,' he said. 'Living a half-life. Living a lie. Never allowing myself to get emotionally involved with anyone. Never having to ask someone to put everything on the line and just… accept me. Asking someone to keep my secret.' He looked down at his hands, resting on the railing. 'It was fine, actually. There was no one I wanted to get close to. No one I wanted to love and have them love me back.' He looked up, his eyes filled with tears. 'Until I met you.'

He turned away. The world suddenly seemed darker, more desolate. Full of loneliness and fear. The light of a human heart flickering, guttering out. She focused on his words. *Until I met you.*

Sarah acted: beyond thought, beyond words. Reaching out, she touched the arm of his coat, brushing the snow away. Turned him towards her.

'Tomas,' she whispered. She put her hands to his face, ran her fingers down the frozen lines of tears on his cheeks. Nothing mattered but the way she felt – the way *they* felt. There was no past for either of them, and the future would be what it would be. But in this moment…

Lifting his chin, she pulled him close to her, twining her arms around his neck. She pulled his head to hers, his lips to her lips. Closing her eyes, she filled herself with the rightness of his kiss. Desire swept through her body and would not be denied. This was what her life had been leading up to. All the pain, all the half-remembered joy, came together and ignited inside her. She was lost, utterly lost to him.

'Sarah…' He pulled away, breathless. 'Sarah, I have to know. That you accept me as I am. It's important. It's everything.' He closed his eyes for a second, steeling his resolve. 'Because I'm thinking of going public. Coming out of hiding.'

'Really?'

'I went to see Jessie. That's where I've been. I wanted to face up to everything.'

Sarah listened in surprise as he outlined the details of his trip to London.

'I was shocked – and delighted – to see that she can walk again. She has a husband and a son, and she's devoted to her charity work. She's a stronger person for what happened. Can you believe it?'

'Yes,' Sarah said. 'I can.'

'Anyway, it got me thinking about making a statement. "Tom Willowfield is alive and well and living in Paris" or something like that. Announce that maybe…'

'What?'

'Maybe he might try and write another book? Someday?'

She squeezed his hand. 'That sounds like a very good idea.'

'I don't know. There may be backlash. Recriminations. I don't know what the reaction will be. Maybe nothing – maybe no one cares about Tom Willowfield anymore. Or maybe, there will be another shitstorm. God… that would be awful.'

'Shh.' She put a finger to his lips. 'You're right – you can't predict what the reaction will be. But I guarantee you that it's worse to fear it than to face it.'

He stared at her like her words were a revelation. 'You're right.'

Sarah turned back to the river, a snowflake tickling her nose.

'I saw Victor when I was in London.'

Tomas's shoulder stiffened. 'I didn't know you were in contact.'

'We weren't. I tracked him down on Facebook and crashed his work party.'

A faint smile crossed Tomas's face. 'Facebook. What an invention.'

'Yes, it is. Anyway, I saw from his photos that he'd moved on. He got help – therapy – and managed to get his life back on track. He's given himself a second chance. And he hopes I'll do the same.' Saying the words, something bloomed inside her. 'Rowan would want that too – I know that. I've got a long way to go, but I'm ready to make a start.'

'I'm glad.' Tomas brushed a strand of hair from her face. 'But a start of what?'

'Trusting my own judgment and instincts. Believing again. In myself – and in you.' She smiled as the words were swept away by the wind. 'I want to love you, Tomas. And I want you to love me back.'

'Sarah... are you sure?'

She looked deeply into his eyes. Saw the hope there – and the fear.

'Let's get this shitstorm started,' she said.

Joy radiated from him as she went into his arms. His lips were soft and yielding as they found hers. Her body melted with pleasure, with love. She was half aware of people passing them on the bridge, giving a whistle or making a remark. But she didn't care one bit. What could be more natural than kissing on a bridge in the enchanting city of Paris? After a few more whistles, though, they came up for air.

'So, what now?' he said. 'If you're not frozen solid, do you want to go to dinner... or something?'

Sarah laughed. He seemed so shy, almost boyish. A different person. The side of him she loved most. The real man inside.

'I'll take the "or something".' She ran a teasing finger over his lips. 'But first, we'd better get the boy back home, don't you think?'

'I think I might die if I have to wait any longer to be with you,' he said. 'But yes, you're right. I'd better make sure Franz can look after Mathilde and Andre tonight. I don't think I'll be free to babysit.'

'No?' Sarah joked. 'We could always stay in, get a takeaway, warm up with some hot cocoa, and watch TV.'

'Um,' he said, 'you may not have noticed, but actually I don't have a TV.'

She laughed heartily. 'I think there's more of Tom Willowfield left inside you than you realise. I had him down as the type not to have a TV.'

Tomas smiled. 'Actually, *he* did.'

Sarah took his arm and they began walking back to the toyshop. 'It will take some getting used to,' she said. 'This idea of two men for the price of one.'

He put his hand over hers. 'Maybe. And I've got some decisions to make too. I'm no longer Tom Willowfield. But I'm not Tomas Mercier either. I'm not quite sure who I am, to be honest.'

She leaned close to him and squeezed his hand. Snow swirled gently around them as they walked off the bridge and crossed the busy road on their way back to the toyshop. 'Then let's find out together.'

86

MATHILDE

FRIDAY, DECEMBER 15TH

She is spinning, dizzy. Music plays, figures move, clocks tick. Children shout and laugh. The Christmas tree at the top of the castle rotates slowly, filling the huge space with the fresh scent of winter pine. Lit up with thousands of flickering candle bulbs, the branches sparkle with silver tinsel and shiny red and gold baubles. On the top, a shooting star made of lights flashes like a wish. Mathilde is swept up by the brightness, spellbound by the magic. And the boy… When Andre smiles, the love inside her unfurls and takes flight.

Sarah comes over and helps her onto a stool. Tomas brings her a comforting glass of *vin chaud* that warms her up inside. So many people… so much love.

Mathilde hooks the heels of her shoes over the rung of the stool. Silver shoes, so sparkly and shiny, so perfect. Just for a moment, the veil of memory closes. How has she come to find them? An attic?

No – not an attic. A cellar. As she was dressing for the grand opening, Tomas had knocked on her door. Apologised again for leaving – he had things to think about, to sort out in his head. Of course he did. He is young and foolish. But Sarah will set him straight.

Tomas found the box in the basement of the building. Of course! Mathilde instantly remembered putting them in the storage locker after Renée died. Not only the shoes, but the special cookbook that her husband and daughter had loved. Mathilde cried when she unpacked the box. But finding lost things – it is a comfort, somehow. Sarah found her giraffe. She has found her silver shoes. The circle is complete.

Mathilde looks across the room to where Franz is handing out silver wands trimmed with sequins and ribbons to a flock of children. He has made this; created this magic place. He did it for her and Andre – and for his sweetheart, Anna, who will never see it. But her daughter and her children are here, and they will see it. And someday, maybe Andre will have children too. His life is just beginning; the cocoon is breaking open. Soon, the boy will spread his kaleidoscope wings and be ready for glorious flight.

Mathilde gets to her feet. The shoes are surprisingly comfortable. She goes over to Franz. The lines on his face soften when he sees her. His smile is as bright as a moon, his cheeks as rosy as a cherub's. And the look he gives her… Her stomach spins. She is a young girl again – a butterfly. It makes her forget what she wanted to say.

'Mathilde.' He takes her hands in his.

And it doesn't matter what she says, because words aren't important. Nor is the memory of anything but this moment.

87

SARAH

Children – running, flocking, shouting, sparring with foam swords; waving wands, butting heads in plastic knight helmets. A thousand coloured lights flashed as the carousel spun, knights jousted, a princess sang to her prince, a cook chased a knave with a rolling pin, and a huge mechanical dragon swooped down from the ceiling. Music played, glasses clinked, and the hired assistants rang up sale after sale of toys, musical boxes, antiques, and doll's houses.

'I thought I was used to hard work,' Tomas said, breathing hard as he carried a huge replica Eiffel Tower into the workshop to wrap up for the lady who'd bought it. 'But this is ridiculous.'

'That hat is ridiculous,' Sarah said, teasing the jingle bell tassel on his elf hat. 'But cute too.'

'Touché.' He tried to nudge her sequined reindeer antlers with his nose, but she pulled away laughing.

'First things first – see to the customers and don't drop the merchandise. Let's nail this happy ending for our shoemaker.'

'Sure, boss.' His eyes twinkled. 'Whatever you say.'

Somehow, the grand reopening of *La Boutique Fantasque* had become the talk of Paris. The place to see and be seen. Between Anne-Marie and her Facebook campaign, and Sarah's own Paris contacts, the launch had spiralled beyond anyone's wildest imagination.

Tomas recognised a few celebrities with their children and nannies in tow. Anna's daughter, Sofia, was there with her children and Andre was there in his ripped jeans, dark glasses, and leather jacket, helping make sure the little kids got their turn riding on the carousel and playing in the upper levels of the castle. He and Sofia's twins had hit it off. It was a delightful thing to explore a toyshop and even better if it was done with friends.

Though shy at first, Franz had found his element talking to customers, and handing out wands, swords, and sweets to the children. Mathilde hovered nearby, her brow a worried frown, tutting that Franz would tire himself out – and how would she get Andre home then? But a glass of warm, spiced wine soon set her right, and she began to relax and enjoy the spectacle.

'It is a success, I think.' Franz was beaming when Sarah and Tomas came back into the workshop followed by Monsieur Rouveau. Rouveau had brought his son and grandson to the launch, and wearing smart-casual clothing instead of his usual impeccable suit, he seemed a little less formidable.

'A huge success,' Sarah agreed. 'And this is just the start.' She gave Franz's landlord a measured look. She'd already had a word Rouveau earlier – it was going to take time before the toyshop's finances were fully restored. They'd agreed a temporary reduction in the rent, on the understanding that increased traffic to the toyshop would benefit the landlord's other properties nearby. Sadly,

Komitov and his consortium had turned their eye away from Paris, to bigger and better projects elsewhere. In fact, Jeanette, also attending the launch, had whispered in Sarah's ear that the source of Komitov's funds were under investigation by the French authorities, and hinted that she too might be looking for a job very soon. Sarah had promised to give her a call in the new year to discuss teaming up on a venture to help out struggling independent shops. She'd even mentioned the idea to Rouveau, and was surprised when it was favourably received.

'You drive a hard bargain,' Rouveau said, looking at her with admiration.

'I hope so.' Sarah laughed. It was early days, but who knew? Maybe she could create a happy ending for other shops and other shopkeepers right here in Paris. Even Rouveau couldn't argue with a plan that created wins for everyone.

The older man turned to Tomas. 'And with this woman, you will have your work cut out for you.'

Tomas moved his hand low on her back. 'I know so.'

Sarah blushed, smiling as they went back out to the theatre. The music played, the carousel spun, the tree sparkled, the children laughed with delight. As the scene changed and blurred before Sarah's eyes, she felt a sudden presence inside her, filling her with joy. A tiny face, a rush of love. Instead of feeling sad, she felt alive with happiness: her heart unlocked, open to possibilities. She leaned close to Tomas and whispered in his ear. 'It's what she would have wanted.'

Tomas drew her close. She twined her arms around his neck and he kissed her deeply. She smiled inside, knowing that he understood.

PART VI

The light, when it shines upon her, is beautiful and pure. It is made more precious by the memories of the dark. Once, she thought the darkness was forever. Once, she would have chosen to forget it. But now, she knows that it is as much of part of her as her long neck, her spots, and her tiny horns. She is made of wood, she is made of memories. Darkness and light woven into the present. And the future…? That is a gift beyond price.

A man places her in a box; she is sent in the post back to the woman who lost her. The woman is different now too. She too has embraced the memories, allowed the space to open up inside her. Like the shards of a vase fused with veins of gold, she is stronger – stronger for the knowledge that the circle will be broken many times, but it can be healed with love.

The woman places the little giraffe back in the circle. Her painted heart lifts in delight as she recognises her old friends. They whisper together in a language that only they can understand. A tear falls from the woman's eyes as she runs a finger over the giraffe's tiny horns and faded spots, once loved by a beloved child. The giraffe was lost and now she is found. The woman, too, has found something beyond price. She has found her future and the space within herself to make new memories; to write new stories and share her love with others. She has given herself permission finally to live again.

EPILOGUE

SATURDAY, JANUARY 6TH

The London Times

A shockwave has gone through the literary world after a statement was released by prize-winning author Tom Willowfield. Following an incident in which his then-girlfriend, Jessie Ripon, was seriously injured, Willowfield disappeared into obscurity, changing his name and adopting a new identity. Tom Willowfield became Tomas Mercier, author of The Art of Death *and other crime novels.*

Willowfield was the one-time winner of the prestigious Curtis P. Whitney prize for literature for his debut novel The Rites of Spring. *At the time, his work was compared to that of literary greats such as William Faulkner and Tom Wolfe.*

Willowfield's relationship with Ripon was described in the press as 'troubled', and the couple was notorious for their decadent lifestyle, that ultimately ended in tragedy.

In his statement, Willowfield said:

'I deeply apologise for any hurt I have caused Ms. Ripon and others through my actions and inactions. I am releasing this statement because I no longer wish to hide from my past and let it define

me. Going forward, I intend to take full responsibility for my life and future career, whatever direction it may take.'

Ripon, now the head of a North London charity supporting disabled women, commented that: 'I appreciate Tom Willowfield's sentiments. I hope that by taking this action, Willowfield will once again be ready to share his great gifts with the world.'

Tom Willowfield has yet to announce his future plans.

FRANZ

TUESDAY, JANUARY 30TH

'Do you believe in happy endings, Mathilde?'

Sitting side by side on the sofa, Franz caressed the delicate veins on the top of her hands. He and Andre had spent the day at the toyshop hard at work – over a month had passed since the grand opening and they were still worked off their feet filling orders. Despite a few setbacks, Andre had taken to the work like a duck to water. He was helping Franz most days, though that would change when eventually he went to school. Tonight, Tomas and Sarah were looking after Andre. It was Mathilde's birthday, and Franz had planned a special evening just the two of them. Outside the window, the lights of Paris glittered in the darkness blurred by gentle snowflakes swirling in the air like dancers. Mathilde looked beautiful – straight and slender in a grey silk dress and her beloved silver shoes. They'd had supper, and Franz had given Mathilde the musical box he'd made for her: polished wood inlaid with gold, with a beautiful ballerina dancing to *Swan Lake*.

'Oh Franz – it's beautiful,' she said as she unwrapped it. Franz was delighted by her delight and the way her eyes lit up like a child's as she wound it over and over. It reminded him of those other eyes that he could still remember from long ago. But instead of feeling sad, Franz felt joyful – Anna's life had meant something, and she'd left behind a positive legacy. Now, he was doing the same.

She set the gift on the table, and they sat together on the sofa, holding hands under a warm blanket. They talked of life and memory; their happiest times… and their saddest. There was always an air of sadness about Mathilde; that was part of who she was. Franz knew it was not possible for another human being to make another human being completely happy. That had to come from within.

'I'm just worried, that's all,' she confessed. 'Worried about what happens with Andre when I can't continue on my own.'

'But you are not on your own,' Franz said. He wished he could get this one idea into her head. Wished she would just give in and trust him. But Mathilde had been on her own for so long – as had he – and change would always be hard.

'I know.' She stroked his hand lightly. 'But still, I worry.'

There were little signs. When he thought back on the time he'd spent with her, he realised they'd been there all along. She would sometimes stop speaking in mid-sentence, as if she'd forgotten what she was going to say. Once or twice she forgot a name. Occasionally she put things in odd places and then forgot. Often, she was aware it had happened. Sometimes she was not.

Now, though, a tear trickled down her cheek. He kissed it away. He'd asked her about happy endings because it had been on his mind ever since seeing Tomas and Sarah together once again. The dancers colliding, putting aside the fear and impossible heartbreak caused by the past. He was happy for them, though he knew that it would take some time for them to work out their path. Since the statement had been released, Tom and Sarah had been involved in a media storm that they were trying to weather. Tom was working on another book; Sarah was helping him work through his self-doubts. She had also been actively speaking to local shopkeepers and landlords, developing a business model to support independent shops. All in all, they were moving forward together.

'I believe that happiness is not an ending or a beginning,' Mathilde said. 'It just comes and goes. Like breathing in and breathing out. Like memory. Like life.'

He turned her wrist over and ran his fingers alone the lines of her hand. 'That's very philosophical,' he said. 'But a little sad.'

She smiled. 'I have had more moments of happiness in the last few months than I can remember in many years. You have given me that.'

'I hope there will be many more to come.' He lifted her hand to his lips and kissed it.

'There will be more,' she said. 'And when I can ease my mind about Andre, then, who knows?'

'And what would ease your mind?'

'Knowing that he can go to school and make friends. Knowing that he can use his gifts and make something of his life.'

'Has he not been moving forward in leaps and bounds to do these things?'

Mathilde smiled. 'Yes, he has.'

'Good.' Franz pulled her close, feeling a rising sensation of desire. An old man's desire, late in life, to be with the woman he loved – not to be young again, or even to feel young – but to give her more moments of happiness than she would have had otherwise.

'I will look after Andre as long as I can, Mathilde. As long as he needs me. If it becomes necessary, he can live with me. I already think of him as a grandson, a son even.'

'You are a good man, Franz Himmelberg,' Mathilde said. She pressed her body closer to his. Though she was too thin, she was warm, with a beating heart that resonated with his.

Before he could get too comfortable, he bent down on one knee, ignoring the creak in his joints and the pain in his hip. 'Mathilde,' he said. 'I am going to ask you a question – and no matter what the answer is, I will look after Andre. So do not feel under any pressure. But I love you. I would like to marry you. To live with you and Andre, if you would have me.' He gave a chuckle. 'Though, maybe in a bigger flat.'

'But Franz,' she protested, 'you know—'

He took a breath and looked into her eyes. 'I believe our lives have come full circle to where we are meant to be. I would like to be with you in your happy moments and your sad ones. To be together with you, and be your memory, for as long as we have. I love you, Mathilde. Will you marry me?'

'You are a foolish old man.' She clutched his hand tightly. 'And you don't know what you are getting yourself into.'

'Maybe not.' Franz smiled. 'But that is my choice. What is yours?'

'Oh Franz, get up.' Mathilde touched his face, her hand trembling like a tiny bird just born.

'Say yes, Mathilde.'

'Well… yes.'

Franz wasn't quite sure how he managed to get up onto

his feet, let alone lift Mathilde and whirl her around as if they were teenagers. She laughed, and he kissed her again and again. Late in the night, he wound the musical box and the ballerina spun on her toes. And two lonely people who had found each other, danced together as a pink dawn rose in the eastern sky.

The End

A LETTER FROM LAUREN

As the characters in The Little Paris Toyshop discover, life sometimes requires us to take a leap of faith. It requires us to show up before we're ready, it requires us to take actions even when full of self-doubt. For me, this was the story of writing this book. When I first wrote it, I was told by agents and publishers that they loved it… but… it didn't fit the right genre, they didn't know how to market it, it was not for them. I listened. I believed them. Ultimately, I shelved the book – gave up on it.

Luckily, the book refused to give up on me. Something about it made me come back to it. Perhaps it was the characters, with their stories that deserved to be told, even in my imperfect cross-genre way. Or maybe it was the quote by Toni Morrison that I use as a guide in my writing: 'If there's a book that you want to read, but it hasn't been written yet, then you must write it.' Or maybe it was because during this time, I began to look at my writing in a whole new way, with a whole new goal. I want to write beautiful books that add value to the lives of my readers. I want to write not just for me, but for them.

Whatever the reason, I took that leap of faith. I became my own first believer in the story, my ability to tell it, and most importantly, my ability to get it out there to my audience. This last part is the hardest. This is the part that requires overcoming the perfectionism, the self-doubt, the imposter syndrome, and the voice inside your head that is constantly whispering: 'It's not good enough'; and the corollary: '*I'm* not good enough.'

Publishing this book required me to stretch myself and move outside my comfort zone. It required me to become a different person – a person who believed the book had value – before I had the result. The rejection and failure required me to evolve, to keep trying new things, to battle through depression, and keep believing. The book required me to transform it into something better than what I envisioned at the start. It required me to become a better writer, and ultimately, a better version of myself.

I would like to thank Debi Alper and Donna Hillyer for their insightful editing, Rory Hadley for his owl-eyed proofreading, and Emma Graves for designing the cover. I would also like to thank my family for their love and support, especially my partner, Ian, my mom and dad, and my daughters Eve, Rose, and Grace, to whom this book is dedicated.

Most of all, I am grateful to my readers for choosing this book and taking the time to read it. If I can reach even one person, then it is all worth it. If you are that person – thank you.

Lx
Surrey 2023

In memory of Monica Yeo, 1928-2023

CAN I ASK A FAVOUR?

Thank you for reading The Little Paris Toyshop. I hope you enjoyed reading it as much as I enjoyed bringing the story and characters to life.

If you loved the book, please can I ask you to leave a review or rating. It helps other readers find my books and might help someone discover their next perfect read.

You can leave a review or rating here: https://geni.us/TLPTReview or scan the QR code below.

Thank you so much!

GET A FREE BOOK

I would love to give you a free book, which you can access by signing up for my mailing list at the link below. Your email address will never be shared and you can unsubscribe at any time.

Here's the link and a QR code:
https://geni.us/LaurenWestwoodWriter

FOLLOW ME ON SOCIAL MEDIA

If you'd like to get up to date news and information on events and new releases, follow me on social media below:

Facebook: https://www.facebook.com/Lwestwoodbooks

Instagram: https://www.instagram.com/lwestwoodwriter/

Twitter: https://twitter.com/lwestwoodwriter

LOVED THE LITTLE PARIS TOYSHOP?

Discover an emotional and intelligent new romance today…

LOVED THE LITTLE PARIS TOYSHOP?

If you save a crumbling mansion,
will it mend a broken heart?

A month ago, Amy Wood had her perfect home, perfect boyfriend, and perfect job in London. Now she's broken-hearted, living in her parents' tiny bungalow, and working in a local estate agents in Bath.

But Amy gets a new lease on life when she undertakes to sell Rosemont hall, a crumbling Georgian mansion riddled with woodworm, dry rot – and secrets.

Amy searches for the perfect owner to restore the house to its former glory, but time is running out. As she clashes with unscrupulous property developers and the enigmatic heir to the house, Amy uncovers pieces of the past that some people would rather remain hidden.

Can Amy unlock the secrets of Rosemont Hall and find the keys to her own happy ending?

A sparkling and intelligent feel-good romance.

Download here: https://geni.us/HouseofSecondChances

LOVED THE LITTLE PARIS TOYSHOP?

Will the secrets of the past be the keys to the future?

Alex Hart loves her job as manager of Mallow Court, a historic Elizabethan house. But the discovery of a precious jewelled locket changes everything, and things are not as they seem.

From an old diary, to a charismatic barrister, a mysterious clockmaker, and the darkest hours of the London Blitz, Alex must uncover the truth about the things she holds dearest. Her heart hangs in the balance, and someone is determined not to let sleeping dogs lie!

A brilliant feel-good romance with a satisfying old-house mystery.

Download here: https://geni.us/HouseofHiddenSecrets

LOVED THE LITTLE PARIS TOYSHOP?

**An old house, a secret heartbreak,
a second chance at love.**

Lizzie Greene is about to lose everything. With no money and no job to pay her late husband's debts, she is resigned to selling her quirky old house, Tanglewild.

But a lifeline appears when Lizzy's house is chosen as a location for a film based on a best-selling romance novel. Her household is turned upside down by a cast of colourful characters: an enigmatic author, a handsome location scout, a brooding director, a heart-throb leading man – never mind her ex-mother-in-law camped out in her drive.

But behind the Hollywood magic, all is not as it seems. Someone has a hidden agenda in coming to Tanglewild and will stop at nothing to keep its secrets hidden. Will Lizzy's desire to save her house lead to new love or to mortal danger?

A delightful and heart-warming story of overcoming past heartbreaks and finding a new beginning.

LOVED THE LITTLE PARIS TOYSHOP?

Download here: https://geni.us/HouseofLoveandDreams

Two strangers, two worlds, one night in London.

Christmas is a joyous time, but not everyone is merry and bright. Nicola is a star at the top of the corporate ladder, but her personal life is a disaster. A night of cancelled trains and festive carols at Waterloo Station is the last straw.

Dmitri loves conducting his pop-up choir during the festive season and spreading joy and cheer around London. But he carries painful secrets from his past that robbed him of his dream to become a concert pianist.

When Nicola and Dmitri's worlds collide on a snowy night in London, their lives will never be the same. But will the power of music and moonlight lead to new love, or to devastating heartbreak?

A hauntingly beautiful romance about the healing power of love.

Download here: https://geni.us/MoonlightOnTheThames

LOVED THE LITTLE PARIS TOYSHOP?